Suzanne Wright lives in England with her husband and two children. When she's not spending time with her family, she's writing, reading or doing her version of housework – sweeping the house with a look.

She's worked in a pharmaceutical company, at a Disney Store, at a primary school as a voluntary teaching assistant, at the RSPCA and has a First Class Honours degree in Psychology and Identity Studies.

As to her interests, she enjoys reading, writing, reading, writing (sort of eat, sleep, write, repeat), spending time with her family, movie nights with her sisters and playing with her two Bengal kittens.

To connect with Suzanne online:

Website: www.suzannewright.co.uk
Facebook:
www.facebook.com/suzannewrightfanpage
Twitter: @suz_wright
Blog: www.suzannewrightsblog.blogspot.co.uk

The Dark in You series

Burn

Blaze

Ashes

ASHES

Suzanne Wright

piatkus

PIATKUS

First published in Great Britain in 2017 by Piatkus

3 5 7 9 10 8 6 4 2

A CIP catalogue record for this book
is available from the British Library.

ISBN 978-0-349-41319-8

Typeset in Goudy by Rules
Printed and bound in Great Britain by
Clays Ltd, St Ives plc

Papers used by Piatkus are from well-managed forests
and other responsible sources.

MIX
Paper | Supporting
responsible forestry
FSC® C104740

Piatkus
An imprint of
Little, Brown Book Group
Carmelite House
50 Victoria Embankment
London EC4Y 0DZ

An Hachette UK Company
www.hachette.co.uk

www.littlebrown.co.uk

To Mrs. D.,
Sorry for laughing when you said I'd be
a writer one day, I just really didn't
expect things to pan out

Acknowledgments

These sections are so hard to write because there are so many people to thank. Like my amazing family, who make room in their lives for the voices in my head. Like my awesome assistant, Melissa, who reminds me to do my calming breathing exercises in social situations. Like everyone at Piatkus, most especially the extremely awesome Anna Boatman. Like my Bengal cats, who clawed at someone I really don't like the other day . . . but we won't talk about that.

Lastly, I want to say a big thanks to you! Yes, you (hi! *waving*) and to all the other people who've read my books. *Thank you so much!*

If you wish to contact me, you can reach me by email at suzanne_e_wright@like.co.uk or via social media.

CHAPTER ONE

———————◆———————

If I were a set of keys, where would I be?

Shoving the drawer closed, Harper Wallis cursed. She'd searched the reception desk, her office, the breakroom, and every tattoo station. There was no sign of her keys, which was a major problem since she couldn't leave without locking the studio.

Having been raised by imps, she was very security conscious. Breaking and entering was merely one talent that imps possessed. They also excelled at lying, cheating, stealing, and identity theft. She might biologically be a sphinx like her mother, but Harper was an imp in every other way that counted.

Speaking of imps ... Harper turned to her teenage cousin. "Did you find the keys?"

"Nope," Robbie replied.

"Well, maybe if you got up off your ass and *looked* instead of lounging on the sofa flicking through the portfolios, you might actually find them."

Heidi, her other cousin who was only five, came skipping

out of the breakroom and crossed to Harper. "They're not back there."

Harper stroked the little imp's white-blonde hair. "Thanks anyway, Heidi-ho." The kid truly did look like an absolute angel. As a demon, she was, of course, far from it.

"Why not just call Raini?" asked Robbie. "She's the co-owner; she must have her own set of keys."

"She does," said Harper. "But I'm not calling her all the way back here." It wasn't exactly a simple location to arrive at. Six months ago, they'd relocated the business to the Underground, a demonic paradise that was pretty much a subterranean, hyperactive version of the Las Vegas strip.

Harper's mate, Knox Thorne, had built the Underground a long time ago, and it was globally popular—mostly because demons were impulsive creatures that had instant gratification issues, loved adrenaline rushes, and were plagued by boredom and restlessness.

"Done," declared Richie, her uncle. Dusting off his hands, he backed away from the vending machine. "It should work fine." He lightly pounded his fist on the side of the machine, and it sprung to life with a whir as it dropped a bag of chips.

Harper shook her head. "It doesn't matter how many times I do that, it never works for me." His daughter, Khloë—who also happened to be Harper's receptionist—did it just as effortlessly. "Thanks, Richie, I appreciate the help."

He frowned at her. "I still don't understand why you want to work here when you could earn a hell of a lot more money working for me," he griped. Her uncle could fix anything. He could also recreate any piece of art. He'd produced and sold countless counterfeit paintings, and he'd passed on his expertise to Harper. As such, it disappointed him that she chose to "waste her artistic talent by drawing with needles".

Harper raised a hand. "I'm not having this conversation with you again."

Richie grunted. "Come on, kids, your mom will be waiting for you." Although he was unmated, he had dozens of kids with five different mothers. He was a good dad, though. Financially and emotionally supportive. Never missed a single baseball game, school play, or ballet recital. In that sense, he was very unlike Harper's nomadic father who could go for months at a time without contacting her, though Lucian did actually consider that to be full-time parenting.

Gathering his tools, Richie spoke. "Where's your bodyguard?"

"Tanner has the night off, since I'm riding home with Knox." Her mate was a busy guy, so their work days didn't always finish at the same time. "I'm meeting Knox at his office and then we're going out for a meal."

Honestly, she didn't feel up to it. She was so tired that her mind was foggy with exhaustion, and all she wanted to do was go home and crash. Not that there would be much point in that. Sleep hadn't been coming easy to her lately. That might not have been so bad since, as a rule, demons didn't need much sleep and could even go days without it. But when she *did* sleep, it was restless and didn't restore her energy.

"Want us to walk you to Knox's office?" asked Richie.

She shook her head. "I can't leave until I find the keys." In general, she wasn't a forgetful person, but it had been a long, tiring day and her brain just wasn't cooperating. "Don't worry, I'll find them. They're here somewhere. Thanks again for your help."

Richie nodded. "Ready, kids?"

"Yep." Heidi peppered Harper's face with kisses and then turned to skip away, but Harper grabbed her by the back of her sweater.

"What?" asked Heidi, blinking innocently.

Harper held out her hand. "I want whatever you've stolen with those sticky fingers of yours."

Heidi pouted and then fished a diamond belly button ring out of her pocket. The little girl could always be counted on to take something shiny. "You're no fun," she said.

Harper gaped at her. "How did you even get this?" The glass reception desk doubled as a display cabinet for jewelry and other products, and Harper always kept it locked.

Heidi gave her a look that said, "Don't insult me." Then she skipped over to Richie.

He patted his daughter on the head. "You make your daddy proud."

Harper rolled her eyes. "I'll see you all soon."

They said their goodbyes, and Robbie then ushered the kids out of the studio.

Determined to find the damn keys, Harper restarted her search. She checked every desk drawer, the spaces between the sofa cushions, and then underneath the table and couch. Once she was positive they weren't in the reception area, she moved onto the tattoo stations and thoroughly searched every one of them—still no keys.

Harper's inner demon huffed at her in sheer exasperation, like she was failing on freaking purpose. It had absolutely no sympathy for her; it just wanted to be with its mate.

Sharing your soul with a dark predator that was essentially a psychopath could be a bitch of a situation at times. The demon had no conscience, no empathy, no ability to love. It also possessed a strong and annoying sense of entitlement that made it a persistent motherfucker.

As Harper made her way through the breakroom and into the stockroom, a mind—dark, familiar, and comforting—brushed against hers. *You're late, baby.* It wasn't a reproach; more like a need for confirmation that nothing was wrong.

She smiled as the velvety, smoky, rumble seemed to slide over her skin. Knox's sinfully seductive voice truly shouldn't be legal. *I'm sorry, I can't find my keys.*

You don't think anybody's taken them, do you? There was a promise of retribution in his words.

No, they're here somewhere. But as Harper scanned the inventory, she didn't see them.

I have a spare set. I'll bring them to you.

She lifted a brow, even though he couldn't see. *And just why do you have spare keys to my studio?*

A vibe of amusement touched her mind. Apparently, her snippy remark didn't bother him. *It used to be one of my security offices, remember?*

Oh, yeah, she'd kind of forgotten that. *Give me ten minutes. If I haven't found mine by then, I'll use the spare set.*

If that's what you—

She frowned when he abruptly cut off. *Knox?*

I need to have a quick talk with Levi, he said, sounding distracted. *After that, I'll come to you if you haven't already arrived.*

If he was doing that "keeping things from her to protect her" thing again, there'd be an argument for sure. But since his mind had already pulled away from hers, she didn't bother saying as much.

Turning her attention back to the mystery of the disappearing keys, Harper looked in the small restroom and gave the kitchenette a thorough exploration. Nothing.

Cursing, she returned to her office to give it yet another search. Looking under her sketchpads, she froze as a prickle of awareness danced across her nape.

She was about to turn when a heavy weight slammed into

her back, propelling her forwards so that she was bent over the table. Just as fast, the back of her shirt was ripped open and a body appeared in front of her as two meaty hands grabbed hers, fisting her own hands and pinning them in place.

"We need to do this quickly," said a gruff voice.

What the fuck? *Knox!* No response. A familiar, protective power rushed from her belly to her fingertips. They prickled as the power fought for release. Harper would be more than fucking happy to release it on her captive, but her hands were trapped. "Get the fuck off me!"

"Do it now."

Someone blew into her ear, and suddenly Harper was at home. She stood in the doorway of her bedroom. It was almost eerily dim. Weirdly, the entire space was bare apart from one thing: a cradle. It would have been deathly quiet if it wasn't for the sound of a baby crying.

For some reason, the sound made her stomach tighten. She crept forward, feeling disturbingly compelled toward the cradle and—

Abruptly back in her office, Harper hissed through her teeth. The flesh of her back felt like it was on fire. Her demon raged, freaking the fuck out. Harper writhed and struggled against her captive's grip, scrambling to understand what the hell was happening.

"You want to release me," she said in a compelling tone that came with the sphinx package.

A dark chuckle. "No, we don't."

Her surroundings shifted once again, and she found herself walking toward the cradle again. Time was slow here. There was no pain, no panic, no anger. But it wasn't real … was it? She didn't know, so she kept her mind focused on the vision in front of her. The crying seemed louder now and—

Finding herself bent over the office table once more, she blinked, disorientated. Her body bucked and writhed as what felt like some sort of magnetic force called to her wings. They snapped to the surface and fanned out around her—huge, gold, heavy, eagle-like, gossamer wings that were silky-soft but strong as steel.

"Look at the black and red streaks running through the gold feathers," said the demon subduing her hands. His shock was understandable—they were the colors of the flames of hell.

A covetous hand stroked one wing. Red-hot rage whipped through her, and she writhed like crazy. "Let me go, you motherfuckers!"

"She shouldn't be partially aware!"

"Well I know that, but she is!"

Knox! Knox! Where the hell was he? Was someone attacking him too and—?

She was back in her bedroom again, closer to the cradle now. The cries had eased a little, as if whatever lay there was calmed by her presence. A part of her wanted to retreat, but she *needed* to see the source of the crying. Needed to know if—

Arching like a bow, Harper screamed around her gag—*gag?*—as something sliced into her back. No, *into the stems of her wings*. The son of a bitch was trying to sever her wings! Tears stung her eyes each time the jagged blade mercilessly cut into the stems. She redoubled her efforts to be free, even as it worsened the pain that was burning her from the inside out. Her heartbeat was racing so fast that she wouldn't have been surprised if it collapsed.

The male behind her cursed. "If sphinx wings were as flimsy as they look, this would be a lot goddamn easier."

"I swear I will fucking kill you!" she growled around the gag.

The males just laughed. *Laughed.*

Her inner demon shoved its way to the surface and pulled back its lips. "You will die for this," it told them in a flat, emotionless voice that was barely audible, but the demon's presence still made both males pause for a moment.

"For God's sake, put her out!"

A warm breath blew into her ear once more, and she was back in her room. Two single steps were all it would take to get her up close to the cradle. She took one step, then another. And there, eyes closed as it fussed and kicked its little legs, was a baby. It looked so tiny and sweet, sucking on its fist.

Harper's smile was slow but real as she tentatively reached out and ran the tip of her finger over the small hand, warmed by the feel of its petal-soft skin. The baby's eyes flipped open, and all she could see were flames.

Harper snapped back to reality, pain ripping through her as someone continued sawing into the stems of her wings. Black spots filled her vision, and the sickly tastes of blood and fear flooded her mouth until they almost choked her.

She wanted to shout. Struggle. Fight back. But she felt paralyzed with the sheer agony that came with each and every slice. Not even the adrenaline pumping through her was much help at this point.

"Now those rings sure are pretty," said her captor, keeping her hands fisted so tightly that her nails bit hard into her palms. "I'll bet there are people willing to pay top dollar for them—maybe even more than this guy's paying us for the wings."

Like hell would she let them take the rings. Knox had given them to her. One was a black diamond; something a demon only gave to their mate. It was a symbol of the ultimate commitment. They meant more to her than even her wings.

"No, don't free her hands. She can cause soul-deep pain, idiot."

"She's trapped in a dream right now. She doesn't even know we're here or where she is."

This was her chance, Harper thought. If nothing else, she could hurt one of the bastards who was hurting her. She didn't move when he slowly lifted her third finger. She remained still, quiet. As she felt him try to tug off her rings, she did nothing more than poke his hand. The dark power prickling the pad of her finger forced its way inside him.

His mouth opened in a silent scream as pain scorched his nerve endings, punctured his organs, sawed through his bones, and battered his soul. He stumbled back and fell, knocking piles of paper down with him. And there were her keys. Grabbing them, she infused hellfire into them and—bracing herself for yet more pain—swung back her arm and slashed at the male behind her.

There was a cry of pain, and then his weight left her. Twisting, Harper spun to face the bastard, breaths sawing in and out of her. Stocky. Dirty blond hair. Scruffy beard. Leather jacket. He also had a saw in his hand that dripped with blood. Not good.

He was glaring at the sizzling slash across his chest as his skin blistered and peeled away, thanks to the hellfire eating at it. Her demon smiled at the sight. His gaze snapped to hers just as Harper tugged down the gag, and he lifted his saw threateningly.

Well, shit.

She thought about snatching the stiletto blade from her boot and infusing it with hellfire, but it was really no match for the saw, was it? Still, if she could touch him just once, he'd be a soul-deep wreck just like his friend. He shifted from foot to foot, and she knew he was preparing to charge at her. Her breathing quick and shallow, she braced herself. But he didn't move.

Eyes cold, mouth set into a sneer, he spoke. "You burned me."

Using the back of her trembling hand to wipe at the sweat

beading her forehead, she snarled, "And you almost *cut off my fucking wings.*" She wanted to bludgeon the son of a bitch with his own weapon. But not before sawing off his arms and mangling him.

Her demon shoved its way to the surface and hissed at him. "I warned you that you would pay. You should have heeded me." Harper forced her demon to retreat and abruptly lashed out with the blazing keys. He jerked back, but they still scored his cheek. His skin sizzled as the hellfire ate at it. Her demon grinned.

"You *bitch!*" He lifted his saw again, ready to attack.

KNOX!

With a battle cry, he lunged.

She sidestepped him, barely avoiding the saw. He crashed into her desk with a grunt, slashing at thin air and—

Fire thundered to life outside the office doorway. He whirled around to watch as the fire spat and crackled. The flames then faded, and there was Knox. Relief flooded Harper so fast, her legs shook.

Deep-set ebony eyes swept over her, and his perfectly sculpted face set into a mask of savage anger. Her attacker took a cautious step away as those dark eyes slammed on him with lethal intent, glittering with a fury that began to pulse around them.

Her attacker made a gurgling sound and dropped his bloody saw, clawing at an invisible hand that lifted him off his feet. Knox's psychic hands had touched her more than once and always given her nothing but pleasure. That had made it so easy for her to forget that they could also deliver a shit load of pain.

Knox stalked to him. Slowly. Casually. Utterly composed. Yet, every step was both predatory and threatening. She shivered a little. It always spooked her when he was so unnaturally calm.

His eyes flicked to the other demon, who was still sobbing in the corner, but his gaze quickly snapped back to the male in his psychic grip. Knox halted in front of him and cocked his head. "Your little friend over there can answer my questions," he rumbled. "Which is a very good thing because there isn't the slightest chance that I could let you live even a moment longer."

Knox's eyes bled to black and the room temperature plummeted as his demon rose to the surface. Harper tensed. It would never harm her, she knew that. But it would be dumb to ever let herself forget how cold, menacing, and old the entity was. It could destroy them all so very easily. And it wasn't particularly interested in the right or wrong of wreaking havoc when it was in a rage. Right then, it was incalculably *pissed*.

The demon glared at its captive. "You hurt what's mine," it said in a chilling, disembodied voice. "Cut her. Made her bleed. Caused her pain." It leaned forward slightly. "Now I will do the same to you."

Straightening, the demon held up its hand. The male's body arched toward it; legs kicking, arms flailing, eyes bulging. His face was red and contorted with an agony that he'd undoubtedly cry out with if his larynx wasn't being crushed. His body violently bucked, and there was a nauseating *crack* as his ribs broke and his chest somehow burst open. His heart flew into the demon's open hand, still beating.

Harper didn't know whether to be impressed or revolted. Her bloodthirsty demon was most certainly impressed, grinning with a wicked satisfaction.

The corpse dropped to the floor like a sack of spuds. Hellfire erupted out of the demon's hand, devouring the organ it held until even the blood was completely gone.

Harper's brows rose. Now *that* was definitely impressive. Her inner demon wholeheartedly agreed.

The entity turned to face Harper, and its black eyes raked over her. Then those eyes changed, and she was once more looking at Knox. But then they bled to black again, and she realized that he and his demon were battling for dominance. She stayed rigid as she waited to see who would win.

Finally, the entity seemed to have agreed to retreat, and suddenly Knox's dark eyes were focused solely on her. Despite that danger clung to him, that his demon was so pitiless and cruel, and that he was every inch the most lethal predator she'd ever met, Harper felt nothing but safe when he stalked to her and cradled her face with his hands.

"Ah, baby, what did they do to you?" Even though his voice vibrated with a rage that was thickening the air, there was a gentle note to it that almost undid her.

"They tried to saw off my wings," she told him, struggling to ease the tremble in her limbs. Now that the adrenaline rush was fading, the pain was like nothing she'd ever felt and she wasn't sure how much longer she could stay conscious.

Knox viciously swore. "Let me see."

Holding herself stiffly, she turned. "How bad is it?" He didn't answer, but fury blasted the air, sending shockwaves sweeping outwards. The walls and ceiling shook slightly. She slowly turned back to face him. His expression was now blank, and he looked the image of composure even as his anger seemed to clog up the room. "How bad?" she asked again, panicking now.

Knox cupped his mate's jaw, wanting to pull her close and hold her tight against him, but he was scared he'd hurt her. She was in enough pain as it was. "The bastards didn't get very far. The saw didn't even make it halfway through the stems." But he knew that every drag of the serrated blade must have been absolutely agonizing. He clenched his jaw, hating the very thought of her in such excruciating pain.

She wasn't bleeding badly, but the cuts on her back were ugly. The saw had sliced into her flesh several times, as if she'd repeatedly jerked and the blade had accidentally nicked her each time.

The front door burst open just moments before Levi came skidding into the office. His gun-metal gray eyes took in Harper, the dead demon, his whimpering friend, and the bloody saw. "Fuck," he bit out.

Knox wasn't surprised to see his sentinel. They'd been in the middle of a conversation when Knox had heard Harper's telepathic scream, whispered her name, and then abruptly pyroported from his office to the studio. Levi had no doubt panicked.

"They tried to steal Harper's wings," Knox told him. "I believe they're hunters."

Levi cursed again. "How successful were they?" he growled, examining the dead body.

"Not very," said Harper. "I'll be okay."

Knox framed her face again, fighting to keep his touch gentle when he was feeling anything but. "You should have called me immediately. I know you want to protect me just as I do you, but why wait until you're so badly hurt?"

"I did call you. You didn't come."

He frowned. "I came as soon as I heard you."

She shook her head. "I called you over and over. You didn't come." She'd started to think that he wasn't going to come at all. "I thought something might have happened to you."

Knox slid a possessive hand around her nape and gave it a comforting squeeze. "I only heard you once, baby. It was like an echo of a scream." And it had pierced a heart he hadn't thought he had until he met Harper. "One of the hunters must be a blocker."

"A what?"

"Someone who can block telepathic calls. If you weren't so strong, I probably wouldn't have heard you at all." And then they'd have taken her wings, he thought. They might have even killed her to protect their identities. He could have arrived here, spare set of keys in hand, only to find her dead. His breath caught in his throat at just the very idea, and his demon bared its teeth, wanting vengeance on the other male who'd dared to harm its mate.

Knox stroked his thumb along her jaw. "We need to get you home." Where she'd be safe, where he could get her cleaned up, where she could heal. Vengeance would come later.

"Are we taking that little fucker with us?" Levi clipped.

Knox cut his gaze to the hunter that was huddled against the wall, shaking and whimpering as what Knox suspected was soul-deep pain reverberated through him. That wasn't good enough for Knox or his demon. No amount of pain would be enough. They wanted to see the bastard bleed, wanted to hear him scream in the sheer agony that he and the other hunter had put Harper through. Neither Knox nor his demon would settle for anything less.

"He's definitely coming with us," Knox replied as he prowled to the hunter. The smell of the male's fear pleased his demon, who tried to resurface again, but Knox pushed it down. Now wasn't the time to play with their prey. Getting Harper to safety where she could heal was his priority.

Knox squatted in front of him. "You and I will talk very soon. You're going to tell me everything I want to know. *Everything.*"

And then he was going to die.

CHAPTER TWO

———◆———

Stretched out beside his mate as she lay on her stomach, Knox stroked a hand over her long, sleek, dark hair and played with the gold ends. Although her cuts had faded to pink lines and the tears in the stems of her wings had partially reknitted, anger still blazed inside him. He took a deep, controlled breath, inhaling her warm, honeyed scent. She was alive. Safe. Healing. But rage was still a living, breathing, clawing thing inside him.

His demon's anger didn't show any signs of abating either. How could it? Their mate had been attacked, for fuck's sake. Attacked in her own studio, a place where she should have been safe. He'd been the one to convince her that she *would* be safe there. She'd relocated her studio at his request, believing he was right, and he'd been far fucking from it.

His eyes fell closed as he remembered the moment he'd heard her telepathic scream. The panicked, pain-filled sound kept replaying in his mind like a broken record, and he knew he'd never forget it. Similarly, he'd never forget the sight of her there in her office; eyes clouded with pain, limbs trembling, and her skin glistening with a fine sheen of sweat.

His demon had almost lost it; had wanted nothing more than to rise and wreak havoc, but Knox had only given it dominance for a short time. He'd needed to check on Harper, had reminded the demon that she was more important than their revenge—something it luckily agreed with. The entity was selfish and merciless, but it would always put Harper first.

The dark entities that lived within demons couldn't love; they simply weren't capable of that emotion. But they could form attachments to people. It wasn't something they did often or easily, but it was always permanent and always intense. Knox's demon had claimed Harper as its mate. It had "collected" her and was every bit as possessive and protective of the little sphinx as Knox was.

Shiny, defiant, and unique, she'd instantly captured his demon's interest the second they met. Knox had been just as fascinated. She was an intriguing creature. Smart. Stubborn. Complex. Elusive. There weren't many things that Knox found unpredictable, but Harper often managed to surprise him. That was something he liked.

It sometimes amused him that someone so small had so easily upturned his life. Innately sensual with mouthwatering curves and a plush mouth that he'd never tire of biting, Harper was a package that he hadn't been able to resist. He craved her on every level—mentally, physically, and even emotionally. She was indelible to him, as both his mate and his anchor.

Demons came in pairs; had fated psychic mates, or "anchors", that could make them stronger and keep them stable enough to prevent them from ever turning rogue. It was impossible for demons to control the dark entity within them, but it *was* possible to resist the entity's persistent attempts to completely take over if a demon linked minds with their anchor.

Knox hadn't planned to claim his anchor, since he was powerful enough on his own. The whole thing had seemed unnecessary and complicated to him. He didn't allow people in his life, but there was no way a person could maintain a distance between themselves and their anchor. Especially since they found it mentally uncomfortable to be separated for long periods.

Although the anchor bond was only psychic in nature as opposed to emotional or sexual, anchors still tended to be close friends and they always protected, supported, and were loyal toward each other. Knox didn't consider himself a person who needed friends, even though a numbing loneliness had begun to plague him back then.

Still, when he'd first stroked Harper's mind and realized what she was to him, he'd thought *Mine*. He hadn't been able to walk away from her. He'd relentlessly pursued her both psychically and sexually. Only once he'd fused their psyches had he understood that she truly was the only thing that could ever keep him stable. For all his power, he could never have been enough to keep himself from turning rogue.

Just like, for all his power, he hadn't heard her calling for him tonight.

The hunters had *cut* her, sawed at her wings, tried to steal them from her ... and he'd been talking with Levi, completely oblivious. Knox had made her promise to call out to him if she was ever in danger. Stubborn and protective, Harper rarely did so—refusing to lure him into dangerous situations. The fact that she *had* reached out to him showed just how scared she'd been. It gutted him that she'd suffered so much pain and had feared that he wouldn't come for her.

He traced the pink lines on her back, needing that proof that she was healing. A vicious sexual need pricked at him, pushing him to follow the primal urge to drive his cock deep inside her;

to take her hard and reassure himself in the most basic way that she was alive. But he didn't. She might be healing, but she was also drained. The last thing she needed was him fucking in and out of her like a man possessed.

She flinched as his finger touched a wound that was obviously still tender. He fisted his hand, infuriated with himself because, dammit, he should have fucking heard her. No, he should have gone to her with the spare set of keys rather than give her a little time to find her own. Then he could have killed the hunters before they even got the chance to touch her.

As he pulled back his arm, her hand loosely cuffed his wrist. "It's not your fault, Knox."

He wasn't surprised by her comment. Of course she'd know where his thoughts had led him. She understood him better than anyone. Sometimes, that made him uncomfortable, but it also felt good to be known so well after centuries of living a mostly solitary existence. He'd had plenty of people *around* him, but not part of his life. "I told you that you'd be safe there."

"Not even you could have guaranteed that."

He let his eyes drift over her face, hating the lines of pain there. "I should have heard you." He kissed her, pouring a silent apology into it.

"You did hear me."

"Not soon enough."

"Through no fault of your own." If Harper hadn't gotten stronger since fusing her psyche with Knox's, she might not have been able to contact him at all. That wasn't something she wanted to think about. Not only because she'd have lost her wings, but because Knox would have subsequently lost all control—something that would have led to so many deaths and so much destruction.

She lightly skimmed a hand over his short, stylishly cut hair;

it was as dark as his eyes and soft as silk. If her back still wasn't throbbing with pain, his otherworldly potent sex appeal would have sent her libido into a frenzy. He was nothing like the guys from her past with his GQ-style, Armani suits, and badass predatory edge. Tall and solid and dominant, Knox had a raw sexual gravity that drew people to him. All that supreme confidence, leashed power, and animal grace *totally* rung her bell.

"Talk me through exactly what happened," he said, stroking her wing. It was like touching hot silk. The feathers might be soft, but they weren't fragile. He found the contrast as fascinating as he did the female beside him.

She grimaced. "Um . . . yeah, I'm not sure that's the best idea." He was already pissed beyond belief and she didn't want to provoke the rage she knew was still simmering beneath the surface. Her demon was just as wary of stoking the fire.

"Harper, this is the kind of situation where *not* knowing is worse." Ignoring her pleading expression, he pressed, "Tell me."

She sighed. "Fine." Inhaling deeply, she took in the scents of clean linen, fragrant oils, and Knox's dark, sensual cologne. "I was minding my own business, searching for the damn keys, when the hunters just seemed to appear out of nowhere. One slammed me over the table while the other stood in front of me and pinned my hands still. I couldn't fight them at first, because the one trapping my hands—the one who's still alive—sent me into a dream. I kept snapping in and out of it."

Knox frowned. "I sensed that he's a nightmare. The breed can sometimes send people into dreamlike states, but they don't control the content of the dreams. What happened in it?"

"I was here, in our room. There was no furniture except for a cradle. There was a baby—I don't know if it was supposed to be a girl or a boy, I couldn't tell. It had flames for eyes."

"Considering a delusional demon claimed you'd have a 'child

of flames' who would destroy us all, it's hardly a surprise that you had a dream about it," he pointed out. Not so long ago, a demon from their lair who was near-rogue had targeted Knox, convinced that killing him before he could breed would save the world. After several unsuccessful attempts, Laurence Crow had then kidnapped Harper and tried to give her a hysterectomy to prevent her from having Knox's child. She'd killed the bastard instead.

They'd soon discovered that Crow's strings had been pulled by a group of demons that called themselves The Four Horsemen—a group that wanted to overthrow the Primes and have domination of the US. They believed that Knox, being so powerful, was in their way.

Knox had also discovered that he'd already killed one of the Horsemen . . . or Horse*woman*, really. Isla had wanted to not only have a US Monarch, but to *be* the Monarch. When her plan failed, she'd attacked Harper. Naturally, he'd killed the bitch.

Isla's death hadn't made the other Horsemen back off, though. Instead, they had tried and failed to cause a political war between the Primes, hoping they would turn on each other. It was only when Harper was bound to a table while Crow stood over her with a scalpel that another of the Horsemen waltzed in—a demon, Roan, from their lair. He was also Harper's half-brother, and he was now as dead as Crow.

It meant that two Horsemen were still out there, and Knox had to wonder if they were behind the attack at the studio.

"They were going to take my rings too," said Harper. "They were going to sell them."

His demon snarled at the idea. "Most hunters sell things on the black market. Sometimes they're hired to obtain something specific. We knew there was a risk that hunters would come for your wings if people were to find out that you could now call them to you." Sphinx wings were widely coveted. Until some of his power had poured into her mind and given her wings whatever push they'd needed to surface, she'd been known as the sphinx without wings. "We kept them a secret for that very reason, so what I want to know is how the fuck someone outside our close circle of people could have found out about them."

"The hunters mentioned a guy; it sounded like they were hired by someone." That suggested the hirer was either stupid or suicidal, in Harper's mind—and not just because Knox was a powerful Prime of a lair that spanned most of Nevada and even some of California. No, it was also because harming the mate of a demon who was thought to be the most powerful in existence wasn't advisable—especially when it was rumored that said demon could also call on the flames of hell.

If the hunters' employer knew just what breed of demon Knox was, Harper strongly doubted they would have fucked with her, no matter how dumb or tired of living they'd become. But very few people knew what Knox was. That only increased the fear that their kind already felt. And since fear and awe came hand in hand in the brutal world of demons, Knox was widely respected and admired.

Being a billionaire who owned a chain of hotels, casinos, bars, restaurants, and security firms, Knox was just as respected and influential in the human world. He hid in plain sight, just like most of their kind. It was hardly surprising to Harper that he was such a powerful figure. Demons loved power, challenges, and control. As such, many were CEOs, politicians, entrepreneurs, bankers, stockbrokers, lawyers, surgeons, police officers, and even celebrities.

"Well, we have someone who can give us the answers that we seek," said Knox. The hunter was currently in the boathouse on the grounds of the estate. Knox was raring to get his hands on the little fucker.

"You're going to talk to him now, aren't you?"

"Talk" wasn't quite the word Knox would use, but there would be a little talking involved. He sifted his fingers through her hair, watching as the hazel irises of her glassy, reflective eyes suddenly swirled like liquid before turning into a deep ocean-blue. He suspected that no matter how many times he watched their shade change like that, it would always fascinate him. "Not until you've fallen asleep. You need rest."

Harper didn't want him to go, but she also didn't want to have to walk him through the rest of what happened tonight, step by step. He was torturing himself enough as it was. "Thank you for somehow hearing me and coming for me."

He kissed her, savoring her taste. "Thank you for being strong enough to make me hear you. I'll always come for you." He held her gaze as he added, "If somebody hired them, I will find out who it was, and I will kill them. I swear that to you."

She smiled. "You don't have to swear it. I already know you will."

As always, her instant faith in him touched Knox. Before Harper, no one had ever looked at him with utter trust—and they'd been right not to do so. He was as ruthless, unforgiving, and merciless as he was rumored to be. He was loyal to very few people, and the only person on Earth who was completely safe from him was Harper. What amazed him about her was that she didn't doubt that she was safe from him. Not even a little.

Truly, no one—not even Knox—could have blamed her if she did have doubts. She'd seen him at his worst, knew the level of chaos and destruction he could cause, and had watched him conjure the flames of hell. There was only one thing that was impervious to the flames; it was the very thing that was born *from* the flames. An archdemon. And that was exactly what Knox was.

Unlike what some human religions believed, archdemons

didn't serve Lucifer; they served hell itself. They were as callous and conscienceless as their inner demons; were born to control, command, and destroy. And yet, Harper accepted him, trusted him, loved him.

It wasn't that she was willfully blind to his power or his true nature—no, she knew exactly what he was, and she'd walked into their relationship with her pretty eyes wide open. But she'd still taken him as her mate, still exchanged rings with him, and still even accepted his inner demon.

In short, she fucking owned him. But that was okay, because she in turn belonged to him.

"No more talking." Grabbing the remote from the nightstand, he lowered the electronic shades, plunging them into utter darkness. "Now close your eyes. I'll stay with you until you've fallen asleep, and I'll be here when you wake up."

Luxuriating in the way his hand gently played with her hair, Harper closed her eyes and let herself drift off.

The boards of the boathouse creaked beneath Knox's feet as he stalked down one of the narrow walkways that separated the three chrome and fiberglass boats. Moonlight filtered through the windows of the building, illuminating the anxious face of the hunter who sat bound to a wooden chair. He didn't struggle, didn't make a sound. All Knox could hear was the water lapping against the hulls and the creak of the taut ropes as the boats rocked slightly.

How's Harper? asked Levi, his tall, broad frame standing near the wall. He was vibrating with anger. The sentinel didn't like many people, but he liked and had a great deal of respect for Harper . . . which was probably why there was one hell of a bruise on the hunter's jaw.

She's fine. Sleeping, thankfully, Knox replied. He came to a

stop in front of the hunter, who Levi had divested of his camo
outfit and combat boots, leaving him in only his boxers and
socks—no doubt to make him feel even more vulnerable than
he already did.

Knox didn't bother to conceal his rage. He let it fill the boathouse, just as he'd let it fill Harper's office. He also allowed his
demon to surface just enough to release a low growl. The stench
of the hunter's fear joined the other smells of water, wax, and
motor oil.

Knox liked the way the hunter's tanned face paled and his
brown eyes flashed with fear, but he much preferred him as a
whimpering mess, huddling in a corner. "Feeling better? That's
a shame." Casually, Knox stuffed his hands in his pockets. "The
upside is ... you can talk. And that's exactly what you're going
to do."

He snorted, but the sound was too faint to be derisive. "Like
I'll believe you'll let me live."

"I don't recall saying that I'd let you live." It was truly laugh-
able that the nightmare would think any differently. "We're not
making a deal here and exchanging information for your life. I'm
telling you that you're going to answer my questions truthfully."

The hunter lifted his chin slightly in a gesture of defiance so
weak that Knox's demon rolled its eyes, despite its anger.

"I've interrogated several nightmares in the past," said Knox.
"I've found that I prefer interrogating your kind. You see, I can
effortlessly thrust my mind into someone else's and find all
the information I need. There are few whose shields present
a challenge. My mate's shields are very unique; they have the
psychic equivalent of steel barbs, meaning I'd have to shred my
own psyche to get past them." That she had such tough defenses
made him proud.

Knox began to circle the hunter as he continued. "Your

shields are solid, but not impenetrable. Still, it's never good to read the mind of a nightmare." But if he delved into the hunter's mind, all Knox would find would be his own personal nightmare. "But I'm not deterred by that, because I like the challenge. I like being able to really enjoy the interrogation process. It feeds my demon's need for violence."

As Knox moved to stand once again directly in front of him, the hunter swallowed hard and said, "I didn't hurt her."

"No, but you pinned her down while another did. You stood by and did nothing while she was in pain. That's just as bad." Knox's demon pushed for freedom, wanting to make the nightmare pay. *Soon*, Knox promised it. "Sphinx wings sure are beautiful, aren't they? I'd imagine that the wings of a powerful Prime like Harper would be worth the sort of money that would set you up for life." Knox cocked his head. "Just who offered you that money?"

"No one. We were just being opportunists."

Knox sighed. "It's always so disappointing when people lie to me. I don't like to be disappointed."

"It's the truth."

"And that's yet another lie, which you will pay for. You went after my mate—that's a hell of a risk to take, considering she's powerful and that you'd have known *exactly* what I'd do to you if you were caught. Besides, most of the demon world believes that Harper's wings never came to her. I don't see why hunters would randomly target Harper unless they believed differently. Very few know the truth, and I'm quite sure that the only way hunters *would* hear about it was if they were told by someone."

His Adam's apple bobbed as he stared at Knox, eyes fairly glowing with fear now.

"I can understand why you'd be so determined to hold back information. Personally, I wouldn't have any interest in spilling everything I knew to the person who was about to kill me. But you really, really should spill it all."

"I already told you, we were just being—"

"For every lie you tell, I'll hurt you that much worse."

"I can say we were hired if that's what you want to hear, but it won't be the truth."

As his cell phone chimed, Knox said, "Hold that thought." He pulled the cell out of the inside pocket of his jacket and saw "Jolene" flashing on the screen. Jolene Wallis was Harper's grandmother, a shrewd and strong Prime, and a woman who would obliterate anyone who threatened her family. He wondered if she'd heard that Harper was attacked. No one had announced anything, but Jolene had sources everywhere.

"I need to take this." Letting the hunter sweat a little would add to his demon's fun anyway. Knox moved a few feet away and answered, "Hello."

"I heard something happened in Harper's office," clipped Jolene, all business. "Is she all right? She's not answering her phone."

"She's sleeping," said Knox. "To put it briefly, she was attacked by hunters who were hired to steal her wings. They didn't succeed and she's healing well."

A hiss. "Tell me they're dead."

"One is. The other will be once he's given me the answers I want."

"I need to see her."

"Not now. Let her sleep. She needs it." Especially since she hadn't been sleeping well recently.

There was a resigned but long, suffering sigh. "Keep me updated. I want to know *everything* that bastard tells you. Make him pay." The line went dead.

Tucking his phone in his pocket, Knox overheard Levi speaking to the hunter. "Don't think that lying will help you. Knox wants answers, true, but he'll happily torture them out of you. This is nothing but foreplay."

It was true that Knox and his demon liked to toy with their prey. Moving back to stand before the hunter, he asked, "Where were we?"

"The more he lies, the more he'll hurt," said Levi helpfully.

"That's right." Knox sighed at the hunter. "And you lied again, as I recall it. Some people are masochistic that way. I suppose it's good for you that you appear to like pain. It'll help you get through the next few hours." Knox conjured a ball of hellfire and bounced it on his hand. "Have you ever eaten one of these?"

The chair creaked as the hunter jerked back, looking shocked by the question.

"It's a standard punishment within our lair, isn't it, Levi?"

"It is," the reaper verified. "I've heard it hurts like a son of a bitch. It burns your tongue, mouth, throat, esophagus, lungs, stomach, and finally your intestines before it sizzles away. Of course, it hurts a hell of a lot worse when it's a high-powered, lethal orb. That will burn a person from the inside out, leaving their corpse a melting, blistering mess until it finally vaporizes."

The hunter's panicked gaze darted from Knox to the blazing orb in his hand.

Knox tilted his head. "You look surprised that anyone would use such a punishment. It's no secret that I'm cruel and ruthless." He looked at Levi. "Maybe some think I've gone soft now that I'm mated."

"You soft?" Levi snorted.

"If anything, it's made me harder," Knox told the hunter, "because my drive to protect my mate is so intense and primal. Many have already died for harming her, so it truly does confuse me that anyone would assume that they could do so and not pay with their life. And yet, you hurt her."

"It wasn't me, I just—"

"Held her down so that she couldn't defend herself while another sawed at her wings; yes, I know." His eyes bled to black for just a moment, and the hunter nervously licked his lips.

"It was nothing personal. Just business."

"Business?" Knox rumbled.

Levi gave a dramatic wince. "Damn, hunter, you're just digging a deeper hole for yourself here."

"I just mean that—"

"There's really nothing you could say that would excuse what you did." Knox took a step closer to him. "As I said earlier, I won't be making any deals with you. You won't die faster if you tell me the truth straight away. I won't spare you any pain—not after what you did to my mate. But it is in your best interests to be truthful."

He swallowed. "Why?"

"Because my demon wants to play with you too," Knox said softly, "and I've decided to let it."

The hunter's face went devoid of all color. Well, who'd want to deal with an entity as dark and psychopathic as Knox's?

"It often gets carried away when it comes to torture," Knox went on. "But there's a possibility that it will get bored quicker if it has the answers it needs. I say 'possibility' because there's really no knowing for sure. If you'd prefer to take your chances, that's fine too. Either way, you'll be in pain and you'll die—this is a win-win situation for me. So, you can tell me what I wish to know immediately, suffer horribly for a little while and then die . . . or you can tell me what I wish to know *eventually*, suffer horribly a hell of a lot longer, and then die." Knox twirled the ball of hellfire. "Now, I'll ask again. Who hired you?"

The hunter opened his mouth and talked.

CHAPTER THREE

Harper woke to the smells of coffee, bagel, and cream cheese. She didn't move or open her eyes, but Knox must have sensed that she was awake because the tapping on his laptop keyboard stopped. Fingers then brushed her hair aside and he pressed a kiss to her temple.

"Morning, baby."

"Morning," she mumbled into the plump pillow. "What time is it?"

"Seven. You had a good, long sleep. It was a relief. You haven't been sleeping well lately."

Taking stock of herself, she realized that her wings had melted into her back, which meant they were healed. She also realized that someone—most likely Knox—had slipped a T-shirt on her while she slept.

Opening her eyes, she found him propped up against his pillows on his side of the massive bed, laptop resting on the legs that were stretched out in front of him. "What did the hunter have to say?"

"I'll tell you all about it while you eat. Sit up."

But she was just so comfortable. The deluxe mattress and super-soft bedding made her feel like she was wrapped in a cloud. The hedonistic luxury wasn't confined to the bed. The whole room was lavish with the high-quality furnishings, rare imported flooring, a huge-ass closet, and the balcony, which was more like a patio with a small pool. Knox did like his comforts.

His finger traced the shell of her ear. "Up."

"Do I really have to?" she whined.

His lips twitched. "Yes, or your breakfast will go cold." He closed his laptop and set it on the nightstand. "Then Meg will lecture you again for not eating well."

It was understandable, Knox thought, that her sleep cycle and appetite was off. Almost dying at the hands of dark practitioners and then again at the hands of a near-rogue demon would shake up anyone. To be responsible for your half-brother's death, even if he did completely deserve to die, would tug on the strings of a heart that felt as deeply as Harper's did. "Come on, baby, sit up."

"Okay," she mumbled, struggling into an upright position. He kissed her. Softly. Gently. Carefully. Harper shot him a scowl. "I'm not a spun-glass princess."

He smiled. "No, you're definitely not that." He placed a tray of food over her lap. "Eat."

Just to annoy him, she sipped at her coffee first. Her demon grinned when his eyes narrowed. It didn't like being treated like it was fragile either. "So, what did the hunter say?"

Knox waited until she bit into her bagel before he spoke. "They were sent an anonymous, encrypted email with a substantial offer if they could get their hands on your wings."

"So we can't trace the email?"

"No. It self-deleted a short time after it was opened."

"Clever." And terribly inconvenient, she thought with a

frown. "How were they supposed to contact this person once they had my wings?"

"They weren't. Their instructions were to leave your wings at a certain destination—a warehouse not far from here—where their cash would be waiting. Once they were gone, someone would come forward to grab the wings. If they didn't appear on time, no cash."

"What time exactly were they supposed to turn up at the drop-off point?"

"Eight pm—I hadn't even begun interrogating him at that time." Knox twirled a strand of her hair around his finger. "Keenan and Larkin went to the warehouse anyway and looked around, but they found no sign of anyone."

"Shit." She bit hard into her bagel. She figured it wasn't fair to take her anger out on the pastry, but what was done was done.

"They were also given strict instructions *not* to kill you."

Harper blinked. "Really?"

"This person wanted your wings, but they didn't want you dead. They were allegedly very adamant about that in their email."

"Any thoughts on why this would be important to them?"

Knox shrugged. "It could be simply that they believe I truly can call on the flames of hell and they didn't want me to unleash those flames out of grief. After all, what use are your wings to them if the world itself no longer exists?"

Harper would like to say that, no, he wouldn't go as far as to destroy the world if she died. But a demon who lost its mate was a dangerous creature, and if that particular demon was powerful enough to very effortlessly annihilate the world, why wouldn't it?

A rogue archdemon had almost done it once before, which was why Lucifer—or Lou, as he liked to be called—agreed to keep the breed in hell. But since he hadn't agreed to round up any archdemons who might still be roaming the planet, he'd left Knox exactly where he was—no doubt pleased about the loophole. The guy was *whacked*.

Lou was also rather insistent that Knox get Harper pregnant fast. Ever since a rogue demon had claimed to have had a vision that they'd produce a child that would destroy demonkind, Lou had badgered Knox to impregnate her. He also wanted them to call the baby Lucifer. *So not gonna happen.*

"Keenan will be obtaining the names of the main wing collectors, since they're the likeliest suspects at this point," said Knox. "I'll pay each of them a visit if I have to, but I *will* find out who sent the hunters after you."

"I'm guessing you don't want me to come along."

No, Knox didn't. He wanted her far away from any who might covet her wings. He chose his words carefully, knowing she didn't like to feel coddled. "Demons like things that are pretty and shiny. These demons might be innocent of coveting your wings, but if I put you in their sights, their interest could then turn to you."

Harper really couldn't deny that, which kind of annoyed her.

"On another note, Larkin and Keenan have removed the corpse from your office and cleaned up the blood."

"Tell them I said thank you." She hadn't been looking forward to facing the mess.

"They felt helpless seeing you hurt, so they were actually happy that there was something they could do for you. They're enraged by what happened. You should know that Tanner is shouldering some of the responsibility."

She groaned. "He has no reason to. Yes, he's my bodyguard, but we gave him the night off, since I was getting a ride with you and Levi. He can't possibly blame himself for not being there when there was absolutely no reason why he should have been."

"Well, he is. And nothing I've said has made him feel differently."

"I'll talk with him about it later." She took a sip of her coffee. "Now, why don't you tell me what it was that made you cut our telepathic conversation short yesterday."

"Or maybe we could watch T.V. for a while." Grabbing the remote, he switched it on.

"*Knox.*"

He sighed. "For the first time in months, you're eating properly. I don't want that to stop."

"I'll keep eating, I swear." To prove it, she took another bite of her bagel. "Come on, tell me."

He took in a long breath. "Carla, Bray, and Kellen are leaving the lair."

"I see," said Harper, her tone even. Given Carla was her mother, that should have hit her where it hurt, right? It didn't. They'd never had a relationship. When Harper's father, Lucian, rejected Carla as both his mate and his anchor, something inside the woman had just broken. Her attempt to abort Harper had failed, as had her request for an incantor—a demon capable of using magick—to trap Harper's soul in a bottle. Jolene had paid Carla to give birth to Harper, at which point the imps had taken her in.

Such cruelty was a perfect example of just how unstable a demon could become if they lost their mate. Still, Carla's pain was no excuse. If the things Roan told Harper right before he tried to kill her were true, Carla was still somewhat twisted. One thing that Harper knew for sure was that Carla—being self-centered, petty, and hurtful—would never play a positive part in her life, so what was the point of her being in it?

"I can't say it's unexpected." In fact, Harper was surprised they'd remained there this long. "I mean, who'd want to answer to the person who killed their son?"

"You're also a person who was almost killed *by* their son," replied Knox. "Roan conspired against all the US Primes, not just you."

"But Carla and Bray don't want to believe that."

"No, they don't. They're leaving Vegas altogether." Knox was glad of that, but he kept his satisfaction out of his voice. "They've bought a house in Washington."

"I guess it makes sense that they'd want to be far away from me."

"I take it that Kellen still hasn't returned any of your calls," he said, referring to her other half-brother.

"Not a one." The teen had initially reached out to Harper, hoping to have a relationship with her, but he had a habit of shutting her out whenever things became strained between her and his immediate family. "I've kind of . . . um . . . given up."

"Because you're not a sucker for punishment." Knox didn't add that there wasn't a chance he'd let Kellen try to squeeze his way back into Harper's life. He'd warned the kid once before that him pulling away from Harper again wouldn't be tolerated; he wasn't fucking kidding. He wouldn't allow anyone to play with her feelings that way.

Knox curled a hand around her chin and turned her face to his. "Don't let them hurt you, baby." He rubbed his thumb over her lower lip. "You can't change that they resent you for Roan's death, but you can change that you're letting them make you feel bad about it."

"It's not that I feel bad about it," said Harper. She'd never liked Roan, and she'd never once thought there was a chance that they could have any kind of sibling relationship, but she also hadn't thought she'd ever have to kill him. Technically, it was her demon who'd done the deed, but the demon was part of her soul, and that meant Harper shared the responsibility.

Her demon hadn't simply killed him. She'd coldly toyed with him before tossing him into the flames of hell—flames she'd somehow been able to conjure since they had, for lack of a better word, "birthed" her wings.

Forced to simply watch as her demon raged and destroyed, high on that power ... Harper would never forget how that felt. The demon had wanted to avenge Harper. It had wanted to make Roan and his co-conspirator feel as helpless as they'd made her feel. What her demon hadn't realized was that its actions had left her feeling utterly powerless too.

She wasn't upset with her demon. The entity didn't think the way she did, didn't "feel" as she did. There was absolutely no point in expecting it to account for any emotional hurt its actions might have caused.

To the demon, it was all very simple: Roan had intended to kill her, therefore he had to die.

Harper understood that, but it still wasn't easy to accept that she was partly at fault for her half-brother's death because, dammit, she wasn't made of stone. So, yeah, maybe she hadn't slept so well for a while and maybe her appetite had suffered. But that was partly because ... "I don't feel guilty about his death. I feel guilty that I don't actually regret what me and my demon did that night. It was him or me—I value my life more than I did his. Still, he was my half-brother." She should feel bad about it.

"Only in a biological sense. He was never once a brother to you, Harper. He never had a kind word to say about you, he repeatedly did things to hurt you, and then he fucking tried to kill you. The imps are your family. He was never a part of it."

Her demon fully agreed. Harper sighed. "You're right."

"I'm always right, baby. You're just taking a while to realize that."

She chuckled. "Really?"

"Yes, really. Now finish your breakfast." He turned up the volume on the T.V., hoping it might distract her from her thoughts. He was about to grab his laptop and finish answering his emails, but the news reporter's words snatched his attention.

" ... when police arrested her this morning after the fire, she told them she'd put her son in the oven because he was a changeling. She allegedly believes that her own child was taken by fairies who left her their child in exchange. Neighbors described Lipton as pleasant and helpful, but they also claimed she was very cold towards her son. Thankfully, the boy was able to escape the house and was relatively unharmed."

Harper scowled. "She tried burning her son in the oven? That's sick."

"Parents claiming their children were changelings was once a common thing," Knox told her. "Mostly, it was a claim made by people whose children had disorders or developmental disabilities. It was said that in order to identify a changeling and undo the switch, you had to do things such as hit, whip, or burn the child in the oven. Some parents used it as an excuse for murdering their own child."

Harper gaped. "And they got away with it?"

"Shockingly, yes." He grabbed his cell from the nightstand and dialed a familiar number. When the demon answered after the second ring, Knox asked, "I saw the news. Anything I need to know?" He wasn't entirely surprised by the response. "All right. I'll be at your home in an hour." Ending the call, he said to Harper, "That was Wyatt Sanders."

"The detective?"

"Yes." Wyatt was also one of the demons in their lair. "It would seem that the little boy is a demon."

Her mouth fell open again. "You mean to tell me that there's truly such a thing as changelings?"

"There was once upon a time," he said, rising from the bed. "They were the days before DNA tests could be done."

Putting the tray aside, she followed him into the walk-in closet. "Seriously?"

Selecting a fresh suit, Knox began to unbutton his shirt. "It didn't happen very often. When it did, it mostly happened with cambions. As they're half-human, their inner demons can sometimes lie dormant, making them more or less human. It was considered a kindness to let them be raised in the human world, where they would be fairly normal, than in the brutal world of demons, where they would be considered weak."

Her response faded into the back of her mind as she watched his muscles fluidly bunching and rippling beneath all that sleek skin. No one had the right to look that good. Seriously. There was no fat whatsoever on that body. He was power and strength and exuded an alpha energy that gave her goosebumps. She just wanted to trace those abs with her tongue—

A low growl rumbled out of him. "You can't look at me like that, baby. If I thought you could deal with just how hard I need to fuck you, I'd be in you right now." Knox couldn't give her soft and slow right then. Not when her fear-filled scream still haunted his mind and a fierce need still beat at him. "But later, when you've had time to properly recuperate, I'll have you."

"Fascinating," she said dryly, irritated that he spoke like she was some delicate flower that needed careful handling. If she didn't know he was still a little shaken after what happened, she'd give him a bucket load of shit for it. Today, she'd cut him some slack.

Taking a seat on the leather sofa in the center of the closet, she said, "Back to the changeling thing ... I can understand why it might be considered a kindness for weak cambions, but it wasn't a kindness to the human children."

Knox slipped on a fresh shirt and began to button it. "Demons

were only permitted to exchange the child for one who was so
ill that there was no way they'd live."

Well, that wasn't so bad. "You said it isn't done anymore, but
Wyatt claims that the kid is one of us."

"Yes. And I have every intention of finding out who dared to
leave a changeling without my knowledge or permission."

She pushed to her feet. "I want to come with you."

He sighed. "Harper—"

"Nu-uh. I'm fully healed, I've had a decent sleep, and there's
too much going on in my head for me to relax. Also, this is no
small situation." Slyly, she asked, "Wouldn't you rather have me
with you, where you can see for yourself that I'm fine?"

He narrowed his eyes. "You play dirty."

"Thanks."

"I'd still rather you stayed here, within these four walls, where
you're safest."

She frowned. "Whatever made you think I'd be staying inside
these walls all day?"

He tensed. "You intend to go to work?"

"Why wouldn't I?"

"Maybe because you were attacked there yesterday."

"If you think I'll let anything or anyone taint my studio, you're
out of your mind. I will *not* be scared in my place of work." It was
her baby; she loved it. "It's sweet—and undeniably irritating—
that you want to wrap me up in cotton wool, but it will *never*
happen. It's not like it was the first time I was ever attacked. And
if this is you trying to distract me from what we were talking
about, it won't work, Thorne."

He ground his teeth. "I just want you safe."

"I know that." Moving to him, she deftly fastened his tie and
smiled sweetly. "But, really, what safer place is there for me to
be than at your side?"

His little sphinx always knew what buttons to push to get what she wanted, Knox thought with an exasperated sigh. His demon wanted to take her with it; wanted her where it could keep an eye on her. If the entity had its way, she would never leave its side.

The demon became very easily bored and had little patience for people. Harper was really the only thing that gave it a sense of contentment. It was totally charmed by her, found her company . . . fulfilling. She never failed to amuse and entertain it. When she was around, the demon was more passive and well-behaved.

Knox traced the tattoo-like collar of thorns on her neck with the tip of his finger. It was one of three brands of possession that his demon had left on her skin. He had to agree with Harper that, yes, putting a brand on her throat where it was so highly visible was the equivalent of an "All Rights Reserved" sign, but his demon wanted it to be clear that she was taken. Any demon who saw the brands on her flesh would know what they were; would understand that she was *his* and his alone.

Just as possessive, her demon had left two brands on him— one on his nape, and one across the back of his shoulders, making each seem more like an extension of the other. Both were tribal and masculine with thick, pointed curves and solid, black lines. Knox wouldn't lie; it was a total turn-on for both him and his demon that they'd been branded by hers.

"Come on, Knox, you know nobody can keep me safe better than you can."

She was right on that. "You're very good at getting your way."

Harper grinned. "I learned from the best." Her mate was damn good at making things go his way. He could certainly talk her in circles at times. She'd had to learn fast how to keep up or he'd walk all over her—it was simply in his nature to forge ahead when he wanted something.

"I'll help you get dressed."

"I don't need—"

"Just let me take care of you."

Sensing that he needed that, she relented. "Okay."

Harper's demon rather liked how carefully and reverently he touched her as he stripped her naked and then dressed her in the blue jeans and black, long-sleeved shirt she chose. He even insisted on brushing her hair—something he did often, as if it soothed him somehow.

When they were both finally ready to leave, he took her hand and guided her down the curved staircase, along the wide hallway, and over to the marble foyer. There, he helped her slip into her jacket before guiding her outside and down the wide steps with a hand on her lower back.

Levi opened the rear door of the Bentley—one of several luxurious cars that Knox kept stored in the garage. Once Harper and Knox slid inside, Levi drove along the long, curved drive; passing the extensive, beautifully landscaped lawn and the security gatehouse.

The estate was bordered by high, brick walls that would have been plain had it not been for the ivy that trailed along them. At first, Harper had felt a little intimidated by the size of the estate. It was a far cry from the many homes she'd grown up in with her nomadic father. But now . . . well, now it felt like home.

The mansion was an expansive, lavish, beautiful piece of modern architecture, but it wasn't excessively extravagant. Wasn't showy or ostentatious. Instead, it possessed a warm elegance and the same undeniable charm as its owner.

It also had blue-tinted, bulletproof windows that Harper found *totally* awesome.

As the black, heavy, metal gates swung open, Knox spoke.

"How do you feel about going somewhere for a few days? Maybe spend some time on the yacht?"

Considering she was used to his overprotective ways, Harper figured she really should have seen this coming. Crossing one leg over the other, she gave him a sideways glance. "Really, Knox, I'm not traumatized by what happened. I don't need to get away from Vegas."

Knox stroked her thigh. "No one would blame you if you did. It hasn't exactly been a relaxing place for you over the past year. Plenty of people would want a break from it in your position."

"I'm not plenty of people. Knox, seriously, I really am fine."

Knox could sense that she truly believed that, but he wasn't convinced—not given that her body was screaming, "stressed!" He knew she was far from fragile, but it was difficult to remember that when she looked so drained and weary. "I need you to promise that if you do feel overwhelmed—" he gently tapped her temple "—you'll call me."

"I promise."

"And I need you to also promise me that you'll be alert. There is a possibility that more hunters will be sent. I doubt it, because, although hunters are greedy, they aren't stupid enough to pursue something that got two others killed. Still, there might be some who'll do it for the right price. Everyone has a price."

"I'll be alert," she vowed.

"Good girl." He kissed her softly, barely resisting the urge to take her mouth hard and feast on her. He held himself in check, but it was a struggle. "I don't know who found out that you can fly. The sentinels know, your family knows—it's possible that someone overheard one of them talk of it. If so, I suspect that someone may have passed on this information to another person who would want it. Either that or they themselves covet your wings. They may also know just how unique your wings are."

"If they do know, they didn't tell the hunters. They were sincerely surprised when they saw the colors of my wings."

"In any case, they obviously have no idea that you can conjure the flames of hell or I doubt they would have risked trying to obtain your wings." The flames of hell could destroy anything aside from archdemons—nothing else was impervious to the flames, which was why Knox took great care in ensuring the demon world didn't discover that he truly could call on them.

As a disturbing thought occurred to Harper, she sat up straighter. "Or maybe that's *why* they did it. If someone was in possession of wings that were sort of . . . birthed from the flames of hell . . . they'd have a lot of fucking power if there was some way they were able to tap into it. The kind of power only you could fight."

Knox twisted his mouth, pondering it. "True, but I don't believe they *could* tap into it. Not unless they have some way of fusing your wings to them—and I'm quite sure that's impossible."

"It doesn't mean there isn't someone who's willing to try it. It's just something we should consider."

"And we will," he assured her. "While we're busy finding who's behind the attack, we'll have to put aside our investigations into the remaining Horsemen."

"Which could be exactly what someone wants," she pointed out. "The Horsemen could have hired the hunters to either piss you off or distract you—maybe even both."

That was something he had already considered. "Yes, but I need to be sure. Any immediate threat to you needs to be eliminated." He tucked her hair behind her ear. "I'd feel a lot better if you'd agree to learn how to call on the flames. Then you could have called on them yesterday."

"I caused a lot of destruction last time." Enough to scare her into never wanting to do it ever again.

"That was mostly your demon."

"Yeah, I remember it got high on the power. It would *love* another try at it." Just the thought had it fairly rubbing its hands with glee.

"But if you don't learn how to call and direct the flames, you could call them by accident—I don't think you want that."

She sighed, knowing and resenting that he was right. "Fine, I'll learn."

"Right decision." He kissed her palm. "Are you sure you won't take at least one day off work?"

"Not happening, Thorne. You know me well enough to know that I can't sit around the house doing nothing—I'll go crazy."

Yes, Knox did know that. He even understood it, but he'd still rather have her at home. Still, Knox knew better than to browbeat her on anything—she'd object just to be contrary. Her obstinateness was typical of both imps and sphinxes. She had many sphinx qualities, despite being more of an imp by nature. Her breed was much like a bird and a lion rolled into one. In addition to being graceful and difficult to pin down, Harper was fierce and strong.

"All right," he said. "I'll trust you to call me if the day catches up with you." He'd also tell Tanner to keep a close watch on her and ensure that she ate well through the day to build up her strength.

A short time later, Levi parked the Bentley outside a small, detached house. As he opened the rear door, he said, "I think it's best if I wait in the car." He tipped his chin toward the group of teens who were staring at the Bentley with covetous eyes.

"We won't be long," said Knox. He took Harper's hand and led her up the narrow, cobbled path. She pressed the doorbell and stood back.

Within moments, Wyatt opened the door. He nodded in

deference. "Mr. Thorne, Ms. Wallis." He stepped aside, inviting them to enter.

A redhead stood behind him, gray eyes bright, smile strained. Her face was narrow and pale, rather unlike her mate's—he had an almost square face that was as tanned as the rest of him. It was easy enough to sense that Wyatt was a cop, Harper thought. It was in his stance, his expression, and the authoritative air about him.

"We haven't met before," she told Harper. "I'm Linda. It's a pleasure to finally meet you face-to-face, Miss Wallis."

Harper gave her a quick smile. "It's good to meet both of you. Call me Harper—the Miss Wallis stuff makes me feel awkward."

Rather than leading them further into the house, Wyatt lowered his voice as he spoke. "The clean-up crew you sent to the hospital to destroy the boy's hospital record and blood samples were almost done when I left."

Knox nodded his approval. "How is he?"

Wyatt jiggled his head from side to side, but his tousled peanut-brown hair didn't move, thanks to whatever gel he was using. "He seems all right, which I didn't expect. His mother didn't just try to burn him in the oven, she tried to burn the house down—as if to be sure he died. McCauley told the police that he managed to get out of the oven before she switched it on and then he scrambled out of the house. Since he has no burns, they believe him." Demons were impervious to normal fire, so the oven would have done him absolutely no harm. "Danielle Riley"—another demon from their lair— "was his appointed social worker; she's going to log in her file that he was placed with relatives and make it all look official."

"Who do you think his biological parents are?" Linda asked Knox, folding her arms.

"I'm not sure yet," replied Knox. "But I'll find them."

"He's welcome to stay here until then," Linda offered, sounding overly casual. "I mean, if that's okay with you?"

"If you'd like to take care of him temporarily, that's fine," said Knox. Linda's relief was clear to see on her face. Wyatt didn't look so delighted, Knox noticed. "Where is he?"

"The living room," said Linda.

"Lead us to him."

With a nod, Wyatt headed down the thin hallway and into a homey room with apricot walls, a lush beige carpet, and a cream leather sofa. In front of the large T.V. sat a little dark-haired boy, eyes locked on the cartoon that was playing.

"McCauley," said Wyatt, "these are the friends I was telling you about."

The boy turned to look at them, his face surprisingly blank. Being part of a large family, Harper was used to being around kids. Used to their nervous energy, their tendency to hop from one thing to another, and their boundless curiosity. But this boy's big brown eyes held no curiosity. No interest, no wariness, no happiness, nothing. And something about that raised her hackles.

Given what Knox had told her about changelings, Harper had expected him to be so low down on the power spectrum that he could pass for human. No demon would ever mistake this boy for human—he was by no means weak.

Knox spoke first. "Hello, McCauley. I'm Knox. This is Harper."

The boy's eyes bled to black as his demon surfaced, making its presence known and sizing them up. It retreated after only a few moments.

Knox tilted his head. "It fears me, doesn't it? The entity inside you. The one that drives you. I have my own, just as Harper, Wyatt, and Linda do."

McCauley didn't react.

Harper caught sight of the drawing on the coffee table. It was a standard family drawing, really—two adults, one boy, one girl, and a dog that looked like a golden retriever. But his pen control and attention to detail were impressive. "You're good. Is that you?"

He nodded.

She pointed to the little girl. "Who's that?"

He shrugged.

"Your mother has been arrested," Knox told him.

"Teri wasn't my mother." It was said with no emotion whatsoever. It didn't even seem like he was *suppressing* emotion. He genuinely didn't seem affected by the matter, one way or the other.

"No, she wasn't," Knox agreed. "Do you know who is?"

The little cambion shook his head. He didn't look particularly bothered by that either.

"I intend to find the answer to that question. In the meantime, you'll stay here with Wyatt and Linda. All right?" A nod. "Good."

"Do you need anything?" Harper asked him.

"No, thank you." Such a well-mannered phrase, yet there was no real "thanks" there. No gratitude. No anything.

"We'll see you again soon," Knox told him.

The kid's demon rose to the surface again; there was a challenge there this time. Knox's own demon surfaced and glared down at the boy, intimidating his demon into submission.

When both entities retreated, Knox warned, "Don't let it borrow trouble, McCauley." Taking Harper's hand, Knox led her to the front door. Before opening it, he turned to Wyatt. "You sure you want to keep him here?"

It was Linda who answered. "Positive."

Knox raised a questioning brow at Wyatt, who gave a simple nod. "All right," said Knox.

"Was there another child?" Harper asked, remembering the picture he'd drawn.

"The only people who lived in that house were him and the human female who'd raised him," said Wyatt. "Her husband left and remarried long ago. He has a daughter with his second wife, but he has no contact whatsoever with McCauley."

Harper thought it likely that McCauley had drawn a picture of himself immersed in that family ... or maybe he'd drawn the family he'd wished he had. "Don't hesitate to call us if you have any problems with him." The couple smiled, but Wyatt's smile was weak.

Once they were back in the Bentley, Knox gave Levi a run-down of what had been said.

"I like kids, I really do," said Harper. "But that kid was creepy. And he's not low down on the power scale."

Knox took her hand. "He's fairly powerful for a cambion."

"And pretty robotic. There's nothing, well, *child-like* about him. No crazy energy, no humming or fidgeting." There didn't appear to be any wasted movements with him at all. "He feels ... *cold.*"

Knox toyed with her hair. "Sometimes I think that demons forfeit emotion for power. I'm an example of that."

Her brows snapped together. "You're not emotionless."

"No, but I don't feel the range of emotions that you do. I'm not capable of many of them."

"You feel love, right?"

The tiny tremor in her voice made his chest tighten. "Baby, one day you're going to be utterly secure in the knowledge that you're a loveable person. I'll make sure of it."

"I don't doubt that you love me."

Knox knew that was true. Giving her a black diamond had crushed any doubts she might have had, but he suspected that it would take a long time to ease the insecurities that had been born when both parents abandoned her as a baby. Her subconscious didn't seem ready to heal. "Good. Never doubt it, because it will never change."

"If you can feel this emotion so strongly, if you believe it isn't something that will ever fade, then we don't forfeit emotion for power."

"That might be a good point, except that I only feel it for you. So maybe it's just that you're my miracle."

She smiled. "I've been called a lot of things. Never a miracle. My family would be so disappointed that I'm not living up to my purpose to annoy all those who cross my path."

Knox's mouth curved. "Oh, you're still expertly good at irritating people. I just get a free pass. For the most part, anyway."

"Very true." She smiled against his mouth when he kissed her. "Back to what we were talking about before, what do we do about McCauley?"

"I'll have Keenan find out how many women from our lair were pregnant back then. We'll find out who she is."

"Are you sure she's from this lair?" Demon lairs didn't claim territories, and their kind sometimes lived in places far from their Prime, so Harper believed it was very possible that the mother belonged to another lair.

"No, but we should look to our own first."

"And if one of ours *did* leave a changeling?"

"They'll pay the price."

CHAPTER FOUR

As Levi pulled up outside one of Knox's upscale clubs, Harper spotted Tanner leaning against the building. As her bodyguard and chauffeur, the broad-shouldered tower of muscle often took her to work and accompanied her to the studio before going off to do ... whatever sentinels did. Since the entrance to the Underground was beneath this very club, he was obviously waiting to escort her to work.

Knox curled his hand around her jaw. "My day will be pretty hectic, but I'll meet you in the Underground when your studio's closing." He kissed her softly. "Remember to—"

"Stay alert, I got it. You be safe too."

He kissed her once more, ending it with a nip to her lower lip. "Always am."

"See you later," she told him. As Levi opened the rear door, she hopped out of the Bentley. "Watch over him for me, Levi." The reaper inclined his head.

Pushing away from the wall, Tanner offered her a wan smile as she approached him. "How're you feeling?"

"Better now that both hunters are dead. Still blaming yourself like a total idiot?"

He ran a hand over his short, dark hair. "I'm your bodyguard—"

"And it was your well-deserved night off." Hearing a car horn beep, she gave Levi and Knox a quick wave as they drove away. Turning back to Tanner, she added, "Now accept that it wasn't your fault instead of being a dumbass. I don't time have for dumb-asses. And I already have Knox trying to blame himself—I'm done with this shit."

Tanner snorted a laugh, his wolf-gold eyes lighting up. "Let's get you to work." He accompanied her inside the club and down the flight of stairs to the basement. At the back of the large space, two demons guarded a door. Recognizing her and Tanner, they parted with a respectful greeting and opened the door. She and Tanner then walked through and, after a short elevator ride, arrived at the Underground.

The place was as busy and noisy as always. Pretty much everything could be found there. Bars, restaurants, casinos, clubs, hotels, a shopping mall—the list was endless. There were also other and much wilder things there such as the rodeo, the combat circle where demons fought for money, and the dog racing stadium for hellhounds.

Stepping out of the elevator, she and Tanner walked down the strip, passing plenty of venues and stores—some were open, some were closed until the evening arrived, at which point the entire Underground came alive.

Her studio, Urban Ink, was in an ideal spot. It was close to not only Knox's office but the best restaurants and even the shopping mall. It was also opposite a hotel wherein she and Knox had a penthouse suite—that meant she could go there to change clothes whenever she and the girls wanted to hit the bars after work.

Ordinarily, Harper met her co-workers in the coffeehouse beside the studio before they opened up, but she was running late so she headed straight to the studio. As she pushed open the glass door, the bell above it chimed. The scents of paint, ink, coffee, and disinfectant hit her, along with the heavenly smell of fresh Danishes that was coming from the coffeehouse.

Rather than leaving, Tanner followed her inside and said, "I'm going to take a quick look around."

Her cousin and receptionist, Khloë, came from behind the desk. "Grams is stressing about something, and you look like shit warmed up. What happened?"

With a sigh, Raini bumped the small, olive-skinned imp aside and handed Harper a caramel latte. "Jeez, Khloë, did you have to jump down her throat?" Raini was a senior tattooist as well as the co-owner of Urban Ink.

Having hung her jacket on the coat rack, Harper gratefully took the latte. "Thanks."

Even wearing a plain white vest with plain pants that hid her wicked curves, Raini was a breathing advertisement for sex—it was a succubae thing, and Raini didn't like it. She could hide her figure, but not her flawless skin or inherent sensuality. And if she'd thought that putting pink highlights in her blonde hair might dull its appeal somehow, it did the opposite.

"Something happened," insisted Khloë, daring Harper to deny it.

"Yes, something did happen, but I don't want to have to tell the story more than once so let's wait for Devon," said Harper, referring to their apprentice who also specialized in piercings. Harper had already told the story to Jolene on the way to work. Her grandmother had predictably lost her mind, even though she'd already known some of what happened from Knox.

Raini pointed behind her. "Oh, Devon's in the—"

A loud hissing sound was followed by a grinning Tanner strolling out of the breakroom with a furious Devon marching behind him, her long ultraviolet ringlets bouncing. Hellhounds and hellcats had an instinctive aversion to each other, and the two demons in question were engaged in a weird war that mostly involved pissing each other off for their own entertainment.

Cat-green eyes blazing with anger, Devon slung a pink ball of yarn at Tanner's head. "You keep buying me this shit, pooch, and I'll snap your neck!"

"But the color matches the pretty cat collar I bought you and—why do you have to hiss at me?" In the reception area, he sank into the sofa with a happy sigh, switched on the wall-mounted T.V., and put his legs up on the coffee table, almost kicking off the tattoo portfolios.

Devon frowned at him. "What are you doing?"

"Getting comfortable."

Harper groaned. "Please tell me that Knox didn't tell you to stand guard all day."

"He wants me to stick by you and make sure you're safe."

You asked Tanner to stay with me? Knox, we talked about this. The hellhound was a sentinel—he had better and much more interesting things he could be doing than babysitting her.

I told him to repeatedly check in to make sure you're fine.

Why would he say you told him to stick by me? But as she watched Devon go a disturbing shade of red, she understood. Knox must have understood too, because Harper felt his amusement as his mind brushed against hers. Harper sighed. *One day, she's going to kill him, you know.*

I've had the same thought multiple times. His mind touched hers once more, and then he was gone.

"Tanner, quit riling Devon and go do sentinel stuff," said Harper.

He rose to his feet. "I get it, I get it—she needs space because it's hard for her to deal with her feelings for me."

Devon gaped. "The only thing I feel for you is a boundless, blinding, glorious hatred."

He smiled. "You know you make me hard when you get all mean, kitten."

Harper pointed at the door. "Out."

Chuckling to himself, Tanner left.

Khloë patted Devon's arm, the image of sympathy. "Just so you know . . . your nipples are hard. Hey! Keep them claws to yourself!"

Harper threw an exasperated look at her shit-stirring cousin. Like all imps, Khloë found an immense delight in fucking with people. "Does anyone want to know what happened yesterday?" Everyone's attention immediately snapped to her.

Eyes glinting with the typical hellcat curiosity, Devon sidled up to Harper—Tanner forgotten. "Do tell."

Harper crossed to her tattoo station and settled in her black leather chair. "Quick warning: you're not gonna like it."

Once Harper had finished recounting what happened, Raini slumped against the glass checkered partition between their stations, amber eyes dull. "I'm sorry."

Harper frowned. "For what?"

"I should have waited with you. We could have locked up together."

"Why would you have waited for me? You never do it any other time. You hold no blame whatsoever for what happened."

"From now on, we all leave at the same time," declared Devon. The others nodded.

"There's no need," Harper assured them, but the words fell on deaf ears.

Khloë folded her arms. "Who do you think sent the hunters after you?"

Harper let her head fall back and took a moment to admire the tattoo flash on the ceiling. "No idea. Apparently, the hunters didn't know their identity either."

Disgusted, Devon shook her head. "I can't believe there are people out there who actually want to hang people's wings on their wall. It's twisted."

"You're fully healed now?" asked Raini.

"Yes, so you don't need to worry or fuss." But Harper suspected they still would.

The doorbell chimed, and Harper's first client for the day entered. Just like that, the girls switched into "work" mode and ushered the client over to Harper's station.

Since they kept the name "Urban Ink" when they relocated the business, they also kept its rock/art/Harley Davidson vibe. In addition, they hung their old metal art on the bright white walls—each of which was an enlarged copy of a tattoo, like the tribal swirls, flock of ravens, and the Chinese dragons. Pretty much everything else, including the lighted tracing tables and vending machine, were new.

She figured she didn't fit a person's idea of what someone who co-owned a tattoo studio would look like. She wasn't covered in tattoos and didn't have dozens of piercings. One of her nipples were pierced, though, and she did have three tattoos, but all three were in white ink and hidden beneath her clothes. Why? Well, Harper didn't have tattoos done for the hell of it. She only did it if the tattoo meant something to her and, as a private person, she didn't want people asking what hers meant.

Later, as Harper was cleaning her equipment after doing a floral tattoo, the door once again opened. Tanner strolled in, bringing with him the scents of freshly baked bread, smoky meat, hot peppers, and mayonnaise.

"I come bearing gifts," he said, holding up a deli takeout bag.

He gave Harper a pointed look. "Knox wants to make sure you eat."

Raini took the bag from Tanner. "Aw, that's sweet of him."

Harper snorted. "He just doesn't want me leaving the studio to buy food." Still, she telepathically thanked Knox and received a soft brush of his mind in response.

"Who can blame him?" asked Devon, sweeping the hardwood floor.

Rather than poking at the hellcat, Tanner turned to Harper, his expression somber. "I just saw Carla walking past here. I think she was about to come inside, but then she saw me."

Great. "Maybe she was coming to say her goodbyes."

"She's leaving your lair?" The hope in Khloë's voice made Tanner smile.

Harper nodded. "It's probably best for all concerned." She tipped her chin toward the breakroom. "Let's go eat, I'm starving."

After Tanner said his goodbyes and left, Khloë locked the door and flipped the sign to "Closed for Lunch". With that, they then settled at the table in the breakroom.

Raini handed Harper one of the deli sandwiches. "I take it Kellen's leaving with Carla and Bray."

Unwrapping her sandwich, Harper nodded, "Yep."

Devon put a hand on her shoulder. "I'm sorry, sweetie. I know you hoped to have a real relationship with him."

"It would have been nice." But Harper was done letting it get to her.

As she grabbed some bottles of water from the fridge and handed them out, Khloë said, "Kellen might be young and grieving, but it doesn't give him the right to mess you around." As if to punctuate that, Khloë bit hard into her sandwich. "You didn't go looking for him. *He* came looking for you."

"I got the distinct feeling that he didn't like Roan much anyway," said Devon. "It could be that he's feeling guilty about it now that Roan's dead. Still, it's not an excuse to be a dick."

Harper was about to say something else, but then the door swung open and several members of her family waltzed in: Jolene, Martina, Beck, and Ciaran. Harper guessed that Ciaran, who was Khloë's twin, had teleported them all into the studio.

As Harper stood, Jolene forced a smile as she studied her from head to toe. "You're really okay?"

"I told you I was fine."

"Yes, but you're a very good liar—I know, because I taught you well." She gently pulled Harper into a one-armed hug. Wearing her usual smart getup of blouse, skirt and high heels, Jolene possessed an effortless veneer of elegance that many would envy. Strong, powerful, and fearless, she was the kind of demon who fit the role of Prime perfectly.

She was also the kind of woman you'd find at the center of a riot—a riot that she'd also quite possibly instigated.

Beck, Jolene's anchor, cast Harper a gentle smile. "Good to see that you're okay. I knew you would be."

Pulling back, Jolene stroked Harper's hair. "It's really a shame those bastards are dead. Snapping their necks would have made me feel a whole lot better."

Martina, her aunt, cupped Harper's cheek. "Tell me Knox made them *hurt*," she growled.

"Oh, they hurt," Harper assured her.

Martina nodded, satisfied. The outgoing, softhearted, entrancingly beautiful imp was a total sweetheart. She also had a bad habit of setting shit on fire.

Ciaran frowned at Harper. "You sure you're okay? You look like cra—"

Harper held up a hand. "Heard it several times, don't need to hear it again."

"Fine, fine." Ciaran ruffled Khloë's hair and said, "Hey, bitch."

"Eat shit, asshole," Khloë shot back. No one outside their lair would ever suspect the twins were very close, since they persisted in antagonizing each other.

Jolene placed her hands on Harper's upper arms. "Tell me *everything* that happened."

"I called you this morning and told you the story, even though you already knew most of it from Knox."

"Yes, and both of you were very vague."

"Of course we were, Grams." Jolene was like a lioness when it came to her family. She was fierce in her protectiveness and would avenge any slight—no matter how small, no matter what it took. Being that she was batshit crazy, she was also the ultimate wild card and couldn't be trusted not to overreact. Stripping someone's home of every valuable they possessed, demolishing entire buildings, and threatening to destroy the Golden Gate bridge were all completely okay in Jolene's book. She *never* let anything go.

Jolene began to pace. "You're my granddaughter—you can't expect me to ignore that this happened to you."

"No, I can't. If you want to look into it, fine. I'd appreciate it. But like I told you on the phone, you can't be the one to dole out the punishment, Grams. It would make me and Knox look weak as Primes if we didn't shovel our own shit."

"Much as I hate it," said Raini, "she's right, Jolene. They're Primes. They can't have others deal with their problems."

Khloë nodded. "We can't be the ones to bring this fucker down, Grams. We can help find who hired the hunters, but then we have to tell Harper and Knox what we know."

Jolene hissed. "All right."

"You promise?" asked Harper. Her grandmother was a terrific liar, but she wouldn't break a promise to someone she cared for.

Exhaling a put-out sigh, Jolene said, "I promise that I won't overstep by killing the person behind the attack if I find them first."

Harper smiled. "Thank you."

"But I won't hide that I'm looking for them. If I didn't seek to avenge my own granddaughter, it would make *me* look weak."

That was true. "Fine."

Jolene kissed her cheek. "You take care. And get some sleep. You look like crap."

"You make me feel so loved, Grams."

"I do, don't I?"

As Knox entered the studio later that day, he saw a yawning Harper do a long, languid stretch. His jaw clenched at the sight. He should have insisted on her staying home. Not that it would have achieved anything. His mate did her own thing. It was something he respected, but it also frustrated him at times.

His demon cheered up a little now that she was close. It had pushed Knox all damn day to go to her; check on her; stay with her.

Spotting him, Harper smiled as she put on her jacket. "Hey. How was your day?"

"Boring." He crossed to her and breezed his thumb along the black smudge beneath her eye. "You're tired again."

"A little."

Tanner snorted at the understatement, and she shot him a narrow-eyed look.

Raini ushered them all toward the door. "I need to lock up."

After the studio was secure and the girls said their goodbyes and headed off, Harper looked up at Knox. "So, where are we going?"

Since Knox would rather she got some rest, he was about to suggest they go straight home when she spoke again.

"I hope it's a place with food. I'm hungry."

"You're hungry?" Well, that made a nice change. If taking her somewhere meant she'd eat a little, then that was what he'd do. "Where do you want to go?"

"You're asking me to choose what we do?"

He sifted his hand through her hair. "I like surprising you, but you're too tired for the surprise I had in mind. You pick what we do."

"You're not going to be pleased about it," she warned.

Knox stilled. "You don't want to go back to the rodeo, do you?" Because that would be a big no.

She gave a soft chuckle. "Nothing as wild as that. I just really feel like ice cream."

"Ice cream?"

"Yeah. And you're more of a 'Five Star restaurant' kind of guy than a simple ice cream parlor person."

"I know a good place to get ice cream."

Her brow furrowed. "There's a parlor on the corner."

"I know somewhere better."

"Really? Well, I don't care where we go as long as there's ice cream. Lead the way."

Tanner and Levi flanked them as Knox led her down the strip to one of his hotels. While some places were closing, others were being opened and street vendors were setting up. The Underground would only get busier as the hours went on.

When they finally arrived at the luxury hotel and the automatic doors swished open, the cool air conditioning slid over them. As usual, some of the employees rushed to him with questions. Hiding his impatience, Knox answered them quickly and directly without breaking stride. He then guided Harper to the rear of the hotel and through a glass door. The quiet chatter of the lobby was quickly replaced by the sounds of children's laughter, spoons scraping bowls, and the whir of a blender. "Well, here we are."

Harper's eyebrows flew up. It was nothing like your standard ice cream parlor, she thought. It was more like a cute, chic restaurant. The décor was white and gold, and had an almost royal look about it.

There were glass-covered cases with several tubs of different colored—and, according to the sign, award-winning—ice creams. But instead of customers lining up at the counter, they sat comfortably while waiters took their orders.

"I had no idea this was here." Then again, she'd had no reason to come to these places before meeting Knox.

Harper plucked the menu from the stand. Damn, there were so many choices—so many different flavors, so many different toppings, and so many different syrups. They had everything, from typical flavors like vanilla and chocolate to others such as cotton candy and piña colada.

When the host appeared, she ordered a waffle cone of salted caramel covered in butterscotch syrup and little chunks of honeycomb. When the waiter walked away, she frowned at Knox. "You're not ordering anything?"

"There's no point," he said.

"Why?"

"Because I'll get so distracted watching you eat that my ice cream would end up melting all over my hand."

Chuckling, she returned the menu to the stand and then rubbed her chilled hands together. It was a lot colder than the hotel lobby, but Harper supposed it had to be or the ice cream would easily melt. It was only right then that she noticed that Levi and Tanner hadn't followed them inside. "Where are the sentinels?"

Knox gestured to the glass wall behind her. "Waiting for us." Giving them some private time while also guarding them.

As a yawn crept up on Harper, she did her best to suppress it. She failed.

"You went back to work too early," he admonished. "You should have taken the day off to fully recover."

She gave a soft snort. "Says the guy who's probably never taken a day off in his life."

"There have been a few."

"I don't mean days where you worked from home. I mean days of no work whatsoever—no calls or texts or emails to business associates. Can you honestly say you've ever had one of those days?"

No, he couldn't. "Point taken. But you still should have taken the day off instead of pushing yourself."

"Those bastards aren't disrupting my life."

He sighed. "So stubborn."

"Proudly."

Tapping his fingers on the table, he said, "I want to ask you something. It's probably not fair of me to ask this of you—it's not a customary thing among demons and is more of a human convention, but I'd like you to do it."

Dubious, she frowned. "You're not going to ask me to get married in a church, are you?"

Mouth curving, he took her hand. "No. These rings say we're bound." He smoothed his thumb over the black diamond, adding, "I'd like you to take my surname."

Her brows almost hit her hairline. "Well, that wasn't something I'd have ever expected you to say. Maybe I should have. Your possessiveness knows no boundaries."

"I won't deny that."

"At least you're admitting it. Changing my surname doesn't

seem necessary. I mean, it's not like people are under any doubt that we're together."

"It's important to me."

"No, it's important to your possessive streak."

It was more than that. "I want my mate to share my surname."

"Keeping my surname doesn't mean I'm not fully invested in this relationship or that I don't believe it will last," she assured him.

"I know that. And I fully admit that I want you branded in as many ways as it's possible to brand someone." Knox didn't even care that that was unhealthy. He'd made his peace with it long ago. "But this isn't about taking possession of you."

"Then what is it about?"

"I understand that your family name means something to you—the Wallis imps supported and loved you while your maternal family rejected you." For that reason, they'd always have his respect and backing. Well, all except for her father anyway. "I don't have a family to welcome you into. We'll be making our own family, and I want us to do that with one name."

Her chest tightened. "Did you really have to put it that way? I don't know how to argue that." It was too sweet.

"So don't." He leaned forward. "At least think about it."

"I'll consider it."

"Thank you."

The waiter then reappeared, and Harper took the bumpy waffle cone with a wide smile. "Thank you." She licked at the piece of art and groaned; the salted caramel ice cream was smooth and cold on her tongue. "You're totally missing out," she told Knox.

Eyes on her mouth, he said, "Oh, I assure you, I'm not." He barely took his eyes off her mouth the entire time she ate. By the end, he was so damn hard he knew it would hurt to walk.

When she was done, she cleaned her sticky fingers with a lemon wipe. "Ready to go?"

He was ready to get her home where he could take her as he'd wanted to since the previous night. He let her see that in his expression, and he had the pleasure of seeing her pupils dilate and her cheeks flush. "I'm ready to go. Are you ready for me?"

"If it involves me coming multiple times, I'm totally ready."

His cock twitched. "You'll come as many times as I want you to."

"I don't know ... maybe I'm still a little too fragile for you."

He snorted, rising to his feet. "Fragile is never a word I would use to describe you." He kept possession of her hand as he guided her out of the parlor. Levi and Tanner fell into step with them as they walked down the long hallway, toward the exit.

Up ahead of them, the door to the hotel's restaurant opened and a bunch of people filed out. Harper recognized three of them: Thatcher, Jonas, and good ole Alethea. The males were both Primes, and Alethea was Jonas' sister. She also happened to be a pain in Harper's ass and liked to flirt with Knox—as if shaking the sheets with him in the distant past gave Alethea some rights to him.

For a while, a whole lot of females had flirted with Knox, but the majority had recently stopped. They'd seen the black diamond he gave Harper and had accepted that it meant there was nothing at all temporary about her place in his life. She suspected they'd ceased to be bitches to her as they'd rather not make an enemy of Knox. Smart move on their part.

Alethea ... well, she didn't demonstrate the same wisdom. In fact, at that very moment, she shot him a sultry smile and said, "Evening, Knox." Her gaze then cut to Harper, and her smile fell. "Sphinx."

"Dolphin." Yeah, Harper liked to call her that since, as an

encantada, Alethea could shift into the form of a dolphin. It was kind of a random ability for the ultimate sex demon, in Harper's opinion, but whatever.

"Knox, good to see you," said Thatcher, bushy eyebrows lifting slightly. It was probably wrong just how badly Harper wanted to pluck them. "How are you?" he asked.

Knox inclined his head. "I'm well, thank you."

Thatcher nodded at Harper—it wasn't so much a nod of respect from one Prime to another as it was a simple acknowledgement of her presence, but she let it go. She wondered how long it would take the Primes to realize she just really didn't give a shit if they accepted her or not. The fact that she was a Wallis would always be held against her to some degree.

Jonas' smiling eyes danced from Knox to Harper. "It's a pleasure to see you both. We haven't spoken since the celebration of the Underground's anniversary, have we?"

"No, we haven't," said Harper. She didn't mind Jonas. He was an okay guy, and he did his best to control his dumbass sister.

"Did the Showcase agree to sell?" Jonas asked Knox.

As the boys started talking business, Alethea examined Harper from head to toe and smiled smugly. Yeah, Harper was quite aware that she resembled the living dead and she hated that the dolphin was standing there looking the image of perfection. Alethea's smug smirk only rubbed salt in the wound. And because Harper could be a bitch too, she said, "So, how's life in the Red Light District?"

Behind her, Tanner snickered.

Alethea's eyes tightened. "You overstep far too often, sphinx. I have to say, you look rather weary."

"And you look rather bitter," said Harper. "Still pissed about the rings, huh?"

Alethea licked her teeth. "I won't lie, I don't think you're the right person for Knox. But my brother is right—Knox is our ally, we should support his choices."

Like Harper would ever believe that. She smiled. "That's good to hear, even if it is complete tripe."

Alethea's mouth curled. "I said we *should* support his choices. I never said that I did."

And that was why Harper still believed that Alethea could be one of the Horsemen. On the one hand, it could be said that surely she wouldn't draw so much of Knox's attention to herself if she was secretly conspiring against him. But Alethea was a she-demon scorned, and scorned she-demons were malicious creatures—especially when they had an ego as wide as hers.

"And I'm not the only one who'll never support his choice to have a Wallis for a mate," clipped Alethea.

"Ooh, I cared for about a ninth of a second. Then I remembered how stupid and insignificant it is."

Alethea leaned forward. "Did you know that in the dictionary, your name is under the word 'bitch'?"

"Not sure why you're smiling. *I'm* not the one who had to look up the word."

Alethea sucked in a breath and went to bark something else, but then the boys ended their little conversation.

Knox put a hand on Harper's back. "Ready to leave?"

"Totally." Harper gave Alethea a winning smile. "Well, it's been great talking to you. You know how much I enjoy these little chats we have."

Slipping his arm around Harper's waist, Knox nodded at the other three demons. "Enjoy your evening." Leading her out of the hotel, he said, "It's hard not to intervene when she speaks to you that way."

"I appreciate that you don't. She needs to understand that I can defend myself just fine. Also, it's really fun to toy with her."

Knox's mouth quirked. "Yes, I've noticed you enjoy it. My demon finds it just as amusing. But we're going to push her and the others out of our minds now."

"I have no issues with that plan, just so you know."

My plan also involves you. Naked. In our bed.

Still have no issues with the plan.

Good to know.

Harper smiled. The anticipation crept up on her and taunted her the entire journey home. But when they finally walked into their bedroom, he looked at her just as he had this morning— like he was afraid he'd break her. She frowned. "You're not going to tuck me into bed, are you?"

"I couldn't even if I wanted to." Knox thrust his hands into her hair, growling. "Open for me." He kissed her, drinking her in. She tasted like Harper and caramel and honeycomb. And he couldn't get enough. He tilted her head, licking deeper, taking more. Taking everything.

Her hands delved into his hair, nails digging into his scalp. Groaning, he shoved his hand under her shirt and bra and closed it around her breast. It was soft, round, and plump. Perfect. Her hard nipple brushed against his palm; he wanted it in his mouth.

Bunching the bottom of her shirt in his hands, Knox slid it up and over her head and then whipped off her bra. The sight of the tattoo-like brand of thorns circling her breast made masculine satisfaction whip through him. She was *his*. Every single inch of her belonged to him. Only he could touch her, taste her, drive deep inside her. No other male would ever have her. He'd kill anyone who tried.

Taking a fistful of her hair, Knox pulled hard, arching her back. He latched on tight to her pierced nipple, flicking the ring with his tongue and tugging it with his teeth. He breezed his thumb over the white ink 'So it goes' tattoo beneath her breast—her own personal reminder not to dwell on things that were out of her control.

"Undo your jeans," he rumbled. "I want them off." He needed to fuck her hard and deep.

Harper's shaky fingers fumbled as she awkwardly snapped open her fly. He helped her shove down her jeans and panties, and then tossed her on the bed. Breathing hard, she watched as he quickly shed his own clothes, eyes drifting over her with sheer unadulterated possession. Naked, he truly was a sight to behold. Not an ounce of fat there. His body was all solid muscle, controlled strength, and sleek skin that hummed with power. Then there was his long, thick cock that was currently standing to attention.

She was just thinking of rearing up to touch him when psychic hands grabbed her thighs and spread them. She shivered. The hands were so icy cold, yet they somehow gave off pure heat—a heat that snaked up her inner thighs all the way to her centre, making her tingle and burn. He reached out and skimmed the tip of his fingers over her folds. The light touch fired the need already taunting her.

Knox crawled on the bed, eyes on her pussy. He wanted her taste in his mouth when he took her. "I want you to be quiet for me."

She blinked. "What?"

"You heard me."

Harper almost gaped. She was noisy and they both knew it. "You can't be serious." But his expression said that he was.

"I don't want you to make a single sound until I tell you that you can."

"And if I do make a sound?"

"You'll regret it."

Oh, she didn't doubt that. He could be a sadistic fucker when he felt like it. To say that he "liked" control would be an under-statement. It was important to him on a fundamental level. She couldn't hand over complete control to him. Her life was her own. But she could give it to him in the bedroom. Most of the time she did, since it always worked out well for her, but she didn't do it easily.

"Remember what I told you, Harper." It was a silkily spoken warning.

"How could I freaking forget?" There was a slight chill in the air as his eyes bled to black. "Can't you be on my side?" she asked the demon.

Its mouth curved. "I like the noises you make. But I also like to play." As if to punctuate that, it sank one ice-cold psychic finger inside her. Instantly, her pussy began to heat until it was burning. Knox resurfaced and shot her a cautioning look that promised retribution. "Not a sound."

Cursing, she grabbed his pillow and put it over her head. Harper bit back a gasp as he danced his tongue over the black, intricate swirl of thorns on the V of her thighs—it was the third brand of ownership that his demon had given her.

As his tongue slid between her folds, she practically melted into the mattress. There were guys who would give a half-hearted attempt at oral and who treated it as a means to an end. Then there were guys who would go down on their partner like it was an Olympic sport, who took their time and enjoyed it. Knox was one of the latter, which made her a lucky bitch.

Every lick and stab of his tongue was almost casual, as if he had no objective and simply wanted to taste her. If it wasn't for how hard his fingers dug into her tremoring thighs, she wouldn't know just how badly he wanted to be in her.

"I know you're hurting, baby," he said against her folds. "I'll take it away soon."

He'd better. That was the thing. The psychic fingers didn't just work to rev her engines, they sparked an ache inside her that only Knox would fill. No one else would take it away. Just him.

He kept on tasting and torturing her, and her orgasm soon began to build. She knew it would be a big one. There was no way she'd keep quiet. She squirmed, dislodging him. Grunting, he repositioned her and latched onto her clit. At the same time, one psychic finger pushed into her pussy, making it blaze unbearably.

"Come, but be quiet." It was an order, and her body automatically responded to it.

She bit into the pillow as wave after wave of pleasure crashed into her, wracking her body. The pillow disappeared, and there was Knox. The ice-cold finger dissipated, making her pussy blaze and spasm. Then psychic hands lifted her trembling thighs, angling her hips.

Knox licked along the collar of thorns on her throat. "You're like a drug."

"Drugs are bad for you."

His mouth curved. "Not this drug. It's new on the street. But only I get to have it." She laughed. Knox placed the head of his cock near her opening, but he didn't push inside. He stayed there, let her feel him, let her know what was coming. She squirmed, trying to impale herself on him. He placed a splayed hand on her stomach and shook his head.

Frustrated that he was making her wait, she snapped, "Okay, what do you want?"

"I have everything I want right here, baby. It's already mine. Now I'm going to take it." He sucked her nipple into his mouth and slammed home.

She inhaled sharply as his cock filled and stretched her just right, making all kinds of nerve endings spark and flame. It was

almost painful, courtesy of the damn psychic fingers that always
left her inner walls hypersensitive. She could feel every ridge,
every vein, every throb.

"That's it, don't make a sound." Her eyes called him evil. Knox
dragged his teeth down her neck and gave her pulse a sharp bite.
Her hot, wet pussy tightened around his cock. "Nothing feels
better than this." Then he fucked her. Hard. Deep. Slamming
in and out of her, loving the prick of her nails on his back. "I've
wanted to do this all fucking day."

Fisting her hair, Knox bit and sucked at her neck, leaving little
marks of possession that his demon loved to look at. Feeling her
pussy flutter around him, Knox thrust harder. Faster. She sank
her teeth around his shoulder as she came, but he didn't stop.
He kept pounding into her, pushing her closer and closer to yet
another orgasm. "Now let me hear you."

"You're a *bastard*!" she burst out.

If he wasn't out of his mind with need, he would have laughed.
Instead, he watched her face, savoring her moans, throaty little
whimpers, and the hot clasp of her pussy. "Let me feel you come."

An ice-cold psychic finger flicked her clit, and Harper arched
into Knox as her release crashed into her, trapping a scream in
her throat. She felt his cock swell as he slammed into her twice,
and then his spine locked and she felt every splash of his come.
Panting and tremoring, she had to ask ... "How are you still
hard?"

He sighed. "You always ask me that. Why?"

"You just fucked me into oblivion. You should have no energy."

He licked at the anchor mark on the hollow beneath her ear.
She'd left a similar mark on his, effectively branding him as her
anchor. "I can't be inside you and not be hard."

He rolled them both onto their sides, keeping her close.
Feeling him stroke her back, Harper knew he was searching for

any slices that hadn't yet completely healed. "They're gone," she assured him.

Though he was pretty sure that was in fact the case, Knox needed to see that for himself. He gently turned her onto her stomach and swept his hand down her sleek back. No wounds, no blemishes, no trace that she'd ever been hurt—there was only the tattoo-like marks of her wings.

Relieved, Knox pressed a kiss between her shoulder blades, silently promising not to allow anyone to take the wings from her. And when he found the person who sent those hunters her way, he'd make what the hunters went through seem like a fucking pleasure cruise.

CHAPTER FIVE

———◆———

The coffeehouse was always fairly busy in the mornings, so Harper was used to standing in the long line. Patience wasn't her strong point, but it would be worth the wait. She didn't need to look at the menu board or the chalkboard advertising the specials. She always ordered a caramel latte—it had become her ritual, and nowhere did lattes better than this place.

So she stood there, surrounded by the sounds of chatting, the hum of the blenders and espresso machines, and the clatter of mugs and dishes being stacked in the dishwasher. She didn't mind the noise, though. She *did* mind that her tongue was burning like crazy for no apparent reason. Hopefully the latte would help with that.

Harper inhaled deeply, taking in the comforting smells and coffee beans. She loved it. Loved how the scents of chocolate, cinnamon, caramel, and nutmeg blended so nicely with it. Usually, she'd be tempted by the pastries inside the glass case. Honestly, she was more interested in snatching the tall canister of whipped cream and eating it all to herself. An interest she would, of course, totally ignore because it was just plain weird.

Tanner and the girls were gathered around the bistro table near the window; it had become their spot. Tanner, as usual, was flicking through a newspaper, but Harper knew he was fully aware of everything going on around him.

Finally reaching the front of the line, Harper smiled at the barista. "Morning."

"Good morning. I placed your usual order as soon as I spotted you—it should be ready by now." It was something the she-demon often did, since they always ordered the same things.

"Thank you." Harper handed her the money and, after placing her change in the tip jar, headed to the end of the counter. There, another barista was placing cups on a tray. This particular she-demon, Wren, reminded Harper of one of her cousins—she was bright, ditsy, and extremely quirky.

She smiled at Harper. "Got your order right here." She placed one of the cups in Harper's hand. "Try this instead of a latte."

Harper sniffed. "What is it?"

"Just frothed vanilla milk."

"But I love my lattes." Harper was ashamed to say she almost whined that.

"I know, but spice is the variety of life . . . or whatever." Her brow creased in concern as she added, "I heard about the attack. How are you?"

Harper wasn't surprised that the news was getting around. The demonic grapevine worked at a seriously fast speed. "I'm fine, thanks. I'll feel even better if you give me my latte."

Wren smiled. "Not scared of a little milk, are you?"

Harper felt her lips quirk. "You can be weird sometimes, you know."

Wren's eyes twinkled. "Maybe we're twins."

Harper laughed. "Maybe." A whistle made her look over her shoulder. Devon was stood at the condiment trolley, tapping her watch impatiently. Harper rolled her eyes and turned back to Wren. "I'll try the damn milk." She took a cautious sip. Harper had always been a caramel girl, but the frothed vanilla tasted super good. Even better, it seemed to soothe her burning tongue. Still, Harper made a put-out huff. "Fine, I'll take it."

Wren chuckled. "You're welcome."

"Yeah, yeah." Lifting the tray, Harper headed to Devon, who then quickly helped her add sugar, milk, and other toppings to the drinks.

"I'll carry the tray," said Devon. "You waited in the line."

Fine with that, Harper turned . . . and almost bumped right into none other than Carla. Well, fuck a freaking duck.

Her inner demon hissed, having no time or patience for this woman who'd abandoned them. It was the first time Harper had come face to face with her since before Roan's death. The resentful glitter in her eyes told her that Carla wasn't there to check that she'd recovered from the hunters' attack. No surprise there.

Harper was conscious that the chatter had died down and everyone was watching, waiting to see how it would play out. Carla would no doubt be thrilled about that. She did so love being the center of attention . . . such was the life of a narcissist.

Part of Harper felt sorry for this person who was so emotionally stunted that she was still stuck at the infantile age where her own wants and needs were more important than those of others. Because of the gaping emotional hole inside her, she'd always perpetually seek the attention that she needed just as intensely as an addict needed crack. And Carla's drug of choice seemed to be sympathy. She was a never-ending victim, and drama made her feel alive somehow. As such, she was milking whatever sympathy she could get for having lost her son.

Maybe Harper's thoughts should have shown a little more sensitivity to Carla's current situation. After all, the woman was grieving. But, honestly, Harper didn't believe that Carla could experience grief the way others did. She just didn't seem truly capable of forming an emotional connection with anyone. Neither of her sons had a kind word to say about her, which was telling. And loving a person often meant putting them first, and Carla was far too self-absorbed to put anyone before herself.

Tanner was instantly at Harper's side, his stance protective. *There an issue here?*

There could be, Harper replied.

"I wouldn't advise you to say whatever it is that's going through your mind, Carla," said Devon. None of the girls had ever liked Carla, particularly Khloë, who insisted on referring to both Harper's parents as merely her "primary blood relations".

Carla's shoulders lifted as she took in a long breath. Apart from their small figure, pointed chin, and dark hair, they didn't share much resemblance at all. It was something Harper, petty though it might be, was thankful for. "I just want to say one thing."

Harper doubted she would only say *one* thing. Carla loved the sound of her own voice.

"Roan … he had his faults," Carla continued. "He wasn't perfect by any stretch of the imagination. But he wouldn't ever have considered being part of some scheme to see the US Primes overthrown. It doesn't even make sense—he would never have benefitted from it."

"Okay."

Carla blinked. "Okay?"

"There's nothing at all that I could say that would appease you. If you wish to believe he wasn't part of it, who am I to interfere with that?" Harper had no intention of giving the woman the argument she was looking for.

"But you don't agree with me," Carla pushed.

"It's possible that he was lying, but I don't see why he would have."

"But maybe *you're* the one who's lying."

Harper's demon snarled. "And would I?"

"Maybe you're jealous that I kept him but I gave you away."

Harper couldn't help it; she laughed. But it wasn't a pleasant sound. "Oh yeah, Carla, you got me there," she said dryly. There were a few snickers.

Carla's expression was hard as stone. "Doesn't it bother you that you killed your own brother?"

Did it bother Harper that she'd been in a position where she'd had to kill him or be killed *by* him? Yes. Did it bother her that he was dead? No. Roan had conspired against the US Primes. Worse, he'd wanted Knox dead. That was something Harper would *never* forgive or excuse.

"You might not have liked him, but *I* loved him. *I*—"

Harper took a single step toward her, eating up her personal space. "Do you know what he did while I was tied to a table? He took a pair of scissors, and he cut into my earlobe ... claiming you'd once done the same thing to him."

Carla's eyes flickered. The twisted bitch *had* done it.

"From what he told me, that wasn't an isolated incident. You'd hurt him before that and you hurt him again afterward. Play the devastated, crumbling mother if you want, Carla, but don't expect me to buy it."

There was a huff, and then another voice spoke. "You never could resist causing a scene, could you, Carla?"

Harper peered over Carla's shoulder to see a small old woman in a gypsy dress. It was Nora, the grandmother of one of the

Primes, Dario. Harper had only met her once before, when they learned that Nora had premonitions. To be specific, she *knew* and *felt* events that would soon occur.

It was through Nora that Harper and Knox had learned about the Four Horsemen. Nora hadn't seen Roan's face, but she'd *known* through her ability what his motivations were. She'd warned them that the person pulling Crow's strings was cold and power-hungry with a void that would always leave him unsatisfied with life.

Frowning at Carla in both disappointment and impatience, Nora added, "Do you not think you've done enough to this girl?"

Looking like she was sucking on a lemon, Carla said, "She killed—"

"A son you mistreated and controlled, from what I heard," Nora finished. "A son you didn't see as a person in his own right—he was only ever an extension of you. It was little wonder he grew to be greedy for power. He spent so many years under your rule that he needed the greatest power possible to feel in control. Or, at least, that is what everyone is speculating."

Cheeks reddening, Carla hissed, "He was *not* one of the Horsemen, if the Horsemen even exist."

"Oh, they exist. And he was one of them—never doubt it. The only person at fault for his death is Roan. He made his choices. They were bad choices that could only ever have resulted in his own demise."

Before Carla could say another word in her son's defense, Tanner forced her to step aside and said, "You've said your piece. Now it's over. Get the fuck out of our way."

Once Carla shuffled to the side, Nora gestured for Harper to move forward and then linked her arm through hers. Instead of escorting Harper to the bistro table, Nora headed straight out the door with Tanner close behind them.

Outside, Nora said, "There. Now take a breath."

Harper settled her hands on her hips as she inhaled deeply, urging her pissed-the-fuck-off demon to calm down. The entity despised Carla and always would.

Nora patted her back. "You were right to believe there's nothing you can say that will appease her. She'll never accept that Roan was virtually responsible for his own death."

"Yeah, I know," said Harper. "I can understand why she wouldn't want to acknowledge what he did."

"It doesn't make it okay that she just confronted you in there," Tanner clipped.

No, it didn't, which was why her demon wanted Harper to go back inside the coffeehouse and bitch slap her. Instead, Harper spoke to Nora. "I hope you're not here because you've had some kind of bad premonition."

The woman cackled, sounding just like Jolene. "No premonition. I heard you were attacked by hunters, so when I saw you inside the coffeehouse I took the opportunity to check that you're healed."

"I'm fine," Harper told her. "Pissed, of course, but otherwise okay."

Nora opened her mouth to speak again, but then the bell chimed as the coffeehouse door opened. The girls all filed out, carrying their mugs. Technically, they weren't supposed to *take* the mugs, but Harper doubted the baristas would give them a hard time about it as long as they returned them.

"You okay?" Raini asked.

Harper nodded. "It's not exactly the first time she saw fit to cause a scene."

Khloë sneered at Carla through the glass window. "It's what attention junkies do."

"Come on," began Devon, leading Khloë toward the studio. "Let's get inside or we'll be late opening up."

Nodding, Harper smiled at Nora. "It was good to see you. Tell Dario I said hi."

Nora patted her arm. "Will do. Take care of yourself, Harper." She waved at the others and then walked away.

Raini unlocked the studio door, and they all strode inside. "You sure you're okay?" she asked Harper.

"Fine." Harper sipped at her drink. "Not looking forward to telling Knox about it, though. He'll be pissed." And he'd no doubt point out that if she'd stayed home, she could have escaped the ugly encounter blah, blah, blah. He'd be wrong, though. Carla would have found another opportunity to confront her.

"You should tell him now before someone else does," Tanner advised. "What's that you're drinking?"

"Frothed vanilla milk, apparently."

Devon frowned. "Since when do you drink frothed vanilla milk?"

"Since the barista gave it to me to try." And since it eased a weird burn on her tongue. "It's good." *Knox, you busy?*

His mind brushed against hers. *Never too busy to talk to you. Everything okay?*

I just wanted to let you know—and it's no big deal, I'm not upset—that Carla caused a little scene in the coffeehouse. It wasn't bad, she quickly added. *There was no yelling or threats or anything. She just made it clear that she doesn't believe Roan was one of the Horsemen.* There was complete silence. *Knox?*

A vibe of anger touched her mind. *I'll deal with it.*

No, I already dealt with it. I'm just telling you because I figured you'd want to know.

She has no right to confront you, Harper.

No, she doesn't, so I dealt with it. She'll be gone from the lair soon. Don't give her the satisfaction of a reaction. Carla was the type of person who found bad attention better than no attention, which was just plain pathetic in Harper's opinion. *She's not important. Let her see that.*

There was a long silence. *Fine, but if she tries anything else . . .* He let the sentence trail, but the threat was clear.

I understand.

His mind stroked hers once again, comforting her, and then he was gone. And as her stomach unexpectedly churned and lethargy quickly crept up on her, she started to wish she'd stayed home.

Keenan sank into the chair in front of Knox's office desk and slapped a piece of paper on it. "I was hoping there would only be a few collectors of demonic wings and that this would be a process of elimination. If only life was that simple."

Knox picked up the sheet of paper and scanned the long list of names, doing his best to shove aside his anger at Carla Hayden. The she-demon had done enough damage to Harper. She had no right to even speak to her, let alone confront her. But he'd respect Harper's wishes as long as Carla kept a distance from her from this point onwards.

"Those people are simply the ones who are *known* to buy them on the black market—there'll be God knows how many more." The incubus pulled a flask out of the inside of his jacket and took a swig. "There's one guy in particular who I think we should be looking at. He's the main collector of sphinx wings. His name is Francisco Alaniz."

Knox frowned. "I recognize the name, but I don't believe I've met him."

"He's a casting agent who runs his own very successful agency in Malibu. He represents a lot of celebrities, sportsmen, and other media professionals. He's also Thatcher's cousin." Keenan's blue eyes hardened. "Funny how Thatcher was one of the demons we were recently investigating as a possible Horseman when—*bam*—Harper was attacked."

Knox stilled as the implications sank into his brain. "I've considered that the hunters were sent as a distraction. We've been actively investigating the identities of the other two Horsemen for some time now. I wondered if maybe we got too close."

The main reason he'd suspected Thatcher was that the Prime was an incantor. Only blood magick could have extracted Laurence Crow from Knox's prison, which meant that either one of the Horsemen was an incantor or that they'd hired one to free Crow. Knox had to explore both possibilities. His demons had been discreet in investigating Thatcher, but that didn't mean the Prime hadn't somehow found out about it.

"Thatcher's a strong incantor who's been known to use blood magick in the past," said Keenan. "But what really interests me about this guy is that he seems to be the only Prime who isn't looking into the matter of the Horsemen."

Levi's eyes narrowed. "That could mean he thinks the theory is bullshit, or that he sees no need to investigate it because he knows exactly who they are. If he did set his cousin's sights on Harper, we may have made Thatcher nervous. But ... I don't see how he could have known that Harper's wings came to her."

"Maybe he didn't know," suggested Larkin, sitting on the sofa near the window that overlooked the combat circle beneath the office. "Maybe he thought he was lying to the hunters."

Knox inclined his head at the harpy. "True, but whoever did it would have known that we'd do our best to track who hired the hunters. That trail has led to his cousin, which puts Thatcher in our sights. He's smart. Would he really do anything to turn our attention to him that way?"

Levi rubbed at his nape. "It could be that he didn't expect you to get your hands on the hunters and find out they'd been hired. Hunters often act alone."

"From what I learned, Francisco isn't known to hire hunters," said Keenan. "I also learned that his father and brother were sphinxes—both of whom he hated right up until the day he killed them. It's believed that *their* wings were the first to be hung on his wall."

"If that's true, they're probably like trophies to him," said Larkin, toying with her long braid. "Maybe the other wings belong to people he wanted dead."

Knox's thoughts exactly. "We need to hear what Francisco has to say, but I don't have the patience to take the trip using the private jet." He needed answers *yesterday*.

Sure, he could pyroport to Malibu, but not many knew he had that ability. Knox liked to keep the demon world guessing on what he could or couldn't do. It made it hard for them to work out just what breed of demon he was. If they ever did, they'd no doubt unite against Knox in the hope of killing him. It wouldn't work, of course, but he'd prefer not to have to wipe out most of the demonic population.

"We could use Armand," suggested Larkin, referring to a member of the Force who had the ability to teleport. "He could take us to Francisco."

Knox nodded. "Summon him."

Moments later, there was a knock at the door. "Come in," said Knox. Armand strolled inside, no doubt having teleported outside the office after receiving Larkin's telepathic summons.

"We need you to teleport us somewhere," Knox told him. "How many can you teleport at one time?"

The tall, bald demon said, "Four, including myself."

Knox twisted his mouth. "Is there a limit to how far you can go?"

"I've yet to have a problem reaching a destination."

Keenan rattled off the address of Francisco's Malibu office. "Can you take us there?"

"Absolutely," said Armand. "When?"

"No time like the present," said Knox.

Resting his clasped hands on his office desk, Francisco Alaniz smiled, making the lines of his tanned face deepen. Knox had always thought that the purpose of fake tan was for it to appear natural, not to look *literally* fake. Maybe Francisco's skin wouldn't have seemed quite so dark if his hair wasn't so light.

Knox accepted the invitation to sit opposite Francisco, but he didn't return the smile. It was possible that this demon was responsible for what happened to Harper. Knox wanted to shove the guy against the wall and threaten to cut him open and yank out each and every one of his organs, but Knox knew better than to ease the reins on his control. He also had to bear in mind that the Horsemen *wanted* him to lose it. They persistently targeted Harper because they believed she was his one weakness. They were correct about that.

He did have the option of simply thrusting his mind into Francisco's to find the truth for himself, but it wasn't an act that Knox enjoyed doing; it meant sieving through a person's thoughts, fantasies, memories, and secrets. It was always an overload of information—information he would often rather not have known.

Also, walking around, thrusting his mind into that of others, would make Knox seem weak, in a sense—make him seem like he didn't trust his own judgement. It would also lose him the respect of many, since it was indeed a violation. He only did it when absolutely necessary.

"I must say it was quite a surprise when my receptionist

announced that Knox Thorne was outside my office," Francisco told him, eyes briefly flicking to Levi, who was stood against the far wall. Only Levi had entered the office with Knox. The others were standing guard outside the door, which Francisco's receptionist wasn't too happy about.

Francisco leaned back in his chair. "So, what brings you here, Mr. Thorne? Do you need representation?"

"No. I have some questions for you."

"Oh? Shame. You've got the face and charisma that would take you far in this industry."

Knox got right to the point. "My mate was attacked recently."

Expression sympathetic, Francisco sighed. "Yes, I heard about that. They were hunters, correct?"

"Yes. They were under the mistaken impression that she has wings. She's fully healed. She fought them, which they should have anticipated. Still, it isn't enough for me that I killed the hunters who attacked her." Knox's voice hardened as he added, "I want the demon who hired them."

Francisco sat up straight. "They were hired?"

"Yes. Someone hired them to obtain her wings. My first thought was that it could be a collector."

Realization dawned on Francisco's face. "Ah, I see. You've heard about the wings that are displayed on my wall at home." He sighed. "The only wings on my wall belong to my dead relatives—demons I despised for one reason or another. In truth, I don't care much for sphinx wings. I'm not interested in collecting them."

"Yet, you display them on your wall."

"I took the part of those demons that defined them. You see, in my family, the sphinxes are considered the superior breed. I'm a reaper, just like my mother. She and I have never been good enough for the others. What makes them so different from us?

Nothing. They're not more powerful. They're not stronger. Yet, some of them felt that they had the right to fuck with me and hurt my mother."

So he'd stolen from them the one true thing that made the sphinxes so very different from Francisco and his mother, Knox realized.

"I don't hire hunters, Mr. Thorne. And I do my own dirty work, no matter how dirty it is. Mostly because I don't like to owe people anything."

Knox's instincts told him that Francisco was telling the truth. "I see. Any ideas on who the demon that hired the hunters could be? They sent the hunters an anonymous, encrypted email that deleted itself soon after being read."

Francisco rubbed at his jaw. "I've heard of the method, but there's only one person who I personally know that uses it."

"Who?"

"His name's Dion Boughton. He's a collector of many things, not just wings. If you're looking for someone who refuses to get his hands dirty but will risk any wrath to add things to his collection, you should look to him. He has a museum inside his home. From what I've heard, he also collects people."

"People?" Knox echoed.

"He likes to surround himself with the unique, which could have a lot to do with him being a very average person."

Both Harper and her wings were indeed unique, so Knox would definitely be having a chat with Dion.

"He won't be easy to speak with. He lives on a private island, which is psychically shielded. If you want to speak to him, you'll need an invite."

"Do you have his number?"

Francisco clasped his hands again. "He doesn't have a phone."

Levi's brows drew together. "Who doesn't have a phone?"

"He's a technophobe—he rejects any advances in technology, especially anything that interferes with personal privacy, like social media," said Francisco. "He's also a bit of a recluse. He doesn't accept many visitors on his island." He turned back to Knox. "If you wish to get in touch with him, you'll need to write to him."

Knox frowned. "Write to him?"

How archaic. Levi chuckled.

"I have his address." Francisco retrieved a small, leather-bound file from his desk drawer and flicked through it until he settled on a specific page. "Just send a quick note expressing your wish to meet with him. He should reply within a few days—a week at most."

Knox took the slip of paper on which Francisco had jotted down Dion's address. "How is your cousin, Thatcher?"

The abrupt change of subject made Francisco double-blink. "I haven't heard from him in a while. We don't talk much."

"Hmm. If you do speak with him, pass on my best wishes."

"I will do, Mr. Thorne."

Knox gave a curt nod and stood. He held Francisco's gaze as he warned, "If I find out that you've lied to me about anything here today, I'll come for you."

Francisco swallowed. "I'd expect nothing less."

"Good. We'll see ourselves out."

CHAPTER SIX

---◦◦◦---

"Why do you always take me to weird places to do lessons?" Harper griped.

"I don't take you to weird places," said Knox, standing in front of her. "I take you to deserted places where they'll be no witnesses."

"Well, this place is certainly deserted." Harper's nose wrinkled at the smells of mildew, chalky dust, and sun-warmed stone.

"Look at the situation this way; you're seeing ancient ruins that have yet to be discovered by humans. That means we won't be seen by tourists, hikers, or archeologists. And if the flames *do* get out of hand, all they'll destroy are buildings, spires, and stone pillars that are already crumbling."

He was right, Harper thought as she glanced around. Everything was weatherworn and covered in moss, thick ropy vines, and other foliage. Even the stone statues were worn to the point that they were faceless.

What worried her was the snake skin she'd spotted among

the rubble. *That* and the fact that it was eerily quiet. All she could hear were dead leaves scuttling along the stone and scrub bushes rustling with the breeze. "Don't you find this place even a little creepy?"

"Stop trying to distract me," Knox gently admonished. He breezed his thumb along her lip. "I know it's been a week since the attack and nothing else has happened, but that doesn't mean we should lower our guard. If it makes you feel any better, I don't think you'll need more than one lesson. As I know from when I was teaching you to fly, you pick things up very quickly. It only took a few lessons before you were flying alongside me without any help. I know you have reservations about calling the flames, but that's a good thing."

She frowned. "How?"

"Calling on them is as serious as anything can be. You should be anxious, and you should be wary of just what kind of destructive power they have. If you weren't, I'd be concerned and disappointed in you."

"I'm not just wary of the flames, Knox. I'm wary of how much my demon likes them. It would have happily annihilated the world because it was pissed off that I'd been hurt. In my opinion, this kind of power shouldn't be placed in the hands of an entity that vengeful." Her demon snarled at that assessment.

"I'm not teaching your demon how to control the ability to call them. I'm teaching *you* how to do it. Then, if the situation merits it, you can call on them well before your demon even thinks to interfere."

Harper wasn't warming to the idea at all, but if she wanted to be sure that she wouldn't accidentally call them, she needed to listen to him. She planted her feet. "Okay. What do you want me to do?"

He dropped his hand and stepped back; the carpet of dead

leaves crinkled beneath his shoes. "First, I want you to just listen. As you know, my kind can call on the flames of hell because we are the flames. They birthed us, they sustain us, and they protect us. They come to me as easily as the protective power inside your belly comes to you."

"Even when you were a kid?"

"Even then, just like your power to cause pain was something that tried to protect you as a child."

Harper's chest ached at the idea of a little boy being expected to handle that level of power. No adult should be expected to handle it, let alone a child.

"Your wings were, in a sense, birthed by the flames," Knox continued. "As such, they're connected to the flames. The power is there. Ready. Waiting. But you emotionally and mentally reject it out of fear of what your demon might do with it."

Which, Harper thought, made her sensible. "It was scary to be a backseat passenger while the psycho went . . . well, psycho. Maybe it wasn't scary to *you* because you still don't have the sense to fear my mighty wrath." She decided to ignore the gleam of amusement in his eyes. "But it was shitifying for me."

"You think I can't relate to that? My demon has lost control more than once, and I was forced to be nothing but a spectator while it wiped out everything in its path. Neither of us can be sure that your demon won't do the same thing again. But if it can trust that you don't need it to protect or defend you, it shouldn't push you too hard for dominance in a critical situation. And one way to be sure you're fully protected is by conjuring the flames of hell."

She poked the inside of her cheek with her tongue. "I don't think this will be as effortless for me as it is for you."

"Maybe not, but we'll see. Call your wings."

Heat briefly blazed down her back as her wings snapped out.

She flexed her back muscles, making them flap a few times. They were heavy, despite being gossamer.

Knox stroked one wing as he said, "They are your connection to the flames. Think of them as the bridge between you and this power that you wouldn't otherwise have access to. As long as the bridge is there, the flames can come to you. Without it, they can't reach you."

"All right."

He began to slowly pace in front of her as he spoke. "Your wings are out. The bridge is there—what happens next hinges on you. The night you called the flames, I tried to calm them. I couldn't, because they weren't answering to me right then. They weren't there for me, they were there for you. They raged out of control, yes, but only because your emotions were out of control."

"You're saying I can control them?"

"Control them? No. You can guide them, ask things of them, even try to direct them. But you can never control them, just like you can never control your demon. It doesn't work that way."

"Bummer."

His mouth twitched. "But if you stay focused, if you channel your emotions into one direction, the flames will do the same." He slanted his head, adding, "Mostly."

She narrowed her eyes. "What do you mean 'mostly'?"

"Like I said, they can't be controlled. I wouldn't go as far as to say they have their own mind. They don't. But they have their own will."

Having been surrounded by their strength and power, Harper could agree with that.

"The point I'm making is that if you give them a target, they will focus on it. If your anger hadn't been so out of control and had instead been focused on Roan, the flames might have swallowed him whole rather than surround the entire trailer and then, traveling outwards, consume whatever they touched."

She narrowed her eyes as the comment triggered the memory of Knox standing there as red, gold, and black flames spouted from the ground to devour two dark practitioners in an alley. No other destruction, no sticking around to burn anything else—the flames had died down as quickly as they'd come. Huh.

"And now we practice." Knox threw an old photograph of Crow onto the ground. "There he is, Harper. There's the bastard that targeted me again and again. He wanted me dead, and he used you to try to get to me—he even went as far as to try to cut out your womb so you could never carry my child. Killing him was almost a kindness, really, considering the pain he deserved to feel."

She licked her lips. "You want me to call the flames to devour the photograph?"

"Unless you'd rather I'd brought a living person. Your ex would be my preference."

"The dolphin would be mine." Harper rolled back her shoulders. "Talk me through what I need to do."

"Tap into the link you have to your wings—the link that allows you to call them to you. It may feel physical, but it's psychic in nature. Find it."

Harper didn't need to search for it. The link was as much a part of her as the wings themselves. "Got it."

"Good, now you're stood on that bridge we were talking about. Crow is your target. Stare at that photograph and think about him. Think of everything he caused, every bit of pain the people around you suffered. Think of what he did to you and what he would have done to me."

She did, feeling fury build inside her like a firestorm. "The link . . . it's getting hot. Really hot."

"I want you to direct every bit of the rage in you at that

picture. *Feel* the rage, and *focus* on the cause of the rage ... and call the power that's on the other side of the bridge."

She glared down at the photo, trying to project her anger onto it. "The link's super, super hot right now."

"Don't break away from it," he said, hearing the wariness in her tone. "The heat can't hurt you. You know that. Focus on the photo, Harper. Focus on Crow."

She sensed the power on the other side of the bridge raring to be released; she called to it. The air buzzed and the ground trembled, making the dead leaves at their feet flutter. It scared her enough that her resolve faltered for a minute.

"They won't hurt you, Harper. They can't. Direct them at Crow. He slapped you, he sliced you open, he tried to remove your womb and—"

Harper winced as an almost unbearable power shot up the "bridge" and flames erupted out of the ground with a roar. She stepped away from the blistering heat, even as she marveled at what she'd done. They consumed the photograph easily, but they didn't die down.

Knox was instantly at her side. "Okay, Harper, I want you to shove aside the rage. Crow is gone now. Dead. He can't hurt you ever again, and he can't hurt me. It's over." He whispered into her ear. "All over. That's it, good girl. The flames did what you needed them to do; now let them go."

The flames slowly eased, and the buzz in the air died away as the power returned to where it came from. The photograph was gone. All that remained were ashes that were dotted with a red residue. Harper gaped at him. "I did it. I actually fucking did it."

"Of course you did it."

She smiled. "Can I do it again?"

"I had a feeling you'd say that."

* * *

Harper clasped the door handle, staring into the dark, mostly bare room. The cradle was shaking in time with the baby's cries. Her heart ached at the sounds. The cries weren't loud, sharp or high-pitched. They were more fussy, whiny "Where are you?" cries that held a little indignation. But they still tugged at her, drawing her into the room.

She walked toward the cradle—each step was slow, careful, tentative. Some part of her wanted to turn and flee, though she didn't know where the wariness came from. But she kept moving purposely forward.

The cries lowered to soft, nasal snorts . . . as if the baby knew attention was coming its way. Harper swallowed as her unexplainable wariness built. Still, her steps didn't falter. And then she was there, staring into the cradle.

So tiny, she thought, with a smile, as she watched the baby writhe and kick. It squinted up at her, eyes dark and familiar. Then those eyes bled to black, and the cradle burst into flames.

Harper woke with a silent gasp, wincing as the spotlights in the mahogany ceiling pricked her eyes. She quickly became aware that she was lying on the living room sofa, covered in a blanket that Knox must have thrown over her. He'd muted the wall-mounted T.V. that she'd been watching before she fell asleep. Well, calling on the flames of hell was tiring.

Double-blinking to clear her vision, she sat upright on the curved, beige sofa that was identical to the one opposite it. A shadow fell over her, and she looked up to see Knox staring at her, his head cocked.

"You're awake."

"You sound disappointed." Watching him slip on the jacket of his suit, she realized . . . "You're going somewhere and were hoping you could leave me behind." Sneaky.

"No such luck, apparently," he grumbled.

"Where are *we* going?"

He looked about to argue, but instead he sighed and said, "To visit McCauley's mother."

"You know who she is?"

"We're pretty certain it's a she-demon from our lair by the name of Talia Winters. McCauley bears a strong resemblance to her. Of course, she can confirm it for us."

He walked soundlessly along the light pine flooring and over to the beautiful fireplace. Grabbing her cell phone from the mantel among her knickknacks, he tossed it to her. She'd added a few other personal touches to the spacious, high-ceiling room, such as the thick oak book shelves and the soft throw blanket that was the same ocean blue as the Persian carpet.

"I recall Talia being pregnant," Knox added. "She claimed that the child died shortly after its birth."

"I'm guessing it was exchanged for a human child who *did* die shortly afterwards." Harper stood and did a long, catlike stretch. "Tell me about Talia. I don't recall ever seeing her."

Knox curled an arm around her and drew her against him. "That's because strip clubs aren't really your thing."

"She's a stripper?"

"Yes. She's unmated, has no other kids, and is rumored to be a junkie. I'm not sure how true that rumor is." He caught her lower lip between his teeth and tugged, smiling at her gasp. "Tanner is coming with us and he's almost here. As soon as you're ready to leave, we'll head to her apartment and find out."

"All I need is a quick coffee; then we can go."

A short while later, Levi drove them to what was a shady part of Las Vegas. Harper thought her old apartment building was bad. This area was way worse. It was the kind of place you expected to find squatters and addicts, and should worry that you might be hit by a stray bullet. The building itself was covered in graffiti and strange yellow stains, and it also looked charred in places. Many of the windows were grimy while others were broken or bordered.

"Again, I'll watch over the car," said Levi.

Since there were small groups of shifty people scattered around, Harper figured that was a good idea.

Tanner opened the rear door so that Knox and Harper could slide out. Knox led the way as they headed to the building, and Tanner remained behind her—they were boxing her in, protecting her. It galled her on one level, but she decided to let it go.

Some dubious-looking juveniles were sat on an old couch outside, smoking and drinking. Humans, she sensed. They boldly stared, but something on Knox's face made them look away. They might not know what he was, but they were wise enough to sense the danger in him.

The front door creaked as Knox pulled it open. Harper's nose wrinkled. The air was dank and dusty. She could smell pot, urine, dirt, and something ... wrong. Rancid. Yep, this place was definitely much worse than her old address. Glass, cans, used needles, and other trash was scattered along the floors and stairwells. It was dim, thanks to the loose wiring hanging out of a hole in the ceiling where a lightbulb should be.

Knox looked at the broken elevator. "She lives on the third floor, apartment B."

"Then up we go," said Tanner.

Knox again walked ahead as they climbed the cluttered stairs. She was almost surprised when no rats or cockroaches skittered past them. The walls sure were thin, because Harper could hear tenants arguing, laughing, and blasting their music.

Finally, they reached Talia's apartment door. Knox knocked, but there was no response. He knocked again, louder this time.

The neighboring door opened, and an elderly human woman

peeked out; face worn and haggard. "You'll have to knock hard," the human told them. "Talia tends to sleep through the day."

"I see," said Knox. "Thank you."

The old woman made a huffing sound and disappeared into her apartment.

Knox banged his fist on Talia's door almost hard enough to make it rattle. The sound of stomping and cursing coming from inside was soon followed by the door being yanked open.

"What?" snapped a tall, almost-wafer-thin blonde. Then she got a good look at Knox and paled. "I'm s-so sorry, Mr. Thorne, I-I didn't know it was you."

"That's okay, Talia," said Knox. "We'd like to speak with you."

She blinked and shoved a hand through her loose, dull-blonde curls. "Um, yeah, okay, sure. Come in."

The floorboards beneath the thin carpet creaked as they walked inside. Harper had been looking forward to escaping the stairwell scents. Honestly, it didn't smell much better in here. Dust. Stale food. Cigarette smoke. And a sickly, cloying perfume.

The apartment was small and sparsely furnished with clothes strewn everywhere. The stained wallpaper was peeling from the walls, revealing cracks in the plaster. Harper could see the tiny kitchen from where she stood. Could see the piles of dishes in the rusted sink, the broken cabinet doors, and the cluttered countertop.

Feeling eyes on her, she cut her gaze to Talia. The she-demon was looking at her, taking her measure, as if wanting to assure herself that she was the prettiest in the room. Whatever. Harper just stared at her until Talia finally averted her gaze. She bore a strong resemblance to McCauley with her dark eyes, high cheekbones, dimpled chin, and small ears that protruded slightly.

Her tank top and shorts bordered on indecent, but that could be because it was seriously *hot*. Even with the sound of voices,

T.V.s, and a dog barking, Harper could hear the air conditioning unit clanking on and off. She wondered how the hell the woman managed to cope in the heat.

Harper knew a lot of people ended up in places like this when they were down on their luck, but she got the feeling that Talia just didn't care enough about her life to respect herself or anything in her possession. Or maybe it was just that she was too fond of drugs to care about much else, because if her sallow skin, bloodshot eyes, and contracted pupils were anything to go by, the whole "Talia's a junkie" rumor was true.

Her cheeks reddened with embarrassment as she glanced around. "The place is a bit of a mess." She shoved aside the threadbare curtain and wrestled open the rusted window. "Sorry I took a while to answer."

"That's fine," said Knox.

She wrapped her arms around herself and lifted her chin. "Um ... so ... what do you need?"

"Did you see the news recently?"

She blinked rapidly. "You mean, like, on T.V.? I don't watch the news. It's always depressing stuff. Murders and assaults and war."

"There was a recent story about a woman who drugged her six-year-old son, shoved him in an oven, and tried to burn him alive."

Talia's brow furrowed. "What?"

"Her effort didn't work so well. Turns out his skin's impervious to fire."

"He's one of us?"

"She seems to believe he's a changeling. That's why she put him in the oven—apparently, it's a surefire way of exposing a changeling child. He's six." Knox watched realization dawn on Talia. Fear flashed across her face. "You didn't ask my permission, Talia."

She licked her lips, shoulders curving inward. "I-I knew you wouldn't give it to me."

"Why did you do it?" asked Tanner.

Talia snorted a laugh. "Are you kidding? Look at this place. Look at *me*. Kids need love and security and all that jazz, right?"

"You could have tried to improve your situation," said Tanner.

Talia shook her head hard and glared at the floor. "I couldn't have loved him," she mumbled. "I wanted to. I just couldn't."

Something about the way she said it made Harper guess, "You were raped."

Talia flinched.

"You should have told us," Knox said through his teeth. "We would have taken care of the situation."

Talia looked at him, eyes wet. "There wasn't anything you could have done. The son of a bitch was human. I took care of it myself."

"You killed him," said Harper.

Her eyes flared. "Hell yeah, I did. It wasn't anything he didn't deserve."

Harper wasn't going to argue with that. "You didn't abort the baby, though."

Talia shrugged, briefly averting her gaze. "He hadn't done anything to anybody. Wasn't his fault. But I'm not, you know, maternal. Never wanted kids. Still don't. Which is a good thing, really, considering I ain't straight." She jutted out her chin. "Judge me for giving him away if you want, but he wouldn't have had a good life with me."

"He didn't have a good life with the humans," Knox pointed out. "What happened to their biological child?"

"It was on life support. I had the midwife from our lair—Sella Monroe—exchange the babies. He wouldn't survive among demons. They'd see him as easy prey."

"There's nothing weak about your son," said Knox.

She stiffened. "What do you mean?"

"He's powerful, Talia."

She shook her head. "I swear to you, there wasn't even a slight aura of power around him. I couldn't sense his demon. I might as well have been holding a human baby. Ask Sella, she'll tell you."

"Maybe the power and his demon stayed dormant for a little while—there's no way to be sure."

Talia sank into the saggy couch, as if her legs were too weak to hold her up any longer. After a few moments, she spoke. "So he's okay?"

"He's fine. He's staying with Wyatt and Linda Sanders at the moment."

Sensing where this was going, she began shaking her head again, eyes wide with panic. "I can't take him. I wouldn't make a good mother. I don't have anything to give him."

"He has nowhere else to go, Talia."

"The Sanders will keep him. You know they will. He'll be happier there."

"Talia—"

"I *can't* take him." Her words broke on a sob. "Don't ask me to. *Please*. I can't."

Knox exhaled heavily. "All right. But I can't guarantee that people won't realize you're his mother. He looks like you. You might even find that he pays you a visit someday."

"He'll hear enough to know I'm not what he needs," she mumbled.

"Take care, Talia. We'll let ourselves out."

As they walked down the stairwell, Tanner said, "I went in there prepared to be pissed at her."

"She genuinely does believe she did right by him." Harper

sighed. "If all she'd have been able to see was her rapist whenever she looked at him, then maybe she did."

"Are you leaving McCauley with Wyatt and Linda?" Tanner asked.

Reaching the front door, Knox held it open. "If the arrangement is working for all concerned, yes." Once in the Bentley, Knox said, "Levi, we need to make a pit stop at the Sanders' home."

"You got it," said Levi. "Is Talia the kid's mother?"

"Yes." Knox quickly told him what was said and then pulled out his phone and dialed Wyatt's number. "I have some information for you, but I don't want to speak of it while McCauley's nearby. Meet me at the end of your front yard in ten minutes." When Wyatt agreed, Knox ended the call.

"Do you think they'll want to keep McCauley?" Tanner asked.

"Linda will," began Harper, "but I'm not so sure about Wyatt."

When Levi finally parked at the bottom of the Sanders' yard, both Linda and Wyatt were waiting there, expressions grim.

The moment Knox and Harper slid out of the car, Linda stepped forward and asked, "What is it?"

"We have the identity of McCauley's mother," Knox told her. "It's Talia Winters."

For a moment, an odd look crossed Wyatt's face. Then it was gone, and he blew out a breath. "He looks a little like her. How did I not see it?"

"Have you come to take him?" asked Linda, voice shaky.

"Talia doesn't believe that her home is the best place for him," said Knox.

"I'd have to agree," clipped Linda. "She's a hooker."

Harper arched a brow. "She's a stripper, which is different."

Linda lowered her gaze. "You're right, of course. I apologize."

Yeah? She didn't sound all that apologetic.

"We'd be happy for him to stay here," Linda told Knox. "I'm sure McCauley would be fine with it." Hearing their landline ringing, she said, "Excuse me."

Once Linda was inside the house, Knox turned to Wyatt. "How has McCauley been?"

"Not an ounce of trouble," replied Wyatt. "Almost painfully polite. You wouldn't think the kid had been through a traumatic experience. He never talks about his human parents or what happened to him." He shrugged. "Maybe he's in denial or something, I don't know."

"Your mate loves him," said Tanner.

Wyatt gave him a weak smile. "She loves that she has someone to love."

"I'm going to be honest with you," began Harper. "If you ask me, there's something not quite right about that kid."

Wyatt sighed. "I know what you mean. Something about him rubs my demon up the wrong way. But he's just a kid, and—whether he's traumatized or not—he's been through something awful."

Harper raised her hands. "If you're happy for him to stay here, we won't interfere with that. But you have to be sure, Wyatt. Because even though the kid freaks me out a little, I don't want him to have to bounce from home to home. He needs stability."

Wyatt gave a slow nod. "I agree. I'm happy for him to stay with us."

Well he sure didn't look happy about it. Harper figured he was doing it for his mate's sake. Noticing movement in her peripheral vision, Harper looked to see McCauley staring out of the living room window. She waved to him, forcing a smile. He waved back, but the move was almost mechanical.

"All right," said Knox. "He can stay with you if you're positive that it's what you want."

"I'm certain," Wyatt told him.

Knox nodded and then ushered Harper back into the Bentley as he spoke to Wyatt. "I'll check in occasionally to make sure this arrangement is working for everyone. I trust that if you have any problems, you will call me."

"I will," Wyatt promised.

As Levi pulled away from the curb, Tanner spoke to Knox. "Leaving him with the Sanders was the right thing to do."

"Yeah, for McCauley," said Harper. "But maybe not for them." Time would tell, she supposed.

CHAPTER SEVEN

Knox glanced around the large living room that was all marble floors and dark woods. When Francisco had said that Dion Boughton liked to surround himself with the unique, he hadn't been understating things. The island upon which his grand, opulent home sat was a tropical paradise. The home itself was filled with antiques, vintage items, unusual ornaments, expensive vases, and servants who were rare breeds of demon.

Dion sat on a throne-like chair opposite Knox, regarding him with a studious gaze that held an excited glitter. Like someone who was giving an antique a thorough appraisal. Knox's demon curled his upper lip, not liking that at all.

He's excited to see you because you're as unique as they come, said Levi, who was the only one to have accompanied him into the room. Armand, Keenan, and Larkin waited outside.

"Are you sure you wouldn't like coffee or some refreshments?" Dion asked.

"No, thank you," said Knox. "We just have some questions."

Dion's smile faltered. "This isn't a social call, is it?"

"I don't do social calls, Mr. Boughton."

Disappointment clouded his expression. "Very well. How can I help you?"

"I don't know how up to date you are on what happens in the outside world," began Knox, "but my mate was recently attacked by hunters."

Dion looked both stunned and incredulous. "I wouldn't have thought anyone would dare risk your wrath. Or her wrath, for that matter. Sphinxes aren't forgiving creatures, and I saw your mate in action on the video footage of the elections when Isla attacked her. I don't watch much television, but the elections weren't something I was prepared to miss. Your mate is powerful."

"She is," Knox agreed. "And yet, someone hired hunters to steal her wings."

Dion's brow furrowed. "But she doesn't have wings."

"No, she doesn't. But it would seem that someone either isn't aware of that or simply doesn't believe it—whatever the case, it means the hunters died a very painful death for no good reason." Knox once more studied the room. "I can't help but notice that you're quite the collector. I hear you have a museum here."

All emotion left Dion's face. "You believe I hired the hunters."

"Did you?"

Dion's back straightened. "No, I did not. Have I hired hunters to acquire things for me in the past? Yes. Did I hire them to steal wings that your mate does not possess? No."

Knox twisted his mouth. "From what I've heard, you lack the sort of ethics that would hold you back from doing such a thing."

"I don't claim to have many morals, but I am not a stupid man. Targeting your mate would be the height of stupidity."

"It would. But maybe you're also a man who feels you're

untouchable. Maybe you feel that sending encrypted emails protects your identity."

Dion's mouth tightened. "I did not hire those hunters."

"If it wasn't you, Mr. Boughton, who could it have been?"

"I truly don't know. I do not concern myself much with the outside world. I prefer my own company. But it seems obvious to me that the Horsemen would be responsible, whoever they are."

"Oh, I believe there's a very good chance that this person is one of the Horsemen," said Knox. "If I can identify who hired these demons, maybe I can identify one of the Horsemen."

"I have no idea who it could be. If I did, I would tell you. I don't like that a group of demons are conspiring against the Primes any more than you do."

"I'd like to believe you, Mr. Boughton, I really would. But it seems quite a coincidence to me that a person who collects sphinx wings also uses encrypted emails to communicate with hunters . . . just as the demon who I seek does."

Flushing, Dion said, "I am not the only person who uses that technique to protect my identity. In fact, I learned it from my old Prime."

Knox's muscles tensed. "And just who is your old Prime?"

"Thatcher."

Son of a bitch.

Sitting on the swing, five-year-old Heidi glared at her brother's back. She'd told him she was hungry and wanted to go home, and he'd promised her they'd leave in ten minutes. That was *ages* ago. Robbie was still at the other side of the playground, leaning against the monkey bars, flirting with girls.

Heidi rolled her eyes and pretended to gag. She could hear them laughing, even though it was kind of loud with the swing creaking, the kids shouting, and the parents talking. She'd bet the girls wouldn't find him so funny if they knew about his "secret" magazine collection.

Maybe she should go over there and tell the girls that he just wanted to "get laid". Heidi might not know what exactly that meant, but she figured it had something to do with him not being a virgo anymore . . . or was it a virgin? She shrugged.

Yeah, she'd tell the girls. Then she and Robbie could finally go home. He wouldn't like it, and that would make it more awesome.

Laughing to herself, she held the bumpy chain links tight and twisted herself around, laughing even louder when the swing bounced back around. And now there was a man standing in front of her, smiling. A demon. She dug her heels into the dirt, bringing the swing to a halt.

"You're Heidi, right?"

She didn't say anything. Just stared at him. He had a nice smile, she thought.

"You're Harper's cousin."

He knew Harper?

"She told me about you," he said. "You really do look like a little angel, don't you? It's all that long white-blonde hair, the rosy cheeks, and those pretty blue eyes."

Her eyes were aquamarine actually, but she didn't say that. She bit her lip and said in a wobbly voice, "You're really tall."

Smiling softly, he squatted in front of her. "That better?"

She nodded and gave him a shy smile.

"My name's Dean. I'm one of Knox's sentinels."

Heidi frowned. "I thought he only had *four* sentinels." She'd met them all. Keenan was the funniest.

"He used to, but now he needs more to make sure Harper's protected. I was just at your grandmother's house. She asked me to tell you that you need to come back inside. Harper was attacked again."

Again?

"Hunters tried to steal her wings. She's okay, but your grandmother is upset and she's worried." He reached out to grab her arm. "Come on, I'll walk you—"

"*Stranger!*" she bellowed in his face. "*Stranger danger! Gun! Fire!*"

"Little bitch," he spat, yanking her off the swing.

Heidi screamed and screamed and screamed until a horrible ringing sound filled the air. Blood started to come out of his ears, and that was why she wasn't supposed to use *that* scream—it could burst people's eardrums and even make windows smash, but Heidi didn't want the bad man to take her. With a loud shout, he let her go. She hit the ground hard, and stopped screaming.

"Heidi!" It was Robbie's voice, and he was close. The man ran into the trees, and some people chased after him.

Robbie helped her stand. "Are you okay? He tried to take you?"

She nodded. "My butt hurts."

Robbie's face went hard. "I'll kill him."

The people who'd ran after the bad man came back, panting. One of them shrugged and said, "He's gone."

Robbie growled. "He's *what?*"

The human shoved a hand through his hair, looking baffled. "It was like he just . . . disappeared. He's gone."

Leaning forward in the overstuffed armchair, Harper lifted her mug of tea from the mahogany coffee table and blew over the rim. "Thanks, Grams."

Jolene smiled from her spot on the couch, one leg crossed over the other. "You're welcome, sweetheart."

Harper took a sip of the tea. She'd asked for coffee, but Jolene had insisted that she needed something to help her "relax". Really, she didn't need the tea to relax—not when she was at

Jolene's house, even though her head was pounding. It was a place she loved; a place where she'd always felt safe; a place that always seemed to smell of coffee, cookies, and lavender.

If the scent of Jolene's infamous cookies wasn't enough to make a person feel welcome, they'd certainly feel put at ease by the homey feel to the place. The earthy colors, throw cushions, fleecy blankets, cherished keepsakes, and framed photos—it was a *home*, not just a house, and that was no doubt what often drew so many of their family and lair there.

Ironically, part of what made it feel so safe for Harper was that it was a constant hub of activity. Her relatives were always coming and going, and it had always made Harper feel protected and secure. It wasn't something she could explain—it just was.

Jolene studied her closely. "You seem better today."

"I feel it." She was still tired, but not weary. If the headache would just fuck off, she'd feel even better.

"Stress has a powerful impact on the body."

"I'm not stressed."

"I would be in your shoes," said Martina, who was beside Jolene with her legs curled under her. "You've been surrounded by danger since Knox walked into your life."

"You blame him?"

"Not at all," said Martina. "He's not at fault for the actions of others. You know better than to think I'd judge him like that."

Smiling, Harper teased, "You mean because you, the wondrous firestarter, isn't in a position to judge anyone for anything?"

Martina grinned. "Maybe."

"Did you find out anything that may help us work out who hired the hunters?" asked Tanner, who was sprawled on the recliner.

"No, none of the people we know who work on the black market seem to have any idea of who it could be," said Jolene.

"But you can be sure that no others will come for you, Harper. The word has been spread among the black market that you survived the attack and that Knox killed both hunters."

Many imps obtained and sold things on the black market, so her family had some contacts there. The imps didn't sell people or wings or anything like that, but they sold rare objects and antiques. Mostly, they sold information. Imps were great at acquiring information.

"Where is Knox anyway?" asked Jolene.

"On his way back from paying Dion Boughton a visit," said Harper. She'd already told Jolene about his meeting with Francisco and that Knox had written to Dion. "He received a letter from Dion yesterday with an invite to his island."

Martina picked up her cup of coffee. "Dion's the one with the museum inside his home, right?"

"That's right. He likes to collect the unique—objects, people, animals."

"You're unique in many ways," said Martina. "That makes him a likely suspect."

"And a convenient person to pin the blame on," Jolene pointed out.

Martina nodded. "That too." She looked about to say something else, but then the front door burst open and a group of kids entered.

"Hi, Grams!" they shouted in unison. They ran down the hallway and into the kitchen. Moments later, they were dashing back down the hallway with cookies in hand, shouting, "Bye, Grams!"

Martina chuckled at their antics and then turned back to Harper, smile fading. "I heard that Carla caused a fuss at the coffeehouse."

Harper shrugged, going for blasé. "Doesn't matter. She'll be gone soon."

"It does fucking matter," insisted Tanner. "The sooner she leaves, the better."

Jolene made an "I'll second that" humph. "Harper, you should know that Lucian's coming to visit next month."

Harper carefully placed her mug on a square coaster. "Yeah, he told me."

"Have you told Knox?" asked Jolene.

"No. I'm not looking forward to them being in the same room again." To say that there was tension between Knox and Lucian would be the understatement of the century. Knox despised Lucian for not being a real father to her, and Lucian wanted "that psychopathic bastard" completely gone from her life. "Maybe one day they'll—" Harper cut off as the front door once again burst open.

Robbie came dashing into the living room with a spooked-looking Heidi in his arms. He was breathing hard, his eyes wild. Like that, everyone was on their feet.

"What happened?" Jolene demanded.

Robbie growled, "Some creep just tried to snatch Heidi."

Harper gaped. "You are *shitting* me."

"I wish I was."

Martina took Heidi into her arms and cuddled her. "It's okay, sweetie."

Jolene clenched her fists. "Who?" The word was like a whip. "Who tried to take her?"

Shrugging, Robbie shook his head. "I don't know, Grams, I wasn't watching her properly. I'm sorry." He looked miserably at his sister. "Sorry, H."

Martina sighed. "Your mom and dad are gonna freak, *especially* your dad."

Yep, thought Harper, Richie would indeed lose his shit. Harper stroked a hand over Heidi's hair. "Did the man say anything to you?"

"He said that you told him about me," she said in her tinkle-like voice.

Bastard. Harper kept her tone soft and calm. "Yeah? What else did he say?"

"That he was Knox's new sentinel, and that he was supposed to bring me here because hunters had tried to hurt you again."

The hairs on Harper's nape rose as a menacing growl rattled out of Tanner. "Did he say anything else?"

"He tried to get me to go with him, but I didn't want to." Heidi looked at Jolene. "I screamed at him, and I shouted all those things you told me to shout if any stranger tried to hurt me, like 'gun' and 'fire' because you said it makes people listen. But he still grabbed me, so I . . . I used *the* scream. I know I'm not supposed to, and I didn't mean to scare the other kids, but—"

"It's okay, sweetheart." Jolene kissed her forehead. "You did what you had to do. You did *exactly* what you should have done."

Harper nodded. "Nobody is upset with you, Heidi. We're all very proud of you."

"You definitely deserve some cookies." Martina carried Heidi into the kitchen, talking softly to her.

Harper shoved a hand through her hair. "I can't fucking believe this," she hissed quietly.

Seeing Robbie stick a finger in his ear, Jolene asked, "Does it hurt?"

"I can still hear the ringing a little," said Robbie. "But it's not bad. She screamed right at the guy, so it only hurt him. Don't get me wrong, it was still loud, but it was directed at him so no one else was hurt."

Well, that was good. Hearing a knock on the front door, Harper said, "That'll be Knox." And, shit, she had to tell him before he came inside or his anger would spook Heidi. "Don't shout for him to come straight in, Grams. I need a minute to talk with him."

"Good idea," said Tanner.

Harper walked out of the room and down the hallway with Tanner close behind. She opened the front door, and they both stepped onto the porch, closing the door behind them. At Knox's frown, she held up her hands. "I need you to stay calm."

Knox stilled. "I hate it when you start a conversation with that sentence."

"Me, too. It's about Heidi." She told him and Levi everything that Heidi and Robbie had said.

Knox's face turned into a mask of savage fury. "Someone tried to take a five-year-old child, posing as *my* sentinel?"

She slowly smoothed her hands up and down his chest. "I need you to stay *completely* calm, Knox. Calmer than you've ever been. She's a little shaken. You don't want to make it worse, so please suck your rage in."

He inhaled deeply, adopting that unnatural calm that she'd never be able to perfect. If she hadn't been able to feel his anger brushing against the edges of her consciousness, she'd have thought he truly had his shit together.

"Let me in," he said. "I need to talk to her a little. Not interrogate or upset her, just talk to her."

Harper nodded, trusting that he wouldn't do anything to frighten Heidi. She opened the door and led the way to the kitchen, where the four imps had gathered.

Knox smiled at Heidi, who was sitting on the countertop, munching on a cookie. "I heard you had a bit of an adventure today. You must have been very scary to make a bad person run away."

"My scream hurt his ears."

Sensing Knox's confusion, Harper said, *She has a sonic scream.*

Ah, I see. "From what Harper tells me, you were very brave. I will find the person who did this, okay? They'll never bother you again. I just need you to tell me whatever you remember about him so that I can find him."

Heidi's little button nose wrinkled. "Well—"

"What did he look like?" Martina interrupted. "Tall? Short?"

"He was tall," said Robbie. "He had broad shoulders."

Heidi nodded. "He—"

"What about his hair?" said Martina. "Blond? Red? Brown? Black?"

Heidi opened her mouth to answer, but Robbie beat her to it. "He had a buzzcut."

"Did he tell you his name?" Knox asked Heidi.

"Yes," she replied. "He said it was—"

"He won't have given her his real name," Robbie scoffed. "He could be anyone. I've never seen him before."

Heidi did a cute little growl. *"Will someone please let me talk? Jeez."*

Harper bit her lip, stifling a smile. "They don't mean to talk over you, Heidi-ho, they're just anxious. Now what is it you'd like to say?"

"He said his name was Dean. I don't know if it's true. Check." She pulled a brown leather wallet out of her pocket and handed it to Knox.

Jolene framed her face with her hands, smiling. "You fabulous little girl!"

Levi grinned and tugged on one of her ringlets. "You told him he was really tall in that shaky voice to make him bend down so you could rob him, didn't you?"

She grinned back at him. "Uh-huh."

Harper kissed her cheek. "Clever girl."

She smiled brightly at Jolene. "Can I get a puppy now?"

Harper looked at Knox, who'd opened the wallet. *What's his name?*

Dean Bannon.

Huh, so he had used his real name. *Never heard of him.*

I have. He's a stray demon for hire. His address is right here on his driver's license. Levi, grab him and take him to the boathouse. Knox rattled off the demon's address, and the sentinel nodded and strode out of the house.

Jolene walked over to Knox, eyes hard. "I want that bastard."

"I have questions for him," said Knox.

"So do I—this son of a bitch is mine."

Harper put a hand on her shoulder. "Levi will get him, Grams. Once Knox is done with his questions, you can have him, okay?"

Jolene's shoulders lost some of their stiffness. "All right. He'd better be alive when you hand him over, Thorne."

Knox couldn't give her any guarantees, since it would really all depend on exactly what the fucker said. "I'll do my best not to kill him."

Jolene snorted. "I suppose that's the best I can hope for."

It didn't take long for Levi to retrieve Dean. In fact, they were already at the boathouse when Tanner drove Harper and Knox back to the mansion. She wasn't surprised that Knox tried to talk her into going inside and leaving the interrogation to him, but she was having none of that shit. Heidi was her cousin and that motherfucker had tried to snatch her. Harper wanted to look into his eyes. She *needed* to do it.

He was tied to a chair, mostly naked, when Knox and Harper strolled into the boathouse with Tanner in tow. The hellhound went to stand beside Levi near the wall while Harper and Knox halted in front of their captive. He didn't look like a criminal, she thought. He looked more like a doctor or a teacher—someone harmless and nonthreatening. She supposed that was his "weapon", so to speak.

No one said anything. The tense silence stretched out until the anticipation had to be almost excruciating for good ole Dean. He spared Harper only a brief glance; his attention was on the predator glaring down at him. He was wise not to look away from anything that dangerous, in Harper's opinion. Knox might look cool and composed, but they could all sense that he and his demon were *far* from it.

Her own demon was just as infuriated. The entity liked Heidi a lot and was very protective of her. The fact that this male had frightened her, manhandled her, and tried to *take* her ... yeah, that was definitely enough for her demon to want him dead and buried. Jolene would most certainly take care of that, and his death would not be an easy or quick one.

"Mr. Bannon, isn't it?" Knox held up the wallet. "You should have thought twice before trying to kidnap a pickpocket."

Dean swore, shaking his head, clearly disgusted with himself.

Harper's smile was all teeth. "Howdy." She tilted her head. "How're your ears?"

"A little better."

"Too bad." She bent forward a little. "How does it feel to be brought down by a five-year-old?" His eyes flared, and she straightened. "Yeah, that's pretty much what I thought."

Knox took an aggressive step toward him. "I don't make deals, but I'll make an exception in this case because I need answers. If you answer my questions honestly, I won't kill you."

Hope briefly flickered in Dean's eyes, but then he shot Knox a skeptical look. "I find that hard to believe."

Knox shrugged. "Then what do you have to lose?" Dean said nothing, but Knox saw capitulation in his eyes. "Now I'm going to take a stab in the dark and guess that you were hired by

someone to take Heidi Wallis. Why did they want her?" Knox
raised a hand. "Don't try telling me you acted independently.
We both know you'd be lying. Not that it will bother me all
that much if it becomes necessary to . . . *persuade* you to tell me
what I want to know. My demon will definitely enjoy it. Just as
it enjoyed killing the two hunters that attacked Harper."

Dean swallowed. "I don't know why they wanted the kid. I
don't even know who they are. I didn't ask any questions. It's
none of my business."

"She's *five*," Harper spat. "It doesn't bother you that you could
have been hired by a pervert? Maybe you were hoping they'd
share her with you."

He jerked back. "What? Hell, no. I was hired to do a job—
that's it."

"A job for who?" asked Knox.

"I don't know. I got an anonymous email. It was encrypted.
Whoever sent it was smart. It self-deleted a few minutes after I
opened it."

Knox exchanged a knowing look with Harper. "How are you
supposed to contact this person?"

"I'm not," said Dean. "I was hired to take her and drop her
unconscious at a specific place, where the money would be waiting. The old quarry near the landfill. Then I was supposed to
leave straight after—no hanging around, and no trying to make
contact with anyone."

Knox thought on that for a moment. Whoever was behind
the attacks was taking many precautions to ensure they couldn't
be identified, which meant they weren't underestimating Knox's
ability to find them. Yet, they obviously considered themselves
smart enough to avoid capture or they would never have fucked
with Harper in the first place. "What did they want with Heidi?"

"They didn't say. I didn't ask. I'm normally contacted by

people who demand ransoms, so I'm guessing that's what this is about."

Harper cast him an exasperated look. "She's a Wallis. We're not exactly billionaires."

"No," agreed Dean. "But *he* is," he added, tipping his chin at Knox.

Knox narrowed his eyes. "You think they were hoping to extort money from me?" It didn't seem likely to him.

Dean shrugged. "Maybe. Maybe not. Maybe it wasn't money that they wanted from you—I don't know. That's really all I can tell you."

Sensing that was the truth, Knox drawled, "All right." He licked his teeth. "You've been very helpful, Mr. Bannon. Cooperative." Which thoroughly disappointed Knox's demon. "If you're lucky, your death might be a quick one."

"Not exactly surprised you're reneging on your deal," clipped Dean.

"I'm not going to kill you. I just needed to question you. No, it's the Wallis imps that are going to kill you. Considering you tried to kidnap one of their own, I'd say they have the right to give you what you've got coming."

Harper nodded. *Grams, he's ready for you.*

Mere moments later, Ciaran, Jolene, and Richie appeared a few feet away. "Thank you, Knox," said Jolene, eyes hard on Dean. "Mind if we take the chair?"

Knox swept out a hand in invitation. "Not at all."

"Grab him," she told the other imps.

"Wait," Dean said to the imps. "I told *him* what you need to know!"

"You also tried to kidnap my daughter," snarled Richie. "At what point did you think that would go unpunished?"

Dean's gaze darted from face to face, as if searching for an ally.

When he looked at Harper, she shrugged and said, "You really should have known better than to fuck with my family." And then they were gone.

Knox turned to Harper and drew her close. Her scent dulled the rage that seemed his constant companion these days. She slid her arms around him and smoothed them up and down his back, comforting him and taking comfort. Sweeping a hand down her hair, he kissed her temple. "I wanted to kill that fucker so bad."

"So did I." Harper leaned into him. "But Jolene needs to do this. It's hard for her to stand back while we deal with the person who sent those hunters after me."

Knox nodded. "Killing Bannon allows her to get vengeance for both you and Heidi. I know she needs that. I know Richie has more of a right to punish Bannon than I do." He rested his forehead on hers. "That didn't make it any easier not to slice his throat open."

She pressed a kiss to his neck. "Your restraint was appreciated."

As the two sentinels joined them, Tanner scraped a hand over his jaw and said, "You know . . . I've been thinking."

"Did it hurt?" Harper quipped, hoping to lighten Knox's mood.

Tanner shot her a mock glare. "As I was saying . . . it's possible that they're not targeting you to get to Knox. Maybe this is about you."

Knox had been considering that since the moment he heard that Heidi had almost been taken. "I'd like to disagree, but it does make sense," he told Harper. "At first, I thought the person who hired the hunters was most likely one of the Horsemen and had made yet another attempt to make me lose my control by hurting the only thing that matters to me. Now, I'm not so sure."

She tilted her head. "You don't think the Horsemen are behind the recent events?"

"I think we've *assumed* that they are," Tanner replied. "Maybe we shouldn't have. If I were one of the Horsemen, I would keep a low profile for a while. A lot of our kind are investigating the matter. Would it be wise of them to strike out at you during this time? I don't believe so."

"He's right," Levi told her. "Look at Heidi—what would the kidnapping have truly achieved? Sure, Knox would have paid ransom money, but it's not a matter that would have hurt him. Pissed him off, yeah, but not hurt him. If the idea was to ask you to switch places with Heidi, you would have been prepared to do it." Levi turned to Knox. "But would you have let her, or would you have found another way to get Heidi back?"

Knox said nothing. That question didn't require an answer. Everyone there knew that Knox would *never* have allowed Harper to trade herself for another, not even for a child, not even for a child of her own blood. He would have done whatever it took to get Heidi back, but he would not have handed his mate over to anyone. Every single demon would know that.

Tanner nodded at Levi. "The hunter said that the person who hired them doesn't want Harper dead. But taking into account the pain she went through and that they wanted her cousin kidnapped, they clearly want her to suffer. That sounds personal to me. Still, I'm not saying we should rule out that Thatcher has anything to do with all this—his name has cropped up twice now. Even if these attacks are personal to Harper, it's possible that he's involved."

"Would Thatcher have any reason to be angry at you?" Levi asked her.

"I don't think so," replied Harper. "I barely know him. I get the feeling he looks down on me, but many demons do—I'm a Wallis, after all. Do you think that whoever's behind all this is counting on us to blame it on the Horsemen?"

"Yes," replied Knox. "That's exactly what we did, isn't it?"

"My main enemy is Alethea—she would *love* to see me reduced to nothing but a pile of ashes. But as Tanner pointed out, this person doesn't want me dead. Could Carla or Bray want to hurt me for what my demon did to Roan? Sure. But I don't think they're smart enough to do all this and remain undetected."

"You're probably right," said Levi. "But we won't dismiss any of them as suspects."

"If the Horsemen are hoping to fly under the radar for a while, they won't be happy that they're being blamed for something they didn't do," Keenan pointed out.

Agreeing with that, Knox nodded. He telepathically reached out to Larkin and informed her of the day's events. After the harpy was done cursing, he said, *We need to explore the idea that this person wants to hurt Harper, not me. Still, everything keeps leading us back to Thatcher. Find out as much as you can about him. Dig as deep as you can go. If he has any link whatsoever to Harper, I want to know about it.*

If there is one, I'll find it, Larkin promised.

Turning Harper toward the exit, Knox said, "Come on, let's get you to bed."

"Who were you talking to?" Harper asked him. As their psyches were connected, she could feel the echo of his telepathic conversations; she simply couldn't understand the words.

"Larkin," he replied. "She's going to search for any possible link between you and Thatcher. If he has any sort of grievance with you, we need to know what it is. And we need to know before he acts again."

Nodding at that, Harper slipped her arm around his waist as they began a slow walk out of the boathouse. "Onto another subject, how did your meeting with Dion go?"

"Well . . ."

CHAPTER EIGHT

———◆———

The sting of teeth biting into the back of her shoulder snapped Harper out of sleep. Before she could wince, a hot tongue lapped and swirled over the mark to soothe the hurt. She realized that she was lying on her stomach while Knox was draped over her like a blanket, caging her in.

"Morning," she purred. Her demon stretched, luxuriating in his attention.

"Morning, baby," he said against her skin.

The throaty rumble made her stomach clench and her nipples tighten. "I hope you're hungry."

Understanding her meaning, Knox smiled. "I'm starving." But he wouldn't give her what she wanted just yet. He wanted to play first. Before Harper, he hadn't "played". Sex had never been anything but a basic need until she came along. He'd never cared for any of his partners. Never needed or craved them. Never been so focused on ensuring that they loved every minute of it. But it was different with Harper. Everything was different with her.

Harper fisted the bedsheet as his mouth traveled lower down her back and left another suckling bite that seemed to send a dart of pleasure directly to her pussy. His mouth explored her back, leaving little marks everywhere and licking along the sensitive lines of her wings. Wet and restless, she squirmed and tried arching into him. A hand pressed down on her lower back, keeping her flat against the bed.

"Don't move." Knox cupped her ass with his free hand. Boldly. Possessively. "I love this ass. Smooth. Pert. Biteable. And mine." He gave it a firm squeeze.

"Knox—"

"Shh." Knox plunged a finger inside her pussy. She tried to arch into him again, but he pushed down on her lower back to keep her flat. "I said, don't move."

"You're a damn tease."

Knox spoke into her ear. "No, I'm just playing with what belongs to me." No one else had ever belonged to him, and he'd sure as hell never belonged to anyone else. That Harper was all his, that he had rights to her that no one else would ever have—both as his mate and as his anchor—intensified the raw possessiveness he already felt for her.

As Knox sank a second finger inside her, he curved it just right, smiling at her gasp. Fisting her hair, he pulled her face to his and took her mouth. Consumed her. Dominated her. Greedily feasted on her as he fucked her with his fingers. "That's it. Take it."

He burned for her. Day. Night. All the fucking time. It took nothing more than for him to shift in his seat and suddenly scent her on his shirt. Just like that, even in the middle of a conference room, he'd be rock hard. Right then, his cock was full and heavy, aching for release. For *her*. For the only thing is his life he'd ever loved.

Harper gasped as ice-cold psychic fingers parted her folds, leaving her clit exposed to the mattress. The finger already deep in her pussy began to thrust in and out, rocking her against the bed, sending shockwaves of pleasure to her clit. It felt so good, but she needed more. Needed him filling and fucking her. "No more teasing."

"I'll give you what you want," he assured her, pausing to swirl his finger. "Soon."

Soon? "I like 'now'." The words came out kind of breathy with need. "'Now' sounds way better."

Knox drove another finger inside her, loving how hot and wet she was. Loving that her scent had become warmer and sweeter as her need built and built—it always did. What he loved more was that she held nothing back; that she was his with no limits or boundaries or doubts. She didn't even hold back from his demon—a fact that the entity treasured.

Kneading her scalp, Knox licked at a bite mark he'd left near the dragonfly tattoo on her nape. The mark gave his demon the same wicked masculine satisfaction that it did him. Knox bit down, and her pussy rippled around his fingers. His cock throbbed as if in envy.

Out of her mind with the need to come, Harper bucked hard enough to get to her knees. "Knox, I'm serious, you need to—" His fingers and body heat disappeared, and then his tongue stabbed inside her. "Oh, God." That talented tongue licked and lapped and swirled. Her thighs quivered, and she wasn't sure how much longer they could support her weight.

She jerked as a psychic finger plunged inside her while another flicked her clit. Her pussy began to burn and spasm until it was almost unbearable, and Harper could do nothing but ride the wave as her orgasm barreled into her with such force that her head spun. But the pleasure didn't fade. No. Because then the psychic fingers dissolved, and her pussy went from burning to inferno hot.

Knox blanketed her back again and growled into her ear, "Tell me."

Cheek to the mattress, Harper licked her lips. "Tell you what?" she asked, just to fuck with him for teasing her.

Knox *tsk*ed at her sass. "Baby, you know better than that." He slid his hand around her throat, covering the brand there. "If you want my cock inside you, you'll tell me what I want to hear."

His hand squeezed her neck in warning, but Harper only smiled. Even then, with his body trapping hers and his hand tight around her throat, she felt safe and . . . cherished. She knew he'd never hurt her. Knew that she was completely safe with both him and his demon. So she gave him those three little words he wanted. His long, thick cock plunged into her—forcing its way past swollen muscles until he was balls-deep in her pussy, exactly where she wanted him to be.

"I love feeling your pussy wrapped around my cock. All snug and warm and slick." Knox gripped both her shoulders, holding her still, as he pounded in and out of her. His pace was feral, his thrusts were savage. Her hot pussy squeezed and pulsed around his cock, showing him that she wanted it, that she loved it. Maybe even needed it.

Every throaty little moan shot straight to his cock. She was so fucking tight. He needed to be deeper. Needed to be so deep that she'd never forget the feel of him; that his name would be imprinted on her soul.

"Knox . . ."

It was a warning, but he hadn't needed it. He *knew* her body. He could sense that she was about to come. He also knew that she was expecting him to force her to wait. He didn't. "Come for me. That's my baby." His balls tightened as she came with a scream, squeezing and milking his cock. He jammed himself deep and exploded, shooting jet after jet of come inside her.

Feeling hollowed out, he pressed a kiss between her shoulders. "I love you too, baby."

"Then life is good," she slurred.

He fully agreed.

The bed beneath her rattled, and Harper's head snapped up. She blinked, realizing she wasn't in bed. She was in her office, and she'd fallen asleep at her desk. Damn.

Raini stood opposite her, one brow raised, lips pursed. She gestured at the brown paper bag she'd obviously plonked on the desk, waking her. That was the second time she'd been woken by someone else that day. She much preferred Knox's method.

Rubbing at the ache in her temples, Harper picked up her take-out cup of frothed milk, disappointed to find the cup cold. "What's in the bag?"

Raini folded her arms. "Open it." There was a challenge in her tone and posture, and Harper didn't like it.

Just to be awkward, Harper said, "Maybe later."

"Don't play with me, Wallis. Open it."

"Or . . . ?"

"Or I'll tell everyone exactly what's in that bag. I haven't mentioned it to anyone else. Don't force me to."

Out of morbid curiosity alone, Harper grabbed it with a sigh. Opening it, she froze. "You have to be kidding me."

"You need to use it, Harper," Raini insisted.

She shook her head and tossed the bag onto the desk. "Not necessary."

"Isn't it? I disagree."

"Well, I disagree that you have a need to disagree."

Raini picked up the bag. "Then it won't do you any harm to

use this and prove me wrong, will it? Come on, Wallis, let's see who's right."

Harper sighed. "I don't have time for this shit."

Eyes softening, Raini put a hand to her chest. "Do it for my peace of mind, if nothing else. *Please*."

"Don't you think you're being a little ridiculous?"

"Some days. Not today."

Again, Harper sighed. "Fine. I'll do it later," she lied.

"Now you're just lying." Raini took Harper's hand and pulled her out of her seat.

"You're stronger than you look."

Raini shoved the bag at her. "Go get it over with."

The urgency in Raini's tone sent a chill skittering down Harper's spine. She cocked her head, watching the succubus closely. "You really do think this is necessary, don't you?"

Raini gave her a wan smile. "Yeah, I really do."

Swallowing hard, Harper strode out of the office and went off to "humor" Raini so she could have that peace of mind she seemed to need. But when Harper walked to her station ten minutes later, she wasn't feeling so nonchalant anymore. Raini took one look at her face and flashed her a small smile that was both anxious and supportive.

Devon's brow creased. "You okay, Harper? You're awful pale."

Harper licked her lips. She wasn't ready to tell them yet. Besides, Knox should be the first to hear the news. "I just feel a little lightheaded, that's all." That wasn't entirely untrue.

"Huh." Devon's expression said she wasn't buying it.

"Knox called me," lied Harper, gently tapping her temple—a temple that still ached like a bitch. "He wants to see me. I shouldn't be more than twenty minutes."

"Take as long as you need," said Raini.

With a nod, Harper cleared her throat. Pretty much in a

daze, she grabbed her purse, and slipped on her jacket. Ignoring Khloë's intense scrutiny, she walked out of the studio with Tanner close behind.

Sidling up to her as they walked along the loud, busy strip, he said, "Where are we going?"

"Knox wants to see me." If the hellhound detected the lie, he didn't show it. He simply stayed at her side, protective as ever, guarding her from pedestrians.

It didn't take long to reach the office that was located above the combat circle. Heading behind the dome, she jogged up the flight of stairs and over to the door where Levi stood like a sentry.

Surprise briefly flashed in Levi's eyes, but he stepped aside and knocked on the door. "Harper's here to see you."

"I could have done that myself," she grumbled at the reaper, but he just smiled.

At Knox's "Come in!" she turned the metal knob and pushed the door open, feeling a little like she was walking to her doom. Leaving Tanner with Levi, she then closed the door behind her.

Mouth curved, Knox rose from his leather chair, rounded the desk, and crossed to her. "Hey, baby." He slid his arms around her waist and kissed her long and hard. "This is a surprise."

Harper almost laughed. If he thought *this* was a surprise, he was going to find her news one hell of a shock. "How are you?" Yes, she was procrastinating—go judge her.

"Better now that you're here." He nipped her lower lip and then laved the mark. "Not that I'm not happy to see you, but what brings you here in the middle of a work day?"

"Um . . . well, we kind of need to talk about something."

"We *kind of* need to do it?"

"Yeah. See, I just . . . Well, the thing is . . . I mean, you need to . . . God, there's really no easy way to—"

The office door burst open, and Levi declared, "Knox, we got a problem."

Knox went rigid. "What sort of problem?"

"Talia's apartment is on fire. That kind of problem."

Harper's mouth fairly dropped open. *Well, shit.*

In no time at all, Harper found herself standing outside Talia's apartment building for the second time in the space of a week. Nobody was sitting on the old couch outside this time. Nu-uh. Everybody simply stood across the street, staring at the blackened section of the building and watching as dark smoke drifted into the sky.

A fireman walked over to Harper and Knox, covered in soot and sweat; she recognized him from their lair. He nodded respectfully. "Mr. Thorne, Ms. Wallis."

Knox inclined his head at him. "What happened here, Blaine?"

"The fire didn't spread beyond Talia's apartment. Oddly enough, it was easing off before we even arrived ... as if it was under the control of someone."

"Hellfire," said Knox quietly.

Blaine nodded. "That would be my guess."

"I'm hoping you're going to tell me that Talia's at work."

"I wish I could. The neighbors heard her screaming. My guess is that it was her dealer. Apparently he paid her regular visits, threatening her with violence if she didn't pay what she owed him. I'm guessing this was about money that she simply didn't have to give." Blaine shrugged. "I can't think of any other reason why she would have been screaming apologies at someone."

"Apologies?" Harper echoed.

"Yes, ma'am. Her closest neighbor claimed that Talia kept screaming that she was sorry over and over." Hearing someone call his name, Blaine gave Knox and Harper an apologetic look. "Excuse me."

Just as Blaine walked away, Tanner appeared and said, "I talked to her closest neighbors. They said they heard her—"

"Screaming apologies," Knox finished. "Blaine mentioned it."

"Did he also mention that she kept begging for forgiveness, promising that if they stopped the fire and let her out she'd make it right—whatever 'it' is?"

Knox rubbed his jaw. "No, he didn't mention that."

Tanner gestured to a curvy, dark-skinned female standing near an ambulance, her face blank, eyes wet. "Rosa just arrived. She's Talia's partner. Want me to talk to her?"

"I'd like to ask her some questions myself." Keeping possession of Harper's hand, Knox headed to the she-demon. "Rosa?"

She blinked up at the three of them, looking dazed and numb. "I don't understand how this could have happened." Her voice was low, soft, defeated. "I just spoke to Talia an hour ago. She was fine."

Harper's chest tightened. "I'm not good in these situations," she admitted. "I don't know what to say, except that I'm sorry."

Rosa swallowed and gave a weak nod of thanks. "Why would someone do this?"

"The police said she's been having trouble with her dealer," said Knox.

"Raymond?" Rosa's brow pinched. "He's a lot of things, but he's no killer. He hasn't got the stomach for it."

"Is there anyone else who might have been upset with her?" Harper asked. "One of the neighbors said they heard her shouting apologies to someone."

Confused, Rosa shook her head. "She didn't have enemies. Outside of work, Talia kept a low profile." Silent tears began streaming down her face. "I just don't understand."

Knox gave her a pointed look. "If there's anything we can do, you let us know, Rosa."

"I will. Thank you, Mr. Thorne." She swiped at her wet cheeks. "Maybe she'll find some peace now. She was never really at peace with life."

"I'd like to think that she will." Harper gave her shoulder a sympathetic squeeze, feeling so fucking bad for Rosa. The female was doing a hell of a lot better than Harper would have done in her position. Losing Knox would destroy her. Wanting to give the grieving female some space, Harper clasped Knox's hand. *Let's leave her in peace.*

"Thank you for speaking with us, Rosa," said Knox. "Remember to come to us if you need anything." He turned to Harper. "Let's go, baby."

As they walked to the Bentley with Tanner, she looked up at Knox. *You think it was McCauley, don't you?*

So do you.

Harper didn't deny it. Couldn't deny it.

Once the three of them were back inside the Bentley with Levi, she said, "If McCauley can teleport, it wouldn't have been hard for him to go there, set the fire, watch her burn, and then ease the hellfire before getting away again without being seen." Hellfire wouldn't burn the demon who conjured it, which meant that McCauley would have gotten away unharmed.

Levi caught Harper's gaze in the rearview mirror, his expression one of disbelief. "You think the kid did this?"

"Talia wasn't alone when she burned to death," Knox told him. "She was apologizing to someone, promising that she'd make it right."

Levi cursed. "That doesn't mean it was him."

"No, it doesn't," agreed Knox. "But it does mean I need to speak with him. Make a pit stop at the Sanders's house."

Levi switched on the engine. "You got it."

When they finally pulled up outside the house, Harper looked at Knox. "Did you give Wyatt a telepathic heads-up that we were coming?"

"No. I want to *see* their reactions to the news."

Levi opened the rear door for them. "You've got me real curious about this kid. I'll come inside with you this time. There are no teens lurking about, eyeing up the Bentley."

Knox led the way up the path, and Harper then pressed the doorbell.

Wyatt opened the door after a few moments. His eyes narrowed as he took in the four of them. "Something's happened."

"Can we come in?" said Knox.

"Come through to the kitchen." Wyatt led the way into a small, bright kitchen. "What's wrong?"

Expression grave, Knox spoke, "Talia is dead."

For a brief moment, Wyatt said nothing . . . as if not comprehending the words. "What?"

"Both Talia and her apartment went down in a blaze of hellfire, but the rest of the building is fine. It was clear that she alone was the target."

"Hellfire?" Wyatt's gaze sharpened. "She was murdered. Jesus."

"Someone trapped her inside and killed her. She was screaming for them to let her out, but they didn't."

Cursing, Wyatt gave a sad shake of the head. "I've watched hellfire burn people alive. It has to be a horrible way to die."

Harper was in perfect agreement with that.

Linda strolled into the kitchen. She almost stumbled to a halt as she studied their faces. "What is it? What's happened?"

Wyatt rubbed at his nape. "Talia burned to death in her apartment. Hellfire."

Linda's face went slack and she gripped the counter. "Oh my God."

"Any suspects?" asked Wyatt, shifting into detective mode.

"Some believe it may have been her dealer," began Knox, "though her partner doesn't seem to think so."

"It's always the same with addicts," said Linda with a sigh. "If the drugs don't kill them, the dealers do. She chose that lifestyle."

Harper didn't like the bite in her voice. "*Nobody* deserves to die like that."

Linda blanched. "Of course not, I wasn't suggesting that she did. I just ..."

She was just glad that Talia couldn't come and take McCauley away, Harper guessed.

Knox glanced at the doorway. "Where's McCauley?"

Linda hesitated to respond. "He's upstairs, playing in his room. Why?"

"Has he been there all day?" asked Knox.

She double-blinked. "Yes. He doesn't spend a lot of time downstairs with us." And that clearly disappointed her. "He likes his space. Privacy."

Harper personally didn't know a lot of six-year-olds that confined themselves to their room and didn't want attention. It would be one thing if he was in an abusive household, but it was obvious that Linda would enjoy showering him with positive attention. "We'd like to talk to him."

Linda's gaze darted from Harper to Knox. "I don't think it's necessary for you to break the news to him. He never knew about her. Maybe we could simply tell him that you've been unable to find out who his biological mother is—it would be unkind to make him lose a mother twice."

"That's not why we wish to speak with him," said Knox.

Realization flashed across Linda's face. "You don't think it was him surely? He's *six*, for God's sake." When no one said a word, she put a hand over her heart. "I swear to you, he did not leave this house. I would know if he had."

"Maybe you just didn't see him leave," said Knox.

Linda's lips flattened. "If he could teleport, he would probably have left his human adoptive parents long ago."

"Not if he had nowhere else to go."

"He doesn't even know that Talia was his mother."

"He could have heard you talking about it."

"But we *didn't* talk about it."

"That's not entirely true," Wyatt objected, ignoring his mate's glower. "He may have overheard our argument with Pamela, Talia's mother. I'm not saying he caused the fire, I'm just saying he may have overheard that conversation."

Knox tilted his head slightly. "You had an argument with Pamela?"

It was Linda who responded. "Talia must have told her about him—probably because she didn't want her to find out from anyone else. Pamela wanted to take him. She was very insistent." From her tone, it was clear that she'd felt intimidated by the woman. "We said no. She threatened to involve you, so I pointed out that it was you who left him in our care and that if she wanted that to change then she'd have to consult you."

"She hasn't spoken to me about it yet." Knox pursed his lips. "When did this happen?"

"This morning," Linda replied. "Even if he did hear the argument, it doesn't mean he did anything wrong. Teleporting isn't that simple. He'd have to have an address or an image in his mind of a person or a place he wanted to go. He doesn't know what Talia looked like or where she lived."

Phone in her hand, Harper asked, "Does he have access to a computer? To the Internet?"

"Not the Internet," said Linda.

"What about either of you?" Harper asked the pair.

Wyatt folded his arms. "We use the Internet, yes, why?"

"Because it would be a simple case of finding her on Instagram." Harper held up her phone, showing them Talia's Instagram page. "She also has a Facebook profile. In other words, there are ways he could have gotten a picture of her. Surely you don't spend every moment watching over him. He could have used your computer without your knowledge."

Linda shook her head. "He's a sweet boy."

Harper inwardly snorted.

"He'd never harm anyone," Linda insisted. "He didn't even harm the human who cruelly tried to burn him in an oven. No, I won't believe that he hurt Talia."

"We still need to speak with him." Knox turned to Wyatt. "Take me to him."

Linda opened her mouth to object, but Knox silenced her with a look.

"This way," said Wyatt. They followed him up the stairs, across the landing, and over to a closed door. He gave it a rhythmic knock. "McCauley, you have visitors." Without waiting for an invitation, Wyatt twisted the knob and let the door swing open. "You remember Knox and Harper, right?"

Keeping Harper slightly behind him, Knox entered first. He briefly scanned the room. It had been decorated and filled with toys and games that any boy McCauley's age would love. Linda and Wyatt had clearly spared no expense.

Knox didn't fail to notice the drawings on the walls—like last time, they were pictures of a family. Two adults, two children, and a dog. In each drawing, they were dressed or posed differently, but the people always looked the same. "Hello, McCauley."

From his space on the carpet, McCauley looked up at them. "Hello." His voice was as devoid of emotion as his expression. He stayed very still, his posture unnaturally perfect.

Cocking his head, Knox studied the Lego tower the boy had

built. Tall, solidly built, and well-proportioned, it looked like a mock model of a building. Very advanced for a child of six. "You must be a smart boy."

McCauley blinked.

Knox used his psychic hand to lift a Lego brick and place it on the tower. "Can you do that?"

McCauley shook his head.

Knox feigned disappointment, hoping to prick at the pride of McCauley's demon. It worked. The boy's eyes bled to black and then narrowed. Suddenly, dozens of Lego bricks lifted from the carpet and started to circle the tower like planets orbiting the sun.

"Impressive," said Knox when McCauley's demon retreated. "What else can you do?"

"Just that."

It was a lie. Knox didn't understand why the child would lie about it. It was as if the demon didn't want to show its power. Was it simply used to hiding, having lived amongst humans for six years? Perhaps. "Did you leave the house today?"

The boy gave a slow, stiff shake of the head.

"Do you know why we're here?"

"No, sir."

"I think you do. I think you know what we suspect happened today." That received no reaction whatsoever. "I killed someone when I was a child," he said, ignoring Linda's gasp. "It's not an easy thing to do. Is it?"

"I don't know, sir."

"Talia apologized. She begged for forgiveness. But you killed her anyway. Why?"

McCauley blinked, still exhibiting no emotion. "I don't know who you mean, sir."

"You're quite the little liar, aren't you, McCauley? And you're not as good at it as you think you are."

His eyes narrowed *ever* so slightly.

Linda shouldered her way into the room and crossed to McCauley. Standing behind him, she placed her hands on his shoulders. "You heard him, he didn't do anything."

Leaning into her, McCauley rubbed at his eyes. "I'm tired."

It was an act, and Linda fell for it hook, line, and sinker—smiling down at him like he was her own, personal angel.

"We'll be back," Knox told her.

Linda's head snapped up. She didn't glare at him, but he knew that she wanted to. Instead, she stiffly inclined her head, as if not trusting herself to speak. She remained with McCauley while the others all made their way downstairs.

In the hallway, Knox spoke to Wyatt. "I think it would be best for all concerned if I remove him from your home."

Wyatt's shoulders sagged a little. "It would devastate Linda."

"I'm pretty certain he killed Talia."

"I wish I could disagree. I look in his eyes, and I see nothing. He's never happy, he's never sad, he's never angry, he's never anything. It's not natural. But Linda wants him here."

"He manipulated her up there," Harper pointed out.

Wyatt nodded. "It's not the first time he's done it. You have to understand ... Linda had several miscarriages. Only one pregnancy went full-term." His Adam's apple bobbed. "Our son was stillborn. We called him Sam."

The agony in his voice made Harper swallow hard. She couldn't even imagine how painful that must have been for the couple.

"It's something that's been eating at Linda for a long time," Wyatt continued. "It's like she feels that she's failed as a woman and a mate—it's ludicrous, of course, but that just seems to be how she feels. She sees McCauley as a chance for us to be a 'real' family. She doesn't care that he doesn't behave like normal kids. As far as she's concerned, we shouldn't expect any element of normality from a traumatized child. And she's probably right about that. It could be that I'm being as insensitive and paranoid as she's accusing me of being."

"You're not," Harper stated. "As sad as it is, your mate seems intent on being willfully blind to the fact that McCauley isn't just a little out of the ordinary. There's something truly wrong with him."

"I know, but it will devastate Linda if you take him. We can't know for sure that he did kill Talia. Innocent until proven guilty, right?"

"I'm not comfortable leaving him here," said Knox.

"Where else does he have to go? Look, you need someone to keep an eye on him. I can do that. Maybe I can even help him. Maybe with time he'll come to trust us and he'll change."

Knox strongly doubted it, but Wyatt was right—he did need someone to watch over McCauley. Wyatt was as good a person as any for that role. "All right, but don't drop your guard with him. You're a strong demon. He might be a child, but he could also be a very dangerous child. Don't hesitate to act in your defense."

"I won't."

Though Knox still wasn't comfortable leaving the Sanders to take on McCauley, he left the house with Harper and the sentinels. Nobody spoke until they were inside the car.

Levi turned on the ignition. "Damn, you weren't kidding when you said that kid is creepy. I'm ninety-nine percent sure he killed Talia."

"And he's not sorry for it," said Tanner.

Levi pulled away from the curb. "He behaves like our inner demons do—it's as if he's taking behavioral cues from it, imitating and obeying it."

"Like the demon is the parent," Harper mused.

Knox looked at her, eyes narrowed. "Exactly."

"His human mother was neglectful, right?" said Tanner. "It could be that his demon sort of . . . stepped in."

Levi whistled. "That would be bad. Our demons don't particularly give a shit when it comes to right and wrong. They're vengeful, they don't feel guilt. If that's the kind of 'parent' that's shaped him, he needs to be watched very closely. Maybe Linda and Wyatt really can help him—they'll be role models. They'll give him the attention and care that, until now, only his demon ever gave him. Do you think McCauley will hurt them?"

"If our theory is right, no," replied Knox. "His demon will be smart enough to know that it needs the Sanders to tend to McCauley's basic needs. It will be happy to use them until it feels that McCauley can take care of himself. It will have urged him to stay with his human mother for the very same reason. She could feed and clothe McCauley—things the demon can't do for him."

"You don't think it will get jealous if McCauley begins to care for the Sanders?" asked Harper.

Knox took her hand. "I don't think there's any risk of McCauley emotionally connecting with them any time soon. If it does happen, it would be in the distant future. Hopefully the demon will be used to the Sanders by then. It may even eventually like them if it feels they're good to McCauley. We can only speculate."

As Tanner and Levi started discussing sentinel business, Harper turned to Knox and asked softly, "Did you really kill someone when you were a kid?"

"They deserved it."

"I'm not saying they didn't. I just hate that you were put in a position where you had to kill or be killed when you were so young." Harper gave his hand a comforting squeeze. He looked at her, and what she saw in his eyes gave her the chills.

"By the time I was done with them, so were they."

CHAPTER NINE

———◆———

Ending his brief phone call, Knox slung his cell on the small bar in his living room and poured himself a gin and tonic. "Want a drink, baby?" Receiving no answer, he glanced over his shoulder. Harper was sitting on the sofa, her gaze inward as she twisted her rings and twirled her ankle absentmindedly.

A sense of unease prickled at him. Taking a swig of his drink, he crossed the room to her. Harper didn't fidget unless something was playing on her mind. And that was when he remembered . . . "Sorry, baby, you wanted to talk to me about something earlier. What was it?"

She looked up at him and blinked. For a moment, she didn't say anything. Then a determination gathered behind her eyes and she licked her lips. "Maybe you should sit down. Yeah, you should definitely sit down."

He'd prefer to stand, but he humored her and perched himself on the edge of the coffee table. "What is it? Tell me. If something's wrong, I'll fix it."

Sitting up straighter, Harper cleared her throat. Her mouth bopped open like a landed fish, and she seemed to struggle for words. "Okay, so I'm just going to say it."

"All right," he said. But she didn't say it. Her mouth opened again, but still nothing came out. "Why are you so nervous?" Dozens of possibilities raced through his mind, and he didn't like any of them. That sense of unease began to swell.

"I'm not nervous ... per se."

Yes, she was. He placed his tumbler on the table and took her hands. "Harper, tell me what's wrong."

"Nothing's *wrong*. Or, at least, *I* don't think there's anything wrong. You might feel differently."

"Harper, you're not making any sense. Whatever it is, just tell me."

"Okay, so, here it is. I'm ... Well, it's ... " Cursing, Harper delved into her purse and pulled out something that she'd stuffed in a sandwich bag. "I have something to show you."

Knox frowned, unable to make out what was in her grip. He held out his hand. "Why is it in a sandwich bag?"

"I didn't want you to have to touch it."

"Why?" he asked, as she finally handed it over.

"I peed on it."

"You peed on—?" Realization hit him, and he looked down at the item in his hand. Even through the plastic bag, the long, white pregnancy stick was clear. And so was the word "Pregnant" on the digital screen.

Harper stayed very still, giving Knox the space to work through the news. She wouldn't lie, she was totally on edge. Sure, they'd talked about having a baby and he'd been fine with it. But it was one thing to talk about a hypothetical baby and a whole other thing to find out that said baby was no longer so hypothetical.

She had a big family; she'd seen how differently males could react to pregnancy. Some were terrified by the prospect of being a father due to their own insecurities. Some felt trapped by the financial burdens, responsibilities, and social restrictions that came with fatherhood. Some, like Lucian, weren't ready to give up their own childhood or independence; they saw the idea of a baby as a loss of freedom.

Even the soon-to-be-fathers who were excited had their worries, and they sometimes did stupid things like act out or throw themselves into work rather than voice those concerns. Harper could understand it, though. She supposed that males probably often felt detached from their partner's pregnancy, since they played no physical part in it. The attention was usually on the women, so they might even feel a little left out at times.

Responsibilities didn't scare Knox Thorne, and he was too much of a confident, competent person to be insecure about his ability to be *anything*, even a father. Still, there was never really any knowing how a person would react to hearing they'd be a parent. And considering he was a total worrywart who constantly fussed over her health and safety, this news could very well send his anxiety levels soaring.

She figured that it could help if the news was delivered at a positive, well-timed moment. So, as they'd driven to Talia's apartment building, Harper had decided to delay breaking it to him. She'd planned to ask Meg to prepare his favorite meal and then fish out his favorite wine—possibly even get him drunk. She could then have broken the news to him gently, and he'd have had the time and privacy to allow it to settle into his brain.

A good plan.

Harper just didn't have the patience to wait like that, but she'd been determined to try. However, when he'd sensed that her head was ... well, up her ass ... he'd leaped on the matter, and she knew there would be no intimate meal. There was really no brushing him off when he knew something was bothering her. He would hound her and hound her until she coughed up the truth.

Although she'd made up her mind to just tell him right then, her nerves were so fried that she hadn't even been able to say the simple words, "I'm pregnant." Now he was staring down at the pregnancy stick, unmoving. And she didn't know what the hell to do.

She wondered how his demon was dealing with the news. Once the shock wore off, her own demon had switched into overprotective mode. Its priority was now the safety of the life inside Harper's womb. And Harper was pretty sure that if Knox didn't take it well, her demon would be thoroughly pissed at him and want to send soul-deep pain shooting up his dick.

As the silence dragged on, Harper barely resisted the urge to wring her hands. Eventually it got too much for her. "Okay, you need to say something or I might freak out."

His head lifted, and he looked at her through unreadable eyes. "You're pregnant?" The words came out choked.

"It would seem so."

He placed the stick on the table and stood. Her stomach dropped. Hell, she hadn't expected him to walk out, but she'd give him space if it was what he needed. Her demon would prefer to just slap him.

Taking Harper by surprise, his hand cuffed her wrist and he gently pulled her to her feet. Then his hands were in her hair and his mouth was on hers. Hard. Hungry. Consuming her.

Freeing her mouth, Knox rested his forehead on hers and splayed a hand on her flat stomach. "You're pregnant?"

She licked her lips. "I'm pregnant."

He swallowed. "We're not calling it Lucifer."

A shaky laugh bubbled out of her. "You're not upset?"

"No. This is my happy face. Can't you tell?"

"No."

"I'm far from upset," Knox assured her. He kissed her again, pouring all the emotions he was feeling right then inside her. Excitement. Wonder. Shock.

He was also anxious. Anxious that Harper would find the pregnancy and the birth difficult. Anxious that something might go wrong. Anxious about the baby's health. Knox was a person who liked to be in control of the things around him. This wasn't something he had any control over.

His demon was having the same internal struggle, and it wanted nothing more than to lock Harper away where no one could touch her or the child growing inside her. It wasn't a bad idea, really.

Knox framed her face with his hands. "How are you feeling?"

She took a long breath. "Okay. Better now that I know you're good with it."

"I guess this explains why you were so tired and lethargic all the time." He knew it was a symptom of a demonic pregnancy, but it hadn't occurred to him to even consider that she could be pregnant. He should have done. He shouldn't have simply assumed it was stress. Knox cursed as he remembered something. "I was rough with you this morning."

Harper smiled. "Rough sex isn't going to harm the baby." Outside forces, however? Yeah, there was a chance they would. Or, at least, they would *try*. "People will come for the baby. That's what Nora said," she reminded him. It made sense that there would be demons who would think to use the baby to control him. Others might even want the child for themselves, suspecting it would grow to be as powerful as Knox, and could be used against him. Her demon snarled, communicating that it would kill anyone who attempted any such thing.

"They won't get anywhere near the baby," vowed Knox. He would never allow it. His father hadn't protected him, and Knox would be damned if he failed his own child. His demon felt just as strongly about it. "We will ensure the baby is safe and protected at all times. Yes, it will mean that they'll be coddled, but better that than in the hands of someone who would harm them."

She nodded. "Whatever it takes."

"You know that the security around you will be stepped up now, don't you? I understand that your pride will balk at it, but it's necessary."

"I know." Harper sighed. "The baby needs to be protected."

Her immediate capitulation took Knox by surprise. "If I'd known that pregnancy would make you accept better security so easily, I'd have knocked you up months ago."

She smiled, sincerely surprised that he was so at ease with the news. "I was worried you might feel a little . . . "

"Jealous?"

She blinked. "Actually, I was going to say 'anxious' and maybe 'excluded'. Some guys feel like you're on the outside looking in—I don't want that for you. *Do* you feel jealous?"

"I'll admit that I'm selfish enough to not want to share your attention with anyone." So was his demon, actually. "But this isn't just 'anyone'. It's our child." He needed to have a doctor confirm that she was pregnant before he could truly believe it. There was still a surreal quality to the situation.

She leaned into him. "You're not upset that a lot of things will change?"

"What's so bad about change?"

"Nothing at all. I'm just checking."

"Does anyone else know?"

"Raini knows. She bought the pregnancy test and urged me to use it. Honestly, I thought she was being dramatic. It turns out that she was right. I didn't confirm that I was pregnant, but she'll have known just by the look on my face. She won't tell anyone, though. Not even Devon or Khloë."

"But you want them to know," he sensed.

"I'll feel bad keeping it from them, especially since Raini knows. Personally, though, I think we should keep the pregnancy quiet from as many people as we can for as long as we can."

Knox rubbed her upper arms. "I agree." Or people might attempt to either kill her to stop the birth of the baby or kidnap her to have access to the baby once it was born. "But you can still tell your closest friends." Mostly because he suspected that it would make them keep a close watch on her. That idea appealed to Knox and his demon a great deal. The more eyes she had on her, the better.

"We'll need to also tell the sentinels," he continued. "And you need to see a doctor. One of the gynecologists in our lair, Dr. Rodgers, is one of the best in the US." Knox fully intended to make sure she had the best of everything throughout the entire pregnancy. "He's odd, but he cares about his patients and he's very discreet."

"We can make an appointment tomorrow—"

"No, we should ask him to come here. Now." The primal part of Knox wanted nothing more than to take Harper to the floor and bury himself inside her—it was an unexpected urge, but it was there all the same. However, the overprotective part of him was in a frenzy and wanted her to be checked out and to have the pregnancy confirmed. "I need to know that you and the baby are fine."

"Then I guess you'd better call him."

Dr. Rodgers was nothing like Harper had expected. Small, gangly, and sporting geeky glasses, the Chinese American demon looked more like a scientist than a gynecologist. Given that he now possessed information about Harper and Knox that the rest of the lair did not yet know, he didn't seem excited or smug as she might have expected. Her demon eyed him suspiciously, too overprotective to trust any strangers around them.

As he stood in her living room, hands clasped, Rodgers flashed her a professional smile. "So, you believe you're pregnant."

Sitting on the sofa beside Knox, she said, "The test was positive."

"Demons can get fake positive results, so the tests aren't always very reliable. What about symptoms? I can tell just by looking at you that you've had trouble sleeping. How's your appetite been?"

"Not at its best."

He pursed his lips. "Your tongue ever feel like it's burning?"

She frowned. "Yes."

"Headaches?"

"Yes."

"Nausea?"

"Yes. But I haven't had morning sickness or anything."

"Some pregnant women don't." He offered her a bottle of water. "Drink."

She didn't take the bottle. "I need to use the bathroom, so I'd rather not."

"Don't pee. I want to do an ultrasound scan, and the images will be better quality if you have a full bladder. Now drink—we want it nice and full."

Knox took the bottle, twisted off the cap, and handed it to her. "Good girl," he said as she sipped at it. They both watched the doctor as he switched on the portable ultrasound machine that he'd brought with him.

"Given what you've told me," Rodgers began, "I'd say you're about nine to ten weeks pregnant. Demonic babies develop at a faster rate than human babies, so the pregnancies usually last around thirty weeks. There are three stages to a demonic pregnancy. I call them infestation, oppression, and possession."

She paused with the bottle close to her mouth. "Aren't those the stages of demonic possession?"

Smiling, he shrugged. "Pregnancy is pretty much the same thing."

"No, it's really not." She cocked her head. "Anyone ever told you that you have the oddest sense of humor?"

"Once or twice." He pushed some of the buttons on his portable ultrasound machine. "Lay back. Let's get a look at this baby."

Knox kissed her temple and then rose from the sofa, but she tightened her grip on his hand. "I'm not leaving you," he told her, perching himself on the arm.

Mollified, Harper lay on the sofa and pulled up her T-shirt. Rodgers squirted cold gel on her stomach and then moved a handheld probe around her lower abdomen, which put pressure on her bladder and made her *really* need to pee. But the sound of a heart beating strong and fast pushed her discomfort into the background.

Knox leaned forward as they watched the screen. He could make out the head and the outline of the baby's body clearly, and his chest tightened. She really was pregnant. Even as he looked at their baby, the whole situation still felt surreal.

Rodgers tilted his head. "Huh."

Knox's muscles went rigid. "What does 'huh' mean?"

"It means I was wrong. You're sixteen weeks pregnant, Harper. Congratulations."

Harper gaped. She was nearing the end of the second stage of her pregnancy? Her demon blinked, shocked for the second time that day. "How is that even possible?"

Rodgers turned to her. "Well, there's such a thing called 'sperm'. During sexual intercourse—"

Knox sighed. "Do you have to be an idiot right now?"

"Sorry."

"You're sure she's that far along? She doesn't look pregnant. Her stomach doesn't even have a slight pouch. If anything, she's lost weight."

"It's not unusual for a she-demon to lose weight at first, especially if their appetite has been suffering. It's usually at around the eighteenth week that the mother begins to actually *look* pregnant. Then things go pretty fast from there." He turned to Harper. "You're approaching the end of stage two, so the tiredness will start to wear off and you'll get your appetite back. *But* you'll have to deal with backache, joint pain, an increase in sex drive, and of course weight gain. Oh, and your demonic abilities might play up a little. The latter doesn't always happen, though, especially if the she-demon is powerful like yourself."

"Sounds grand," she said dryly. Most of her attention was still on the monitor. She suspected that the image would just look weird to anyone who wasn't emotionally invested in the situation. For Harper, the little bundle on the screen was a marvel. Her throat felt tight and she had to cough to clear it.

"Does everything look okay?" Knox asked the doctor, keeping his fingers linked with hers.

Rodgers turned back to the monitor and moved the probe a little. "It all looks good. Although . . ."

Tension gripped Knox. "Although what?" he prodded when the doctor fell silent.

"The fetus is smaller than it should be, though that can change. It could have a growth spurt at some point." Rodgers' mouth curled as the baby started wriggling around, looking like it was trying to do the breast stroke or something. "Quite the little mover, isn't it? It's small, but it's feisty. Ever feel a little fluttering in your stomach, Harper?"

Now that she came to think of it ... "Yeah. The fluttering has gotten more ... pronounced. Sometimes it feels like bubbles popping." She'd just thought it was, well, gas. And she was paranoid that she'd let it all go in public.

"That's the fetus moving around. In the next couple of weeks, there'll be a noticeable difference in the strength of the movements."

Rodgers removed the probe—*thank God*—and turned off the ultrasound machine. He then gave her a paper towel to wipe off the gel. Knox helped her clean it up, and then Harper righted her T-shirt and sat up. "Is there anything I can do to make sure that the baby grows as it should?"

"Just ensure that you take care of yourself," said Rodgers. "If you take care of your body, your body will take care of the fetus. We'll have regular scans so we can monitor how things are going and make sure it's developing just fine."

Knox nodded. "What will happen if the baby *doesn't* grow like it should?"

"That depends on a few things. Harper may have to be induced and have the baby early, but I don't think it will come to that." The machine whirred as it printed out a small picture of the screen. Rodgers handed it to her.

Glancing at the smooth black and white picture, Harper swallowed hard again. That was her baby. Hers and Knox's baby. It was growing inside her. She was ... it was just ... wow. Until a few hours ago, she hadn't even suspected that she could be pregnant. It was honestly hard to wrap her head around it.

She gave the picture to Knox, who looked down at it with

such an intensity of emotion that she sucked in a breath. If she'd have had any doubts at all that he was happy about the pregnancy, that one look would have eradicated them.

Rodgers grinned. "Feeling manly now, Thorne? This is the ultimate proof that you're a virile man."

Knox shot him an impatient look that made the doctor's grin deepen.

Gathering his things together, Rodgers pointed at Harper. "No alcohol, no raw fish, ease up on the caffeine, and don't overexert yourself." At her nod, he said, "Call me if you have any questions or concerns and ... well, congratulations once again. Don't worry. This matter will be confidential and there will be no records."

Knox inclined his head. "Thank you."

"I appreciate you coming so soon," said Harper.

Equipment in hand, Rodgers gave her a gracious smile. "It was no problem at all."

Knox dropped a kiss on Harper's head and then accompanied Rodgers to the front door. "Is there anything I should watch out for? Any complications I should expect?" He hadn't wanted to ask in front of Harper.

"All pregnancies can have complications, but they don't always do so," Rodgers told Knox. He patted his arm. "Don't worry so much. Try to enjoy it. And smile. Your life is about to be turned upside down and be forever changed." With that, he walked out the door and down the steps, where his black sedan waited.

Knox closed the door and returned to the living room. He sat next to Harper and pulled her close, looking down at the scan picture she was staring at. Sweeping her hair away from her face, he asked, "You okay?"

She met his eyes, puffing out a breath. "I didn't think I'd be so far along. In fourteen weeks, we'll be parents." Panic rose sharp and fast as it truly sank in. "We're so unprepared for this it's not even funny. Babies need lots of stuff and we have literally nothing. We'll need a cradle, a stroller, a—"

"Ssh." He massaged her nape and kissed her gently. "You're getting yourself all worked up, and that's not good for you. We'll get everything we need. We'll be as prepared as any set of parents can be. I know this has come as a shock to you—I can very much relate to that—but you don't need to stress about anything." He'd do enough of that for both of them anyway. "Just do what Rodgers said and concentrate on taking care of yourself. Now, why do you look guilty?"

"You heard Rodgers. The baby's too small. That's my fault. I wasn't eating well."

"I also heard him say that it's not unusual for a she-demon's appetite to suffer at first. That is not your fault." He rubbed her back. "Everything will be fine. I won't have it any other way."

She bit her lip. "Don't hate me if I turn out to be a really shit mom, okay? It won't be something I did on purpose."

He curled a hand around her chin. "You could never be a bad mother. Have we not already been over this?" If either of them were likely to make a bad parent, it would be Knox. But he had every faith in himself and Harper as a unit. "Like I've pointed out once before, Lucian didn't raise you; he relied on you because he isn't able to meet his own needs. You were the parent in that relationship, so you already know a thing or two about parenting. You're also as caring, responsible, and protective as any mother should be."

"Speaking of Lucian ... I don't even want to wonder how he'll react." Hearing she was pregnant would mean he'd have to accept that Knox was a permanent fixture in her life. She wasn't like Lucian, she wouldn't walk away from the father of her child unless she absolutely had to—Lucian would know that. "Jolene and the girls will be ecstatic. I have to say, though, that I'm thinking the person who'll be most excited is Lou."

Knox exhaled heavily. "Yeah. He's going to be a pain in the ass once he finds out." Glancing once more at the ultrasound image in her hand, Knox stroked the baby with his thumb. It still wasn't quite sinking into his brain that there was a little person inside Harper; that that little person was his child. *Their* child. Still, every protective instinct that he and his demon had was on high alert. "No one will ever harm the baby," he swore.

Harper squeezed his hand. "No, they won't. And if anyone tries, we'll string them up by their intestines. We'll make an example of them to send a message of just how dumb it would be for anyone else to try."

Knox looked into her eyes, saw the promise of retribution right there, and nodded. It was a vow. "Come on, let's go to bed."

"I really don't think I could sleep right now." She was too wired.

His mouth set into a lopsided smile. "Who said anything about sleeping?"

CHAPTER TEN

———————◆◆◆———————

Knox paused with the fork halfway to Harper's mouth, his forehead wrinkling. "You're going to work?"

Harper arched a brow. "What, you thought I'd spend the rest of the pregnancy sitting around, twiddling my thumbs?"

"A man can dream."

She rolled her eyes. "I took three days off, even though I didn't need them." She'd agreed to spend the time catching up on her sleep, but she'd really done it so that he had a little time to adjust to the idea that she was pregnant. Honestly, she'd also needed that time to adjust. Now that she had, the anxiety had been replaced by a scary anticipation. But it was a *good* kind of scary.

It was amazing just how different her world now seemed. Everything other than Knox had taken an emotional backseat to the life inside her. And that was the way it should be, she thought. It hadn't been that way for her own parents, but it would damn well be that way for her.

"I will admit that having your undivided attention during my time off was quite enjoyable." Obligingly, Harper ate the chunk of grapefruit that he offered her.

Since discovering that Harper was pregnant, a delighted Meg had tried filling her with fruit, vegetables, and other healthy foods. Knox often insisted on feeding her, which Harper would have quickly lost her patience with if she hadn't understood why exactly he was fussing. He was worried for her, and it got to him that he had no control over the matter. It made him feel helpless. She didn't want that. If letting him fuss over her made him feel more involved and not quite so powerless, she'd deal with it.

"And I enjoyed being able to give you my undivided attention for the past three days," said Knox. "Why not allow yourself to enjoy it a little longer?"

"You can't be with me all the time." She took a sip of her orange juice. "We both have businesses to run."

"I know." Knox sifted his fingers through her hair. "But my protective instincts are in a frenzy right now and it's making me paranoid over your safety."

She gave him a reassuring kiss, humming because he tasted of coffee, porridge, and brown sugar. "I get that. My own protective instincts are a little hyper at the moment too, and my demon is on edge—seeing everything and everyone as a potential threat, which is going to get old *fast*. I need you to be the rational one. Besides, I have Tanner."

Knox wasn't so sure he could give her "rational". His demon snorted at the idea. "Keenan will now also be guarding you. One bodyguard for you, and one for the little person in there." He gently rubbed her stomach. "Do it for me. I need that peace of mind, Harper."

"I do understand that we need to tighten the security. I'm not going to fight you on it." Especially if it meant that her demon would relax just a little.

He nodded in approval and fed her a piece of kiwi. "Invite Jolene and the girls to the mansion tonight. We'll get them and the sentinels in the same room and give them the news all at once."

"You haven't told Keenan why you've assigned him to me?"

"Not the full truth, not yet. I didn't want to tell him before I told Levi, Tanner, or Larkin—they're immature enough to be jealous about it. And no, I'm not kidding."

Harper's mouth quirked. "Okay, so we'll tell everyone at the same time."

"Keenan thinks I've asked him to guard you because I'm a little paranoid about your safety, which is actually true. Both he and Tanner will remain inside the studio with you all day. When you leave, they'll leave with you."

Despite knowing it was necessary, her instincts reflexively balked at that extent of the overprotectiveness—they were sentinels, they shouldn't be lumbered with babysitting duty—but she didn't argue. Common sense told her that it was better to be safe than sorry. The baby's safety came before her pride and touchy independent streak.

"Since the person who's targeting me tried kidnapping Heidi, do you think they've accepted that it would be too difficult for them to get to me?" she asked. "If so, it's possible that it will be the other people in my life that they might consider harming."

Knox thought on that for a moment. "Since their plan to get their hands on Heidi fell flat on its face, I doubt they'll try touching your family or anyone in their lair again—that will include your co-workers."

Full to her stomach, Harper shook her head when he offered her a slice of apple. "I can't eat anymore. I'm stuffed."

Knox didn't lower the fork. "You're eating for two now, remember."

"I ate a lot more than I usually do," she pointed out. "And the last thing I want to do is vomit it all back up, which is exactly what will happen if I try forcing more food into my stomach."

"Valid point." He put down the fork, which displeased his demon. Still, the entity could accept that she was right and, like Knox, knew there would have been no sense in pushing her. "I just worry about you."

"I know you do, and I love you for it. But I'm honestly stuffed."

He gestured to her orange juice. "Finish that, at least. For me."

With a huff, she picked up the glass and downed the juice like it was tequila. "There. Done. Happy now?"

"I was already happy. Now I'm happier." Knox kissed her, licking into her mouth, taking his time to gorge himself on her. She tasted like fruit and that sweet unique taste that was all Harper. Pulling back, he watched as her amber irises clouded and swirled before changing into a striking cobalt blue. "I wonder if the baby will have your eyes."

Just the possibility of that had the potential to put Harper in a bad mood. "I don't want our child to have freaky eyes."

Knox shot her a mock glare and gave her lower lip a punishing bite. "Your eyes are not freaky." He spoke against her mouth. "They're beautiful. Unique. Fascinating. Just like you."

"It's good that you think so, but I don't." According to Carla, Harper had inherited the weird trait from Carla's sister. It was possible that it could be passed on to the baby, especially since it was guaranteed to be a sphinx. Archdemons weren't born from a womb. "I'd like it to have your dark eyes." They made her think of black velvet. Just because the baby could only be a sphinx didn't mean it couldn't share any physical resemblances to Knox. The baby in her dream had looked up at her through dark eyes, she remembered . . . right before it blew up the cradle.

"What's making you frown? Tell me. I'll make it better."

She smiled. "I was just remembering that odd dream I had about a baby, courtesy of the nightmare hunter."

"Ah." Knox sipped the coffee he'd almost finished. "It's possible that some subconscious part of you considered that you could be pregnant. That might have sparked the dream. Like I said, nightmares can only cause dreams, they can't fabricate the content."

"That's what I was thinking."

At that moment, Meg walked into the room. She looked at Harper's plate and clucked in disapproval, settling her hands on her wide hips.

"I ate as much as I could," said Harper defensively.

"She did," Knox confirmed. "She can't spend much more time sitting here anyway, since she has to get ready for work."

Meg glowered at her. "You are going to work?" She went on to lecture Harper, just as Knox had known she would.

Ignoring the rant, Harper scowled at him. "Throwing me under the Meg bus was just plain mean, Thorne. And it won't make me stay home, if that was your end game."

Knox shrugged, mouth curving. "It was worth a try."

Harper rolled her eyes at him. "Thank you for caring," she then said to Meg, "but I can't stay in this house for the rest of the pregnancy. *I will go insane.* Do you really want a crazily bored imp-by-nature-sphinx for company? 'Cause I gotta tell ya, they're not fun to have around."

Meg humphed and snatched Harper's plate. "I will prepare you healthy snacks to take with you to work, and you will eat all of them."

Harper sighed at her retreating back. "I'm not looking forward to telling the others, because there's a good chance they'll react just as protectively. I can't handle that level of fretting. They'll swarm around me like locusts."

Knox drank what was left of his coffee. "I'd say I'm sorry that they'll coddle you, but I'm not." The more people protecting her, the better, as far as Knox was concerned. Eyes narrowing, she flipped him the finger. Knox just chuckled.

In the coffeehouse later that morning, Harper stood at the end of the counter while the barista prepared her order. Hearing the bell chime, she glanced at the door. Not Carla, she noted. Good. She'd checked each time she heard the bell. It would be just her luck that the woman sought another confrontation. Her demon *really* wouldn't do well with that right now.

"How are you feeling today?" asked Wren.

Harper smiled. "Good, thanks. You?"

"I'm fine." Wren put the last of the cups on the tray. "Frothed vanilla milk for you again, I suspect," she added quietly with an odd gleam in her eyes

Harper stilled as the implication of that comment sank into her brain. "You knew?" All this time, she'd known? "How?"

"I sense these things. I wasn't sure if you knew or not, but I've noticed you're scanning the room as if potential threats may be lying in wait. Your demon's paranoid, huh?" Wren leaned forward to make the conversation private. "Don't fear that I'll share what I know. You've had to deal with many people who would like to see Knox fall. It means you haven't quite realized just how many people wish him to thrive."

"Thrive?"

"Knox is everything a lair could want in a Prime. There are many who would defend him with their lives, though he doesn't need their protection. If he produces a child who might one day take his place, our lair will continue to be strong. I won't do anything to put that child at risk. And it *would* be at risk, but you're smart enough to already know that."

Harper gripped the tray tight. "Does anyone else suspect the pregnancy?"

"Not that I'm aware. I'll let you know if any whispers begin to spread. I can assure you that the lair will close ranks around you, Knox, and your child. Most will be happy for him, just as they were happy for him when he took you as his mate. We want only good things for our Prime. Oh, there are those who have their grievances with him, but all will support him in this. As I said, they want the lair to be strong for their children, their grandchildren, and their grandchildren's grandchildren, and so on and so on."

"In other words, don't worry so much?"

"A child is always a blessing. A pregnancy should be a time of celebration, not fear."

She had that right, thought Harper. "Thanks." Lifting the tray, she walked to the condiment trolley, where Raini was waiting.

As they added milk, sugar, and toppings to the drinks, Raini asked in a low voice, "How did Knox take the news?"

"Very well, thank God. I'll tell the others tonight." Harper had already invited everybody to the house later. "Um, thanks for pushing me to take the test."

Raini smiled. "You can thank me by taking things easy. I get that you'd rather be at work, but pace yourself and work shorter hours."

"God, you sound like Knox."

Raini just snickered. "You don't look as tired today."

"According to the doctor I spoke to, the fatigue will start to wear off. It's no wonder I looked like shit the past few months. Every bit of goodness I took in was going to the baby."

"And you weren't resting like you should have."

Harper held up her hand and pledged, "I will not overdo it. My demon wouldn't allow me to anyway."

"Good. Then let's get moving."

As his visitor entered the office, Knox rose from his seat. "Pamela," he greeted simply. Ever since Linda and Wyatt mentioned that Talia's mother had appeared at their home, he'd anticipated that Pamela would eventually come to speak with him about McCauley. Pamela Winters wasn't a she-demon who backed down. She was a hard, strong-willed woman who could crush a person's confidence with just a look. In that sense, it wasn't surprising that she intimidated Linda.

Pamela was also very conscious of public opinion, so he'd imagine that Talia's lifestyle had been deeply embarrassing for the judge. That may have been why she rarely spoke of her daughter but raved about her son—a very well-known defense attorney who lived in Chicago.

Pamela gave him a gracious nod. "Mr. Thorne. Thank you for seeing me."

Knox gestured for her to take the seat opposite him, and they both sat down. "It seems an inadequate thing to say, but I'm sorry for your loss."

Pamela's smile was brittle, and he got the feeling she'd heard the words so many times that she was tired of hearing them. "Thank you. I know Talia was an addict and had her problems, but she wasn't a bad person."

"I never thought that she was."

"Even when you heard about the boy?"

Knox leaned back in his chair. "From what I understand, Talia had her reasons for giving him to humans to care for. I do not at all condone that she switched him for a human child, especially since she didn't seek permission, but I do understand what motivated her to do so."

That seemed to ease the tension in Pamela's shoulders. "McCauley has been through a lot."

"It would seem so."

"Being with his family, his *real* family, would help him heal. Help him feel he belongs somewhere."

"I hear you went to see the Sanders."

"He's my grandson; of course I did." She let out a long, steadying breath. "I know that Linda and Wyatt are good people. I can see that Linda would be happy to keep and raise him. But she wants him for the wrong reasons. I've watched them together. He could be anyone to her. It's not so much McCauley that she wants, it's a child to care for."

Knox couldn't deny that. Linda clung to McCauley because she wanted a child, not because she loved him. That wouldn't be good for the boy in the long run.

"I truly sympathize with Linda," Pamela went on. "But there are plenty of children out there who need a home and have no family to care for them. McCauley *does* have family who can care for him. He does have somewhere to go. Linda could foster or adopt one of the others."

Elbows braced on the arms of his chair, Knox knitted his fingers together. "I'm not opposed to him going to live with you, Pamela. But I won't abruptly remove him from the Sanders' home. It would not be good for him." And it would be risky, considering there was every reason why Pamela might not want to keep him. She wasn't the type of person who would blind herself to a child's nature. "I'll arrange for you and your mate to meet him and spend time with him. We'll take it slow. If and when McCauley feels comfortable going to live with you, he can do so."

Pamela's fingers flexed. "With all due respect, he is much too young to make such a serious decision."

"His demon is very tense right now, Pamela. It wants to protect him. It won't appreciate you pushing McCauley to do anything he's not ready to do. Win his demon's trust and approval."

Her forehead wrinkled. "Talia said she believed that his demon was latent."

"It may have been latent for a while, but it isn't any longer."

After a long pause, Pamela spoke. "When can we meet him?"

"I'll speak to the Sanders and ask what time would suit them best."

"Linda will put off the meeting for as long as she can."

"I suspect she will try to do so, but I will make it clear that the meeting must happen no later than Sunday."

"Thank you," said Pamela with a slight bow of her head.

"I have to warn you, Pamela. He may not be what you're expecting. It seems that his demon has acted as a parental influence."

Pamela was silent for a moment as she digested that. "Once it realizes that my mate and I will care for McCauley, it may settle down."

"Let's hope so." After she left his office, Knox grabbed his cell and called Wyatt. It rang four times before the demon finally answered. "I've just had a visit from Pamela," Knox told him.

A brief silence met that statement. "She wants to take McCauley." Wyatt sighed. "She may change her mind once she speaks with him."

"I don't want to pluck him from your home, Wyatt. But the Winters want to be part of his life. I'd like him to meet Pamela and her mate, and to let him get comfortable with them. It may be that he doesn't wish to leave you and Linda, but they're his family. They should have the chance to build something with

McCauley, even if it doesn't result in him going to live with them."

A long exhale. "You're right. It can only be good for him to have family around him."

"How has he been?"

"No different. Linda's tried to form some sort of relationship with him, but it hasn't worked. I worried that the longer he was with us, the more attached she'd become to him. But she's not attached to him as a person, she's attached to the idea of him."

"Which is why it will definitely be good for him to meet his maternal family," Knox pointed out.

"I'll speak with Linda and get back to you with a good date and time."

"No later than Sunday, Wyatt," Knox warned. "For McCauley's sake."

"Right. No later than Sunday."

Later that day, the girls, Jolene, Tanner, Keenan, and Larkin were scattered around the living area of the mansion, talking and laughing. At first, Harper's demon was on its guard while so many people were on its territory, even though it knew and partially trusted them. After a while, it lost its tension, though it remained alert.

The day had gone by pretty fast, which could have been because Harper found herself disappearing into her mind between jobs—mentally listing everything she'd need to buy and do to be ready for the baby's arrival.

Devon and Khloë had commented on her "acting weird", not at all appeased by her promise to tell them everything later. Tanner and Keenan hadn't commented, but they had watched her closely. *Too* closely.

Everyone in the room quieted when Knox and Levi finally

joined them. Even as they all exchanged greetings, Knox made a beeline for Harper.

Sitting on the sofa, she smiled up at him as he bent down and dropped a lingering kiss on her mouth. "Hey," she said simply.

"Hey." Knox sensed her nervousness and gave her nape a comforting squeeze. His demon relaxed now that she was close—it had harassed him all damn day to find her and stay with her. He'd telepathically checked in with her many times, but it hadn't done much to placate his demon. *I missed you.*

And I missed you. "How was your day?"

"Relatively good." Knox nodded in thanks as Raini and Devon shuffled along, making room for him on the sofa. He took the seat next to Harper, draping his arm over her shoulders. *How're you feeling?*

Nervous, Harper replied. *I know they'll be happy for us and I'm confident that they won't spread our little announcement, but it's hard not to be . . . protective of the news.*

I understand. We can keep it to ourselves a little longer if that's what you want.

No, it's better that they know. Hearing a throat clear, Harper realized that everyone was looking at them expectantly.

"Well, don't keep us in suspense, Harper," said Jolene. "You know I don't like that."

Harper crossed one leg over the other. "We only want to do this once, so we figured it would be easier to just get you all in one place." She took a deep breath, but no words came out.

Linking their fingers, Knox took pity on his mate. "She's pregnant."

"I knew it!" crowed Devon, a huge smile on her face.

The whole room pretty much descended on Harper and Knox, excitedly passing on their congratulations . . . aside from

Keenan, who said to Knox, "Quick, run. I'll hold her down if she tries to chase you."

Harper sighed at him. "You're an idiot."

"I've known this for a while," said Keenan.

"I can't wait to be an aunt!" Raini clapped her hands a few times. "How pregnant are you?"

"Sixteen weeks," replied Harper.

"Ah, that explains so much," said Khloë. "I should've seen it."

Devon's eyes widened. "Ooh, we get to go shopping for baby clothes!"

"Um, actually, you don't," said Harper. "If a bunch of you buy baby clothes all at the same time, people will guess pretty quickly who they're for."

They all fell silent for a moment. Then Khloë spoke. "We'll take Aunt Kayla with us. She's pregnant. People will just think the stuff is for her."

Devon pursed her lips. "That would work."

"Have you had an ultrasound scan yet?" asked Jolene.

"Yes." Harper took the picture from her purse and handed it to Raini, who cooed over it before passing it on.

"The baby's fine," said Knox, "albeit slightly on the small side."

"So was Harper," said Jolene, her smile nostalgic.

Harper raised her brows. "Really?"

Jolene nodded. "You had a growth spurt near the end of the pregnancy. You were still tiny, but not dangerously tiny. There was no need for you to go into an incubator or anything."

"Are you going to find out if it's a girl or a boy?" Larkin asked, eyes lit up.

"Personally, I'd rather have the surprise." Harper looked at Knox. "You?"

"Whatever you want," he told her. He truly didn't mind either way.

On the sofa opposite them, Khloë leaned forward. "Got any names yet?"

Harper scratched her nape. "I haven't even thought about names." Of course, everyone then helpfully started reciting their favorite names. It wasn't long before they then all began criticizing each other's choices.

Knox spoke above all the noise in the room. "We plan to keep the news quiet for as long as it's sensible to do so. I'm sure we can trust you all to keep it to yourselves."

"Of course," Jolene told him, sobering. The others nodded.

"No one," Knox stressed. "You share it with no one—not even members of your family or lair. Do it for Harper and the baby's sake."

Raini put a hand over her heart. "We won't say a word."

Satisfied, Knox nodded.

Jolene and the girls stayed for a while, arguing with Harper about throwing a baby shower. Harper saw it as yet more "fuss". They weren't sensitive to her plight, however, and seemed determined to arrange the shower. Once that argument had past and Tanner was done riling Devon, Jolene drove the girls home in her Mustang.

Finally alone with Harper and his sentinels, Knox poured himself a gin and tonic and then returned to Harper's side. "I don't think I need to tell you all that we need to tighten the security around Harper."

"The problem is that if she has several guards, people may guess why," said Tanner, sprawled on the sofa opposite. "Now that I *know* she's pregnant, I can *see* it. The fatigue, the weight loss, the dark circles under her eyes that show she's not sleeping well—they're obvious signs. We attributed it to stress, so others probably did too. But if she suddenly has several guards, people will speculate."

Beside the hellhound, Keenan nodded in agreement. "That will spread like wildfire."

Tanner looked at Harper, expression almost apologetic. "I know you love your job but, not to be an asshole, it's going to be hard to adequately protect you when you're constantly around strangers."

Harper sighed. "Tanner—"

"You have to admit," the hellhound began, "now that you're pregnant and don't just have your own safety to worry about, you're going to look at everyone suspiciously, wondering if they're Horsemen or if they hired the hunters. Your demon definitely will be."

Harper wiped a hand down her face. "All right, I won't deny that. But I have a business to run."

"It's a business you *co*-run," Knox softly corrected. "You can afford to take some time away from your job. It's true that you're the main draw for the studio, but it's also true that your co-workers are completely capable of running it in your absence."

"I know that, but I also know that I'll get restless and bored and start taking things apart."

Larkin's mouth quirked. "Maternity leave is a good thing." She paused to frown at Keenan, whose arm bumped hers as he dug out his flask. "Demonic pregnancies aren't easy, Harper. The last stage is particularly hard."

Standing near the fireplace, Levi added, "By then, it will be easy for people to tell that you're pregnant. That's when your safety could really be at risk."

"Don't forget that people are reluctant to fuck with pregnant demons," said Harper. "We can be vicious and moody creatures when crossed." She looked at Knox, adding, "And then maybe you'll finally fear my mighty wrath."

One side of his mouth lifted. "I really don't see that happening."

Harper sniffed. "Fine, blind yourself to the truth."

"Back to the point at hand," said Knox. "Larkin made a valid point. The next few months will be hard on you. Do you really want to make it even harder? And maybe you should bear in mind that being at the studio every day will not make things easier for you—there, you'll have your co-workers constantly coddling you. The further along you get in the pregnancy, the worse that coddling will become."

Pissed that he was right, Harper barely held back a growl. "I'll make you a deal. The doc said that when I hit the eighteenth week, I'll actually start to look pregnant—that will be in just under two weeks' time. On that very day, I will start maternity leave. It's a good compromise." And it would stop her demon from stressing too much.

Knox gave a slow nod. "I can live with that."

"Good, because I don't want to have to hit you."

Levi snorted a laugh. "In the meantime, it would be a good idea to keep Tanner and Keenan close to you at all times."

"I wouldn't worry so much about our lair finding out," said Tanner. "They'll rally around you both."

"That's what Wren said." Harper told them all about the barista.

"I'm not worried about our lair's reaction," said Knox, "but I still want to be in control of when others find out."

Tanner inclined his head. "Then we keep it quiet for now."

"You know," began Harper, "I have the distinct feeling that finding out I'm pregnant may draw out the remaining Horsemen." She looked at Knox. "What better way to make you lose all control than to take your pregnant mate from you?"

A muscle in Knox's cheek ticked. "I know that, and I hate it."

Yeah, so did she.

CHAPTER ELEVEN

———◆———

As Harper took her jacket from the coat rack, the girls gathered close—their expressions sad, eyes shiny with unshed tears. She rolled her eyes. "For God's sake, I'm not going off to war or anything."

"It just won't be the same without you around," said Devon, shoulders drooping. "I'll bet Knox is delighted that this was your last day at work for a while."

"Oh, he's ecstatic," said Harper. "He doesn't even have the courtesy to pretend differently." Earlier that morning, he'd given her a self-satisfied, lopsided smile as they parted ways. She'd bet he'd been doing a mental countdown, ticking off each day with utter pleasure.

"You decorated the nursery yet?" asked Khloë.

Slipping on her jacket, Harper flicked her hair out of her collar. "No, I decided to leave everything until I started maternity leave or I'd have nothing at all to do."

"If you need any help with anything, just let us know," said Raini.

Harper smiled. "Thanks." The days since she'd found out she was pregnant had passed so fast. It had also passed without incident. Nonetheless, her demon had become edgier and edgier as time went on. It looked upon each stranger as a threat, and craved Knox's company more than usual—he was the one thing that made her demon feel safe and secure. The entity needed that sense of safety right now.

Tanner raised a brow at Harper as he and Keenan rose from the sofa. "Ready to go?"

She grabbed her purse. "Yep." Each of the girls pulled her into a hug one at a time.

Raini bit her lip. "It's going to be so weird not seeing you every day."

"Same here. And it's also going to be weird not coming here every day. I'll pop in occasionally." At Tanner's disgruntled growl, Harper shot him a hostile look. "I will not confine myself to my home, no matter how totally cool that home is."

"I'll miss you." Devon patted her arm. "But one good thing will come from you not being here so much. It means the pooch won't be here so much either."

Tanner grinned. "Ah, kitty, we both know you'll miss me. Want a tissue?"

"For my tears of joy? No."

"We went shopping for baby clothes." Raini held up her hand. "Don't worry, we took Aunt Kayla, so it didn't look suspicious. Next time we come see you, we'll bring the little outfits with us. Wait till you see how cute they are!"

Khloë tilted her head, frowning at Harper. "You don't look good."

"I don't feel good," she admitted. She felt a little flushed and just . . . *off*.

"And you didn't say anything earlier?" Raini shook her head

in frustration. "I know you're used to soldiering on, no matter what happens, but you don't have just *you* to think about now. Your body's telling you it needs to rest, so listen to it."

"I didn't say I was tired, I said I didn't feel good. But I haven't exactly felt 'right' since the moment I conceived." As Dr. Rodgers had predicted, the fatigue was gone, her appetite was back, and she no longer had a problem sleeping. She'd also regained the weight that she'd lost and had a noticeable pouch going on. She'd so far been able to conceal it with baggy clothes, but she wouldn't manage that much longer, so it really was best that she started her maternity leave now.

"Fine," said Raini. "Just take care of yourself, okay?"

Harper saluted her. "Sure thing, Mom." Slinging her purse on her shoulder, she gripped the strap as she gave the studio one last look. She was going to miss her job big time.

Tanner opened the door for her, but he didn't usher her out. He just stood there, patiently giving her a few moments.

Harper shot the girls one last smile. "Don't be strangers." With their goodbyes ringing in her ears, Harper followed Keenan out of the studio. The two sentinels flanked her as they stalked down the strip. The Underground was busier than usual, making both her and her demon feel crowded, and she found herself repeatedly blowing out a long breath to stay cool and calm.

Soon enough, they were heading up the elevator and then leaving the club. The valet waited outside with the Audi. As usual, Keenan rode shotgun as Tanner drove them back to the mansion. Taking off her jacket, Harper slung it aside and fanned her face. The cool leather and the blast of cold air from the vents felt *so* good.

She relaxed in the seat, feeling ... conflicted. While she knew that spending the last stage of her pregnancy at home was the right thing to do, it was going to be damn weird. Since the age of fourteen, she'd had one job or another—even when she was attending many of the different high schools during her traveling years with Lucian. It would be strange to not have her days filled with work, to not have her own money, and to not be doing what she loved.

She wasn't going to renege on her promise—she'd made the right choice for her, Knox, and the baby. But being at home all the time was going to take some adjusting to.

Feeling a jab on the left side of her stomach, she smiled. Now that the baby was bigger, its movements were more noticeable—just as the doc had predicted. The fluttering sensations had become light jabs, thuds, and sometimes she could swear she felt it turn and roll. She put a hand on her stomach, feeling yet another jab. The kicks weren't hard enough to be uncomfortable, but they soon would be. It was scary to think that in another twelve weeks, she'd be holding the baby in her arms. Yep, seriously scary . . . but she was looking forward to it. Couldn't wait to see what this little person looked like; whether it was a boy or a girl; what abilities it would have.

A dark, familiar mind touched hers. *I'm on my way home. Where are you?*

She knew from Knox's telepathic check-in earlier that he'd attended a long-ass meeting in one of his Vegas hotels, where he'd fired a board member who'd been doing a little inside trading. Her mate was known for being ruthless, so she had no idea why anyone would even *try* to cross him, but whatever. *I'm in the car, on my way back too.*

A vibe of contentment tinged her mind. *Good. I'll see you soon.*

Soon. Puffing out a long breath, she said, "Tanner, could you turn up the air conditioning please?"

"It's already on full blast."

Twisting in his seat, Keenan eyed her curiously. "You all right?"

She shifted against the leather, which seemed to be heating beneath her. "Just feeling a little warm, that's all."

By the time they drove through the iron gates of the estate, she was no longer feeling just "warm". Harper scrunched up her hair to bare the nape of her neck. "God, I'm hot. Isn't it hot?"

"No, it's not hot." Keenan reached over and put his palm to her forehead. "Shit, you're burning up. I mean *really* burning up. Tanner, check her."

Once Tanner braked outside the steps of the mansion, he turned to press his hand to her forehead. "Your temperature is *way* too high."

Keenan cursed. "I'll tell Knox she seems to be running a fever." He opened the rear door, helped her out of the car, and guided her inside, passing a concerned Dan. "Knox and Levi are almost here," Keenan assured her as he tossed her jacket at Dan, so she guessed he'd contacted Knox telepathically.

"Is something wrong?" asked Dan, following them into the living room.

"Yes. She's fevered." Keenan led her to the sofa and urged her to lean back as Dan disappeared down the hall, calling out to Meg.

Harper almost jumped out of her skin as fire burst to life in front of her. It crackled and popped as it died off, and then Knox was there—the image of concern.

He crouched in front of her. "What is it, baby?"

"I'm just hot."

Anxiety skittered down Knox's spine. Heat seemed to be literally radiating from her. Knox touched her cheek with the back of his hand and almost snatched it back with a wince. "You're dangerously hot. Feverish." Alarmed, his demon snapped to full alertness.

She shifted restlessly. "My blood feels hot. Isn't that weird?"

Knox blinked. "Your *blood* feels hot?"

"Is it a pregnancy thing?"

"Not that I'm aware of." He'd never heard of such a thing in his life. Meg rushed inside with a glass of cold water, and Knox took it from her gratefully and handed it to Harper. "Baby, drink this."

Harper took it, but her hand was shaking so badly that he had to help her guide it to her mouth. She was thirsty, but it was hard to drink because it felt like the water was curdling in her stomach like sour milk. Still, her demon urged her to swallow more.

Knox took the glass from her when she gagged. "Are you going to be sick?"

She shook her head and leaned back, taking deep breaths. "I'm okay."

No, she damn well wasn't. "I need to call Rodgers." Knox stood and pulled out his cell phone just as Tanner entered the room and headed straight for Harper. The moment Rodgers picked up the phone, Knox said, "Harper's running a fever. She says her blood feels hot."

A pause. "Her *blood* feels hot?" The doctor's words rung with confusion and disbelief.

"Yes. What's wrong with her?" The question came out through gritted teeth.

"I can't say without examining her. Put me on speakerphone so I can talk to her."

Knox did as he requested, and then crouched again in front of Harper as the doctor addressed her—asking her various questions that she drowsily answered. The whole time, Knox rubbed her thigh. He could feel the feverish heat of her skin even through the denim of her jeans. Insane with a worry it wasn't used to feeling, his demon snarled and roared.

A moan slipped out of Harper as she began to tremble. "It's like my blood's sizzling."

"Sizzling?" Rodgers echoed. "That doesn't sound good."

She scratched at her skin, eyes wide. "Shit, I feel like my veins are going to explode."

"That's not good either," said Rodgers.

Knox's hand tightened around the phone. "We're fucking well aware that it's not good. I'm going to send a teleporter to collect you. Are you home or in your office?"

"Home."

"They'll be there in a minute. Be ready." Ending the call, Knox spoke to Tanner. "Send Armand to collect Dr. Rodgers and bring him to the mansion."

Levi jogged into the room, expression hard. Watching as Harper reluctantly sipped more water, he asked, "What's wrong with her?"

"I don't know." Knox urged her to drink more. "Does the water help, baby?"

"Yes, I'm okay." Harper handed him back the glass. "I'm cooler now."

Knox looked at her, dismayed. "No, baby, you're not. I swear, I feel like I'm sitting next to a damn radiator."

Shaking her head, she pulled her knees to her chest and wrapped her arms around herself. "I'm cold. Ice-cold. But my blood still feels hot."

Knox's jaw clenched. "Your skin is still burning. You're not cold."

There was a knock at the front door, and Dan left the room only to swiftly return with Rodgers. The doctor pushed his way past the people gathering around and spoke to Knox, "Armand says he will come back when you need him."

Standing, Knox nodded. "Find out what's happening to her so we can fix it and make her better."

Harper looked at Rodgers through squinted eyes. "Something's wrong, Doc," she said, teeth chattering.

Rodgers put his hand to her clammy forehead and grimaced. "You say your blood feels like it's hot?"

Harper nodded. "But I'm *freezing*. Where's the damn blanket?"

"As you've seen for yourself, she's roasting hot to touch," Knox said to Rodgers. "Tell me you know what kind of fever this is."

Levi's brow creased. "Give me a second." At that, he fished his cell from his pocket and backed out of the room.

Knox stood there, arms folded, as Rodgers used a penlight to check her eyes and pottered around, checking her temperature and other things. Knox fisted his hands, impatient for an answer. Harper seemed to have drifted off, which only increased his worry. "Rodgers . . ."

The doctor sighed. "I truly have no idea what's the matter with her." And he was now panicking.

Knox's demon growled and shoved its way to the surface. "How can you not know?" it demanded of Rodgers. "You are a doctor. Do something. Make her better."

Rodgers paled. "Th-there's nothing physically wr-wrong with her," he stammered. "I'm a gynecologist. This sort of thing isn't my specialty, but I know enough to be sure that this isn't pregnancy related."

Knox forced his demon to retreat before it scared the doctor away. "What would normally cause a fever this intense?"

Rodgers seemed relieved to be once again dealing with Knox. "Honestly? Nothing I've ever come across."

"Could it be some kind of allergic reaction?" asked Meg, hovering close enough to stroke Harper's hair. "Some demons develop allergies when they're pregnant."

Rodgers shook his head. "It's too extreme to be an allergy."

Levi dashed into the room. "Knox, you need to get her in a cold bath *fast*."

Knox's muscles went rigid. "Why? What is it?"

"She's been hexed."

A shocked silence hit the room, and everyone froze. The word "hex" could instill fear in just about any demon, because there was no way to counteract it. Knox knew that a hex was no small, simple, common thing. It was nothing like in books or movies. Hexes were rarely used and extremely serious, which was why Knox shook his head. "She can't have been hexed."

"Want to bet her life on it? Because that's what you could be doing if you ignore this." Levi turned to Meg. "Could you run her a bath?"

With a nod, the housekeeper hurried away.

"You spoke to Mia," Knox guessed. She was Levi's friend and an incantor.

"Yes," said Levi, a manic glint in his eyes. "I'll tell you everything she said once we get Harper in the bath, I swear. Mia said you need to do it now . . . unless of course you *are* willing to bet Harper's life on it."

He wasn't. Knox wasted no time in scooping Harper up and carrying her through the house and into their bathroom upstairs. Knox held a limp Harper in his arms as, with Meg's help, he whipped off her shirt, jeans, and socks before lowering her into the shallow bath. Her eyes snapped open and she tried literally throwing herself out of the tub, splashing cold water everywhere. It took Knox, Meg, and Tanner to hold her there.

Knox kissed her, hoping to soothe her. "No, baby, you have to stay in the bath. We need to cool your skin."

Breathing hard and fast, she struggled to be free, tears in her eyes. "It's hot!" she said through chattering teeth.

Guilt tightened his chest. "It's not hot, it just feels that way to you because you feel cold." Knox swiped her tears away with his thumbs. "Ah, baby, you're breaking my heart here."

"I need to get out," she sobbed, still struggling against their hold. "*It's burning!*"

"I swear to you, it's not. If I could let you out, I would." It was literally killing Knox to keep her there, knowing she was hurting. The plea in her teary eyes made his stomach churn. "As soon as—" He cut off as she abruptly hunched over, pressing down on her stomach as if it were cramping.

Tanner glared at Levi. "What did Mia say? Tell us what's happening."

"According to Mia," began Levi, "*this* kind of fever is a sign that a body is fighting a hex. She's sweating it out. Mia said she may have cramps or vomit. We need to cool her down and keep her hydrated, and she needs sleep."

"Sleep?" Keenan echoed, incredulous. "How the hell is she supposed to sleep through that?"

Levi thrust a hand into his hair. "I've no idea. I'm just telling you what Mia told me."

"What hex exactly is this supposed to be?" demanded Knox.

Levi shrugged. "All I know is that the worse it hurts for Harper to fight it, the worse the hex was meant to be."

Knox watched her shaking, sobbing, and clutching her stomach while Meg whispered reassurances. "Could it have been a death hex?"

"Possibly." Levi shrugged again. "There's just no way of knowing unless she fails to fight it off."

"She won't fail," Knox clipped.

Tanner's jaw hardened. "No, she won't."

"Mia is *sure* that she's been hexed?" Keenan asked. "Absolutely sure? Because from what I understand, cursing someone isn't whatsoever easy and it can't be done by just anyone."

"You're right," Levi confirmed. "It's not a petty case of burning someone's photo with a black candle and whispering some bitchy chant. Only incantors and practitioners can cast hexes. To successfully hex someone, they need to do four things: one, go without food and water for three days. Two, feed a few drops of their blood to their victim. Three, take something that belongs to their victim and burn it into ashes. And four, sprinkle those ashes around their altar before performing the hex, which can take hours and very easily rebound back on the incantor or practitioner. That's why demons rarely take the risk of trying to perform one."

Tanner rubbed his nape. "I can't imagine Harper drinking someone's blood."

"It could have been put in her drink at work," said Levi.

Keenan clicked his fingers. "One of Harper's jackets went missing from the studio last week. She thought Khloë had taken it. Maybe an incantor or practitioner got their hands on it, or maybe someone nabbed it for them."

Which would mean the motherfucker or one of their minions might have been in her studio. Knox ground his teeth at the thought, and his demon let out another roar. "Could a hex harm the baby too?"

"I asked Mia that," said Levi. "She said no. The hex is directed at Harper—it will only harm her. But, obviously, if it *is* a death hex and it manages to kill her, the baby won't survive."

Knox looked at Rodgers, who was pale and looked completely out of his element. "She's in pain and has a fever. Will that harm the baby?"

Rodgers hesitated to answer. "It's more serious in human pregnancies. If you keep Harper hydrated and get her fever down soon, the baby should be fine." He didn't say there were no guarantees, but Knox could hear it in his voice. And it spooked the shit out of him.

"She'll be okay, Knox," said Keenan. "She's a fighter."

Harper again tried to get out of the bath. "Let me the fuck out! It's too hot!"

Again, Knox held her down. He *hated* to force her to stay there, *hated* the accusatory glitter in her eyes. "I'm sorry, baby." His head whipped around to look at Levi. "How long do we have to keep her in cool water?"

"Mia didn't say. I'll ask." Digging his cell out of his pocket, Levi left the room to make the call.

Harper grabbed Knox's arm. "Something's happening to the baby, isn't it?" Her shoulders shook, eyes tearing. "I'm losing it, aren't I?"

"No, no, no," Knox quickly assured her. "Someone tried to hurt you with magick. Your system is fighting it. That's a good thing."

She grimaced. "It doesn't feel like a good thing." She sucked in a breath and then hunched over again.

Knox rubbed her nape. "If I could do something, if I could help, I would." But despite how powerful he was, he couldn't do a damn thing to take away her pain. He was built to destroy, not to heal. And for once in its very long existence, his demon regretted that.

Levi re-entered the bathroom. "Once her skin cools, you can take her out of the bath, but you need to keep her covered with a towel or blanket. Basically, we just have to wait it out."

It took half an hour for her fever to break so that they could take her out of the water, but the cramps lasted for over an hour. It was a further forty-five fucking minutes before her blood no longer felt hot. Then, wrapped in her snug terry robe and huddled under the bed coverlet, she finally fell asleep.

Stood over the bed, Knox scrubbed a hand down his face. His jaw ached from how hard he'd clenched it as he'd fought to keep his demon from rising. The entity was a little calmer now that she no longer suffered, but it demanded vengeance.

"Thatcher," Knox spat. "It fucking has to have been him."

"Maybe, but we can't just go to his house and grab him, Knox," said Levi. "He's a powerful Prime. His lair is almost as large as ours."

"I don't fucking care. *Look* at her, Levi. He's an incantor; she was hexed. Are you not seeing the correlation here?"

"I'm seeing it. But I'm also seeing the consequences of you killing him without proof. You remember what happened to the last demon when he killed another Prime without evidence of wrongdoing, don't you?"

Yes. Most of the other Primes had united against the demon and killed him. "You don't think it's Thatcher," Knox sensed.

Levi sighed. "You said yourself that he's too smart to do anything that would cast suspicion on himself. Think past your anger, Knox. I know it's fucking hard, but try. For Harper."

Knox inhaled deeply, rolling back his shoulders. Before Harper, he'd never let emotions get in the way of his decisions—mostly because he hadn't felt many. He called on that practical side of himself as he paced, thinking it through. "The person who sent the emails was very careful to conceal their identity. Hexing her would *not* be a careful move for Thatcher; it would be damn stupid. He's not a stupid person. And, yes, it would be odd for someone who's been so cautious to then repeatedly act in ways that led back to them—I know all this. But what do you want me to do? Sit back and wait for whoever it is to make another move? If it is Thatcher, he's notorious for being like a dog with a bone. When he has an issue with someone, he doesn't let it go. He won't just stop."

Larkin, who'd arrived half an hour earlier, raised her index finger. "Um ... about people with issues."

Knox turned to her. "Did you find a direct link between Thatcher and Harper?"

"Not one, so I checked to see if he'd had any problems with Jolene. I wondered if maybe he had beef with her and he was using Harper and Heidi to hurt her or something like that. Thatcher's never had any major issues with Jolene, from what I can tell. But Jonas has."

Keenan's brows snapped together. "Jonas?"

Larkin nodded. "And it was very recent. It's not clear what happened. Just that he wanted something from Jolene and she refused him, so he threatened to make her pay for it—something along those lines. I'm not saying this is related to everything that's gone on lately, but I thought it was worth mentioning."

Tanner's eyes narrowed. "Jonas may have planned to hurt Jolene by taking Heidi and by hiring hunters to steal Harper's wings."

Larkin shrugged. "Possibly."

"Fuck." Knox pulled out his phone, dialed Jolene's number, and stalked out of the room. He was in the hallway when she answered. He got straight to the point. "Why didn't you tell me you had problems with Jonas?"

There was a silence of sheer surprise. "Why would I? That's my business, not yours."

"It is my business if he has something to do with your granddaughters being targeted, since one of them is my mate."

Jolene sighed. "Knox, I've had problems with many Primes. It's the curse of having a small lair. What's this about? You really think Jonas is responsible?"

"I don't know. Maybe. But I'm not willing to rule out any possibilities. I need to know what problem you two had."

"Jonas saw me and members of my lair talking with Lou at the anniversary shindig you threw at the Underground."

Knox ground his teeth. "It wasn't a shindig."

"In any case, he later came to me with a rather surprising request."

As Jolene repeated her conversation with the Prime, Knox's jaw hardened until it ached. "How long ago did he approach you with this?"

"A few weeks before the hunters went after Harper."

"And you didn't think the two things could be linked?"

"No. I assumed it was the Horsemen, given that they'd already targeted both of you twice before."

Knox couldn't even fault her for that, considering he'd done the same damn thing. "It was a reasonable assumption for you to make," he allowed. "Jonas was no doubt counting on people to blame the Horsemen."

"Can we be sure he's our boy? We have to be completely certain before we take action, Knox."

Halting, Knox inhaled deeply. "At the moment, no, we can't be sure. I'll be calling for all the Primes to meet with me tomorrow. I need to look him and Thatcher in the eye. I need to see how they react to me and what I have to say." While the practical side of him believed that Thatcher wasn't at fault, Knox's emotional side wouldn't allow him to take chances.

"I'll be there. Now, why don't you tell me what this has to do with Thatcher and why you sound as though you'd like to see someone drowning in a pool of their own blood?"

And here was where Jolene would lose her mind.

CHAPTER TWELVE

———◆———

A steady, rhythmic beat woke her. A heartbeat, Harper quickly realized. She didn't need to open her throbbing eyes to know that the arms wrapped around her, keeping her cradled against a warm solid body, belonged to Knox. She'd know the feel and scent of him anywhere.

Swallowing, Harper winced. It felt like someone had rubbed at the back of her throat with sandpaper. Her mouth was dry as a bone. Forcing her eyes open, she realized they were in their room and Knox was sitting upright against the headboard. "Why do I feel hungover?" she mumbled.

Knox kissed her hair and tightened his arms around her, so fucking glad she was awake. He'd known that she was fine, but he'd needed to hear her voice and look into her eyes before he could relax. At the moment, the eyes squinting up at him were a pretty amethyst shade. "Hungover has got to be better than fevered."

Memories of the previous evening flickered through Harper's

mind. She tensed, sure she'd dreamed half of it, because it was simply too surreal. "Did someone really try to hurt me using magick?"

"Yes, you were hexed," Knox confirmed, curling her hair around her ear. His mouth twitched as she let out a string of inventive curses that would have made even a sailor blink in shock. "We don't know what type of hex it was. There's no way of knowing because you fought it off before it could work."

Sitting upright, Harper studied him closely. "But you think it was a death hex, don't you?"

Knox shifted her to straddle him. "I don't know. The hunter said that the person who hired him was very adamant that you weren't to be killed. It could be that they simply wanted to weaken you, but the hex was so intense and you were in so much pain . . . I'm more inclined to think that they're no longer so concerned about whether you're alive or dead. Maybe because they're pissed that their previous plans were foiled—I can only speculate." His jaw hardened. "You should know that it's possible that you were in close contact with whoever cast the hex—or, at least, with someone who worked for them."

"Seriously?"

"They needed to possess something of yours and to have fed you a little of their blood—it could have been in your drink; you wouldn't have known."

Harper grimaced. "Their blood? Really?"

"Really."

Both she and her demon shuddered. The entity was more uptight than usual, which was pretty understandable in Harper's opinion. She put a hand to her stomach as she voiced the question she'd dreaded asking for fear of the answer. "The baby's fine, right?"

Hearing the slight tremor in her voice, Knox cupped her face.

"The baby is fine, I promise you." He'd spent much of the night with his hand on her stomach, feeling the baby move and kick, letting it calm his demon. "Other than a little hungover, how do you feel?"

"Not bad, considering. I don't feel weak or anything."

"Good, because I want to take you somewhere."

She arched a brow. "Oh yeah? Where?"

One corner of his mouth lifted at the dubious note in her tone. "It's a surprise."

A snort popped out of her. "It's you wanting to whisk me away from here—*that's* what it is," she corrected.

"You can't tell me you're not feeling a little anxious. You've been attacked, hexed, and you're pregnant. A little downtime will do you good. And, yes, I want to whisk you to someplace safe. Somewhere where you can relax."

"For how long?"

"For as long as it takes for you to get better and emotionally recover." And for his demon to calm the hell down. "Be honest— your fever might be broken and the pain might have gone, but it's left you weak and weary. It's also spooked you a little and left you shaken."

Unable to deny any of that, Harper puffed out a breath and said, "Okay, you can whisk me away somewhere, but I'd like to see Jolene before I go. She'll be worried."

Knox nodded. "About Jolene . . . you should know that she destroyed a number of derelict buildings last night."

Harper winced. "You told her I'd been hexed? Damn, Knox, I thought you were smarter than that."

"She would have found out from someone. It was better that she heard it from me."

"Hmm."

"Did you know that she'd had trouble with Jonas?"

"Jonas?" Harper echoed, surprised. She listened intently as he relayed the things he'd heard from Larkin and Jolene. "If we were talking about anyone other than Jonas, I'd understand why you might link him with what's happened to me and Heidi. But Jonas likes you," she pointed out, absentmindedly tracing the brand her demon left on his nape. "He wouldn't go after your mate."

Knox's mouth kicked up into a smile. "Nobody likes me, baby. They fear me and so they're civil toward me out of respect and a sense of self-preservation—that's it."

"You're wrong. Your sentinels like you. My family likes you." She smiled. "I like you."

His cock twitched at the sensual note in her voice. "Later, when we're alone, I'll have you."

"Why later? What's happening now?"

"Now I go talk with the Primes. I called an emergency meeting. You can't come, Harper," he quickly added. "One of them can sense pregnancies, and we're not ready for people to know yet."

She snorted. "You'd expect me to stay behind anyway."

"I would," he admitted, unrepentant.

She blew out a long breath. "I guess I'll pack while you're gone."

"Good girl." He kissed her forehead. "We'll be gone a couple of weeks, so don't pack light."

"Okay. Try not to kill Thatcher or Jonas. I want to make sure the *right* guy dies."

"I can't make any promises, but I'll try. For you." Sliding his fingers into her hair, he kissed her—a soft and slow exploration that still left her panting. "Shower."

Sensing he needed to take care of her, Harper didn't protest as he washed, dried, and dressed her. She even let him comb her hair, knowing it calmed him. Still, when he set down the brush and she turned to face him, anxiety lingered in his dark eyes. "I'm okay."

Cupping her hips, he pulled her close. "Of course you are. It's the only reason my demon isn't destroying its surroundings." He gave her a quick kiss. "I have to leave now, so I can't have breakfast with you, but I won't be long. Be good for Tanner and Keenan. Oh, be warned that Meg may fuss over you like crazy. She was scared seeing you in that much pain. Be patient with her."

"I will, if for no other reason than she won't make me muffins anymore if I'm not." She melted into him as he brushed his nose against hers before kissing her yet again. "Love you."

"And I love you, baby." They were words he'd never thought he'd ever give to someone. Words he didn't think he *could* give, since there was no denying that he was emotionally stunted. But they were the truth. She was everything to him. And now she was carrying his baby. A child that would probably always be in danger for the simple reason that Knox was its father, just like Harper would probably always be in danger for the simple reason that she was his mate.

Maybe Knox should feel some regret, feel some sense of guilt, for having taken her as his mate and brought this level of danger to her life. But he couldn't. He'd never have any regrets about Harper, even if it meant that a cloud of menace would always hang above them. It was no doubt selfish and unfair of him, but he'd never claimed to be good. Never would be "good".

Likewise, his demon had no regrets. But then, it wasn't capable of remorse. It had no conscience, no pity, no sense of fair play. Demonkind had been very wise to ask that archdemons remain in hell. It was where they belonged; the only place that beings so destructive and cruel should be allowed to inhabit.

Knox wasn't sure if Harper truly grasped that his demon's

sanity rested on the mere fact that her heart beat in her chest. She anchored it in so many ways that it would literally be lost without her. It was exactly the same for Knox.

The person targeting her truly had no idea just what fate they were tempting. Oh, they no doubt suspected that Knox would snap and cause a mass amount of destruction if she died, but they might also believe that it would turn demonkind against him and, as such, many would come together to take him down.

They didn't understand that none of them would even have a chance to take him down, let alone the ability. Really, they'd better hope to fucking God that their plans didn't succeed, or the Earth would be nothing but wasteland by the time Knox and his demon were done with it. The remains would make hell look like a damn paradise.

Standing at the entrance to the boardroom, Knox watched as Thatcher approached with one of his sentinels. His demon sneered, just as it had at every other person who neared it. Anger still had a tight hold on the entity, and all it wanted was to be with its mate—but not before delivering a special brand of vengeance. And since the male heading toward them could quite possibly be responsible for her pain ... yeah, the demon wanted to butcher him with a boning knife.

Unlike Knox, it didn't care if it punished the wrong person in its quest to discover who hexed their mate—collateral damage was nothing to the entity.

Thatcher nodded. "Good to see you, Knox." He didn't seem to be the least bit nervous or worried about what reason Knox could have had to call for the meeting. "I don't suppose you'll give me a hint of what this is about."

"You'll find out soon enough," Knox told him, just as he'd told all the others who asked.

Thatcher's mouth curved. "It was worth a try."

Knox gestured for him and his sentinel to enter, and they joined the other Primes, who were gathered around the long table. Many were leaning into each other, speaking in low voices—no doubt speculating on what Knox had to say.

More and more people arrived, making his demon more and more restless. When it saw Jonas and Alethea with two sentinels, it unexpectedly settled. No, not settled, he quickly realized. It was putting aside its anger to study them carefully. Very, very carefully. Apparently, it suspected them more than it suspected Thatcher.

Knox gave them a nod of greeting. "Jonas, Alethea."

Jonas' smile was as cordial as always. "I must admit, you have me curious. I'm assuming this is about the Horsemen."

"Have the decency to wait for the meeting to start," Alethea playfully admonished her brother. She then leaned forward as she shook Knox's hand, and he got a whiff of her trademark rose perfume that never failed to make Harper's nose wrinkle.

Knox could see that she was waiting for him to kiss her cheek as he would have done long before meeting Harper, but tonight he didn't. And it scored a hit, because she narrowed her eyes as she straightened.

"Where is your sphinx?" asked Alethea, the words tightly spoken.

"At home, resting."

"Resting?" Concern creased Jonas' brow. "I heard about the hunters. Did more strike?"

"I'll explain everything once the others arrive."

Jonas reluctantly walked away without asking additional questions. Alethea shot Knox an unreadable look before trailing after her brother, hips swaying provocatively. Knox subtly inhaled, allowing the scents of coffee, polish, and citrus air freshener to drown out the perfume.

Standing near the far wall, Levi exchanged an impatient look with Knox. The reaper was still fuming about the hex and seemingly had no tolerance whatsoever for Alethea's brand of petty behavior right now.

Turning, Knox smiled at the sight of two imps approaching. "Jolene, Beck—glad you could make it."

Jolene's mouth curled. "Knox, always a pleasure."

"No Martina?"

"She's terribly upset about Harper. I couldn't guarantee that she wouldn't set anything in your beautiful hotel on fire."

Knox nodded in understanding. "I appreciate your foresight."

Jolene's smile widened. "I thought you might." *I paid Harper a visit before I left for the meeting. Other than tired, she seems reasonably well, all things considered.*

The hex doesn't seem to have caused any lasting effects.

Which means I don't have to blow up any more buildings. Jolene linked her arm through Beck's. "Ah, I see dear old Malden. It will be fun to have someone to toy with." She headed for the table, and Knox knew she'd undoubtedly tease the other Prime much like her granddaughter usually did.

After the last three Primes arrived, and all were seated, Knox closed the door. His footsteps were silent as he stalked along the carpet toward the head of the table, passing light-gold walls that were bare, aside from the media screen at the front of the room. The voices fell silent, until all Knox could hear was the steady hum of the air conditioning.

Knox slowly sank into the seat at the head of the table, the media screen at his back. "Thank you all for coming. I appreciate you taking a break from your schedules to attend the meeting on such short notice."

"Did you find out something about the Horsemen?" asked Jonas.

"Did *you?*" Knox returned.

Jonas blinked. "If anyone knows anything, they're not talking."

Raul grabbed the pitcher and poured himself a glass of ice water as he spoke. "There are whispers of who they *could* be, but they seem to be merely speculation fueled by paranoia."

Knox leaned back in the chair, making the leather creak slightly. "What about you, Thatcher? Heard anything interesting?"

Thatcher adjusted his tie. "I confess, I haven't investigated the matter much."

Knox lifted a brow. "And why is that?"

There was a long pause. "I'm not convinced they are real," Thatcher finally admitted. "I am not calling you a liar, Knox. I just don't trust the words of a delusional, near-rogue demon."

Ordinarily, neither would Knox, but . . . "It wasn't Laurence Crow who told me about the Horsemen. He wasn't aware they were using him like a puppet." Knox had learned of them from Dario and Nora, but since many back then had suspected that Dario was near-rogue, Dario had believed that to voice such a conspiracy would simply make him seem paranoid—a symptom of a rogue demon. As such, it would have then given credence to the near-rogue rumors.

Although the Primes wouldn't be so disinclined to believe Dario now, Knox thought it likely that they would be angry at Dario to hear that he'd warned Knox but not them. He had no interest in causing friction between the Primes or shifting their attention from the real issue—Harper's safety was at risk. As such, Knox said, "Roan talked of the Horsemen to Harper. He was cruel, but not delusional."

"Are you willing to trust the word of a dying, treacherous demon?" asked Malden, though there was no judgement there— merely curiosity.

"My mate believes he was being truthful," said Knox. "I trust her judgement."

Malden inclined his head. "In any case, I personally have no information about the Horsemen."

Knox twisted his mouth. "Shame. But I did not call you all here to discuss the Horsemen. I'm sure most, if not all, of you heard that my mate was recently attacked by hunters."

"I heard," said Dario. "Is she all right?" There was genuine concern in his voice.

"Fine. She fought them hard. They wanted her wings. In fact, they were hired to acquire them. Since my mate's wings have never come to her, it was a waste of their time and earned them nothing but an early and excruciating death."

"The Horsemen hired them?" asked Raul.

"That was my first thought," said Knox, tapping his fingers on the smooth glass table. "Then her cousin was almost kidnapped. The demon who attempted to take the little girl had also been hired by someone."

Jonas' brow knitted. "That doesn't mean the two events are necessarily related."

Jolene spoke then. "Both the hunters *and* the kidnapper were hired by someone who sent an anonymous, encrypted email that self-deleted shortly after being opened. That's not a technique that's widely used, but I know of some people who do use it."

Thatcher sat up straighter, looking resigned. "You might as well know that I am one of those people."

"Oh, I already knew that," Knox told him. "Just as I already knew that the main collector of sphinx wings is your cousin, Francisco Alaniz."

Thatcher's mouth pinched. "Francisco does not collect them for collecting's sake."

Knox held up a hand before the demon could explain further.

"The wings on his wall belonged to his relatives and are trophies—I know. Don't worry; Francisco didn't mention you. He did, however, mention Dion Boughton. I was surprised to learn from Dion that he once belonged to your lair."

Raul's eyes slid from Knox to Thatcher and back again. "Are you accusing Thatcher of something?"

Knox arched a brow. "Should I?"

"I don't deal on the black market," Thatcher stated. "And I don't hire minions."

A ringing made them all turn toward the sound. Flushing, Malden pulled out his cell and quickly tapped the screen, quieting the device. "I apologize. I'm curious, Knox— does Harper blame Thatcher? Is that why she's not here?"

"She's not here because I insisted that she rest. Being hexed takes a toll on even the strongest of demons."

Raul paused with his glass halfway to his mouth, gaping. "Your mate was hexed?"

"Just yesterday," Knox confirmed. "She survived it, of course."

Mila raised her brows, looking impressed. "She's strong."

"It astonishes me that people fail to see *just* how strong she is." Knox steepled his fingers. "She wasn't too weak to attend the meeting, but I want her at top strength for our trip. We're not willing to miss our vacation for someone who stupidly assumed she wouldn't fight off a hex." He didn't want anyone thinking that the hex had sent him and Harper running, so he felt it would be simpler to imply that the trip was organized prior to the magickal strike.

Thatcher sighed, face hard. "I suppose this makes me an even likelier suspect. I'm an incantor, after all."

"Yes, Thatcher, it does," said Knox.

"Why would I harm your mate?" Thatcher's hand clenched, and Knox half-expected him to thump the table. "Considering you're quite adamant that the Horsemen are real, I would have thought you would be blaming them. Or are you also accusing me of being one of them?"

"I'm not so blinded by the Horsemen situation that I believe they're responsible for everything that happens. If I were one of them, I'd lie low."

"As would I," said Jolene.

"If you're looking for someone who would mean your mate harm, you should be looking at the other side of the table." Thatcher's gaze drilled into Alethea, who gawked at him.

"You bastard," she hissed. "Don't you point fingers at me."

Thatcher raised his hands in a helpless gesture. "I only speak the truth. Everyone here knows that you would see Harper dead, given the chance."

Jonas held up a calming hand. "Alethea and Harper do not get along, that is true, but—"

Thatcher snorted. "That is a complete understatement."

Jonas' jaw hardened. "My sister has nothing to do with this."

"You're sure of that, are you? You would bet your position of Prime on it?" Thatcher snickered when Jonas fell silent. "Didn't think so."

Nostrils flaring, Jonas said, "Just because a person dislikes someone doesn't mean that they wish to cause them physical harm."

Thatcher's gaze returned to Alethea. "But *you* would if you thought you could get away with it, wouldn't you? You know, I heard that Jonas' new girlfriend is an incantor."

Shock flashed across Jonas' face, but he buried the emotion quickly.

"Maybe, Alethea, you got her to hex Harper for you," Thatcher suggested.

Alethea bared her teeth. "You're just looking to divert everyone's attention from yourself."

I didn't know Jonas was dating an incantor, Levi said to Knox. *Interesting.*

It is, agreed Knox. *Particularly since he seemed so shocked that outsiders would know about it. For some reason, he was hoping to keep it private.*

Thatcher pointed at Jonas. "Or maybe it was *you* who asked your girlfriend to hex Harper. As I understand it, you're not too happy with Jolene right now. Maybe you wanted to punish her using her granddaughters."

All eyes moved to Jolene, but she was staring hard at Jonas when she spoke. "Thatcher seems to enjoy playing devil's advocate, but he makes a good point. Promising me that I would regret not giving you what you wanted ... well, that certainly implicates you."

Dario narrowed his eyes. "What did he want from you, Jolene?"

She continued staring at Jonas. "Why don't you tell them, Jonas?"

After a moment, Jonas cleared his throat. "I wanted to meet with Lucifer. I asked Jolene to arrange a meeting. She refused."

"You want an *alliance* with him," corrected Jolene calmly. "I told you that I couldn't guarantee you an alliance with Lucifer or that he would even meet with you. The devil doesn't ally himself with anyone. I told him that you wanted to meet him, but he has no interest in speaking with you. That's hardly my fault. Yet, you blame me."

"It's brave of you to be prepared to, literally, make a deal with the devil, Jonas," Knox told him.

Dario squinted at Jonas. "Why would you want to meet with Lucifer? What do you want from him?" At this point, everyone was eying Jonas suspiciously, including his sister, who seemed sincerely surprised by the news.

"That was my question," said Jolene. "After all, Lou likes loop-holes. Any deal he makes always has a catch—and it's always one that makes the demon sorry they made the deal in the first place. That's common knowledge. A demon would have to want something very, very badly to be prepared to make any kind of pact with Lou. I said as much to Jonas. I asked him just what it was that he was so desperate to have."

"What did he say?" asked Thatcher.

"Just that I'd be sorry I hadn't cooperated, which makes me think that it was *very* important to him or he wouldn't be so resentful about it." She looked at Jonas. "At the time, I thought you were full of hot air. Now I'm thinking that you might have had Harper hurt as a warning to me to do as you'd asked. You could have then later thought you could use Heidi to make me cooperate."

Neck stiff and corded, Jonas lifted his chin. "I would never cause any harm to Harper or a child. I wanted to meet with Lucifer, yes, but that is my business. I don't have to explain myself to any of you. And if you're done making accusations, Knox—"

"I don't recall accusing you of anything," said Knox. "Do I consider you a possible suspect? Yes." He glared at Jonas, but kept his voice pitched low and calm. "I don't need to tell you what will happen if I discover that you're behind all this."

"I'm done here." Jonas shot to his feet. "Let's go, Alethea." Looking a little lost, she followed him as he stiffly strode out of the room with their sentinels.

One by one, the Primes began to leave the room. Each said polite goodbyes to Knox, and all appeared to be in deep thought. He suspected that hearing Jonas wanted an alliance with Lou unnerved them a little.

Jolene was one of the last to leave. *My gut says it wasn't Thatcher. Everything points to him, yes, but that's what bothers me.*

Knox sighed. *Last night, I was ready to kill him. But the more I thought about it, the more unlikely it seemed to me that someone so intelligent would continually leave evidence that led me right to him. I can't afford to dismiss him as a suspect, though.*

Of course not—this is Harper's life we're talking about. And I won't dismiss him as a suspect either, but I don't believe it was him. Jonas is known for parading his girlfriends around—he treats them like accessories. But I've not seen him with an incantor, yet he didn't deny that he's dating one. A pause. *Did you notice how startled Alethea was to discover that her brother wanted to meet with Lou?*

I did. I also noticed that it seemed to worry her.

Jolene shook his hand. "The meeting was certainly ... enlightening. Take care of my granddaughter, Knox."

"I will." He nodded at both Jolene and Beck, and the two imps then left.

Finally, the last of the Primes came to the door. "Well, that was eventful," said Dario. His brows lowered as he added, "I'm sorry to hear about what happened to Harper. You will kill who's responsible." The Prime, unlike many others, liked and respected Harper.

"Don't doubt it. I don't suppose Nora knows anything worth mentioning."

Dario scratched his head. "Actually, she asked me to pass on a message to you: When it's time to kill the child, don't hesitate—no matter what."

A cold finger trailed down his spine, and Knox and his demon stiffened. "The child?"

Dario shrugged. "She said you would know what I meant." With that, the Prime left with his sentinel in tow.

Knox closed the door and turned to Levi, who was now perched on the edge of the long table. "Well?"

"Either Thatcher is an incredible actor or he has nothing

to do with neither the attacks on Harper or with Heidi's kidnapping. He was defensive and tried diverting your attention to others, sure, but he had a lot of people staring at him with suspicion. It's only natural that he'd want to point out that others have motives to harm Harper."

Knox nodded. "Jolene thinks it's unlikely that the blame belongs to Thatcher." He quickly told the reaper what Jolene telepathically said.

"She's right that it's odd for someone who treats girlfriends like they're accessories to keep any relationship quiet. I don't see what motivation Jonas would have for doing so. Even if it were *she* who wanted things to stay low-key, it makes no sense that Jonas would agree. He'd be more likely to simply move on to someone else."

Knox rubbed at his jaw. "If we can find out the name of this incantor he's dating, we may be able to figure this out."

"Keenan and Larkin can look into it while you and Harper are on vacation. Do you think it's possible that Jonas is our boy?"

"What I think is that someone would have to be desperate to be prepared to make a deal with Lou, and that makes me wonder just what Jonas must be desperate to possess."

CHAPTER THIRTEEN

━━━━━━━━━━◆━━━━━━━━━━

As the engine fired up and the aircraft began to move, Harper sank deeper into the leather reclining seat. Damn, she really did love the private jet. Black and sleek, it made her think of Knox with his dark designer suits and smooth polished shoes. The white and gray interior was business-like without being bland or insipid. Again, it made her think of Knox; it didn't matter that he never wore much color, he could never be accused of looking plain.

The beverage cart creaked as the attentive stewardess appeared, smelling of hairspray and hand sanitizer. After giving Harper a bottle of water and preparing Knox a gin and tonic, she disappeared behind the curtain. Harper kind of liked her, especially since she never flirted with Knox—apparently, she was happily mated to the captain.

Levi and Tanner were in the cabin near the front of the craft, which meant Harper and Knox were alone when she opened her bottle and asked, "So, why don't you tell me what happened at the meeting?"

Sitting opposite her with his thighs bracketing hers, Knox did exactly that. He would have preferred to simply pyroport them to his privately owned Caribbean island, but he needed to be seen by others to leave Vegas and arrive on the island. Otherwise, people would definitely talk. The less they knew about his abilities, the less they could predict what he could or would do.

Harper sighed. "I wish I'd been there. I don't like that I didn't see their reactions for myself." As his shoulders tensed, she added, "I'm not saying I *should* have been there—it was for the best that I didn't go."

Like that, his muscles lost their stiffness. Knox drummed his fingers on the armrest. "As I reminded you earlier, one of the Primes can sense pregnancies, just like Wren. I want to be in control of when the demon population discovers you're pregnant."

She snickered. "Of course you do. You're all about control." She rummaged through her bag until she found the plastic box that Meg handed her as they were leaving. Curious about what was inside, she peeled off the lid and found a gorgeously prepared fruit salad. It was sweet of the woman, but . . . "I miss chocolate."

Knox's mouth quirked. "I thought you might." He pulled a Hershey's bar out of his pocket, almost chuckling at the way her eyes lit up. His demon's sour mood lifted at the sight.

"Have I mentioned how much I love you?"

"You said it this morning, actually, but it never hurts to hear it again."

"Then I love you, Knox Thorne. Now gimme that chocolate."

He handed it over. "I have an ulterior motive."

She paused in tearing it open. "Oh yeah?"

"You know I love to watch you eat. It's even better when you're eating chocolate—you make those little moans that wrap around my cock like a fist."

Her demon liked that comment a lot. Harper grinned. "I kind of like watching you eat . . . certain things."

The sexual implication had all kinds of images flashing through his head and made his cock harden almost painfully. Another time, he might have ordered her to come to him and do something about the hard-on she'd caused. He could see in her eyes that it was what she expected him, *wanted* him, to do, but . . . "I have plans for you. They don't include you riding me on the jet—not today. So be a good girl and eat your chocolate and fruit."

With a humph, she bit into the bar. "So where are we going anyway? Don't say it's a surprise. You know I don't like them."

A smile tugged at his mouth. "I know."

"You told me to pack plenty of bikinis, so I'm guessing it's somewhere warm."

"Good guess."

Impatience flared in her eyes. "Come on, give me *something*."

"All right. We'll be staying in a beach hut."

She blinked. "Beach hut? You mean, like, at a resort?"

"No. I own the island."

"Well, of course you own an island," she muttered dryly. "Meg gave me a list of the foods that I can't eat to give to whoever's cooking for us. She cried while I was packing. She said she wants me to stay close to her so that she can keep an eye on me and make sure I eat properly. Personally, I think she was just trying to guilt me into taking her along." She broke off a chunk of her chocolate bar and offered it to him, but he shook his head. "She fusses even more than you do, and that's saying something. But, of course, that no doubt suits you just fine."

Knox partially lowered the window shade to protect her eyes from the glare of the sun. "I like knowing there's always someone watching over you."

She slanted her head. "I wonder if you'll ease up on me a little when the baby's born. Maybe all that hyper-protective energy will then be concentrated on them."

Knox leaned forward and curled his hand around her chin as he spoke, voice grave. "I will be very protective of the baby— make no mistake about that. But nothing will ever make me less protective of you. Not a thing." He kissed her hard and deep, tasting Coke and chocolate and Harper ... which was a bad move, really, because it only made his cock even harder. "This is going to feel like a really long flight," he grumbled.

"I bet I can improve your mood," she said with a smile. "Lucian's postponed his trip. Apparently, he met some Thai woman and she's keeping him rather occupied right now."

That *did* improve his mood. "Hopefully she keeps him occupied for a long, long time." Knox took another swig from his glass. "Like a century, for example."

She rolled her eyes. "I can't say I'm disappointed by his news. I don't think he'll react well to my being pregnant, so the delay is most welcome. Not that I want or feel that I need his approval. But you've seen how he gets when something upsets his little world. It's excruciatingly annoying. And I know that if he has a tantrum and says something offensive, my demon's going to want to shove my stiletto blade right up his rectum."

Knox licked his teeth. "My demon will want to do worse." The entity already despised Lucian for his neglect of Harper.

"Which means the whole thing has the makings of a clusterfuck." Harper fell quiet as she finished off her Hershey's bar and drank more of her Coke. "Oh, I meant to ask before: was Dario at the meeting?"

"Yes, he seemed angry that you were hurt and he wants to be sure that whoever's behind the attacks will soon be dead."

"Aw, that's sweet."

"I asked him if Nora had any warnings to deliver. She said that when it's time to kill the child, we shouldn't hesitate. For a moment, I thought she meant *our* child. But I think she meant McCauley."

Frowning, Harper swallowed. "The kid creeps me out, but I don't want to have to kill him." Just the thought made her stomach churn. Even her demon wasn't keen on the idea.

Knox rubbed her thigh. "Neither do I, baby. Neither do I."

"You said it was a beach hut."

"It is."

Hut, my ass. "Knox, aside from having a thatched roof, it is nothing like a hut." The white, two-story building was more of a luxury villa. Situated on a beautiful tropical beach, it was surrounded by tall palm trees and white sand. The sun glittered off the rippling turquoise-blue sea, and she just wanted to dive right in it—it was seriously freaking hot.

It had only been a short walk from the jet to the "hut", but already her skin was sticky and sweat was trickling down her back. As they'd walked along the man-made path through the jungle, she'd seen lots of colorful birds, a few snakes, and heard what she suspected were monkeys in the distance. Not a big fan of monkeys, she hoped they *remained* in the distance.

She almost sighed in relief as the cool breeze swept over her and ruffled her shirt. "Did you ever rent out the island?"

"No. It's mine."

He said it with such finality that she smiled. "And you don't share what's yours."

Knox drew her close and spoke against her mouth. "No, I definitely don't share what's mine." Neither did his demon. He licked at her lower lip and then gave it a sharp, possessive nip. "Come on, let's go inside so I can show you the place."

Knox first introduced her to the housekeeper and mainte-
nance guy—both of whom were natives of a neighboring island
but also belonged to their lair. It was clear to Harper by the way
they chatted to Tanner and Levi that the sentinels had accompanied Knox here plenty of times.

The interior of the spacious, stylishly furnished villa was
beautiful. Bright walls, gleaming floors, and high windows that
took advantage of the idyllic ocean view. The bedroom was her
favorite part of the villa. It had a hot tub, a canopy bed with
white drapes that kept out the mosquitos, and a gorgeous balcony
that overlooked the sea.

Each of the sentinels had their own room at the other side of
the villa, which gave Harper and Knox plenty of privacy. She
was glad of that, because she could be kind of noisy in bed and
the sentinels would no doubt immaturely tease her about it.

Dressed in a neon-pink bikini, she'd just finished applying sun
lotion when Knox walked into the bedroom. His eyes darkened
as they roamed over her, and her demon stretched languidly.
Harper let her own gaze explore his powerful build, lingering a
little on the growing bulge in his shorts. "I'm happy to skip the
swim and take care of that, just so you know."

Knox stalked over to her and trailed his finger over the swell
of her breasts, inhaling the fruity scent of her sunscreen. "Very
magnanimous of you," he quipped.

"I'm all heart."

He dropped to his knees and kissed her stomach. "I don't
know why it turns me on knowing that I put a baby in you. I
really don't."

She swallowed. "I'm not complaining, in case you were
wondering."

He stood, mouth curved. "Come on." He linked his fingers
with hers and led her downstairs and out onto the deck, facing

the beach. Tanner and Levi were already sprawled on sun loungers, soaking up the sun.

Harper almost winced at the smothering heat. "That sand's gonna be *hot*."

"Want me to carry you to the water?"

Pride made her spine snap straight. "I can manage."

Knox's demon chuckled. "If we run, it'll hurt less."

"Then we run. Ready?"

He nodded. "Go."

Harper took off and, *God*, it was like stepping on hot coals. She rushed to the shoreline and pretty much sloshed into the sea rather ungracefully. She'd braced herself for the shock of cold water, but the water was surprisingly warm as it lapped at her body.

She watched as Knox dunked himself and then stood straight. Water poured off his head and slid down his body in a way that made her mouth dry up. "You should do that again. And again." Chuckling, he guided her deeper into the water and pulled her against him. He kissed her gently, softly . . . then dunked them both, the bastard. She coughed as their heads broke the surface. "You could have warned me!"

Knox and his demon smiled. She always made him think of a hissing, spitting kitten when she snapped at him. He smoothed his hands up her back. "Sorry, baby."

"No, you're not." She saw a dark shadow under the water and almost leapt out of his arms. "Jellyfish!"

Tightening his arms around her, Knox looked around. "There are no jellyfish."

"I saw jellyfish."

"There are no jellyfish. Relax," he soothed. "Breathe. Take in the view."

Harper took a long breath. Under the scents of salt water and seaweed were the smells of tropical flowers, sunscreen, and the food coming from the villa. Hooking her arms around his neck, she looked around as they bobbed in the sea, water rippling around them. Waves tumbled into rocks, tossing up foamy sprays of water. There was a dock nearby where jet skis and powerboats idled. Beyond the green mountains, in the far distance, were other small islands.

"Well, does it have your stamp of approval?"

"It does." Even though the heat of the sun pricked her skin and felt oppressive on her chest, she absolutely loved the place. "But if you're hoping I'll agree to stay here for the rest of the pregnancy, you're out of your demonic mind. I don't hide."

"It wouldn't be hiding." He kissed her shoulder, fingering her bikini strap. "Stress is not good for you or the baby."

"Oh, don't play the baby card with me, Thorne."

"This—quiet, peace, safety—is what you need right now."

"And staying here for a few weeks would be awesome. But I would lose my mind sitting around here for the rest of the pregnancy with nothing to do."

"There's plenty to do and see here. Rivers. Creeks. Jungle. Mountains. Waterfalls. Ancient ruins. You could not be bored." He paused at the cry of a pelican that flew overhead. "Your friends and family can visit you. I'll be here."

"Not all the time."

"I can be, if that's what you want."

She almost snorted, but then she realized . . . "You're serious."

He sighed at her astonishment. "Harper, when are you going to realize that you're my priority? You come first to me. If you want me to take the next twelve weeks off work to be with you every moment of this pregnancy, that's what I'll do." His demon would love that anyway.

Touched, she swallowed hard. "I wouldn't ask you to do that."

"Being with you twenty-four seven would be no hardship." Beneath the water, he traced her hipbone, knowing her little raven tattoo was right there. Being that ravens were cunning, strategic tricksters, she felt she could relate to them. Knox suspected they also made her think of her family. "I'll do whatever it takes to make sure you're happy and safe."

"And I love you for that, but I still can't stay holed up here." She smiled, adding, "We can, however, relax here for a little while. That sounds like an awesome plan to me. Besides, we have a nursery to design and baby . . . stuff to order."

"Stuff?"

She shrugged. "I've never cared for a baby. I don't know a great deal about what that entails, what we'll need, or how much of it we'll need. What I currently know is courtesy of the Internet."

"We'll be fine. If we weren't delaying the announcement of the pregnancy, we could have hired people to prepare the nursery for us."

She welcomed the ocean breeze as it tugged at her hair, which hung in wet ropes down her back. "No, I'd rather be part of designing and readying it anyway."

"All right, that's what you'll do." He dipped his hand inside her bikini bottoms, cupping her ass. "So, you're happy to stay here for a little while. How about a month?"

She frowned. "A week."

"That's too short."

"All right, two weeks."

"Still too short. Three weeks. And if you *do* get bored, we'll leave earlier."

"Fine, three weeks."

"Good girl." Of course, he'd do his best to convince her to stay longer. It was that fact alone that stopped his demon from sulking.

"Don't think I don't know you'll try and talk into me stay—jellyfish!" She pretty much tried to climb up his body, not appreciating his chuckles *at all*.

"There are no jellyfish."

"I saw one!" But the bastard didn't stop chuckling. Instead, he pulled her deeper into the sea. They stayed there for a little while, just talking and enjoying the uninterrupted time. "You know, I could really do with an ice cream right now."

"Ice cream? I think I can make that happen." He scooped her up, shocking a little squeal out of her, and traced their footprints in the hot sand as he headed to the villa. Once on the deck, he gently put her on her feet. "Shower first."

"Good idea." Although she hadn't lain on the beach, the sand had somehow found its way inside her bikini and was chafing her skin. Inside the villa, he took her straight to the bathroom attached to their bedroom. Without removing their swimsuits, he backed her into the walk-in shower and then turned on the spray.

Harper hissed through her teeth. The hot water stung her skin, which was sensitive from the sun, but the discomfort quickly faded. And then Knox was kissing her. His mouth was hot and greedy and it totally swept her away.

"So many times a day, I look at this mouth and think about what it feels like wrapped around my cock. Heaven. Fucking heaven." Knox tugged down her bikini strap, letting it sweep over her shoulder. He licked over the cluster of freckles there, then bit hard. "Mine." He stripped off their swimsuits and squirted soap onto his hands. As she shampooed her hair, he soaped her down; tracing her, shaping her, teasing her, until the smell of salt was gone and there was only coconut soap and Harper's honeyed scent.

She gave as good as she got—her touch sexual as she ran her

hands all over him, lathering him with gel. Finally, he pulled her fully under the spray, rinsing off shampoo, soap, and sand. As the water poured down on them, he kissed her again, licking and biting. "I fucking love your mouth." He bit the fleshy part of her lower lip. "And I love fucking it."

She narrowed her eyes, and he knew why. The idea of kneeling on the tiled floor didn't hold a lot of appeal. Still, he knew she'd do it if he asked. It was a total fucking turn-on to know that she'd do whatever he asked—she wouldn't do it easily or meekly, which made it hotter, but she'd do it. He knew exactly what he wanted right then, but it wasn't his cock in her mouth.

It happened so quickly that Harper found herself blinking rapidly. One minute she'd been pliant against him; the next thing, her back was against the tiled wall and one psychic hand was pinning both of hers above her head. "What are you doing?"

Knox fisted his cock. "Watching."

Harper gasped as an ice-cold psychic finger slipped inside her. It didn't matter that she'd been ready for the heat that flared, it still zapped every one of her senses as her pussy began to blaze. "I'm already wet."

"I know that. But I want you even more wet. And I want to stand here and watch while I play with you until you're so wet you're dripping. You want me to have that, don't you? You want to give me what I want."

Her mouth quirked. "It's in my best interests."

He smiled. "It is." He cupped her breasts, molding them. They'd grown bigger, fuller. As he used a psychic finger to fuck her pussy, he tugged, twisted, and plucked at her nipples. He swooped down and sucked the unpierced one into his mouth, flicking it with his tongue. She moaned his name—a feminine demand. "What do you want, Harper?"

Her chin lifted. "I'm not going to beg."

"You don't need to beg," he said softly. "I'll give you whatever you want"—he tugged on her piercing— "but you have to tell me what it is."

"You."

He sucked at her pulse. "You have me."

"*In* me," she ground out.

"I am in you." He gave her a particularly hard thrust with his psychic finger.

Her demon hissed, irritated by his teasing. "Your cock," Harper clipped. "I want your cock in me!"

Keeping her hands pinned above her head with one psychic hand, Knox hooked her legs over the crooks of his elbows. "Then you'll have it." He thrust into her, and her scorching hot pussy clamped and rippled around him. She was coming, he realized. And the "oh shit" look in her eyes meant that she was expecting punishment for not having permission. "It's okay, you can come."

It was a really good thing he thought so, because there wasn't a chance Harper could have held back that orgasm. The moment his long, thick cock had stretched and filled her oversensitive walls in one smooth possessive stroke, sheer bliss had washed over her. She slumped against the wall, eyes falling closed, as her strength seemed to drain out of her.

"Look at me," he rumbled.

She opened her eyes to find him staring at her with that very familiar savage possessiveness. Her pussy clenched, and he gritted his teeth. Knox slowly pulled back. Frowning, she tried curling her legs around him to keep him with her, but he held them tight.

"Don't worry, baby, I'm not going anywhere," he said softly, silkily. "I'm nowhere near finished with you." Jaw clenched, Knox mercilessly slammed into her over and over, knowing she could take it. He'd angled her hips so that his cock brushed her clit with every brutal thrust, and he knew from many, many past experiences that her body wouldn't hold out long against that. Already her pussy was becoming tighter and hotter.

Possessiveness spurred him on, kept him driving deep and hard. His demon wanted to crawl inside her until she'd never be free of him. "It won't matter how many times I have you," Knox growled, "I'll always want more of this pussy. My pussy."

She flexed her hand, wanting to be free to touch him, to scratch him, to pull at his hair. "Let me go." He shook his head, and her demon reached for the surface and glared at him. "Release me," it ordered. But he didn't, and Harper resurfaced with a snarl. The air chilled a little as his eyes bled to black, and the hairs on her nape stood on end as she looked at his demon. "Let me go."

"No," it told her in that disembodied voice. "You'll take what you're given." It mercilessly powered into her at a frenzied pace. Where Knox always clung to his control, the demon didn't. Each slam of his cock was rough and territorial. Knox resurfaced, and the pace and force of the thrusts eased just a little. But then the demon was back, and once again it was feverishly slamming into her. They repeatedly switched, each tormenting her with their own personal brand of fucking.

"Not gonna last," she warned then.

With a growl, Knox leapt to the surface. "You'll last because I want you to last." He thrust harder, literally driving his point home. Violet eyes glared at him, calling him a bastard. "You like it when I don't give you what you want. You like it when I just take what *I* want. Like you're my little toy."

Fuck if he wasn't right, the asshole. It probably made her a little weird, but Harper had made her peace with that. She was about to demand that he just made her come for God's sake, but then she felt it starting to happen again out-of-fucking-nowhere. And since she hadn't waited for permission, there was a good chance she'd pay for that. "Don't stop." He was sadistic enough to do it, but his eyes softened.

"I won't stop, baby." Knox fucked her harder, faster, driving as deep as he could go. "Make me come, Harper." Her pussy clamped down on him as her eyes went blind and she choked out his name, and Knox came so fucking hard it almost blew the head off his cock—it went on and on and on, so intense that it should have hurt.

Shuddering, he slumped against her, breathing hard. "Let's get you cleaned up so I can get you that ice cream you want."

"I'm down with that," she slurred.

Floating on her post-orgasm cloud, Harper was barely aware of him turning off the shower, grabbing towels, and carrying her into the bedroom. It wasn't until he set her on her feet and began drying her off that she partially snapped out of her buzz. She tried to take over. "I can do it."

"I know you can do it." But he kept on patting her dry, and she made no more protests.

"You know, you really should—" Harper froze as a mind slid against hers. Unfamiliar. Small. Young. She gasped in wonder, gripping his arms. "Knox . . . I just felt the baby's mind. It was the tiniest touch, but it was there."

He stroked his hand over the small bump as he reached out with his mind, searching for another. And there it was. He gently "touched" it, felt an answering flutter.

"Did you feel it?"

He nodded, chest squeezing. "It has a vibe of . . . contentment." Knox rested his forehead against hers. "I watched the scan and I've felt the baby move countless times, but touching the baby's mind, feeling it respond . . . that's something else altogether."

She smiled knowingly. "And your protective levels just went up another notch, huh."

"They did." Knox curled his arms around her. "I'll do everything I can to make sure that the baby stays content. I'm wondering if maybe all those endorphins rushing through you have mellowed it out. If so, it might be a sound idea to just spend the next twelve weeks fucking the hell out of you."

"You'll do that anyway." Her stomach clenched as he gave her that lopsided smile that did interesting things to her body.

"You're right. I will."

CHAPTER FOURTEEN

At the knock on the door, Knox called, "Come in." He looked up from the multiple computer monitors on his desk as Keenan strolled into his home office.

The incubus flicked a brief admiring glance at the three abstract art canvases of mechanical clockwork on the gray wall. "How was your vacation?"

"Good. Harper needed it." She'd also enjoyed it enough to stay the full three weeks and had agreed to return there at some point. First, she naturally wanted to be sure that everything was ready for the baby.

Keenan nodded. "I just caught her on her way upstairs. She seemed happy, relaxed. Looks like the break did her good." His brows lowered. "She was eating a raw carrot."

Knox rubbed his nape. "Yeah, she's had a few cravings lately. Mostly ice cream and raw carrots. I'm just hoping she won't start wanting to eat them both at once."

The sentinel shuddered at the idea. "Her stomach is more rounded. Amazing what a difference three weeks can make."

"Rodgers warned us that things would move pretty fast after she reached week eighteen." She was now twenty-one weeks pregnant and there was no way to hide it.

"She let me feel the baby kick." Keenan grinned. "That kid's feisty."

Knox smiled in agreement. "Just like its mother."

Keenan chuckled. "Yep. I'll bet you'll panic if it's a girl."

"Probably." Knox placed his hands on the desk. "Moving onto the reason I called you here . . . what did you find out about Jonas' girlfriend?"

"Her name is Kayce Willard. She's from his lair, she lives with her roommate, she works as a model. And she's missing."

"Missing?"

"She hasn't been seen by anyone since the night after the boardroom meeting."

Knox swore.

"It could be that someone told her you suspect that she may have done some dirty magickal work for Jonas so she's lying low for a while. Who could blame her? But it could also be that someone . . . *disposed* of her. I have members of the Force searching for her as we speak."

Knox nodded in approval. "Anything else I should know?"

"Everything's been pretty quiet. No disturbances within the lair. The studio hasn't had any problems. McCauley has met with his grandparents three times since you left. He was his usual cold self, but they apparently didn't seem put off by it. They also haven't pressured Linda and Wyatt to give him up. In fact, according to Wyatt, they've been very cooperative and civil."

"Good. Keep me updated on the Kayce Willard situation."

"Will do." With that, Keenan left.

Knox made a few calls and answered a few emails, catching up on some of the work he'd missed. Guessing that Harper was in the nursery, he rounded the U-shaped executive desk and left the office to seek her out. Hearing a noise downstairs, he followed it to the kitchen. But it wasn't Harper he found sitting on a breakfast stool, drinking one of her strawberry smoothies while candy wrappers and empty chip packets littered the breakfast bar.

Knox sighed. "Lou, what are you doing here?"

The devil shrugged. "I was thirsty and a little peckish. Yes, I remember we had a chat about you not liking me just showing up, eating your food and stuff. Well, *you* chatted, looking at me with cruel intent. I think it was cruel intent. Could have been a promise of death. Maybe both. Although I would consider both at one time to be an excessive reaction." He peeked around Knox's body. "Where's your mate?"

"I was about to go find her and—Wait, are you stoned?"

"No, of course not. Really. You can trust me. Drug users always tell the truth."

Knox just sighed. He wasn't sure what exactly humans expected the devil to look like, but Knox suspected that it wasn't the version in front of him. Lou was wearing a baseball cap, scruffy jeans, sneakers, and a T-shirt that featured a picture of Inigo Montoya from *The Princess Bride*. Knox didn't know why, and he wasn't about to ask.

Lou was also wearing a denim jacket that had pink sequins stitched onto it. Harper liked to personalize her clothes by sewing diamonds, lace, and other appliques on them. She would also vengefully do it to your clothes if you pissed her off. When Lou had asked her to "jazz up" his jacket, she'd hoped the pink sequins would annoy him. Nope. The crazy bastard liked them.

Knox would bet that most humans would be surprised to find that Lucifer was not actually the ruler of hell. Lou moved there and brought order to it after having some sort of dispute with God. He wasn't a one-dimensional malevolent being either.

Harper had once described him as a psychopathic child with bi-polar and OCD. That about summed him up.

Lou didn't ask much of people, but he did have three laws. One, demons needed to conceal their existence from humans. Two, they must not be caught breaking human laws. Three, they must never cause harm to a child—human or demon.

"You have a nice tan going on. I hope you spent your vacation trying to get our Harper pregnant."

Knox rubbed his forehead. "This again?"

"Why wait? It's a logical step to make in a committed relationship." Lou narrowed his eyes. "You *are* committed to her, right?"

"Of course I am. Now why are you here?" Hearing footsteps, Knox turned to watch as Harper walked into the room.

Lou took one look at her round stomach and grinned like a loon. "Well, would you look at that." He stood. "We're gonna have a baby! Score!" He patted Knox's back. "I knew you'd come through in the end." Crossing to Harper, he bent down. "Well, hello there, baby Luc—"

"*Don't* say it," she snapped.

"You haven't yet told me why you're here," said Knox.

Lou looked affronted. "Do I need a reason to visit my friends?"

Knox shot an impatient look at the most antisocial being he'd ever known. "You don't consider us your friends. You don't *want* friends."

"I told you, I'm branching out from cold and pure evil." He turned back to Harper, smiling. "How far pregnant are you?"

"Twenty-one weeks."

His excitement was quickly replaced by irritation. "You have nine weeks left and you're only telling me this *now*?"

She pursed her lips. "Well . . . yes. But you're still one of the first to know."

And now, mercurial as ever, Lou was once again delighted.

"How've you been? Cravings? Backache? Nausea? Mood swings? I've heard that eighty percent of pregnant women have *seriously* bad mood swings. Like *scary* bad."

"I am not having mood swings."

Knox folded his arms. "While you're here, Lou, answer me a question. Why do you think Jonas wanted to meet with you?"

"No idea," said Lou, retaking his seat.

"You're not even curious?"

"Nope." Lou drank some of his smoothie. "Earth business does not interest me."

Yeah, Knox knew that, but still . . . "We need to know what Jonas wants from you. Talk to him. Find out."

"I can't. See, I have this thing. I don't do things that bore me." Lou set down his glass. "Deals are boring. Jonas wants to offer me a deal. Ergo . . ."

Knox ground his teeth. "Lou—"

"I don't concern myself with what goes on between the Primes. It's all mind-numbingly dull. Now a baby who can single-handedly lay waste to the universe, on the other hand, has me *fascinated.*"

Harper's mouth tightened. "He or she will not lay waste to anything—nor will you attempt to teach them to do so."

"We're keeping the pregnancy quiet for now, Lou," Knox told him. "We need you to do the same."

Lou lifted his hand, as if to pledge an oath. "You can be sure that I will do nothing to threaten the upcoming birth of our little Luc—"

"*We are not calling the baby Lucifer,*" growled Harper, fists clenched.

Lou leaned toward Knox and said quietly, "Notice the mood swing? The stats don't lie."

Harper let out a long breath. "Why are you even here?"

Lou lifted a brow. "Expecting someone else?"

"Preferably someone who doesn't come uninvited, rifle through our kitchen, and help themselves to stuff. It's like having a stray dog turn up all the time."

Lou sniffed at her. "That's unfair. I don't shit on your floor."

"It's important that we find out what Jonas wants from you," Knox interrupted. "It could be related to the attack on Harper."

Straightening in his seat, Lou frowned. "What attack?"

"Someone hired hunters to steal her wings."

His eyes widened. "Get out of town! Really? Someone out there is honestly *that* stupid?" He pouted as he looked at Harper's stomach. "Poor baby must have been in such distress."

"I'm fine, in case you were wondering," she said dryly.

"I don't need to wonder. I can see that you're fine." Lou turned to Knox. "What I *don't* see is how the attack could have had anything to do with Jonas. It's highly unlikely that he knows she has wings."

Knox narrowed his eyes. "How do *you* know?"

"I know lots of things." Lou poked his temple. "I'm a well of information."

Knowing from past experience how tight-lipped the devil could be, Knox didn't bother pushing for an answer. "Jonas is upset with Jolene right now. The person who sent the hunters after Harper also hired someone to kidnap Harper's cousin."

Lou's mouth fell open. "Risking Jolene's wrath? Oh, well, then they really are stupid. Or suicidal. Both works. That woman is *mean*. Giving me packets of chips that open upside down and putting her T.V. volume on an uneven number just to see me cry. How can someone be that cruel?"

Yeah, her grandmother really did love to poke at his OCD streak. Still, Harper frowned. "Do you really feel that you, the devil, are in a position to judge people? You know what, don't answer that. Look, I get that 'helping' people isn't really your thing. But if Jonas wants to make a deal with you, it can't be good. Even if he has nothing to do with the attack on me or the attempt to kidnap my cousin, it's still important to know what he wants. It could be something really bad. You could stop it from happening."

Head tilted, Lou looked at her curiously. "Are you ... are you trying to appeal to my conscience?" He snorted. "That inner voice gave up on me a *long* time ago. Honestly, trying to make me feel bad is more pointless than the 'ay' in 'okay'. If self-centeredness could bounce, I'd be in orbit. And wouldn't that be fun?"

Harper sighed. "At least you're honest about it."

"My shrink says I shouldn't hold things in or pretend to be what I'm not. He says I should just be myself."

"Yeah, that was bad advice."

"And yet, I have a fan club," Lou said smugly. "Several."

"You mean you have Satanic cults that worship you."

"Yeah," he muttered, seemingly unimpressed by them. "Most of the weirdos are like diapers—self-absorbed, full of shit, and need to be disposed of. But I do appreciate that they use symmetrical symbols. Not crazy about their obsession with six-six-six, though. The number six is founded on odd numbers. My favorite number is eight—perfectly symmetrical. They should try eight-eight-eight."

The guy truly was out of his mind. Harper simply said, "Well, if I meet any Satanic people, I'll let them know."

"That's sweet of you." His head tilted and his gaze turned inward. "Hmm. I'm needed elsewhere. Must go. Harper, you take care of our little munchkin. Knox, no, before you ask again, I'm not meeting with Jonas. Even if I tried to help, I'd somehow make it all worse. Tell me I'm wrong."

The thing was . . . Knox couldn't.

"Besides, you don't need my help. You have this. You can manage just fine." He saluted Knox. "*Carpe diem!*" And then, in a blink, he was gone.

Harper exhaled heavily. "Was it just me or was he stoned?"

"He was stoned." Knox frowned at the candy wrappers and empty chip packets on the table. "I think he had a case of the munchies." Knox crossed to her and softly stroked her stomach. "I was looking for you when I heard him down here."

"I was looking for you, too. I want your advice on something." She led him up the stairs and into the bedroom next to theirs, which she'd decided would be the nursery. She gestured to the wall, where she'd brushed three different stripes of paint along the white wall. "Which shade do you prefer?" She'd ordered three samples online and had been delighted to get back from the island and find them waiting.

Knox looked around the spacious room. "You cleared this room out all by yourself?"

"Hell, no. I roped Tanner and Levi into helping me."

"I'm assuming you're going to elect them to paint the walls, too."

"They agreed to help me with the painting."

The word "help" had him frowning. "I'm not sure if I like the idea of you—"

"I'll be painting walls, not knocking them down," she said as patiently as possible, reminding herself just how hard it was for him while his protective instincts were riding him hard. "I promise you that if at any point I need to rest, I will stop—for the baby's sake, if nothing else. Trust me."

"I do trust you," he stated firmly, needing her to know that it was true. "You're the only person that I trust." His demon also trusted her, and that was a major thing.

She smiled. "Good. Now which color do you prefer?"

He pointed to the soft yellow strip of paint. "That one."

She smiled. "Me, too. Great minds think alike. Hey, Rodgers should be here in half an hour."

"I know. Why do you look so nervous? I thought you'd be excited to have another scan."

"I am. I'm just worried he'll tell me that the baby's still smaller than it should be."

He stroked her upper arms. "I'm sure everything will be fine."

"I hope you're right."

A short while later, the doctor was setting up his portable ultrasound machine in their living room again. "Nice tan. I heard you went on vacation. Lucky you. Tell me, Harper, how have you been?"

Sitting on the sofa, she replied, "Fine. I don't feel drained anymore. I'm eating fine. Having a couple of cravings, but nothing weird."

"Any back pain yet?" he asked.

She jiggled her head. "A little. It's not so bad."

"Sadly, it will get worse. What about the baby?"

"It's hyper. Never seems to sleep. We feel its mind sometimes."

His brows lifted. "Really?" he asked, seeming impressed.

"It reaches out by itself," said Knox. "It first happened three weeks ago."

"Interesting," Rodgers drawled. "Lie back. Let's take a look at the baby."

Like last time, Harper lay back as he moved a handheld probe around her gel-covered, lower abdomen. The baby didn't seem to like it any more than she did, because it kept kicking at the probe.

Rodgers chuckled. "It doesn't like me poking and prodding, does it?"

Knox watched the screen, fascinated as the baby wriggled around. It was bigger, and its features were more distinct. It now looked like an actual baby as opposed to a peanut with a head. "Well?" Knox asked the doctor. "Is everything okay?"

"Everything seems absolutely fine," replied Rodgers. "The baby is still a little small, but it's clearly not behind in its development. Babies don't usually psychically reach out until the twenty-third week."

Knox stroked a hand over Harper's hair. "Why do you think it's still smaller than it should be?"

The doctor pursed his lips. "It could be due to any number of things. The baby isn't small enough for me to be worried; its size is just something we need to monitor. Now, I'd like to do a few tests." He held out a little tub to Harper and smiled. "Pee for me."

Harper reached out to grab the tub, but then she froze as Knox's face hardened. She could feel the echo of a telepathic conversation, knew he was speaking with someone. When he finally met her eyes and she saw the anger there, she said, *I'm not going to like this, am I?*

It's Pamela and Rupert.

Talia's parents?

He nodded. *They're dead.*

Knox blinked. "Stabbed to death?"

"Several times," said Keenan. He gestured at the uniformed officers that were urging the growing crowd to step away from the crime scene tape as he added, "The cops might have thought that it was Talia's dealer, looking for her parents to pay whatever she died owing him. But he has an airtight alibi—he's dead, too."

"When did that happen?" asked Knox.

"Last week. It was a gang territorial dispute that went too far." Keenan paused. "I know you probably suspect the kid has something to do with the attack on Pamela and Rupert, but it was pretty vicious, Knox. It would have taken someone with more strength to have made the knife penetrate so deeply. I don't think it's something a kid could have done."

"It can't be a coincidence that Talia's parents were killed." Knox glanced at the house, where a continuing flow of people were passing in and out—some were clearly forensic analysts while others were likely police officers. "How many times were they stabbed?"

"Both were stabbed in the chest six times."

"And McCauley's six years old." Knox could imagine what Harper would make of that. He'd left her at the mansion, where the doctor could finish running his tests. As they hadn't yet announced the pregnancy, she'd needed to stay home. The last place he'd want her to be was a crime scene anyway.

"I agree that it seems like the kid is somehow connected to this, but I truly don't think that he has the strength it would have taken to subdue them and cause such injuries."

"Who else would have a motive to do this?"

Keenan shrugged. "The cops have finishing speaking with their son. He's over there, if you'd like to talk to him. Maybe he knows something."

Knox hadn't realized that Daniel was in Vegas. The demon had long ago moved away, though he remained part of their lair. "All right. Let's see what he has to say." Knox walked through the throngs of uniforms and ducked under the tape. No one tried to stop him; not even the humans. Knox had found that if you appeared to know exactly where you were going, people were very unlikely to bother you. Knox crossed to the tall demon staring at his parents' home and greeted simply, "Daniel."

The male slowly turned, eyes tormented. "Mr. Thorne. It's been a while." He exchanged a nod with Keenan.

"I know it seems like an almost mechanical statement, given

how often it's used in these circumstances," began Knox, "but I'm sorry for your loss."

Daniel nodded. "Thanks."

"How long have you been in Vegas?"

Pain flashed in his eyes. "I came here for Talia's funeral and decided to stay a while."

Knox inwardly winced. The guy hadn't just lost his parents, he'd lost his sister—and all in the space of a few months. "Where were you when this attack occurred?"

Daniel adjusted his glasses. "My hotel."

"You haven't been staying with your parents?"

"I love—*loved*—them, but living under the same roof as them never worked for me. My mom and I argued a lot. You might as well know that we argued the last time we talked. The neighbors heard it, so they'll tell you anyway. And I know how that looks, but I didn't kill them."

Knox doubted that he had, but he kept his expression blank. "What were you arguing about?"

"They wanted to take Talia's kid and adopt him. I didn't think they should."

That sure surprised Knox. "Why not?"

Daniel seemed to choose his words carefully. "They weren't good at parenting. They weren't abusive or anything," he hurried to add. "They loved us, but they didn't discipline us or support us—they let us go our own way."

A little like Lucian had done with Harper, Knox mused.

"Maybe they thought it would be good for us, or maybe they were just too lazy to be bothered guiding us because they had such busy social lives; I don't know. Talia went through the typical teenage rebellion, but it's hard to rebel against people who don't care if you do it. She kept pushing them, wanting a reaction. All she did was mess up her life."

"Whereas you cut your losses and moved on."

Daniel shrugged. "Yeah, I guess you could put it that way. Look, I didn't want the kid to go down Talia's road. He's been through enough, considering what his human mother did. So I told them they should just let him stay with Linda and Wyatt. Besides, if my parents had really wanted him, they'd have taken him when he was a baby."

For a moment, Knox said nothing. "They knew about him?"

Daniel seemed surprised by the question. "Oh yeah. My mother was there for his birth. She pressured Talia to switch him for a human baby. It didn't take much pressure, but it was still a shitty thing to do."

Knox exchanged a look with Keenan. "Why do you think they wanted him now, Daniel?"

"Because they were all about appearances. It would have looked bad to others if they hadn't tried to take him in. They wouldn't have wanted a black mark from society."

Knox could easily believe that. "Is there anyone who may be upset with your parents?"

"Linda Sanders, but I don't believe she did it. Linda came to the house, trying to pay my parents to back off and let her keep McCauley. They refused, but it didn't lead to a major row or anything."

Frowning, Keenan spoke. "I was under the impression that things were going well."

"They were," said Daniel. "Everybody seemed to be working together for McCauley's sake. But then Linda came here Thursday night and declared that she and Wyatt were taking McCauley away for the weekend to Florida, so my parents would have to miss their scheduled visit with him. My mother said she'd never begrudge McCauley a trip but that she didn't appreciate Linda giving them such short notice. Linda seemed . . .

disappointed by the response, as if she'd hoped to draw my mother into an argument—Pamela Winters wasn't a woman who was easily riled."

"When did Linda offer her money?" asked Knox.

"As she was leaving. She was almost at the front door, and then she just turned and said she'd give Pamela forty grand if she'd agree to stay away from him."

Keenan whistled. "Linda meant business."

"My mother was pissed, but she didn't raise her voice. She just turned down Linda's offer and ordered her to leave. Linda apologized for offending her, said she just wanted what was best for McCauley, and then she left." He paused. "Like I said, I don't think Linda hurt them. My mom was a judge and she got a lot of hate mail. It was probably someone who was either pissed at her for sentencing someone they loved *or* it was someone who wanted revenge because she sent them to prison."

After a moment, Knox nodded. "Thank you for answering our questions. If you need anything, let me know. Take care, Daniel."

"He's right, you know," said Keenan as they walked back to the Bentley, where Levi waited. "The attack was most likely related to one of Pamela's cases."

"Most likely," agreed Knox. It made the most sense, after all. But he couldn't bring himself to fully believe it. "Let's get back to my mate."

Back at the mansion, Knox found her in the living room, watching some kind of quiz show. She slowly stood and walked straight to him. He curled his arms around her. "Before I answer your questions, what did the doctor say?"

"He did the tests," she said. "Everything came back normal. Now what happened?" Harper's eyes widened as he told her about the murders. "Hell. Do you think it could have been McCauley?"

Knox grimaced. "I'm not sure it's something he could have physically done."

"He could have enhanced strength like my cousin. Or he could have somehow mind-fucked someone into doing it for him. Its seems weird that he would, though. I mean, Keenan told you earlier that his visits with Pamela and Rupert had gone just fine. I suppose the demon could have still been pissed at them for not taking McCauley in as a baby. It's not their fault that they hadn't known about him, but our inner demons often see things in black and white."

Knox rubbed her back. "It turns out that they did know about him." He relayed his conversation with Daniel.

"Well, shit. That's definitely a reason for McCauley and his demon to be pissed at them. Are you going to at least talk to him about it?"

"Yes, but he's in Florida right now. Linda and Wyatt took him there for the weekend. That means I can't talk to any of them face to face until Sunday."

"Someone will notify them about the deaths, so we can't monitor how they react to the news," she pointed out.

Knox arched a brow. "We?"

"Yes, we," she insisted. "By Sunday, we'll have announced the pregnancy, so it won't be a problem if they see me. They won't be there for the announcement, but they'll still hear about it from someone." She propped her chin on his chest. "We can't keep it a secret any longer, Knox."

He brushed his nose against hers. "We could if I just hid you here," he joked. Well, it wasn't entirely a joke.

Harper rolled her eyes. "Have you thought about where you'll make the announcement and how you'll go about it?"

"Yes. This is what I was thinking . . . "

CHAPTER FIFTEEN

Beneath the sounds of people talking and laughing was the hum of the ceiling fans and the clinking of flutes. Harper peeked through the black curtain to take a good, long look at the ballroom. "There's a whole lot of people out there, Tanner." Not the *entire* lair, which was unsurprising. Their lair was particularly large, so many families often sent one or two of their own to represent the family and hear whatever announcement was made. It meant that the events weren't too hectic and crowded, which worked out best for everyone.

"You don't need to be nervous," Tanner assured her, like, for the tenth time. "The lair won't respond badly to the pregnancy."

Harper turned back to him, hiding once more behind the curtain on the small dais. "Probably not, but I'll have to, you know . . . *talk* to people. *Mingle*." Harper was dreading it. She simply didn't have the people skills required for it. Luckily, her mate did.

She hadn't seen Knox since breakfast, and she knew he was currently dealing with some issues within the hotel. As hiding her rounded stomach while walking through the Underground wouldn't have been the easiest thing she'd ever done, she'd had Ciaran teleport her and Tanner from the mansion to the penthouse suite. There, she'd showered and changed into a long, white, chiffon dress that wasn't loose-fitting yet cleverly made her baby bump a lot less distinctive.

Tanner, Keenan, and Larkin had then walked her to the dais of the ballroom. Keenan and Larkin were circling the ballroom, on guard. Everyone was ready and in place. Now, all they were waiting for was for Knox to show up.

The last time she'd telepathically spoken to him had been twenty minutes ago, when he'd informed her that he was heading to the penthouse to quickly shower and change. Since Knox was wicked fast at getting ready, she could only assume that he'd been waylaid by his staff yet again or he'd be here by now. *Where are you?*

Within moments, his mind brushed against hers. *Dealing with a minor matter before the concierge starts to cry.*

She chuckled. At Tanner's questioning look, she waved a hand and then peeked through the curtain again. People mingled as they sipped wine and nibbled on appetizers being served by waiters that circulated the room. Other guests were gathered around the tall, high tables on which bowls of pretzels and flickering candles were placed. Keenan and Larkin were patrolling the room, their eyes sharp. "I don't see Carla, Bray or Kellen."

"Did you expect to?" asked Tanner.

"No." In fact, she'd been hoping that they wouldn't attend. Maybe that was mean of her, but she simply didn't trust them not to cause a scene.

"They're leaving in three weeks anyway, so nothing you say tonight is anything they need to hear."

He was right, she thought, as she closed the curtain. Harper smoothed a hand down the side of her dress. "I wish we didn't have to make a huge, public announcement."

"The lair needs to know."

"Yeah, I know that, but I would have preferred it if we didn't have to make a big thing out of it. It would have been easier to just ask you and the other sentinels to pass on the news."

"You're their Prime, and there are certain expectations that come with that position. Making public announcements about key information is one of them. Celebrating important events is another. Your pregnancy is both of those things."

"Yes, but have you not seen how people respond to a pregnant woman?" By the way his brow furrowed, no, he hadn't. "Everyone's suddenly an expert on babies and they're all full of advice and nosy-ass questions. I'm glad my stomach's not that big—people are a hell of a lot worse if there's a bump. They try rubbing it like it's a damn genie-infested lamp."

"Genie-infested?" he chuckled.

"You get my point."

"I do. How about this? If anyone seems like they're about to say anything inappropriate or touch your belly, I'll step in and interrupt the conversation."

"That would be good."

"Then that's what I'll do." Tanner folded his arms. "On another note, Keenan said you called Lucian earlier."

Harper nodded. "I thought it best that he found out about the pregnancy from me."

"How did he take the news?"

She pursed her lips as she thought back to the conversation . . .

"Are you freaking kidding me?" Lucian burst out.

Harper sighed. "Lucian—"

"It's not enough that you mated the psychopathic bastard, you're now going to have his psychopathic spawn?"

"*Hey! My child is not psychopathic.*"

"*Don't kid yourself. If it takes after you, it'll be a treasure. If it takes after him, it'll be a living nightmare.*"

Harper scratched her chin. "He took it pretty well."

Tanner snorted in disbelief.

The door behind her creaked open, and Knox's cologne drifted to her. She turned as he and Levi entered the small space. She couldn't stop a smile from curving her mouth as she got a good look at him in all his GQ motherfucking glory. No one had the right to exude so much sex appeal. No one. But as he crossed to her, emanating raw power and masculine intensity, a hot and heavy need unfurled inside her.

And he's all mine, she thought to herself. Her demon was just as smug about it.

Knox actually stopped in his tracks as he absorbed the sight of her. Standing there in the pure-white sleeveless, ankle-length, one-shoulder dress, she made him think of a mythological Greek goddess. Her ivory skin had tanned into a pretty gold shade that matched the ends of her dark hair and gave her skin a healthy glow. Her hair was currently bunched up into some kind of elegant updo that appeared to look deliberately tousled.

Best of all, he could see part of his brand on her breast.

Knox crossed to her with a smile and slid an arm around her. "You look beautiful. Sorry about the delay." He fingered one of her white-gold earrings. As always, seeing her wearing something he'd bought her stoked the possessive streak in him. He gently rubbed her stomach as he reached out and gently touched the baby's mind. All he sensed was contentment. "You ready?"

"Not really."

"It will be fine." He kissed her. "Now, we need to be clear on a few things. At no point tonight will you be on your own. When it's time to work the room, I'll be with you. When you need to use the restrooms, Larkin will accompany you. It's not that any of us believe you're in danger from our lair—it's that we refuse to take any chances."

"I don't want to take chances either."

"Good." He stroked her stomach again. "I'll go begin the announcement. You know when to join me, don't you?"

"Don't worry; I haven't forgotten anything."

Let your anxiety go, baby. Don't let them see you nervous.

She nodded and breathed away the tension in her spine.

"That's my girl." Knox released her and slipped out from behind the curtain. The murmurs and laughter died down as people spotted him, and all eyes turned his way as he crossed to the stand in the center of the dais, where a microphone waited.

His amplified voice came over the sound system as he spoke. "First of all, thank you all for making it here tonight. I'll begin by assuring you that this isn't a gathering to discuss the Horsemen or any issue within the lair. I've called you here because I have some good news to share." He paused for effect. "In approximately two months, there will be a new addition to the lair."

There was a rustle of fabric as the curtain opened and then Harper and Tanner stepped out. Tanner and Levi melted into the shadows while Harper crossed the space to Knox. In that dress, her bump wasn't at all obvious, but enough of the crowd caught his meaning to study her closely. Then applause and cheers rang throughout the room.

"It isn't something you need to keep secret," Knox told them when the applause faded. "But news travels fast among our kind, and we wanted you all to hear it first."

A waiter stepped up onto the dais and handed Knox two glasses. One was filled with champagne and the other with water, at Knox's earlier request. He gave Harper her glass and they both then raised them to the crowd, who raised theirs right back.

Knox clinked his glass against Harper's, and they both sipped at their drinks. "Now we mingle," he said. "Just a couple of hours; then we can leave."

Bracing herself, Harper inhaled deeply. The scents of perfume, cologne, fresh flowers, and scented candles washed over her, making her nose wrinkle. "Let's get it over with." Her low heels clicked along the glossy hardwood floor as she walked off the dais. People immediately came forward, faces beaming.

"Congratulations!" one of them fairly sang.

Harper returned the smile. "Thanks."

The two words were repeated over and over as a continuous flow of people passed on their best wishes. Harper's face soon began to ache from smiling. As Knox charmed them all, Harper mostly just sipped from her glass. She had to admit, her mind occasionally drifted, especially when any of them tried chatting business. Hell, even watching champagne bubbles rise in the flutes was more entertaining than that at times.

Of course, the boredom was often alleviated by those people who—just as she'd predicted—had some "advice" to impart. Some were nice about it and seemed to mean well. Others spoke with a smugly omniscient voice that grated on her nerves and pissed off her demon. By the sheer force of her will, Harper had held her smile in place and accepted their wisdom with a nod.

As he'd promised, Tanner stepped in when it became too awkward. Thankfully, no one tried touching her stomach, because she wouldn't have been able to bite back any snarky remarks if they had.

The whole thing might have been easier if it wasn't so damn hot. Knox must have sensed that it was getting too much, because he moved her to stand directly beneath one of the ceiling fans. She gave him a grateful smile ... and then people once more appeared at their side. Again, Harper mostly stayed silent and just sipped from her glass.

"Here," said Larkin. She exchanged Harper's nearly empty glass of water for another. The ice cubes tinkled against the deliciously cold champagne flute.

Harper eagerly sipped from it, and a cube of ice bumped her lip. "You're a gem."

The harpy smiled. "And you're doing well, considering you're probably screaming inside your head."

Harper couldn't deny it. If it hadn't been for the reassuring pressure of Knox's warm hands, she would have undoubtedly snapped at someone by now. If his fingers weren't splayed on her back, they were cupping her elbow or massaging her nape. Sometimes he kept his arm curled around her waist, as if suspecting that she wanted to bolt—which she did. He also laid the occasional soothing kiss on her temple, palm, hair, or wrist.

Each touch was a reminder that he was there; a reassurance that she was doing fine; and a reward for not complaining. Those touches and kisses also helped keep her demon at ease. It didn't like crowds or mingling any more than Harper did.

At that moment, the concierge appeared and spoke quietly into Knox's ear. He then gave him a helpless shrug and waited patiently.

Sighing, Knox turned to Harper. "I'll be back in just a minute." *You'll be all right?*

"Okay." *I'll be fine. I need to go pee anyway. Too much water.*

Mouth curving into a smile, he kissed her. "I won't be long."

Her demon hissed at the sight of him leaving, feeling abandoned. Harper turned to Larkin. "Restroom?"

The harpy gestured ahead of them. "This way."

Harper followed her, trying not to make eye contact with anyone for fear that they saw it as an invitation to approach. But, sadly, it wasn't enough. Mere steps away from the restroom, a small woman with a beehive appeared in her path. Harper recognized Polly as a regular at the coffeehouse. She was nice enough, but she was also a terrible gossip.

"Congratulations!" said Polly, beaming. "I'm just so happy for you. When is the baby due?"

Harper had been asked that question so many times throughout the night that she found herself grinding her teeth. "I have eight weeks left to go."

"Eight weeks?" Polly's eyes widened. "Really?" She assessed Harper carefully. "Your belly is quite small for someone so far along."

It wasn't a compliment; it was a judgement ... like Harper was deliberately depriving her child of the nutrition it needed or something. At her side, Tanner stiffened, so Harper put a hand on his arm to stay him.

Polly smiled at her again. "I'll bet you're hoping it's a little girl."

Um no, Harper was just hoping the baby was healthy.

"Are you scared about ... you know ... the labor?"

Of course she was, but she'd obviously rather not discuss it with someone who was essentially a stranger.

Polly moved closer and spoke in a low voice. "I won't lie, it's not a walk in the park. I told myself that I wouldn't have any pain relief and I'd do it all natural. But God, the pain! Honey, I don't envy you at all, you poor thing." She patted Harper's hand. "My Aliyah—her head was *huge*—tore me right open until my vagina and anus was just one big hole. I had to have so many stitches, I could hardly walk afterwards. What made it worse was that I lost so much blood, I had to have a transaction."

"A transfusion," Harper corrected.

"That, too. Don't you worry none about putting on weight. Some men ... well, they like a woman with a bit more cushion."

Harper forced a smile. "That is a comfort. Now I don't mean to be rude, but I need to use the restroom."

"Oh, of course, I apologize for keeping you."

"Have a good evening." Harper raced to the door. Tanner then leaned his back against the wall, on guard, as she and Larkin headed inside. Larkin entered first, and she'd only taken three steps when she came to an abrupt halt. "Well, well, well. I didn't expect to see you here."

Harper peered around her, and inwardly cursed as she saw Carla leaning over the sink, chest heaving. Her demon hissed, wanting to claw the bitch. Carla stood upright, her movements stiff and awkward, eyes flaring.

In all the times she'd come across Carla over the years, Harper hadn't seen the woman experience any real depth of emotion. Oh, she'd seen flashes of feelings such as irritation or anxiety in Carla's eyes, but nothing *deep*. Right then, however, Carla was seething. And that, Harper thought, was bad. A narcissist in a rage was an irrational creature ... though perhaps not as irrational as a she-demon that had an unborn child to protect.

Not wanting to appear as though she was cowering behind the sentinel, Harper moved to Larkin's side. The harpy went rigid, not liking it, but she didn't argue. Harper was their Prime; it was her right to deal with whatever came next. She was about to advise Carla to scamper when she spoke.

"I came because I needed to know if you'd found out something about the *real* Horsemen—I want my son's name cleared. Imagine my fucking surprise when I heard that you're ... " Carla cut off, as if the sentence would be too hard to finish.

Larkin jutted out her chin. "You should leave." It wasn't a suggestion.

Carla gave a mocking smile. "But I should be part of the celebrations, right? I'll be a grandmother," she said bitterly.

Larkin arched a brow. "How can you be a grandmother when you're not even a mother?"

Carla flushed, and her gaze cut to Harper. "Nothing to say?" She huffed. "Well, that's a first."

"Larkin's right," said Harper, tone flat. "You need to leave." Harper might not have particularly wanted to make a public announcement, but she sure didn't want anyone spoiling the evening.

Fingers flexing, Carla crossed to Harper. "You took my baby from me." Her lips trembled and then pressed into a flat line. "How is it fair that you now get to have your own?"

Fair? The woman wanted to talk about "fair"?

"And I was your baby once," began Harper, "but you gave me away—you *sold* me . . . but that was only after aborting me and trapping my soul in a jar didn't work. So, with all that in mind, how is it fair that *you* would think to judge me for *anything*?"

Carla scowled. There was no flicker of guilt, no ounce of regret, just sheer fury. "Roan—"

"This isn't about him," Harper scoffed, voice hoarse as she fought her demon from surfacing. "Oh, I'm not denying that you're upset by his death—he was your son, you cared about him in your way. But this isn't why you're standing here, shaking with rage. No. You're pissed because you wanted the lair to turn against me for killing Roan, but they didn't."

Carla's eyes flickered.

"You want, as the grieving mother, to be the center of attention, but you're not. For you, that's hell in its purest form." Because Carla needed attention like she needed to breathe—it gave her a feeling of worth that nothing else ever would. "Especially since the person getting the attention you desperately want is me—someone who sees right through your bullshit. Isn't that right, *Mother*?"

Just as the concierge had said, Malden and one of his sentinels were waiting near the boardroom where Knox had held a meeting with the Primes only weeks ago. He gave Knox and Levi a courteous nod, lines of strain marking his face. "Knox, I'm sorry if I've disturbed anything. I heard you were here and hoped I might have the chance to speak with you. It's important."

"All right." Knox swiped his key in the door lock and opened it, allowing all four of them to slip inside the boardroom. Closing the door, he turned to Malden. "What can I help you with?"

Malden hesitated. "I've been arguing with myself for weeks about whether or not to tell you this."

Knox's brows lifted. "Tell me what?"

Again, Malden hesitated. "I know what Jonas wants from Lucifer."

Knox hid his surprise. "Go on."

Malden sighed, looking sad. "I've known Jonas a long time. I've always respected him as a person and a fellow Prime. We often have dinner together at each other's homes. A few months ago, we had dinner and drank a little too much hard liquor. We got to talking about the Horsemen. Like Thatcher, Jonas is not convinced that they're real. He said no one would be stupid enough to go up against you without having the kind of back-up that you could never hope to fight. I'll admit, I thought he made a valid point."

"What else did he say?"

"He said a lot of things—not all of them made sense. Like I told you, we were drunk. He talked about how tired he was of conspiracies and bullies and people always hungry for power. He said he could understand why some might be prepared to make a deal with Lucifer; said that he himself was tempted. I was shocked."

Impatient, Knox asked bluntly, "What does he want from Lucifer?"

"An archdemon."

Everything inside Knox stilled, but he didn't betray his shock. He and his demon studied Malden closely. Had the Prime guessed what he was? Had he come here with a bullshit story to test Knox's response to the mention of his kind? Knox didn't believe so, but he wasn't ready to dismiss the idea. "An archdemon?" he echoed flatly.

"You can understand why, can't you? Archdemons are cruel, brutal, pitiless. They can't be harmed by the flames of hell because they *are* the flames of hell. But I remember how the rogue archdemon nearly destroyed the world. I believe in the old adage that what's born in hell should stay in hell. I told him that. He said that I was right. Said that it would take a deal with Lucifer to have possession of an archdemon anyway, and that he had nothing that the devil could possibly want. But what if he has thought of something that Lucifer could want? After all, why else would he request a meeting with him?"

Knox folded his arms. "Have you talked to Jonas about it?"

"Yes. After the boardroom meeting, I went to his house. I asked him if he had something to do with what happened to Harper and her cousin. He denied any involvement in it. But he admitted that, yes, he was prepared to make a deal with the devil. However, he wouldn't tell me what it is that he's prepared to give Lucifer. He said that it would never happen anyway, so what did it matter?"

Knox narrowed his eyes. "Why didn't you come to me with this straight away?"

"You went on vacation." Malden sighed, admitting, "And I struggled with the idea of betraying someone who's been a friend to me all my life. I shall be honest with you, this is not me showing my loyalty to you. This is me being concerned that my friend is going to do something very stupid that leads to his own death. You talk to Lucifer. I am hoping you will ask him to turn down whatever offer Jonas makes him."

"I won't need to," said Knox. "Lucifer has no interest in Jonas or any other Prime."

Malden's shoulders relaxed a fraction. "That is good to hear. I hope it will remain that way, for all our sakes. Whatever you are, Knox, I doubt even you would be a match for an archdemon." With that comment, he signaled for his sentinel to follow him out of the room.

Once they were gone, Levi raised his brows. "For a minute there, I thought he suspected what you were and he was here to test his theory."

"So did I," said Knox. "But I think he's telling the truth. For some reason, Jonas wants an archdemon. I'd like to know what that reason is, and if it's at all related to what's been happening to and around Harper."

Knox, said Tanner, voice brisk. *I went to check on Harper in the restrooms, since she was taking a while. It turns out that she's having a verbal standoff with Carla.*

He swore, and his demon went ape-shit. *I'll be right there.* "Carla's here."

Levi's face hardened. "Tell me the bitch is nowhere near Harper."

Knox wished he could. Storming out of the room, he locked it with a swipe of his key card and headed for the ballroom. He reached out to Larkin. *Why am I hearing from Tanner that Carla's confronting Harper?*

Harper's co-Prime, Knox, replied Larkin. *She has every right to put one of her lair in their place.* It was a gentle, respectful reminder. *If I thought she needed my protection, I'd jump in.*

"She'll be all right, Knox," said Levi, hot on his heels.

"She'd better be." Knox pushed open the ballroom door and went straight to the women's restrooms. He shoved open the door in time to hear Harper say, "Isn't that right, *Mother?*"

Unwilling to give Carla the satisfaction of seeing just how infuriated she'd managed to make him, Knox hid his rage behind a blank mask as he stalked inside. No one said a word. Tanner and Larkin, who were stood slightly behind Harper, gave him a respectful nod as they moved aside to let him pass. Carla's gaze skipped to his, and he was surprised by just how much anger blazed there.

Harper didn't react at all to his presence. She hadn't moved an inch, and her stare remained fixed on Carla. His demon respected that. But it also wanted Harper to move very far away from the threat in front of her.

Knox sidled up to Harper, glaring down at the she-demon who'd birthed her yet was nothing at all like her. "And just why are you here?" Even he heard the lethal note in his tone.

Carla's mouth tightened. "I have every right to be here."

"Do you?" he drawled.

"I have three more weeks—"

"No, you don't. As of this moment, you are no longer part of this lair."

Shock flashed across her face. "What?"

"I'm unsure why you're so surprised. This is the second time you've confronted one of your Primes. That level of disrespect isn't tolerated by this lair. As Harper's mate, I'll *never* tolerate it. Consider yourself lucky that you're not being punished before being cast out. Not that I'm taking pity on you. No, I just refuse to waste any of my time or attention on *you*." His demon surfaced, delighting in the way she paled and cowered. "Leave," it ordered. "Never bother what's mine again."

Fists clenched, Carla hurried out of the room with her head held high.

Knox's demon signaled for both sentinels to leave, but they lingered, clearly worried for Harper.

"I'll be fine," she assured them. When the door closed behind the sentinels, she turned to the demon and held up her hand. "Don't tell me I should have called for you and Knox. I wasn't in physical danger, and I had Larkin with me."

"Not in physical danger," it allowed. "But the child needs you relaxed, not stressed. Luckily, it is sleeping."

Harper tilted her head. "How do you know that?" Demons could touch each other's minds, sure, and they could even pick up surface vibes of emotion, but that was all. Even anchor bonds weren't invasive—it wasn't possible to sense emotions, pick up private thoughts, or know if the other was sleeping ... yet the demon before her claimed to know something it not only shouldn't, but that *she* didn't know.

"I know plenty," it told her. "Be more alert and cautious, little sphinx. The child will not respond well to you hurting."

Harper's stomach dropped. "What does that mean?" Because it sounded like a warning.

"It is best that you have no cause to find out." It skimmed its thumb along her jaw. "I don't like the smell of your fear."

"I don't fear you." But his words ... yeah, they were freaking her out.

Its black eyes softened ever so slightly. "No, you don't." It kissed her hard and long, hand clasping her nape possessively. Finally, it retreated. She swallowed as she looked up at Knox. "What did it mean, Knox?"

Hearing the tremble in her voice, he pulled her close and kissed her hair. "Ssh."

She grabbed his arms. "*What did it mean?*"

Knox's jaw clenched. "It's not sharing the answer with me."

Confused, she shook her head. "Why would it keep things from you?"

"It thinks that we're not ready to know."

Harper's breath caught in her throat, and her demon felt the urge to slap his demon *seriously* hard. She put a hand to her chest. "I really don't like the sound of that."

Knox couldn't say he much liked the sound of it either. "The demon might simply have been trying to scare you into being more careful."

Maybe, Harper thought. But the demon claimed not to like the smell of her fear, and she couldn't imagine it deliberately frightening her. Still, it was the answer that made the most sense, because there was literally no fucking way that the demon should have an invasive bond with the baby. "Can we go home now?"

"Yes, we can go home."

CHAPTER SIXTEEN

——————◦◦◦——————

Knox was buttoning his shirt a few days later when Harper walked into the closet, streaks of lemon paint on her face and clothes. She looked so damn cute that he had to smile. Then he noticed she was carrying a hamper. "What's that you have there, baby?"

"It's a gift basket from Lou." She held up a card that read, 'Some stuff for Baby L.' "I found it on the dining room table."

It was the third gift that Lou had sent. Knox sighed. "I'm not sure there's any way to get him to stop."

Harper pulled out little white hats, booties, bodysuits, mittens, and sleepsuits from the basket. As she unfolded one particular bodysuit, she sighed and then turned it to face him. It read, '*This* Baby Got Back.'

His mouth quirked in spite of his annoyance. As she put down the hamper, Knox pulled her close and breathed in her scent. "I missed you." He kissed her, licking into her mouth, enjoying her taste. He'd been in his office most of the night while Harper enjoyed a visit from Jolene, Martina, and Beck. His demon had been an absolute pain in the ass the whole time because it didn't like not being near her.

Harper let out a little grunt and put a hand to the side of her rounded stomach. "This kid sure can kick."

Knox smiled. "Did you think there was any chance that you and I would produce a docile baby?"

"I guess not."

He replaced her hand with his, feeling a thud. "Personally, I think it's protesting that you want to leave the house," he joked. He'd hoped to visit the Sanders and McCauley without her, but he hadn't expected her to stay behind.

Harper's jaw set. "I'm coming with you. Deal with it, Thorne. If it makes you feel any better, the stuff I ordered for the nursery will be delivered tomorrow. That means I'll be pretty busy over the next couple of days, so you won't have to worry about me leaving the house."

On the one hand, that did make him feel better. On the other hand . . . "I don't want you to feel confined or suffocated."

"So far, I don't."

"Good." Looking at the streaks of paint on her face, he smiled. "You have no idea how cute you look right now." He kissed her again, ending it with a bite to her lower lip. "Finished painting?"

"There's a little left to do. Keenan's agreed to finish it for me while we go visit the Sanders." She rubbed Knox's upper arms. "I need to take a quick shower."

"If I wasn't almost dressed, I'd shower with you."

She smiled and pressed a kiss to his throat. "I won't be long."

It was no more than an hour later that they pulled up outside the Sanders' house. Like last time, both Levi and Tanner decided to accompany them inside. Wyatt opened the door, looking weary and resigned. He'd clearly been expecting them.

Having led them into the kitchen, he said, "Congratulations on the pregnancy."

"Thank you," said Harper.

"We heard what happened to Pamela and Rupert." Muttering a curse, Wyatt scrubbed a hand down his face. "I saw the crime scene photos. It was bad. Look, I'm guessing you suspect McCauley of being involved and I'm not surprised. If they'd died from a house fire, I'd suspect him too. But stabbing them to death?" Wyatt shook his head. "He's just a boy."

"You're right, he is," said Knox, positioning himself close to Harper—protective and possessive. His demon didn't like her being around these people, and it watched Wyatt as it would a cobra.

"But . . . ?"

"But it's odd that the family seems to be dropping like flies."

Harper absentmindedly put a protective hand on her stomach. "How's he been?"

"No different." Wyatt sighed. "Linda dotes on him, but she gets no thanks for it."

"Where is Linda?" Harper glanced at the doorway.

"In the backyard, hanging up the laundry. She doesn't know you're here yet."

"Somebody does." Harper tipped her chin toward the doorway, where McCauley's shadow could be seen, plain as day. "You might as well come in, kid."

The boy slowly entered the room, his movements mechanical.

Knox turned to face him, still staying close to Harper. "Hello, McCauley."

"Hello," he said simply. He looked up at Wyatt. "May I have a drink of water, please?"

Harper almost shuddered. He was so polite it was actually freaky.

Wyatt's smile was forced. "Sure." As Wyatt filled a glass with water, McCauley turned to Harper.

She felt his mind brush against hers and narrowed her eyes. "That was very rude." Demons might be tactile, but they were fussy about who had the permission to touch them, whether physically or psychically. That was largely why her own demon was *pissed*.

What did he do? Knox asked.

Touched my mind. As Knox went rigid beside her, she curled her hand around his arm. *Don't give him a reaction.* "You should be careful," she told McCauley. "A lot of demons would retaliate big time over something like that."

The kid seemed completely unaffected by her warning. "You won't hurt me."

Harper arched a brow. "You sure about that?"

"You won't," he stated confidently. "But your child will."

The words chilled her blood, but she didn't jump to the baby's defense, curious if that was what the little cambion wanted. Her demon bared its teeth—it didn't like the boy one teensy, weensy bit.

He took the glass of water from Wyatt. "Thank you."

Knox spoke before McCauley could turn to leave. "I came to tell you that, unfortunately, Pamela and Rupert won't be coming back to see you."

"I know, sir. Linda and Wyatt told me that they're dead."

Knox tilted his head. "You must be very upset to hear they're gone."

The boy nodded, then turned back to Harper. "Are you going to give your baby away?"

She shook her head. "No."

"Even though it's bad?"

"The baby isn't bad," she told him.

"My demon says it is."

"I'll bet your demon says everyone's bad," she said. "It doesn't want to share you. Does it want to hurt the people who are good to you? Does it get jealous?"

McCauley didn't answer, but his shoulders stiffened.

"Was it jealous of your relationship with Pamela and Rupert?" she asked.

"Of course not," he said, tone flat. "Why would it be?"

Harper exchanged a look with Knox. *At first, I thought he and the demon wanted revenge,* she told Knox. *What if the demon just wants rid of any competition to its parental role?*

At that moment, Linda walked into the room carrying a laundry basket. She'd obviously heard their voices, because she didn't look surprised to see them. Her smile of greeting was strained. "McCauley, why don't you go on upstairs?"

With one last look at Harper, he turned and left the room as robotically as he'd entered. Only once they'd heard his bedroom door close did Linda speak again.

"I suppose a 'congratulations' is in order." Envy was stamped all over her face as she stared at Harper's baby bump. Before anyone could thank her, Linda quickly added, "I'm guessing you're here about the Winters." She placed the basket on the table. "Stabbed to death in their own home . . . Awful. Tragic." She swallowed. "McCauley already knows. We told him. It's sad that he won't have his biological family in his life."

"Is it?" asked Knox.

Linda's attention snapped to him. "Of course."

He twisted his mouth. "You had no problems with him building a relationship with Pamela and Rupert?"

Linda tugged on her sweater. "I won't deny that I'd like to keep McCauley here, but I wouldn't begrudge him a relationship with the Winters."

"Then why did you offer them money to stay away from him?" Knox sensed Wyatt's surprise, but he kept his eyes on Linda.

She spluttered. "I did no such thing."

"I have a witness that says you did."

Realization flashed across her face. "Daniel is mistaken. It wasn't like that."

"You *didn't* try to bribe them?"

"It was a test. I wanted to know if they wanted him in their lives for the right reason. Pamela turned down my offer, and I apologized for making it." She gestured to the doorway. "So, if that's all—"

"Don't *ever* dare dismiss me, Linda," Knox clipped. The woman blanched, but it didn't appease his demon at all.

Wyatt straightened, reflexively bristling, but he was wise enough not to interfere.

"You've overstepped a few times since McCauley came to stay here," Knox added. "They were minor slips, so I overlooked them. It appears that I shouldn't have."

Linda's eyes darted from Knox to Wyatt and back again, but her mate didn't speak up for her. "I'm sorry. Truly. I'm just a little emotional right now. He's just a boy. I want to protect him, as any mother should—biological or adopted."

"I never once led you to believe that McCauley would stay here permanently."

Her mouth fell open in surprise. "He's happy here."

"Happy?" echoed Harper, frowning. "What makes you think so?"

Linda licked her lips. "He's settled. He's content. Tell them, Wyatt." But Wyatt didn't. He looked at the floor, clearly knowing better than to lie to his Primes.

Knox stared at Linda. "You truly believe that you have a bond with McCauley?"

"It was slow coming but, yes, I believe we're starting to connect."

"Then you're in danger. Surely you've noticed that McCauley's behavior is not normal." Seeing that she was about to object, Knox snapped, "Don't try bullshitting me, Linda. Open your fucking eyes. He is nothing like your average child, not even a traumatized child."

"He has trouble connecting with others, yes, but should we really expect anything else? His biological mother gave him away, and his human mother both neglected and tried to kill him."

"Yes, neither of his mothers were there for him," said Knox. "From what I understand, his human father was no better. So, taking into account the behavior he displays, who do think stepped in and raised him?"

The implication sank in, and Linda shook her head sadly.

"Maybe you're right and McCauley isn't dangerous, but his demon is. And I think his demon wants rid of anyone it believes is a threat to its parental role. You and Wyatt are threats."

She wrapped her arms around herself. "But he hasn't tried to hurt us."

"Really? Not once."

Her eyes slid away. "They were accidents."

"He burned her hand with hellfire when she tried to stroke his hair," Wyatt said. "He shoved her hard when she once tried to kiss him. Just yesterday, she tumbled down the stairs mere moments after he growled at her to get out of his room."

"It was his demon, not him," Linda insisted.

"Which supports my point." Knox stepped forward. "You want a child, Linda? There are plenty out there who need a home and would accept and return the love you have to offer. McCauley can't be that child for you. If you were honest, you would admit that you don't love him; you love the idea of having a child."

Squeezing her eyes closed, Linda said nothing. Finally, she opened them. The denial had been replaced by a sad acceptance. "Where will you take him?"

"It's best that you don't know that," Harper told her.

Flicking a look at Harper's rounded stomach, she said, "If he's really a danger, I don't think it would be a good idea for him to stay with you."

No, neither did Harper. "He won't be staying with us."

Linda swallowed. "I'll go to him, explain what's happening, and pack him a bag."

Knox nodded. "Go with her, Wyatt."

"No, please, I'd like some private time with him to say goodbye."

Knox inclined his head, and she scurried out the room.

Harper's brow pinched as she sensed Knox telepathically chatting with someone. When it seemed to have ended, she asked, *Who was that?*

Larkin, Knox replied. *I was checking that she was nearly here. We need her to give McCauley a ride to his new home.* Knox didn't want the cambion around Harper.

Wyatt rubbed at his forehead. "I know this is the right thing to do for everyone, so why do I feel like a bastard?"

"Because he's six years old," said Harper. "And you have a heart."

It was a good ten minutes before Linda and McCauley returned to the kitchen. Linda appeared hesitant and sad. McCauley seemed to be completely unaffected.

Wyatt crouched down to him. "Hey, buddy. It's a real shame that you have to leave. If you tell us that you're happy here, we can sort something out and you can stay." But McCauley didn't say a word, so Wyatt nodded and added, "Wherever you go, take some time to decide whether you'd like to come back here. You'll be welcome if you do. Take care of yourself."

Linda helped the boy slip on his coat and then handed a rucksack to Knox. "Here's his bag. I packed some clothes and things."

"Thank you," said Knox. "I'm sorry it has to be this way, but it's necessary."

Linda rubbed her arm. "I know, I just wish it wasn't."

Knox gestured for Levi to leave the house first. McCauley easily followed the sentinel outside without even a backward look at Linda or Wyatt. Linking his fingers with Harper's, Knox led her down the path with Tanner close behind them.

Larkin was stood near an SUV where a few members of the force were waiting, having responded to Knox's summons. *Is everything all right?* she asked.

Yes. I need you to take McCauley to Elena and Andre's house. They're expecting him. Knox then turned to McCauley. "This is Larkin, one of my sentinels. She will take you to a house not far from here. It's a place where many children stay who have no family to care for them. You'll have your own room, and you'll be safe there. Harper and I will keep an eye on you, make sure things are going well for you. Does that sound good?"

"Yes, sir," replied McCauley with no emotion whatsoever.

"You'll only be brought back here if you decide that it's what you want." Knox wanted McCauley and his demon to understand that Linda and Wyatt wouldn't push for him to return, just in case the demon viewed them as a threat.

McCauley nodded and then hopped into the SUV with Larkin.

Harper waved to McCauley as the SUV drove away, and he gave her the slightest wave. She turned to Knox. "You arranged this with Elena and Andre in advance?"

Knox nodded. "When you pointed out that the demon could be eliminating threats to its role, I knew I had to get him out of there."

"You think he'll be okay with them?"

"Neither Elena or Andre will try to 'parent' him, so the demon shouldn't see them as competition. They're used to difficult children, and they're both powerful enough to ensure that McCauley causes no harm to himself or anyone there." Knox waited until they were inside the Bentley before he added, "He touched your mind?"

"Yeah. It wasn't a shy touch, either. It was bold, deliberately rude."

"As if he was provoking you?"

"I got the feeling it was more like he was testing me." But Harper had no idea what the test was supposed to be.

"His demon thinks you won't harm him."

Harper snorted. "It's wrong. If the kid was any threat to me or mine, I'd disable him, no matter what it took. Considering I have an unborn child to protect, no one would blame me for it." Not even Lou, despite his law that no child of any species should be hurt.

Knox laid a hand on her stomach. "Our child isn't bad."

"I know that, but McCauley's demon seems determined to make him believe that everyone around him is a threat."

"Except you," Knox pointed out. "It told him that you wouldn't hurt him. Why?"

"I don't know."

As Levi began to drive, Knox's phone chimed. His conversation was short and sweet—one he felt like he'd had a dozen times over the past few days. "That was Mila," he told Harper as he ended the call and tucked his phone back in his pocket. "Many of the Primes have called to pass on their congratulations. In most cases, they're just courtesy calls really. But some sounded genuinely pleased for us."

That surprised her. "Like who?"

"Dario, Raul, Malden, even Thatcher. But, like all the others, they also sounded a little rattled by the news."

That *didn't* surprise her. "We knew they wouldn't like the idea that there might soon be another being that's as powerful as you. There's nothing to say that our baby *will* be, but I doubt they'll take comfort in that." She rolled back her shoulders. "I'm nervous now that I know how widespread the news is. Have you heard from Jonas?"

"Yes. He also congratulated us, but his message was stiff and formal."

"I doubt Alethea will be pleased." Ha.

"She may not care. She's had a long time to adjust to the idea of you and I together. She may be impulsive and petty, but she's not stupid. She knows that I see you as mine and that I have no intention of letting you go—the fact that I gave you a black diamond spells it out loud and clear for her. Personally, I think the only reason she still flirts with me is just to upset you."

"I'd agree with that," said Levi.

Harper frowned at the reaper. "Eavesdropping, are we?"

Levi ignored that. "One thing Alethea was never good at was letting go of an insult. I don't mean the sarcastic insults you like to shower her with. I'm talking slights to her character or ego." He paused to take a sharp turn. "You already know that Knox's demon quickly got bored with females in the past. He warned them it would happen, but most still caused a fuss over it. Alethea didn't get upset that he didn't commit to her. She accepted it. *But* that was because Knox didn't commit to others either.

"Then you came along and he claimed you in a matter of

months. Alethea had known him for *centuries*. To her, you're an imp, a Wallis, someone completely beneath her. She can't understand why he could possibly want you when he could have her. Knox giving you something he'd never given to her—especially the ultimate commitment—is something she feels insulted by. She's tried to intimidate and manipulate you into leaving him, but nothing ever worked. That only makes it worse for her."

"So you don't think she wants Knox?" Harper wasn't so sure she agreed with that.

"I think she wants him," said Tanner. "But I think she also knows it's not going to happen. Still, that doesn't mean she'll ever accept you as his mate. She'll hurt you however she can just because it makes her feel better."

Harper thought about it a minute. "It's like she entered us into some kind of imaginary competition. Knox wasn't really the prize, though, was he?"

Knox sighed. "I'm right here, you know."

Levi's mouth quirked, but he responded to Harper's question. "No. She might have 'won' Knox, but the real prize was that she'd then feel like the goddess she believes herself to be. Alethea's kind can enchant and seduce any human. That's why she spends so much time around them—it makes her feel powerful to be the object of so many fantasies, to be able to manipulate and control people that way. For her, the ability to make any man want her equates to power."

Tanner nodded and threw Harper a brief look over his shoulder. "She's not used to being turned down. It makes her feel like she's without that power that she's become so used to. But Knox chose you, not her. You took away her power, you made her feel weak—just as it would make you feel weak if she took away your ability to fly or strike out at people with soul-deep pain. She'll never let that go."

Harper tossed Knox a look of irritation. "Did you really have to shake the sheets with such a fucking egotistical nut job?"

Knox chuckled. "I sincerely regret it, and I'm sorry that she tries so hard to hurt you. I'd offer to kill her, but you'd just tell me that you would rather deal with the matter yourself." He pressed a soft, apologetic kiss to her mouth. "Forget about her. She's not important. Never was."

Tanner grinned. "Aw, that was cute."

Knox shot him a scowl. "It's really no wonder that Devon wants to kill you."

Tanner's grin widened. "The little hellcat wouldn't do that."

Harper snorted. "You persist in believing she's some cute little kitty that you could easily handle. One day, that attitude's going to come back and claw you on the ass—literally."

That didn't seem to bother Tanner at all. In fact, he looked like he'd enjoy it.

Twisted.

CHAPTER SEVENTEEN

———— ❧ ————

Leaning against the doorjamb of Knox's home office a week later, Harper waited as he finished his call. He'd begun to spend more and more time at the mansion, doing meetings via teleconference whenever he could. She knew it was because his protective instincts were becoming harder to deal with, and she was guessing that his demon was also more at ease when she was around. Her own demon certainly preferred being at home and having Knox nearby.

As he finally ended the call, she arched a brow. "You busy?" He didn't just stand; he sort of . . . gracefully uncoiled from his seat, and she had no idea why she liked that so much.

"Never too busy for you. You know that," said Knox. The baby's mind lightly touched his—it often responded to his voice that way, and it got to him every time. Rounding his desk, Knox tilted his head, tension mounting inside him as he took in her nervous expression. "Something wrong?"

"No. I just have something to show you."

He smiled as realization dawned on him, and the tension in his muscles fell away. "You're finally letting me see it?"

She pushed away from the doorjamb. "Yes. It's ready."

Knox draped his arm over her shoulders. "Lead the way." She hadn't let him in the nursery even once since she'd began painting it, wanting it to be a surprise. She'd let him do a few things, such as assemble the pretty dragonfly mobile—and he suspected that was because she wanted to be sure he felt involved to some extent—but that was pretty much it.

He hadn't complained. He'd sensed that she'd made it her project and that designing it meant something to her. Since he wanted her happy, and since Meg had explained that it was a "nesting" instinct that was perfectly natural, he'd given Harper that.

Once they reached the closed door of the nursery, she said, "Don't forget; if there's anything you don't like, we can change it."

"I'm sure I'll like it just fine." Twisting the knob, Knox pushed open the door ... and his mouth almost fell open. Damn, the woman had been busy, and her hard work had paid off.

He walked silently along the plush, cream carpet and skimmed his hand over the side of the crib. Like the dresser, changing table, and rocking chair, it was a light, smooth pine. Woodland murals decorated the lemon walls and closet doors, matching the woodland-themed quilt. The most striking artwork was the large, white, tree mural that spanned from floor to ceiling.

The pine shelves were lined with the gifts she'd been given at the baby shower—stuffed animals, baby monitors, and a photo frame that held the baby's first ultrasound picture. A diaper pail and baby chair, both of which were also gifts from the baby shower, sat in the corner.

The breeze coming through the open window fluttered the

white curtains and jingled the dragonfly mobile that hung over the crib. The room felt bright and airy, especially with so much natural light. When the sun shone on the lemon walls, they turned into a deeper, sunbeam shade. She'd created a warm, serene space that was as inviting as it was cozy. He was now extremely glad he'd accepted her request to leave the whole thing to her.

"I was startled when the delivery guys assembled the furniture before they left," she said. "I'm used to flatpacks." Still, it had taken Harper a week to get the room exactly the way she wanted it. She'd bet Tanner and Keenan were ecstatic that the manual labor was over, because she'd really put them to work. "Well, what do you think?" He turned to face her, and the pride on his face warmed her.

"I think you did an amazing job." Knox placed his hands on her shoulders. "And I think you made the best decision when you chose to design it yourself."

She smiled, relieved. "I'm glad you like it."

He cocked his head. "You were worried that I wouldn't?"

"Well, you're a very selective guy. Hard to please, in many ways."

He breezed his mouth over hers. "It's never hard for you to please me. Really, I love what you've done with the room, and I think the baby will love it too. I meant to ask, why the dragonfly mobile? I like it. I'm just curious."

"For the same reason that I got the tattoo of one on my nape. I admire them—despite having a short lifespan and being very delicate, they don't let either hold them back. Plus, they're master fliers. Any sphinx would love to be a master flier." And she wanted that for the baby; was a little worried that, like her, its wings wouldn't come to it naturally.

"Ah, I get it." Knox gestured at the box and bag near the closet. "I see that you have everything ready."

"Yep. All we have to do on the big day is take it downstairs to the living room." She'd chosen to have a home birth, which wasn't uncommon for demons. She liked the idea of being in her own home, a familiar place where she felt comfortable, relaxed, and safe, while she went through what would no doubt be a hell of an experience.

Her main reason for choosing a home birth, however, was that she wouldn't feel safe in a hospital. It would be a time when she was vulnerable, when Knox was distracted, and when the baby wouldn't be all that difficult to get to—no matter how many precautions were taken. As such, people might think it was a good time to attack. At home, she and the baby would be a hell of a lot safer.

Everything she needed for the birth was ready in the box, thanks to Meg—old sheets and towels, blankets, and plastic sheeting among other things. Meg had also gotten hold of a portable heater to keep the baby warm—apparently, her daughter had used one and it had been ideal.

Harper had still packed a bag with toiletries and clothes for her and the baby, just in case there were complications and she needed to be transferred to a hospital. It also meant she didn't have to send Knox and Meg on errands to seek out the stuff she wanted during the home birth; all they'd have to do was grab her bag.

Rodgers hadn't advised against a home birth, since the last ultrasound scan had showed that the baby had indeed had a growth spurt. It was no longer smaller than it should be and, in fact, was a little bigger than he'd expected.

"Nervous about the birth?" asked Knox as they left the nursery, closing the door behind them.

She bit her lip. "Yeah. I've read about it, heard countless stories about it, and I'd like to think I'm prepared, but I still have my worries."

Hating that he couldn't fix that for her, Knox said, "I'll help however I can. Tell me what you want and I'll make it happen. Whatever you need me to do, I'll do it."

"I don't need you to do anything complicated. Just be there." If she could feel close and connected to this person who made her feel safe, Harper knew she'd get through it okay.

He rested his forehead against hers. "I will be with you every step of the way, I promise. And speaking of the baby, I have some news. The lair is organizing a parade in the Underground."

Her brow furrowed. "A what?"

"A parade in honor of the baby."

Harper groaned. "Knox, you saw what people were like at the announcement—full of questions, horror stories, and unwanted advice. The further along a woman is in the pregnancy, the worse it is. When Heidi's mom was pregnant, I felt so bad for her. It's like people see a baby bump and forget the existence of etiquette. They commented on everything—her boobs being bigger, the weight she'd gained, her face being plumper, her ankles swelling up."

Knox raked his gaze over her. "I don't mind that your breasts are bigger. The only weight you've really gained is the weight you initially lost. And your face isn't plump. Your ankles don't look swollen either."

"Not the point, Thorne. Heidi's mom gracefully ignored it, but I don't have her easy temperament. I'd rather have the damn baby shower again, and *that's* saying something."

"I thought baby showers were supposed to be relaxing events."

"Not when they're thrown by imps, they're not."

When Jolene had told him that she'd organized a baby shower for Harper, he'd envisaged a relaxing get-together that involved silly games, finger foods, a diaper cake, and lots of oohing and ahhing as the guests sat in a circle watching the mother-to-be open their gifts. But it turned out that an imp baby shower was *nothing* like that.

Although Harper had warned him that it would be a rowdy event, he hadn't realized just what she meant until he'd later pulled up outside Jolene's house to hear "Ice Ice Baby" filtering through the open windows. The imps had a mimosa bar, a DJ, karaoke, and a BBQ going, and everyone other than Harper had been absolutely smashed by the end of it.

Curling his arms around her shoulders, Knox brushed her nose with his. "All right, I'll ask the lair to cancel the parade." He tilted his head when her brow creased. "Why don't you look happy about it?"

"Because part of me now feels guilty and ungrateful. I don't want to offend the lair."

Knox almost chuckled. In her shoes, he wouldn't have felt guilty at all, but Harper had a marshmallow center that meant she'd never be as selfish as he was. "I'd sooner offend our lair by canceling the parade than ask you to do something that you don't want to do."

"Stop being so nice when I'm being so whiny."

"You're not being whiny. Even if you were, I'd say you had every right to be. You're hormonal and heavily pregnant, which is making you feel edgy. No one who's edgy wants to deal with anything that annoys them. You're also feeling hyper-protective of the baby, so it's perfectly natural that you wouldn't want strangers around you—especially strangers who might try touching your stomach." Neither Knox nor his demon liked the idea either.

"You really don't think I'm being stroppy and unreasonable?"

"No, I don't. I'm guessing your demon's just as restless and close to snapping—from what I've heard, that's pretty normal during pregnancy. I just thought you might like to get out of the house. You've worked so hard on the nursery that, aside from attending the baby shower, you haven't been anywhere. You were adamant that staying in the house all the time would make you crazy."

Harper frowned. "I would have thought you'd be happy that I haven't been anywhere."

"I find that I don't like you doing anything that seems out of character for you—it makes me worry. Meg assured me that you were nesting and there was no need for me to be concerned, but I'll always worry about you."

Harper thought about it for a moment. "It might actually be good for me to leave the house and get some air. And it might be best to let everyone see that I'm pregnant and satisfy their curiosity so they're not all staring at me if I need to go to the Underground for any reason."

"It might be," he agreed, careful not to push her either way.

"It bothers me that people might think I'm hiding—that would give whoever's fucking with us a *real* kick. It would also make us look weak." Which was exactly why she hadn't wanted to stay in the villa for long, she reminded herself.

"Personally, I don't much care what other people think. But I do care that people might believe I don't trust in my ability to protect you."

Harper sighed, and her shoulders drooped. "When's the parade scheduled for?"

"A week's time."

And that meant her stomach would be even bigger for the event. Great. "I'll go, but I can't promise I'll last long or that anyone who upsets me will walk away unscathed."

"Don't worry; I don't think anyone will really want to tangle with a pregnant she-demon." Hormonal and intolerant, they didn't deal with bullshit well at all. Harper was impatient with bullshit at the best of times.

"I'm gonna need a new dress."

"Most women wouldn't utter those words with irritation."

"I'm not most women. I'm also not in the mood to go to the mall. My back hurts and my joints ache."

He gently rubbed her back. "So have Raini pick something up for you, like you did when you needed a dress for the announcement."

Raini was indeed good at choosing outfits for people. Harper wondered if part of the reason the succubus enjoyed choosing pretty clothes for others was that she very rarely bought any for herself.

"Fine," relented Harper, smoothing her hands up his chest. "But I expect a chocolate reward of some kind."

"I can arrange that." He gave her a quick kiss. "Tomorrow." Another kiss. "Now we shower."

"I'd rather play Naked Twister."

He laughed. "Keeping up with your sex drive might kill me."

"There are worse ways to die."

There were indeed. "You know what I just realized?"

A shiver worked through Harper at the sound of his "sex voice". It was all dark, dominant, and hypnotic. "What?"

He scraped his teeth over her earlobe. "We haven't christened the closet."

Harper swallowed. "That's a bad oversight on our part. Terrible, even. I'm thinking we should rectify it."

"It wouldn't be right if we didn't." Thrusting his hands into her hair, he kissed her. Licked into her mouth. Sucked on her tongue. Bit at her lip. Took and tasted and dominated. All the while, he was backing her into their room and then through to the closet. Stopping near the sofa, he said, "I want what's under these clothes. Take them off."

A little dazed by that hot, heavy kiss, Harper nonetheless

managed to shed her clothes without stumbling or losing her balance. She was rather chuffed with herself for that. "This is the part where you get naked too."

He skimmed his knuckles down the column of her throat. "There's something I like about you being naked while I'm fully clothed. I don't know what it is." He closed his hand around her breast, squeezing it just the way she liked. She arched into him, gripping his arms. "I'm going to fuck you, Harper. I want you to come hard for me. Want you to feel my cock throbbing inside you. Want you to feel my come shooting deep in you. But first, I want to watch you suck my cock." He tipped his chin at the black leather sofa behind her. "Sit."

Well now. Engines revving like crazy, Harper backed into the sofa and sat.

Knox moved to her. Without being asked, she undid his fly—not quickly and clumsily, but slowly and deftly. His cock sprang out, but she didn't move. She waited for his direction. He slid his fingers through her hair. "You can be such a good girl when you want to be, can't you?"

Harper smiled. Oh, she could be a very, very good girl. It just didn't happen often.

Bunching her hair in his hands, Knox tugged. "Open for me." She did, and he thrust into her hot mouth. "Suck hard. That's it." He didn't need to tell her what to do or how to do it. She knew exactly what he liked and exactly how he liked it. And she gave it to him. Danced her tongue around his cock. Sucked hard enough to make her cheeks hollow. Swallowed so that he felt her throat contract around him.

Using his grip on her hair to hold her still, he took over and fucked her mouth. She didn't object, didn't fight him. Didn't move other than to drag her nails down the back of his thighs. He felt the telling tingle at the base of his spine and knew he had to stop. Pulling out of her mouth, he snatched her head back and traced her swollen lips with his finger. "How wet are you?"

"Why don't you find out for yourself?"

"I think I will. Up." He helped her stand and kissed along her neck. "I want to know how wet you are. Show me."

Understanding, Harper dipped her finger inside her and then held it up to him. Eyes locked with hers, he took the glistening finger into his mouth and sucked it clean. She licked her bottom lip, watching as the raw need in his dark eyes flared. God, she hoped he didn't start teasing her. Since reaching the last stage of the pregnancy, she'd had a quicker trigger than usual. Right then, she needed to be fucked. Not teased. Not toyed with. Fucked.

"Kneel on the sofa and hold onto the back."

Doing a happy dance in her head, Harper turned and did as he'd asked. She let her eyes close as he dragged his tongue up her spine, ending his journey with a nip to her nape. "Knox—" Her mouth fell open in a silent gasp as he sank a finger inside her and swirled it around.

"Soaking wet, exactly how I like you." He twisted her hair into a ponytail, jerked her head back, and drove his cock deep into her pussy. He swore as her walls squeezed him tight and she let out one of those throaty moans that made his balls ache. "I love that sound. Let's see if we can make you do it again." He slowly pulled back and then plunged inside her. "And there it is."

Knox rode her hard. Pumped into her fast and deep, like he'd never get enough. And he never would. Never. He'd always need and crave her, crave *this*. It wouldn't matter if they were together years, decades, centuries—the longing that burned inside him for her would never leave. And he never wanted it to.

As her pussy started to quake around his cock, he stilled and gave a slight tug on her hair. "Not yet. You don't come until I've come, and I'm not ready to leave this pussy yet."

Harper shook her head, sure she couldn't hold on for long. "This is gonna happen with or without you, big guy."

"Wait for me," he rumbled into her ear. He knew she would. Knew she'd hold on if he asked her to. Knew she'd do it just because it pleased him, and he fucking loved that.

Harper hissed as his teeth dug into her neck and he started plowing into her again. Not because the bite hurt, but because she liked the sting of pain and it pricked at the orgasm she was fighting. Each slam of his cock was smooth, sure, and possessive. Every now and then, he'd slow his pace and give a few gentle thrusts, but then he'd resume pumping into her fast and hard— keeping her off balance. "Knox, seriously, I can't fight it."

"But you will." He thrust harder, gritting his teeth as her pussy heated and tightened. His own release came tumbling towards him, and Knox's fingers bit into her hip. Yanking on her hair, he erupted inside her, growling, "Now."

Harper let go of the stranglehold she'd held on her orgasm. The friction within her snapped like an elastic band. Her release blasted through her, violent and intense. She screamed, riding it out until, left with the strength of a noodle, she slumped over her sofa.

Knox kissed the back of her shoulder, enjoying the feel of her pussy fluttering around him as she came down from her orgasm. "You okay?"

"Your cock is awesome."

Startled, he chuckled.

Harper just smiled.

CHAPTER EIGHTEEN

———◆———

Looking out of the floor-to-ceiling window of the penthouse that gave her an incredible view of the Underground, Harper bit her lip. "They really didn't have to do all this."

Knox came up behind her and rested his hands on her stomach as he nuzzled her neck. "The lair's excited for us. They want to show their support."

"Well, they've certainly showed it." There were balloons, streamers, and congratulations banners everywhere. The Underground was *packed*. The sidewalks were crowded with pedestrians that stood shoulder to shoulder behind the ropes. Some balanced children on their shoulders while others encouraged their kids to sit on the curb. A few groups of juveniles had climbed onto the rooftops of the stores, where they could get a better view.

Harper could easily see Raini, Devon, Khloë, and Jolene standing at the front of the line not far from the studio, eating burgers. Martina, Beck, and Ciaran stood behind them, munching on hotdogs. In fact, most of the crowd was eating vender food. The street sweepers were gonna be busy later.

Knox gently turned Harper to face him. "You look beautiful. Raini chose well." He thought the silky, ice-blue dress suited Harper perfectly. "I like that you have your hair down." He loved her hair; loved sifting his fingers through it and feeling it brush over his skin. "And I like that you're wearing the new earrings I bought you." He tapped one of the dangly diamonds.

"They're pretty. Thank you." Harper skimmed her fingers along his smooth jaw, breathing him in. Beneath the scent of his heavenly cologne were the smells of wood wax, fragrant oils, and clean linen. "It's not fair that you can look so mouth-wateringly hot so effortlessly." No hair gel, no fake tan, no cosmetic products of any kind other than cologne—he'd basically just put on one of his tailored suits, briefly combed his hair, slipped on his gleaming shoes, and—bam—he was ready and edible.

Knox's lips curled. "Mouth-wateringly hot? I like that."

"Yeah? I only speak the truth." Really, he was out of her league, but Harper wasn't going to dwell on that. If he said that she was what he wanted, who was she to argue? Still, it would take time for her to get used to his way of life—to all the attention, luxuries, and social power.

Before Knox, she'd never experienced the kind of decadence that he surrounded himself with. The penthouse they stood in was a perfect example. Like the mansion, it was the height of luxury with high ceilings, a marble floor, beautiful paintings, and custom furniture that fit Knox's elegant, masculine style. It didn't just have the usual amenities. No, it also had an office, a gym, and a sauna.

Feeling a particularly sharp kick to the hand he'd rested on the side of her stomach, Knox said, "I can't work out whether that was a greeting or the baby just doesn't like the pressure of my hand." In any case, his demon found it amusing.

"Nah, I think the kid is just trying to kick its way out."

Knox gently massaged her stomach. "It's amazing to think that in just five weeks, we'll be able to hold it." It was a scary yet exhilarating thought, and he was looking forward to it. He was also anxious. He'd heard so many stories of demon births going wrong and he hated the thought of her in pain. Still, he'd never let her see that anxiety—that wasn't what she needed from him. "The time has flown by so fast."

"It has, which is surprising because I expected to feel as if the whole time dragged. You know, I'm also kind of surprised that a being who's as old and sexually active as you are doesn't already have at least one kid."

"I've always been extremely careful to use protection. I don't think I could have trusted anyone other than you to carry and care for my child." His demon certainly couldn't have.

"Don't be sweet. You'll make me cry."

He curled a hand around her chin. "Don't cry. I hate seeing you cry, even when I know it's just hormones at work."

"Then get back to the current matter and distract me."

"Okay. The parade itself won't take long. We'll do a quick lap of the Underground—"

"Tell me we're not riding in a sparkly float," she begged.

He chuckled. "Not a sparkly float. After we've finished the lap, we'll go to the Ice Lounge and relax there for the rest of the celebration. I've no doubt that people will come talk to you, but at least you'll be sitting comfortably and be well-guarded when they do."

"Can Jolene, my family, and the girls meet us there?"

"Yes, I've already put them on the VIP guest list. They should already be in the VIP section by the time we get there."

"Thank you."

"You don't have to thank me. You're mine. I'll always give you what you need." He felt the baby move again. This time, it was as if it rolled beneath his hand. "This little one sure is active tonight."

"Like I said, it wants out."

"In five weeks, it will get its wish." He kissed her and spoke against her mouth, "Love you, baby."

"And I love you." Hearing a ping, Harper twisted to look at the private elevator that was a direct entrance into the suite. The doors slid open, revealing all four sentinels looking smart and alert.

"Everything's in place," Levi told them. "Time to go."

"We're ready." Knox threaded his fingers through hers and led her through the spacious entryway and into the elevator. The sentinels backed against the four walls to make room, all giving them brief nods.

As the shiny metal doors closed behind them, Harper let out a breath. "Looking good, guys." The sentinels each shot her an impatient glance. "Sorry, sorry, you're concentrating on looking scary and unapproachable. Don't worry; you've got that down."

The elevator hummed as they descended. It came to a very smooth halt with a chime, and the doors then slid open once again. Without a word, two sentinels took the lead while the others took up the rear as they all walked through the reception area and out of the automatic doors.

Harper gave a low whistle at the sight she found. Many people were waiting, all dressed up in glitzy costumes. There were acrobats, cheerleaders, stilt walkers, dance troops, and baton and flag twirlers. Even better, there were a bunch of demons on Harley Davidsons. Harper was totally jealous that she couldn't ride one of those . . . right up until she realized that Knox was leading her to a beautiful carriage that was pulled by two white, fine-boned horses.

"Wow," she breathed. Harper inhaled. She loved the smell of horses—hay, wood chips, sunshine, dust, and a hint of leather.

Tanner opened the carriage door and held out his hand. "I'll give you a boost, since you're size-challenged."

"Hey," she playfully whined, allowing him to help her into the carriage. She wasn't at all surprised by the lavish cream-leather interior; Knox always traveled in style.

Knox slid in beside her and arched a brow. "Well?"

"This is pretty awesome," she told him. "I've never been in a horse-drawn carriage before."

"Really? Good. I like to introduce you to new things."

"Well, you massively succeeded." She noticed that the four sentinels flanked the carriage; Levi and Larkin stood on the right while Tanner and Keenan stood on the left. "I'm guessing they'll be guarding us the entire time."

"You guessed correctly. I won't ever take chances with your safety, Harper. The performers are part of our lair, but that doesn't mean I trust them so close to you. Throughout the parade, some of the performers will precede us; the others will follow. That means that, essentially, we're boxed in if there's a threat, which is why the sentinels are here and members of the Force are on patrol."

She wasn't the least bit surprised by how tight his security measures were. "Then you've done all you can do. Let's get this done."

Knox nodded to someone, and then a voice came over the loudspeaker, announcing the beginning of the parade. A big applause rang through the Underground. Then everyone around them began to move.

Harper almost jumped as the marching band roared to life.

The drumbeat seemed to vibrate in her chest as the carriage smoothly pulled onto the strip. There was hooting, whistling, shouting, and laughing. Some threw confetti while others threw candy, snapping pictures with their cell phones.

When the carriage neared the studio, Harper beamed as she caught sight of the girls and her family. Hooting and jumping, they waved like crazy people. Jolene did a very regal wave that made Harper's demon smile.

As the performers and carriage continued down the strip, the members of the Force worked to keep the spectators behind the ropes and ensure that all the performers moved in a timely fashion. All the while, their eyes searched for potential threats.

She leaned into Knox. "Considering I'm nervous, the smells of popcorn, frying onions, and grilled meat shouldn't be making me feel hungry." Her words were almost drowned out by the shouting, the marching band, the clip-clop of the horses' hooves, and the rumble of the Harley engines.

Knox brushed confetti out of her hair. "We'll eat once this is over."

Satisfied by that, Harper carried on waving as the parade went on. Her face actually hurt from fixing a smile on it as they passed what seemed like a never-ending row of bars, restaurants, stores, coffeehouses, hotels, and casinos. People waved from their hotel balconies, and some even dangled cotton "congratulations" banners. Harper waved back, which felt totally weird but it would have been rude not to.

With all the noise, the sparkly costumes, and the delicious scents of vender food, it was a sensory overload—her demon was impatient to get it over and done with. Harper suspected that she might collapse in relief when it was over.

She tried to make eye contact with the kids, amused by how excited they looked. One particular child caught her attention, because he wasn't jumping or waving. Taking a closer look, she realized it was McCauley. He stared right at her, his eyes as blank as always. It gave her the chills, and she shivered.

Knox put his mouth to her ear. "What's wrong?"

"Nothing. I just saw McCauley."

"Elena must have brought him."

"Yeah, I guess so." Shaking off her discomfort, Harper went back to waving and smiling at the crowd. It was a further half an hour before the parade was finally over, and she was so happy to be able to lower her aching hand and drop that Barbie smile.

At Knox's request, the demon steering the horses dropped them off at the Ice Lounge. It was an upscale bar that Harper hadn't actually been to before. When she entered, she could only gasp. It was like walking into a giant Alaskan cave, only the ice was completely synthetic and the temperature was warm.

The curved-back chairs were the same white leather as the swivel stools lining the bar, but it seemed that they were the only, well, *normal* furnishings. The dome bar, the tables, the glasses, the sculptures, and even the walls themselves were all made of artificial ice.

The ceiling shimmered with the colors of the Alaskan Northern Lights—it was seriously beautiful to watch. The colors reflected off the walls, making the ice seem tinted at times. Also, there was some kind of light inside each of the tables, making the fake-frosted cubes glow.

In sum … "This place is fucking awesome." Even her demon was impressed.

"Glad you like it," said Knox as he led her past the crowded tables to the VIP area, where leather sofas lined the walls. As he'd anticipated, Jolene, Beck, and Harper's co-workers were already there, drinks in hand. They all rose, grinning.

Jolene pulled Harper into a one-armed hug. "Hello, sweetheart. Relieved it's over?"

"So relieved I could cry with joy," said Harper honestly.

Jolene cackled. "Knox, always a pleasure."

He nodded. "Jolene, good to see you." After everyone exchanged greetings, Knox guided Harper to the corner of the eternally long sofa, where she'd be surrounded and out of reach. The sentinels joined them in lounging around the VIP area, but they also watched the crowd closely with shrewd eyes.

Harper glanced around. "Where's Martina and Ciaran?"

"Martina's working the crowd," replied Jolene. Translation: she was pickpocketing. "And Ciaran's chatting up some girl at the bar."

At that moment, the server appeared, took Knox and Harper's orders, and then left.

Raini stirred her cocktail as she spoke to Harper. "God, it's been super weird not seeing you every day."

Devon nodded. "Don't take this the wrong way, but I genuinely didn't expect to miss you this much."

Harper snorted. "Thanks, I guess."

Tanner grinned at Devon. "You've missed me too. Admit it."

The hellcat sneered. "Or I could just punch you in the dick instead."

"So you've been thinking about my dick, huh. Don't worry; it thinks about you all the time."

Devon turned to Harper, her hand gripping her highball glass tightly. "If you don't end him, I will."

Harper sighed tiredly. "Tanner, stop risking your life." He ignored her, of course, and proceeded to sniff Devon's hair.

"Come on, we need a picture," Khloë announced. Keenan literally dashed out of the way, and the imp rolled her eyes. "Chill, Keenan, I just want one of us girls. Larkin, that includes you."

The she-demons all grouped together and smiled while Khloë snapped a few photos. Raini and Devon then also did the same with their phones.

"I heard about the baby shower," Larkin said to Khloë. "If Harper were talking about anyone but you, I'd have thought she was kidding when she said that you strapped diapers to your feet and tried skiing down Jolene's hallway."

Keenan shook his head in judgement. "She wasn't kidding. I was there." He'd been on bodyguard duty with Tanner.

Khloë glared at the incubus. "Don't look at me like that. As you can see, I have a smartphone with a camera and I ain't afraid to use it."

The server neared them, holding the tray high as he weaved through the crowd. Finally reaching their table, he put two square coasters on the artificial ice table and then carefully placed down Harper's water and Knox's gin and tonic. Leaving the area, he almost bumped into Mila, who had a group of people with her that Harper didn't recognize.

Levi only allowed Mila to pass, but the others didn't appear to take offence.

"Knox, Harper, I just wanted to say congratulations in person." Mila gave Harper a genuine but reserved smile. "It's good to see that you're well. And your hair looks so shiny and healthy."

See, said Knox. *Not everyone will have harsh things to say.*

"My breasts went a lot bigger than yours when I was pregnant," Mila continued. "There's still time for yours to grow, though. But your backside does seem a little bigger, so at least there's that."

"Yeah, at least there's that," Harper said.

Told you this would happen.

Knox tactfully changed the subject and, before long, Mila and her guests were gone. Harper gave him a grateful smile. Over the next half hour, he had to do it several more times. It didn't always work, however. Some people were totally undeterred, such as Raul's girlfriend who rambled on and on about her friend's pregnancy and then asked, "Can I touch your belly?"

"Depends if you're willing to pay the fee," said Harper, deadpan.

Her brow furrowed. "What?"

"Nothing."

Raul covered his laugh with a cough. "It was great talking with you both. Hopefully we'll do so again soon."

Harper couldn't bring herself to return the sentiment, which only seemed to amuse Raul more.

Devon shook her head in wonder once they'd left. "Some people can be so rude."

Khloë snorted. "Says the person who keeps reaching out to stroke her baby bump."

"Well, at least I pull my hand back."

It was a good thing that she did, thought Harper, because her demon wouldn't react well despite the fact that it trusted Devon to an extent. It was currently on edge and wanted to get out of the place, away from all the strangers around it. *Soon*, Harper assured it.

As the hours went on, more and more people approached to pass on their congratulations and ask after Harper's welfare. Of course, they were also filled with questions—did she know the sex of the baby? Had they chosen any names? Wouldn't it be funny if it turned out that Harper was carrying twins? No, actually, it wouldn't be funny. Not at all.

Her demon tensed when Polly approached—it remembered her from the announcement, and it didn't like how nosy she was.

Polly's eyes widened. "Wow, your belly is big."

Harper blinked. "This somehow surprises you?" Hello, pregnant.

"It's just that you're bigger each time I see you."

Um, wasn't that how it was supposed to work?

"You look as though you're gonna burst any second now."

What a stroke to the ego that was. "Well, don't worry; the baby's not quite ready to make its debut yet."

"I'll bet your sex drive has gone through the roof. My sister's did."

"Really?" *Please stop talking*, Harper barely refrained from adding. She sensed Knox's amusement and wanted to smack him.

"Oh yes. You know, my Raymond said he'd always fantasized about having sex with a pregnant woman. We all have our fantasies, but some of Raymond's do surprise me. Personally, I don't understand what the attraction could possibly be in having sex with a pregnant woman, but . . ." She cut off, as if just realizing she could be offending Harper.

At this point, Khloë, Raini, and Devon—who were all absolutely shitfaced after hours of drinking shots—were practically folded over with silent laughter.

Taking a deep breath, Harper said, "Right, well, I think it's safe to say that we've officially arrived at the end of this conversation."

"Yes," said Polly with a shaky laugh. "Before I go, let me give you a little advice . . ."

Oh God, please don't, Harper wanted to say. Instead, she chugged down her water like it was tequila. As she listened to Polly talk about her son's wide shoulders, the use of forceps, and a consequential cone head, she gripped Knox's arm. *As much as I love unsolicited advice, you need to make her to stop.*

Knox massaged Harper's nape as he expertly redirected the

conversation by involving Jolene, who soon managed to guide Polly away. *Okay, you were right*, he relented. *People do see baby bumps as a green light to say inappropriate things.*

Harper nodded, taking a calming breath. It worked, but that calm quickly left her when she saw none other than Thatcher, Jonas, and Alethea approaching. The dolphin was smiling, but her eyes were hard. That wasn't what caught Harper's attention, though; it was how close she was to Thatcher—they invaded each other's space in a very intimate way. *I think Thatcher's banging the dolphin.*

Knox blinked. *That sounded wrong on several levels.*

Levi reluctantly allowed the three demons to pass, giving each of them a warning glare that they didn't fail to miss. Apparently, though, Alethea chose to ignore hers, because she pointed at Harper's stomach and said, "So, *that's* what happened to my beach ball!" The others all sucked in a shocked breath.

Total. Fucking. Bitch. Harper just stared at her blankly. *She wants me to hit her, doesn't she? I totally get that now.* Her demon snarled, wanting to rise and deliver a warning of its own. Harper barely managed to keep it from surfacing.

Knox rubbed her thigh soothingly, but he didn't say a word to Alethea. He didn't need to—his icy glare was enough to make her pale.

The girls slid forward on their seats, looking ready to pounce. Khloë even shoved up imaginary sleeves, as if readying herself to deliver a solid punch.

"Alethea," Jonas reprimanded under his breath. He then shot both Knox and Harper a wide yet awkward smile. "I apologize for my sister's behavior."

"I've noticed you do that a lot," clipped Jolene.

Jonas' mouth tightened. "We're here in peace. I came to see how Harper was doing."

"I'm good, thanks," said Harper.

"I'd imagine that you're eager to see the end of the pregnancy," hedged Thatcher, the shadow of a smile on his face. He seemed to be genuinely trying to make conversation.

Harper nodded. "It's hard to cart the beach ball everywhere," she said dryly, taking Alethea's joke and making it her own. The others laughed and, as Harper had hoped, Alethea flushed in anger. Awesome.

"I don't think your stomach's actually that big," said Raini. "Not for someone who only has five weeks left before the baby comes."

Devon nodded. "I was thinking the same thing."

Knox lay his arm across Harper, resting a possessive hand on her thigh. *The baby's annoyed.* Just a brief touch of its mind was enough for Knox to pick up a vibe of irritation.

I know, said Harper. *I don't know whether my emotions rub off on it or it just gets annoyed by* me *being annoyed.*

Thatcher looked at Knox, his expression nostalgic. "Watching your child be born is an amazing thing. Becoming a father . . . it changes you. For some people, that's a good thing. For others, it's not. But I have a feeling it will affect you in a good way. You're a man who has his priorities straight and takes care of what's his." He slid a meaningful look at Alethea and said to her, "There's really only so many times your brother can save you. One day, you'll push them too far. There'll be no one who can help you." He walked away.

Cheeks reddening, Jonas gave a courteous nod. "Enjoy your evening. Time to go, Alethea."

"Thatcher's right," Knox told her before she had the chance to leave. "Your petty comments are designed to make Harper feel bad about herself. They don't work, which is the only reason you breathe." His eyes bled to black and his demon said, "If there ever comes a time when you do hurt her, there will be no one who can keep you safe from me."

To Harper's shock, Alethea's own demon rose, but before it could say a single word, Jonas swiftly propelled it away. It was a few moments before Knox's demon finally retreated.

"You okay?" Harper asked him.

"I should be asking you that. It was *you* who she tried to hurt."

Jolene made a dismissive sound. "Ignore her. And ignore all this 'advice' you've been given—it's just verbal junk mail. And to think that they'd risk upsetting a pregnant she-demon ... there are lot of people who are simply, well, stupid. Don't listen to any of the others either, sweetheart. Pregnancy is a personal, subjective experience. What people can forget is that everyone experiences it a little differently. It's challenging and it can be scary, but it's a gift and a privilege. Enjoy it."

Harper smiled. "I will. Thanks, Grams." Scooting to the edge of the sofa, she said, "Larkin, I gotta pee." And the tension was broken.

The harpy chuckled. "Come on."

Harper gave Knox a quick kiss and then allowed Larkin to help her stand.

"Ooh, I'll come too." Khloë rose. Swayed. Double-blinked. Larkin put a hand on the imp's shoulder and sat her back down. Khloë didn't even seem to notice.

"I'll stay here," slurred Raini. "You know I don't like it when the room spins."

Devon tossed back the rest of her Cosmo and stood. "I'll go with you. I got your back."

Harper didn't bother pointing out that the hellcat could barely walk. It was an unspoken rule that none of them ever went to the restrooms alone. It wouldn't matter to Devon that Larkin was coming along; Devon would feel the need to come too.

Larkin remained in front of Harper as they headed to the restrooms. There was no need to weave their way through the throngs of people—they easily moved aside at the "don't fucking test me" expression on the sentinel's pretty face.

Mere feet away from the door, Larkin came to a halt. "*Motherfucker.*"

"What is it?" Harper tracked her gaze. And winced. "Oh."

"What?" asked Devon from behind.

"Carla's heading to the restrooms, with one eye on Harper," said Larkin. "Why this bitch seems to like waylaying you in restrooms, Harper, I don't know." Larkin pushed open the door for the ladies' room and peeked inside. "Coast is clear. Go."

Harper walked in, but Devon remained with Larkin.

"Go, Harper," said the hellcat. "We got this."

Larkin frowned at Devon. "I'm a sentinel, I will deal—"

"*We got this.*"

Harper sighed. "Whatever. Just keep Carla away from me." Her demon would go ape-shit if the woman confronted Harper again.

Alone in the restrooms, Harper quickly did her business—all the while, Larkin and Devon argued with Carla outside. Their voices were muffled, thanks to the closed door and the loud music, so Harper couldn't make out what was being said.

After washing her hands in the sink, she turned to grab some paper towels ... and there was McCauley. She almost jumped out of her freaking skin. "Jesus, kid, what's with the sneaking around?" Her demon stirred, anxious and ready to defend.

He blinked. "You need to run."

Harper's body went rigid. "Run?" It didn't sound like a threat, but ...

"She's going to hurt you."

All right, that was unexpected. And damn creepy when

spoken in that toneless voice. She licked her lips. "Who?" But the boy just stared at her with those chillingly blank eyes. "I don't understand, McCauley."

"I didn't kill them."

Harper didn't have to ask who he meant. "Was it your demon?"

He shook his head.

She frowned. "Do you know who did it?"

He nodded slowly.

God, trying to get info out of the kid was like trying to get blood out of a stone. "Who was it?"

"Linda."

"Linda?" Harper found that she wasn't quite so surprised by that answer. A part of her had always thought something was . . . *off* about the woman. Still, a whole lot of things were *off* about the kid laying accusations at Linda's door, so Harper wasn't totally convinced. "Why?"

"She wanted me to stay with her. And she hated Talia."

The latter didn't made sense. "Why did she hate Talia?"

"I don't know." He paused. "She kept calling me Sam. I told her that's not my name, and she yelled at me."

Wyatt's voice came to Harper . . . *Our son was stillborn. We called him Sam.* But Harper also remembered the warning that Nora had delivered via Dario—*when the time comes to kill the child, don't hesitate.*

Was the kid fucking with her head, gearing up to hurt her? Her gut said no, but Harper didn't know what to think or believe. Her demon was too wound up to think straight and help her work it out.

"I didn't like it in her house," he told her. "My demon said we weren't safe there."

"Why didn't you tell me this before?"

"I don't know you."

It was a simple yet very adult answer, Harper thought, as she inclined her head. Nobody with trust issues asked for help from perfect strangers. And a child who'd found out his whole life had been a lie and whose human mother tried to kill him would definitely have trust issues.

"Linda says you're bad," McCauley added. "But my demon thinks you'll protect me from her if I warn you."

"Why would Linda think I was bad?"

"She said you killed someone she loved."

All right, that made no sense to Harper. Unless, of course, Linda had some affection for Roan, which didn't seem likely. "Where's Linda now?"

"I don't know, but she wants to hurt you."

Harper opened her mouth to ask just why he wanted protection from Linda, but then a new voice joined the others outside the door. It was familiar, yet too muffled for Harper to place it. "Hide," she hissed.

McCauley dashed into one of the stalls and closed the door behind him. His little feet disappeared, and she figured he was standing on the toilet. She wondered if he'd been there when she'd first entered the restrooms.

The door creaked open, but it wasn't Linda who walked in. It was Nora.

Harper relaxed. "Hey, Nora. How are you?"

"Good, good." She gestured to the door with a huff. "Carla's up to her old tricks again. The sentinel and your friend are taking care of it. Look at you. You're glowing."

Harper grabbed some paper towels and dried off her hands. "Aw, thanks."

Nora came close. "Pregnancy's an exciting yet frightening time, isn't it?"

"Definitely."

"But you look happy."

Harper nodded, a smile spreading across her face. "I am. I really—" She flinched as a zap of energy shuddered up her arm.

Nora raised her hand in apology. "Good ole static electricity."

Oddly uneasy, Harper said, "Well, it was good speaking to you, but I have to go." She also needed for Nora to go inside one of the stalls so that McCauley could sneak out with Harper.

"Give the sentinel and your friend a chance to scare Carla away first," Nora advised.

"Doesn't sound as if they're having much luck with that."

"They're toying with her—mocking her and giving her a lecture on her failure as a mother and as a person in general."

Harper chuckled, shaking her head. "I shouldn't find that funny." She figured she also shouldn't feel so tired all of a sudden, but a wave of fatigue hit her hard. "Damn, I should have headed home earlier."

"Yes, you should have. But I'm glad that you didn't. That would have made things much harder."

Harper frowned. Nora's voice sounded tinny and far away. Her sight began to blur and everything seemed hazy, but she felt calm. Totally serene. Her demon felt just as peaceful.

A breeze built behind her, and Harper turned, morbidly fascinated by the swirling circle of red and black smoke that had come out of absolutely fucking nowhere. A portal, she realized. "What the—"

A hand grabbed her arm and shoved her into the smoke.

CHAPTER NINETEEN

—◆—

Opening her eyes had never been so hard, but damn they stung. Harper licked her chapped lips. Her mouth was bone dry and it hurt to swallow. Her skin felt cold and dewy, especially the skin of her back—which was no doubt thanks to the damp soil beneath her.

Soil?

Memories slapped her. The restrooms. McCauley. Nora. The portal. Fingertips digging into her arm and shoving her.

Well now.

Apparently, Nora had a fucking death wish. Obliging her would be a pleasure.

Forcing her sore eyes open, Harper awkwardly sat upright and blinked a few times to clear her vision. She almost wished she hadn't, because finding that she was sprawled on a patch of land encircled by eight, tall boulders wasn't an uplifting sight.

A cold mist hovered above the ground. It was thin, so it didn't haze her view of her surroundings. And it had to be said that her surroundings were pretty bleak.

It seemed like an endless stretch of green, bumpy land. There was the occasional puny bush, mossy rock, or twisted tree, but the weedy land was otherwise plain and bare. No blossoms. No mountains. No landmarks. No real color. It was the kind of place where you could just walk and walk and walk, and nothing would look any different.

There was an unnatural quiet that was broken only by the creak of tree branches and the eerie sound the cool wind made as it rushed over the barren land and whistled through the brittle shrubs. It brought with it the scents of grass, soil, and decay.

Shit, she needed to get away from here. Fast.

Knox?

Nothing.

Knox, please say you can hear me.

Still nothing. Crap.

Adrenaline began to pump madly through her veins. Harper kept her cool, knowing it wouldn't do the baby any good if she lost her shit. Besides, her demon was panicking enough for both of them.

Harper braced her hands on the damp soil and pushed to her feet with a moan. It was no easy feat with a baby bump. She brushed her hands together to get rid of the dirt and then gave said bump a small rub. Her limbs trembled, yet she didn't feel weak.

The mist gave the place an eerie feel, but that wasn't what had the hairs on her nape and arms standing on end. No, the uneven ground vibrated beneath her feet, and those vibrations echoed through her body. She didn't like it, because they didn't make her feel charged—they made her feel dizzy. Sickly. Soiled, even.

The wind came again, brushing against her skin and ruffling the dress that was now damp and stained with streaks of dirt. She shivered, rubbing at her cool arms, as she gave her surroundings another thorough scan. Just where the fucking hell was she? The gray clouds were low, so she guessed she was somewhere high. Had she been dumped here with the hope that she'd never find her way home? And why, exactly, had the old woman sent her *here*?

All valid questions, but Harper nonetheless didn't intend to wait around and find out. Planting her feet, she called to her wings—

White-hot pain streaked down her back, and she spat a vicious curse. She tried calling to them again, but that only earned her more pain. Her heart began to race as fear skittered down her spine. Despite that fear, the protective power that lived in her belly didn't rush to her fingertips. There was the briefest spark inside her, but nothing more.

Something was interfering with her abilities—possibly the same "something" that seemed to be blocking her attempts to contact Knox.

Well, it looked like she'd just have to get out of there the old-fashioned way. Her back protested the idea of walking, but it didn't take a genius to work out that Nora didn't have good things in mind for Harper; she couldn't afford to hang around. There was no dirt path, so it was highly likely that she'd get lost in the mist. Knowing her luck, she might even fall into a bog or something, but she'd be *damned* if she'd stay put.

Harper quickly chose a random direction and started to walk, every step brisk and—

With a gasp, she stumbled back and put a hand on the cold, rough boulder to steady herself as vines suddenly spouted from the earth and began to slither menacingly along the ground. She watched as they twisted around each of the boulders, forming one big foliage fence.

Okay, so she was trapped. Good to know.

Her demon hissed loudly, wanting out so it could attack the vines. Harper fought the entity. It wasn't the first time she'd been a prisoner, but it was the first time that she'd had someone else's safety outside her own to consider. If she hadn't been pregnant, she would have taken her chances with the enchanted vines, but she wasn't sure if they'd retaliate or something weird like that.

She froze as static energy suddenly filled the air. Her hair seemed to lift, and a low droning sound split through the unnatural quiet. Harper turned toward the sound, and that was when a familiar swirl of red and black smoke appeared beyond the boulders. *Well, shit.*

Mere moments later, Nora stepped out of it, dressed in a black robe, her hands joined as if in prayer. Worse, the old bitch was followed by a group of hooded figures. What. The. Fuck?

Given that Nora had opened a portal, there was one thing Harper knew for sure. "You're an incantor," she clipped.

Nora bowed her head with a smile, like she'd been delivered a compliment. "That is correct. I suppose you mistakenly assumed I was the same breed as my grandson. No. But if you *had* known I was an incantor, would you have suspected me as you suspected Thatcher of being involved in the attacks on you?"

"Yes," said Harper truthfully. "I don't trust many people."

"Sensible."

Yeah, but it hadn't fucking helped her much in this case. Harper flicked a look at the hooded figures and asked, "Fellow incantors?"

"Most, but not all," one of them said, sidling up to Nora and lowering the hood. *Linda.* She spared Harper a dispassionate glance before looking at Nora. "When do I join her in the circle?"

Nora held up a hand. "Not yet."

Linda glanced around. "Where's McCauley?"

"I didn't see him anywhere, so I left without him."

Linda's mouth tightened. "Did you even look?"

"Forget about the boy. You can deal with him another time."

Harper glared at Nora as she said with a distaste her demon shared, "I'm guessing you're one of the Horsemen." It would explain how she'd known so much about them.

"In the flesh," said Nora proudly.

Yeah, flesh that her raging demon would love to peel off like an onion. Harper could sort of see the attraction in that idea. "Where are we?"

"Someplace special," Nora replied with a dreamy smile that was kind of creepy. She spread out her arms and inhaled deeply. "You feel it, don't you? This place is an energy vortex."

An energy vortex . . . Okay, so Harper had heard of those. Put simply, they were swirling centers of energy that were said to be uplifting, spiritual, and able to heighten people's own inner positive or negative energy. That would have given her hope, since she could work with energy; could potentially use it to boost her abilities. But this particular vortex . . . there was something very *wrong* about it. The energy wasn't simply negative, it was dark. Ominous. Almost malevolent.

Her demon didn't discriminate when it came to power. Good, bad—the entity didn't care. Power was power, as far as it was concerned. But even the demon was wary of the vortex, and that said *a lot*.

"It was here where I had my vision," Nora told her.

Harper frowned. "You have knowings, not visions."

"Ah, but this place can strengthen a person's abilities. It can also weaken their abilities—it all depends."

"On what?"

"On what the vortex is asked to do."

"And you've asked it to keep me weak and contained," Harper accused.

Knox's mind breezed over hers—the touch was faint, but there. *I hear you, baby. Where are you?*

Relief flooded Harper in a heavy rush, despite that the telepathic voice was weak. Working to keep her face blank, she responded, *I don't know exactly, but I'm stood on some kind of energy vortex, thanks to fucking Nora. It's stopping me from using my abilities*. And Harper needed to keep Nora talking until he got here. "You hired the hunters? Why?"

"Because I had a vision of you giving birth, of Linda and I being close by, and of you releasing beautiful wings and escaping us. I needed those wings taken from you. Sadly, that didn't work. I tried hexing you to weaken your abilities—that didn't work either. But using the vortex to contain and weaken you is probably best in any case."

What would be "best" would be for Nora and her pals to be sliced and diced by a real-life Hannibal Lecter. "Why try to kidnap Heidi?"

"Ah, I didn't. I'm not sure who did. Perhaps it was the last of the Horsemen."

Harper frowned. If Nora wasn't sure whether or not her only remaining partner in crime was responsible, then that would suggest that ... "You're not working together anymore, are you?"

"Let's just say I didn't agree with their belief that we should lie low for a while." Her face hardened. "I'm old. I've waited long enough for the Primes to fall. I was once a Prime, you know. Now I answer to my grandson because a Prime will be challenged by others if it isn't fit to hold its position. Because I aged, I was deemed *unfit*." The latter word dripped with venom. "And now I'm nothing more than a demon within a lair. If there were no

Primes, if there were equal rights for all demons, I wouldn't be thought of as an antique," she added bitterly.

Harper shook her head. "Our kind craves power too much to ever simply exist alongside each other and be content as equals. The hierarchies within each lair exist for that reason, and they work." But Nora wasn't listening. She was gazing around her, wearing a serene expression, like she was in a freaking meadow or something.

Nora clasped her hands. "This truly is a fascinating place. Time is different here."

Not liking the sound of that, Harper warily asked, "Different how?"

"An hour in the vortex is a minute in places beyond it. Think of what that means. You've been here for, say, an hour. To anyone away from this place, you've only been here a minute."

As the implications of that sank in, Harper's stomach dropped and panic fluttered through her. Even if Knox was able to get her at a pace that was supremely fast to him, enough time would have passed here for Nora to end Harper's life first.

"In other words, don't be counting on a rescue, Harper. Call out to Knox all you like—he won't hear you. Not while you're trapped in the vortex."

Huh. Well, that wasn't actually correct, but Nora didn't need to know that. "He'll find a way to get to me."

"Oh, I doubt that."

"You shouldn't. People have hurt and taken me before—he's always come for me." And both Harper and her demon trusted that he'd come for her again.

"He won't come, Harper. As I said, time is different here. Let's say that Larkin goes into the restrooms and finds you gone—she'll sense the leftover magickal energy, but she won't understand it was from a portal. Of course, she'll run to Knox.

He'll feel the magick too, but it's highly unlikely that he'll sense there was a portal. Still, he's smart enough to know he'll need an incantor to 'read' the magick."

He'd be aware that there was a portal for the simple reason that Harper had told him—that was yet another thing that Nora didn't need to know.

"I'm sure he'll find one, and I'm sure they will be willing to reopen the portal for him. However, that process takes up to fifteen minutes to complete. Now add all that time together and, for Knox, that will be—at the very least—twenty minutes before he even steps through the portal. That's twenty hours to us, sweetheart. By then, you'll be dead, and we'll all be gone."

Okay, that was bad. Really bad. Dammit, she had to get *the fuck* out of there.

Nora's expression turned sober as she spoke to her companions. "Get into position."

While Linda stayed still, each of the others copied Nora in moving to stand near a boulder so that they surrounded Harper.

Another shot of adrenaline pumped through Harper, and she flexed her fingers. "I suppose you intend to kill me now before Knox has the chance to get here." And, heartbreakingly, there wasn't a single thing that she could do to stop it.

"Not just yet," said Nora as she and the others sat cross-legged. "I want you dead, but I want the baby first. If we can't destroy Knox, we can at least control him. What better way than through his child?"

Harper's heart slammed against her ribs, and her knees almost buckled. She put a protective hand to her stomach. "You can't have the baby."

"Oh, but I can. You have to understand, Harper, that there's no real way for demons to exist as equals while someone so powerful lives. Knox could take complete control at any time.

Trying to kill him hasn't worked. Holding the baby's safety over his head, though . . . yes, that would keep him under my thumb."

Nora raised her hands and began to chant under her breath. The others joined in, and the stale air suddenly turned heavy and oppressive. The clouds thickened and darkened, making the sky look almost bruised.

"What are you doing?"

It was Linda who spoke. "Inducing labor, of course."

Harper shook her head, stomach plummeting. "The baby isn't ready yet. They'll kill it."

"No," said Nora. "I have a team of people on standby who can give it whatever care it needs to ensure it survives."

"And I'll be there to care for the baby," declared Linda, chin up.

Nora's smile faltered. "Yes, and you'll be there." She went back to chanting, and the wind picked up, whipping the snarled trees and making dirt swirl in the air.

A gust of wind sailed at Harper, making her dress flap against her legs. Panicking, she called to her wings again, and yet more pain wracked her. The baby's mind touched hers. She felt its fear, and that almost broke her. "No, you don't get to take my—"

She cut off as what looked like black drops of rain sprung from Nora's fingertips and, quick as lightning, hit Harper right in the chest. She tried to wipe them off, but they sank into her skin. She felt the magick inside her, then. Felt it slither around her bones, snake around her organs, and settle over her womb like an oily blanket. "What the fuck did you just do?"

Pain blasted through her abdomen, and her womb contracted so hard that she dropped to her knees. It hurt like *holy hell*. She'd never felt pain like it—not when Knox's power poured into her mind, not when the hunters sawed at her wings, not even when her body spent hours fighting the hex.

The wind rushed at her again, stealing her breath and knocking her right on her ass. Vines sprouted out of the earth and shackled her wrists, pinning her hands. She managed to fight their hold just enough to stay sitting upright, but she couldn't free herself. She tried infusing hellfire into the grass, hoping the vines might catch fire, but only smoke left her palms. *Motherfucking vortex.* She could feel its sinister, repelling energy slithering between her fingers.

Another spasm wracked her womb, making her spine arch like a brow. All the breathing exercises she'd read about went completely out of her head. She gritted her teeth against the pain, clenching her trapped hands and unintentionally scraping the soil. Her shoulders slouched as the pain finally faded. Her heart thudded in her tightening chest, her breaths burst in and out of her. "I'll kill you all, I swear to God, I will!"

"No, you won't," said Nora calmly. "You won't even get the chance. Once the child is born, that magick you absorbed will attack every cell in your body—you'll be dead within moments."

A ghostly finger of fear trailed over Harper's nape, but she didn't let that fear show. Her demon leaped to the surface and said, "You *will* die tonight. Do not doubt it."

Nora's eyes flickered. "Linda," she said, her voice a whip, "get in the circle."

The vines bordering the boulders parted to let Linda pass, and then the bitch crouched in front of her. "*Don't* touch me," Harper spat.

"You're safe from me until that baby is out." It wasn't a reassurance, it was a statement of fact that lacked any compassion. She put her hands on Harper's rounded stomach. "The baby's in position, head down."

Harper felt a blazing heat briefly flare from her stomach—it was the oddest fucking thing and had an almost vengeful feel to it.

Linda yanked her hands back, as if burned. "Damn vortex," she grumbled.

But that hadn't been the vortex. Nor had it been Harper or her demon. She snarled at Linda. "You'll never take my baby from me. Never."

Linda's mouth curled into a cruel smile. "Of course I will. And there's not a damn thing you can do to stop me."

Knox took another swig of his gin and tonic, watching for signs of Harper approaching. She'd been gone for a good five minutes now, and he was guessing that she'd been waylaid by nosy demons who were both congratulating and quizzing her at the same time.

He'd take her home as soon as she returned to him, he decided. They'd been there for a courteous amount of time and wouldn't look rude leaving at this point.

"Shit," muttered Levi, going on high alert.

Knox put down his glass, tension mounting inside him. "What?" But then he saw Larkin and Devon fast approaching . . . without Harper. Anxiety flared through him. He stood, meeting Larkin's anxious stare. "Where is she?"

"I"—Larkin swallowed— "I don't know." She spoke in a rush. "She went into the restrooms while Devon and I dealt with Carla, and then she just disappeared."

The words rocked him, slamming into him so hard his breath caught in his throat. On the outside, he didn't move a muscle. On the inside, he fumbled, scrambling to absorb the words. His demon let out a guttural roar. Harper had been right there with him mere minutes ago. How the fuck could she be gone?

Harper? Harper? He reached out to stroke her mind, but he barely managed to touch it—as if there was something trying to get between her mind and his. *Harper, baby, tell me you're okay.*

She was alive; he knew that much, and he clung to it like it was a lifeline ... because it *was* a lifeline. He needed her, wouldn't be able to exist without her.

He wanted to move, to act, to do *something*, but he felt rooted to the spot.

"Harper's gone?" Jolene bit out. The ground and walls began to tremor, and that snapped Knox out of his zone.

He advanced on Larkin. "How can she just disappear?" His voice was a low rumble that vibrated with rage, but she didn't cower.

"The only person who was in the restrooms when I walked in looking for her was him," said the harpy. "He claims to know who took her."

It was only then that Knox noticed McCauley at her side. A dark suspicion whispered in his mind. Could the child have harmed her? Dario had warned them that he may need to be killed. Knox crouched in front of the boy. "You know who has Harper?"

McCauley nodded, eyes blank. "An old woman."

Not an answer Knox would have expected to hear. "An old woman?"

"Harper called her 'Nora.'"

Knox didn't show his surprise, but Jolene did by letting out a string of foul curses that made him think of Harper—and thinking of his mate, missing and possibly hurt, made his stomach churn.

"Nora passed us to go into the restrooms," said Devon, eyes damp. "She was gone too."

Which meant that either the boy was telling the truth or that Nora had been taken too. Leaning towards the first explanation, Knox asked, "Where did she take Harper, McCauley?"

"There was smoke," said the boy. "It was red and black, and it swirled."

"A portal," said Levi.

"Nora took Harper through a portal?" asked Raini, voice shaky.

"Then it vanished," McCauley added.

Knox stormed out the VIP area, crossing to the restrooms with purposeful strides. He shoved the door open, hoping he'd find Harper standing there smiling; hoping it was all one big sick joke that he'd spank her ass for later. But there was no Harper. There was, however, the energy residue from a portal—it was like static electricity in the air.

He whispered his fingers over the lingering energy. "I can feel it," he said through gritted teeth, knowing the others had followed him inside. "The portal was right here."

"There's no telling where it led," growled Tanner, voice hard as stone, muscles stiff. "They could be anywhere."

Knox? Knox, please say you can hear me.

His eyes closed at the sound of Harper's voice, even though their telepathic link seemed weak and almost distant. *I hear you, baby. Where are you?*

I don't know exactly, but I'm stood on some kind of energy vortex, thanks to fucking Nora. It's stopping me from using my abilities.

"Harper says she's stood on an energy vortex," said Knox, curling his hands into fists. The back of his throat hurt, and it was difficult to swallow. "It's preventing her from using her abilities." Leaving her defenseless, just as she'd been once before not so long ago.

"You can hear her?" asked Jolene, brows drawn together. "I keep calling out to her, but she's not answering me." The sentinels and she-demons nodded, claiming the same.

"Maybe it's because they're anchored or something," Raini suggested, hands jammed under her armpits.

"I warned Harper to run," said McCauley, tone flat. "She didn't run."

Knox frowned. "To run from Nora?"

He shook his head. "Linda," he said simply, none of the urgency or fear in his voice that Knox was feeling.

Bastard though he was, Knox itched to shake the boy and drag everything he knew out of him.

Maybe he sensed that, because McCauley took a step forward and said, "Read my mind."

Because Knox's touch was invited, it didn't cause McCauley any pain when Knox thrust his mind into his. Knox delved into his memories, saw the boy watching the parade. Saw Linda slap a hand over his mouth and drag him into an alley. Heard her speak over the phone that then began to ring.

"What?" Linda snapped at her caller. "Not yet. I'll meet you once I've killed the brat . . . Of course this is important to me—I want that baby even more than you do, but this kid will pay first. It's not like you need me to grab Harper for you or induce labor; you might be old, but there's nothing weak about you . . . Fine." Linda then ended the call and turned her attention to the boy in her arms. "All you had to do was love me. But no, you wouldn't do it. You left me. No one leaves me."

Knox watched as McCauley bit her hand and then ran as she screamed, "Ow! Get back here you little bastard!"

Knox then sped forward through the memories, watching a fast-forward version of McCauley fleeing from Linda, hiding in the restrooms, and finally getting to Harper. "You need to run," he said.

Heart in his throat, Knox then watched as Nora talked with Harper before forcing her into a portal. Swallowing hard, Knox withdrew his mind from the boy's. "Thank you for trying to help Harper, McCauley. You can tell your demon that she and I will keep you safe from Linda." Standing, Knox gave the others a rundown of what happened.

Devon put a hand to her mouth. "Oh, God, no. The baby's not ready to be born yet."

Jolene rubbed the hellcat's back, her eyes hard. "It would seem that they don't care about that." There was a wealth of lethal intent in her tone.

"Linda's a midwife," said Keenan. "Nora probably recruited her to help with the birth."

The door burst open, and Thatcher barged in with his sentinel-slash-bodyguard behind him. His gaze ran over everyone. "My sentinel saw you all rush inside like you were being chased by a pack of wild hellhounds. What has happened?"

Knox would have sent him out, only he wanted to see Thatcher's reaction to the news. "Someone kidnapped Harper. They took her through a portal."

Shock flashed across Thatcher's face, and it seemed genuine. "You're sure?"

"Does it look like I'm fucking kidding?"

Thatcher weaved his way through the others and held up his hand, no doubt reading the magick in the air. "You are right. I could reopen the portal for you. Do you trust me?"

"No."

Thatcher let out a short sigh. "Will you allow me to reopen it for you?"

Knox narrowed his eyes. "Why would you?"

"No one likes living under a cloud of suspicion. Maybe if I help you, you'll no longer suspect me of meaning your mate any harm."

Knox, said Harper, voice still faint. *I'm scared.*

Her fear pierced his soul and almost knocked him back a step. *It's going to be fine, baby. I'm right here with you. I'm going to find some way to get to you, I swear. Just hold on for me, okay? Hold on.* Knox nodded at Thatcher. "How long will it take?"

"Ordinarily, the process would take fifteen minutes. I'm a strong incantor. I should be able to do it in ten."

It was too long, Knox thought. But so far, it was the fastest way to get to her. He stepped aside, giving the other Prime room. "I need it done fast."

With his sentinel now at his side, Thatcher immediately got to work.

"Do you think Dario's working with Nora?" Jolene asked Knox.

"My gut says no, but that doesn't mean he can't know something." Knox turned to Tanner. "Bring him here, but don't let him know there's a problem—I don't want his sentinel interfering."

The hellhound nodded and then disappeared from the restrooms.

Muscles tight, Knox remained in position. He wanted to pace and curse and punch a hole through the stall door. Instead, he held himself completely still, even though he felt twitchy, restless, and dangerously on edge. His chest was so tight, he was surprised he could breathe without wheezing.

As the she-demons began to talk, expressing their worries for Harper, Knox blocked out their conversation. He couldn't allow himself to think of what could be happening to Harper—if he did, he'd lose his ability to focus. But despite his best efforts, images of what Nora could be doing to her kept flickering through his mind, slicing at his frayed control.

There wasn't just fury flooding his veins; there was guilt. He should have protected her better. He should never have let her leave his side for a single moment. In being careful not to make her feel suffocated, he'd put her and their child in danger. And he knew he'd never forgive himself for it.

His demon's cold rage echoed through him. Oddly, the demon

wasn't ranting and raving. It wasn't demanding vengeance or pushing for control. If the entity was capable of feeling guilt, Knox would have wondered if it blamed itself the same way that Knox blamed himself. He didn't know why the entity was so unnaturally quiet and still—it wasn't inclined to communicate with him right then.

There had only been one other time that the demon had been so silent despite its rage ... the very day it had taken it upon itself to destroy the cult in which Knox had been raised as a child. Usually, the demon didn't plan or strategize—it acted on emotion alone, and it didn't care to maintain its composure. The fact that it seemed to be silently strategizing now didn't relieve Knox. Harper had told him that it spooked her when Knox was so deceptively and unnaturally calm. Just the same, his demon's unnatural calm worried him.

"Knox," said Larkin, voice sheepish, "I'm so sorry. I should have come in here with her. This is all my fucking fault."

Khloë shook her head. "No, harpy, it's not. The fault lies with Nutty Nora and whoever might be helping her. Harper would tell you the same thing if she could."

Jolene nodded. "Nobody blames you, Larkin. You were told to protect Harper and that was exactly what you did by keeping Carla away from her. You couldn't have known that Nora would mean her any harm, especially since the woman defended Harper against Carla in the coffeehouse not so long ago."

Larkin looked at Knox, eyes still clouded with guilt. "I understand if you want to execute me for failing Harper, but please allow me to help you find and save her first."

"I have no intention of executing you, Larkin. You're not at fault." That was the most reassurance that Knox could offer her while rage and terror were pumping through him. He rolled his neck and shoulders, trying to ease the tension in his muscles, but it didn't work. Nothing short of having Harper in front of him would calm him.

He'd worried enough about how smoothly the birth would go, though he'd hid those concerns from her. He'd sworn to her that he'd be with her the entire time. The thought that she'd be facing it alone, even if only for the short time it would take for him to get to her, flayed him.

His gaze snapped to the door as it swung open and Tanner entered with Dario.

The Prime looked around, seeming both curious and confused. "Tanner said you needed my help, but he didn't say what was wrong."

Knox pinned him with an unblinking stare. "Do you know what she's done? Are you part of this?"

Dario blinked. "What are you—?"

Knox lunged and fisted his shirt. "Do *not* fuck with me right now."

"I swear to you, I do not know what you mean." Dario looked to his sentinel for help, but the male was being held back by Tanner and Keenan.

"Nora took Harper," Knox rumbled.

Dario's eyes snapped back to him and he stilled, brows drawing together. "No. No, she wouldn't do that."

"Oh, but she did. I have an eyewitness that says she took her through a portal." Knox released him with a shove. "Harper herself has telepathically informed me that Nora is with her and wants the baby. She's inducing labor as we speak."

Righting his shirt, Dario frantically shook his head. "No, my grandmother would never do something like that. She has no reason to do it. She could not possibly gain anything from it."

Levi spoke, "There are plenty of reasons why someone would want Knox's child, and you know it."

"She's old—"

"Just because somebody's old doesn't mean they're frail or harmless," said Jolene. "She also has help. She's not working alone."

Dario's mouth fell open. "Don't tell me you think she's one of the Horsemen," he scoffed.

"It's possible," said Levi. "She knew plenty about them. Maybe this was why."

Dario shot him an impatient look. "If she was one of them, why would she ever make you aware of them?"

"For the same reasons that serial killers tip off the police," said Levi. "For attention. To create fear. If people aren't aware that something or someone exists, it doesn't have any power over them."

"Face it," Knox snapped, "your grandmother kidnapped Harper. She wants my child. Make me believe you're not part of this plot and tell me where Nora would take her."

Scrubbing a hand down his face, Dario said, "I just can't believe that she would—"

"Believe it, because she has. Convince me you had no part in this, or I swear I'll end you right now."

Dario stood tall, looking ready to challenge Knox. Wisely, he didn't. "I have played no part in whatever has happened to your mate."

Knox, where are you? I don't want to do this alone.

He almost flinched. The pain in those words gutted him. "How much longer is this going to fucking take?"

"The process is slow-going, I know," said Thatcher, "but I'm going as fast as I can."

Knox softly brushed his mind against hers. *You're not alone,* he soothed. *I'm right here, and I'll be physically with you very soon.*

"Is there a limit to how many people can step through the

portal?" asked Levi. When Thatcher shook his head, Levi turned to Knox and said, "I'm going with you."

"All four of us are going," said Tanner, referring to each of the sentinels.

Knox looked at Jolene. "I need you to stay here."

"You need me to guard the portal and ensure that Thatcher doesn't attempt to trap you there," said Jolene in understanding.

Yes, because Knox couldn't rely on his ability to pyroport if the place where Harper was being held would weaken him.

"I'll kill him on the spot if he does," Jolene vowed.

"And I'll help," said Khloë.

"The portal will remain open," Thatcher assured Knox. "No one else will get in or out of it, and you need not worry that I will try to trap you."

"I hope that's the case, Thatcher," said Jolene, "because I'd rather not kill you."

Biting her lip, Raini came forward. "Do you think the baby's coming tonight?"

Knox nodded. "I'll need to arrange for Rodgers to be waiting at the mansion, ready for Harper. There's nowhere else she'll be completely safe while she gives birth."

"I'll arrange all that," Jolene told him, pulling out her cell phone. "Everything will be ready. Ciaran can teleport the doctor and whatever he needs to your home. You just concentrate on getting to Harper."

Knox might have protested, but he sensed that Jolene needed to be proactive, needed to feel that she was doing *something*. She might look calm, but she'd undoubtedly be far from it.

He reached out to Harper. *We're almost done reopening the portal, baby, just hold on for me.*

CHAPTER TWENTY

———◆———

The agonizing contraction passed, and Harper almost slumped to the ground. Her knees, back, and shoulders felt stiff from being in the same position for so long. But she wouldn't give in to the urge to lie down. No, she wouldn't make herself even more vulnerable than she already was.

Her movements clinical, Linda used a cloth to dab the sweat from Harper's forehead. She was a panting, moaning, sweaty mess, and she knew that her face was probably haggard and pasty. Her eyes watered with both the pain and the harsh wind that kept slamming into her face, stealing her breath. At least the haunting sound of it helped her block out the hideous, droned chanting that grated on every nerve she possessed.

Tied down while surrounded by chanting hooded people, she might have felt more like she was having an exorcism than that she was in labor if it weren't for the excruciating spasms that continuously wracked her womb.

She wasn't sure how long she'd been at this. The minutes

had soon become hours, and the hours felt like days as cramp after cramp assailed her. As time went on, the intervals between them became shorter and shorter, and the pain had become more intense.

She kept reaching out to Knox, but she only heard from him occasionally. She knew the long gaps in those conversations was due to the difference in how much time passed for each of them. For Knox, he was talking with her a few times per minute. For Harper, it was a few times per hour and his responses were always delayed reaching her.

Of course, he didn't know any of that. She'd kept it to herself because she knew that the truth that she'd been in agony for hours would torture him, just as she knew from the other times that she'd been taken from him *exactly* how hard his demon would be riding him.

God, she really was sick of being kidnapped. The first time, it had been *Knox* that the culprits wanted to capture—she'd been nothing but bait. The second time, she had in fact been the target. This time, the baby was who the kidnappers wanted. If they thought they'd get their hands on her child, they were out of their ever-loving minds.

"Here," said Linda, holding a bottle of water to Harper's mouth.

Throat dry and lungs burning with every breath, Harper gulped down the water, not worried that it could be drugged. They wouldn't give her anything that would kill her—the dark magick would do that for them once the baby was born.

Well, Linda probably *would* be tempted to kill her beforehand, considering she now sported one whopper of a bruise on her jaw. Her demon absolutely loved the sight of it. Shame the vines had restrained Harper's feet to stop her from kicking the bitch again.

"I'll bet you're wishing you were in a hospital right now having an epidural," said Linda with a smirk. "Sorry, no pain relief for you."

Harper narrowed her eyes. "I hope I shit on you." She'd heard women sometimes did it during labor, and she'd hoped it wouldn't happen to her. Now, however, it would be a fucking treat.

Linda's lips pinched together. "It won't be anything I haven't seen before."

"I wouldn't be so sure of that. I haven't shit for about two days. I've got lots stored up there." Her demon might have chuckled at that if it wasn't so wound up.

A crippling pain once again rippled through her womb, sending her back arching. She tasted blood and distantly wondered if she'd bitten her tongue. It didn't matter. It was the baby that mattered, and she figured that it had to be even harder for the baby, since it was pretty much stuck in what couldn't be a comfortable position.

"How dilated is she?" asked Nora, voice a little hoarse due to chanting non-stop for God-knew-how-long.

Ignoring Harper's curses, Linda checked and replied, "Four centimeters."

"*What?*" clipped one of the figures—Harper had nicknamed him "Whiner" because he moaned constantly about her slow progress. "This has gone on too long!" Like the others, his face was pale and his expression was pinched. They were all tired and weakening. Ha.

"Labor can be slow, especially when it's a woman's first pregnancy," Linda explained. "I've told you time and time again that it may help if we let Harper change positions, but you're set on keeping her still."

Whiner humphed and then spoke to Nora. "We need to find a way to speed it up. *You* might be sure that Knox can't get to her in time to help her, but I'm not." That was the first bit of wisdom he'd shown.

"If we speed it up, we risk hurting the child," said Nora.

That didn't seem to bother any of them, Harper noted. *Fucking bastards.*

"And if we don't," began Whiner, "we risk finding ourselves in the hands of Knox Thorne—*no thank you.*"

Another incantor—who Harper called "Jumpy" because he seemed to be a nervous wreck and constantly scanned the landscape as if expecting Knox to jump out at him—said, "He's right, Nora. We can't take any more chances than we already have."

After a long pause, Nora said, "Then take a brief break and recharge."

Hoping to delay them from resuming their horrible chanting, Harper spoke to her. "I don't understand. If you're one of the Horsemen, why did you even tell us about them?"

Nora twisted the cap off a water bottle and took a long drink. "Because people need to know about us, and the Primes need to fear what's coming."

"But you described Roan, you basically handed him—" Realization smacked Harper right in the face. "You wanted him dead, didn't you?"

Nora merely shrugged. "He had to go. He became a liability. He'd lost control of Crow and was too blinded by his hatred of you to be efficient. He knew about my vision, knew a baby would come, but he wanted you dead too badly to see the bigger picture. I couldn't risk him killing you." She took another long swig of water and then recapped it. "Everyone ready?"

Harper went to speak again, but another contraction hit. When it faded, she was shaking feverishly ... and too late to engage Nora in more conversation. The old bitch resumed that horrible chanting, and the others quickly joined in. The chanting was louder now, and the words came faster. There was a frantic edge to them that hadn't been there before.

The wind howled as it picked up in intensity, whipping up and tangling Harper's hair. The trees creaked under its brutal force, and she hoped one would snap and smack one of the incantors right over the fucking head.

She flinched at the sharp crack of thunder, and had the satisfaction of seeing Linda almost jump out of her skin. That satisfaction left her when yet another contraction made her almost double over—this one more painful than any that had come before it. When it stopped, she panted, "Tell me about Sam."

Linda reared back as if she'd been slapped.

"I'll bet it hurt when you lost him," Harper said gently. "I'll bet you've never felt pain like that before or since. The worst day of your life, right?"

"By far."

"And yet you want to take my baby from me. You of all people should know what an injustice it is to lose your own child."

Guilt flashed in Linda eyes for a brief moment. "They won't let you live to keep it anyway. I'll only be taking it because there's no one else."

"There's Knox," Harper pointed out. Another contraction came along and stole what she was about to say. As she moaned and panted, lighting repeatedly flashed within the clouds. It was an isolated electrical storm that seemed too close for Harper's liking.

Knox, where are you? I don't want to do this alone. She hadn't envisioned it happening this way. Not once.

Her demon paused in its raving, sending Harper an impression of them being one—telling her that she wasn't alone. It was the first time the entity had ever offered her any support of any kind. But then, they had a common goal: they had to protect the baby. They just weren't sure how they'd do it.

The terrible facts were that she was outnumbered, restrained, in no physical state to fight, and she couldn't access her abilities. Moreover, she'd been infected with some kind of dark magick that would kill her pretty much instantly after she'd given birth.

In sum, she was fucked. But that didn't mean she'd give up hope. That wasn't who she was.

We're almost done reopening the portal, baby, just hold on for me.

Hope flared. She closed her eyes, imagining him standing right there, being calm and supportive to keep her own fears at bay. *Hurry, Knox.* She must have said that aloud, because Linda snorted.

"No one's coming for you. Even if they did, they'd be too late—just like Nora said."

"Nora's batshit."

Linda inclined her head. "Possibly."

"Yet, you're working for her."

"Working *with* her. She needs me."

Harper couldn't imagine Nora needing Linda. What she needed was a midwife; one who would risk going against Harper and Knox; one who was expendable and could be manipulated into helping. But Harper didn't get why she'd been so easy to manipulate. "Why help Nora?"

"You shouldn't have taken McCauley from me, Harper. And you definitely shouldn't have killed Jeanna. She was my best friend."

All right, that was a shocker. "She was also a demon for hire who tried to kill me and led Knox into a trap."

"I know. I'm not really doing this because of them anyway. I'm doing it because Nora made me a very good deal. If I help her, I get to keep your baby." Linda smiled, but it was a creepy smile. "Nora will hold it over Knox's head, but she can't take care of it herself. That's where I come in."

Harper's demon snarled. "What about Wyatt?"

Linda snickered. "Oh, don't feel bad for Wyatt. He's had plenty of affairs over the years."

"Talia," Harper guessed, remembering what McCauley had said about Linda hating the she-demon.

Taken aback, Linda blinked. "Yes, she was one of them. How did you know that?"

"Wild guess." Harper gritted her teeth as another contraction wracked her womb. When it finally eased, she asked, "If you hated Talia, why would you have kept her son?"

Affronted, Linda glared. "I would never punish a child for someone else's mistakes. If I was that sort of person, I wouldn't be willing to raise this baby, would I? I'll raise it as mine, Harper," she taunted. "It'll believe I'm it's true mother. And I'll raise it to hate you and Knox. I will. I'll fill its ears with stories of what horrible, pitiless people you are. It will grow into someone who despises you both."

Just the very idea of that was a knife through Harper's soul.

"It might even one day kill Knox for us," Linda continued. "It won't matter if it's as powerful as Knox or not—he'd never harm his own child, especially when it's part of you. And that right there will give it power over him."

She was right, the bitch. But . . . "You can't think Nora will really give you the baby, Linda. *Think.* Think past how badly you want a child. To Nora, this baby will be a weapon she can wield over Knox's head. She'll keep it hidden but close and highly protected. She won't want it to be loyal to anyone other than her. She's not going to give you the baby and then send you on your merry way. She also won't let you live to tell anyone what she's done."

Linda's smile faded, but then she snorted. "You won't divide and conquer us, Harper. Now, why not just concentrate on delivering my baby, hmm?"

"My baby."

"No, *mine*."

Harper hissed, wishing she could kick the bitch again. But that hiss turned into a moan as yet another contraction hit. Then there was another. And another. And another.

Once again, the minutes bled into hours. She groaned. She cried out. She whimpered. She cursed a blue streak that made Linda jerk back in horror at one point. And now she was more of a sweating, shaking, moaning mess than she had been before.

Her head drooped forward as another contraction eased off. God, it was so tempting to collapse on the ground and give her aching back a break. She was more exhausted than she'd ever been in her life. Her limbs and eyelids felt so damn heavy, and it was a wonder she didn't fall asleep between contractions.

She felt all hollowed out, like she had nothing left in her. She wanted the pain to end, but she also didn't want the labor to end—the thought of her baby in the hands of these neurotic motherfuckers . . . she couldn't stand it.

She'd truly thought that Knox would have got there by now, but there was still no sign of him. If her demon had been able to call the flames, it would have taken over and done so, but neither of them could do a damn thing. *I'll think of something*, she told it.

"How dilated is she?" Nora asked.

Linda checked. "Nine centimeters."

"Not good enough," Whiner snapped. "We can't afford for this to go on any longer. And I don't know about any of you, but I'm tired and uncomfortable. This ground is solid."

Was this asshole for real? She'd been in pain for hours, prodded and poked by Linda, had nothing but tepid water, and was stuck in the same awkward position for way too long—her legs spread in front of multiple people as she waited for her cervix to dilate to the size of a freaking ball while her body felt like it was splitting in two . . . and *he* was tired and uncomfortable?

"Her water broke not so long ago," Linda reminded him. "That's progress."

"We need more than 'progress,'" he clipped. "We need the child in our hands."

Harper shrugged. "You can't blame the baby for not wanting to come out."

Jumpy honed in on her, a glint of fear in his eyes. "What do you mean it doesn't want to come out? How would you know what it does or doesn't want?"

"It told me," she lied, delighting in the way his face paled.

"Nonsense," Whiner scoffed. "It doesn't yet have the capacity to speak in either thought or voice." But he didn't sound so sure. He exchanged wary glances with the others.

"Ignore her," Linda advised. "It's just a baby."

Jumpy spoke again. "It's not *just* a baby. It is Knox Thorne's baby. We have no idea what he is, which means we have no idea what we're dealing with." He looked at Harper. "It talks to you?"

"Not with words, but with images and impressions," Harper replied.

Jumpy swallowed. "I would like to disbelieve you, but you have shown too little fear for my liking."

Because she'd wholeheartedly believed that Knox was coming . . . but she was beginning to think he wouldn't get there in time. Heat seemed to build behind her eyelids, and a lump formed in her throat. But she'd never been a person who accepted defeat. Never. No self-respecting Wallis ever would. She could see only one way to fight the incantors that were holding her captive. Just one. It would be a huge risk because she had no idea what would truly happen, but she had to take it.

Harper dug her fingers into the soil, felt the vortex's menacing energy sizzling beneath her. Instead of fighting the vortex as she'd done since she arrived, she worked with it. It was definitely not the best idea to work with a malevolent, indiscriminate energy, but she was out of options.

Hoping it would be strong enough to help her, she sucked it in. Absorbed it. *Welcomed* it—and maybe that was why it didn't hurt her. The dark energy mixed with the protective power in her belly, which painfully shot to her fingertips like zaps of electricity. Without a second's hesitation, she called to her wings. She felt them respond, felt them begin to rise ... but they didn't. *Damn.*

"You think the child will save itself, don't you?" Whiner asked.

Ignoring him, Harper sucked in more of the vortex's energy. Took it, filled her metaphorical power tank with it even as it made her feel soiled inside and caused her head to pound like a bitch. A contraction caught her off-guard, breaking her concentration. Shaking, she breathed and moaned through the excruciating pain. Once it passed, she took yet more of the vortex's energy, seeking out the "bridge" between her wings and the flames. And there it was.

"You *do* think the child will save itself, don't you?" Whiner pushed.

Harper glared at him, smiling inside as the ground began to shake. "No, I don't." The air buzzed and thickened with power. "I think it will kill you all."

Flames exploded out of the ground in front of her—red, black, gold, and hungry. They devoured Linda whole, and Harper couldn't help finding immense satisfaction in the bitch's screams. Yeah, maybe the vortex's energy had fed her vengeful streak a little.

The unbearable heat radiating from the flames burned Harper's skin, but they left no blisters. Despite their strength and power, they wouldn't harm her. Instead of spreading as she'd hoped, the flames returned to where they came, leaving only ashes behind. *Shit*. It was hard to concentrate while battling with panic, pain, and rage.

Head still pounding, Harper infused hellfire into the grass, making the enchanted vines restraining her wrists catch fire. They released her with an animal-like squeak, and she sat up and did the same to the vines restraining her ankles. Finally free, she forced herself to get to her knees. The others were all staring at her in horror—no, at her belly in horror.

"It was the child," Jumpy cried out. "It called the flames!"

"We're leaving," declared Nora. "Get her."

Whiner frowned. "But—"

"We didn't go through all this to leave her here," Nora hissed. "She comes with us."

Harper struggled to her feet and waited, ready to make her move. Her last reserve of the vortex's energy strained against her skin, wanting freedom, wanting violence. Dark, revolting images flashed in her mind—images of all the things Harper could do to the people around her. Images that both tempted and sickened her.

She shook her head, needing to think clearly. Her heart jumped as Nora lowered the enchanted vines that surrounded the boulders. *Yes, that's it, bitch, send your little helpers this way.* As two robed figures raced toward her, Harper called to the—

Pain thundered through her womb, sending her to her knees once more. *Motherofgoddamnholyfuck.* The incantors reached her, and fingers dug into her arms. "No!"

A blast of energy swept out of her body—a beautiful gold, sheen of light—and knocked every single incantor to the ground. Harper's mouth fell open, and she got to her feet once more. *Oh, little baby, you're gonna be a handful.* Because Harper had *not* done that.

That familiar dreaded, droning sound filled the air again, making everyone freeze. A portal burst to life ... and several figures stepped out of it. The sight of the dark demon leading them, danger in every line of his body, made her knees shake.

"Knox," Harper breathed in relief. A sob almost choked her. He looked at her, his eyes fevered and glittering with rage. They softened with relief for the briefest moment ... then his body jerked as his eyes abruptly bled to black, like the demon had *forced* its way to the surface. It stared at her, and then she could almost feel its soul-eating rage from there. The incantors must have felt it too, but they didn't act. They stayed frozen, like prey hoping not to catch a predator's attention.

A buzz vibrated the air, and her stomach churned. She knew what was coming. It wasn't like when Harper called to the flames of hell—that "buzz" was the power gathering as it came to her. For Knox, the power lived *inside* him ... the demon was simply letting it free.

A tremor rumbled through the ground, and she planted her feet. The power purred against her bare skin; the force of it burned her eyes, rattled her teeth, tightened her chest, and caused a low ringing sound to blare in her ears.

As the air seemed to pinken, she looked up, unsurprised to find that the moon behind the frothing ugly cloud was now blood-red.

She jumped as flames burst from the ground with a roar. They didn't devour the incantors. No, the blinding, tri-colored, ten-foot high flames swirled around Knox's demon, engulfing it. They hissed, crackled, and spat as they danced and swayed— wild and angry, meaning that the demon was wild and angry. Her heart raced as a figure of raging flames stepped out of the fire. No eyes, no facial features, no clothes—just flames.

Knox was gone. The archdemon had come out to play.

Shit.

That was when the incantors seemed to snap out of their shock, hit by their "fight or flight" instinct. And they fled. The ragged line of fire headed straight for the running incantors, leaving a trail of ashes in its wake. Hell, she'd never have thought that Nora could run that fast. The archdemon followed the incantors, its movements almost mechanical.

The sentinels then raced over to her, Tanner in the lead. "Fuck, Harper, you look like shit." He curled an arm around her, helping to take her weight. It was a good thing, because a contraction hit her so hard, her legs almost gave out. Her moans were barely heard over the screams of pain and terror coming from the incantors.

She gripped Levi's arm. "I am so fucking glad you're all here, even if our archdemon has lost its shit."

She winced at a high-pitched screech—a gold flame had hooked around the neck of a fleeing incantor and tossed him into the fire. At the same time, a black flame circled Whiner, cutting off his retreat and trapping him; he screamed from the searing heat alone, and she could imagine how his skin would be blistering and eating away at itself.

Keenan whistled as a third flame wrapped around Jumpy's body and slammed him into the ground once, twice, three times. There was a nauseating crack, and the incantor's cries died abruptly. The archdemon could have killed them all outright, but it was toying with them first.

"Where's Nora?" But then Harper saw her gripping a boulder, screaming as a red flame repeatedly lashed her. At any other time, Harper would have marched over there and dealt with the bitch herself. Right then, she could barely stand on her own. She groaned through her teeth as another spasm assailed her womb. "I am *not* having this baby here!"

Keenan scratched his nape. "I don't think leaving here is going to happen any time soon."

No, neither did Harper. The archdemon was out of control, drunk on power. She knew exactly how that felt, because her own demon had experienced the same invigorating, intoxicating, high. No demon came down from that easily, especially not one on a warpath. As for an archdemon on a warpath ... well, that was a whole other thing, and she wasn't equipped to talk it down. It had a habit of developing tunnel vision when it thought she needed avenging.

She'd managed to talk it down once in the past, but not before an entire building and a bunch of dark practitioners were destroyed. Hell, it had almost killed Tanner and Larkin that night, too set on getting to Harper and slaughtering those who'd taken her from it to really *think*. It couldn't happen again. It—

Harper froze at the familiar droning sound. *Fuck*. She spun to see that Nora had opened another portal and was reaching out to it with one hand. "Oh God, she's going to get away."

"No, she won't," Levi growled. He flicked a hand, and Nora's head suddenly slammed against the boulder. The portal disappeared with a pop.

Harper released a sigh of relief. She'd forgotten the reaper had a telekinetic ability. "Thank you, Le—" She cut off as she spotted the archdemon walking toward Nora. She was the only incantor still alive, Harper then realized.

The flame whipping Nora paused. Like a snake, it slithered up her body and contracted around her. Then it dived down her throat. Eyes bulging, she choked and jerked as more and more of the flame shoved its way inside her—no doubt searing, burning, and consuming everything it touched.

Agony blazed in her amber eyes and her face scrunched up into a silent scream, but Harper had no pity for her. None at all. And when Nora's body spontaneously combusted, Harper's demon grinned with pleasure and satisfaction.

She let out a long breath. It was over. They were all dead. The fire hadn't died, though, she realized with a frown. No, it was still blazing, fierce and furious. It was also spreading along the landscape, consuming the snarled trees and frail shrubs. The mist was gone, and now heat waves shimmered in the air. The archdemon turned away, apparently not done playing.

"*Stop!*" Harper shouted. "They're dead. Thank you. They're gone . . . I need Knox right now. Let him come to me."

But it didn't. The demon walked away. The vortex was feeding its anger and ill-intent, she realized, and that was not at all good. "We need to get Knox away from here. This place . . . "

"I know, I feel it," said Levi. "But getting the demon to leave will be a big fucking job, and I don't think you're up to it right now."

He was right, but . . . "I have to be." Harper sighed. "I guess I'm gonna have to fight fire with fire."

Larkin stilled. "What?"

Locking down on all her out-of-control emotions, Harper used the last of the dark energy within her to tap into her link to her wings. As Knox had taught her, she used it as a bridge . . . and she called to the power waiting on the other end of it. The ground trembled and the air buzzed as, at Harper's will, flames of hell sprouted out of the ground in front of the archdemon. They acted as a barrier, got its attention. The demon tried to lower them but it couldn't, because these flames were answering to her, not the entity.

It slowly and stiffly turned to face her. Although there were no eyes, she *felt* it looking right at her. It knew what she'd done, and it wasn't happy with her. Then it stalked toward her, and she lowered the flames before her panic could send them out of control.

"Harper, get behind me," said Tanner.

She resisted his attempts to move her and instead stepped aside, putting a little distance between them, hoping another contraction wouldn't make her double over. "Don't be stupid. If it thinks you're trying to keep it from its mate, it'll hurt you—sentinel or not."

Tanner growled. "And what if it hurts you, huh?"

"It won't."

"Ordinarily, no, it wouldn't. But this place is feeding its anger and warping its mind. Right now, it's got vengeance on the brain, and you just pissed it off. What if it now wants vengeance against you?"

Harper swallowed. "Then we're all fucked." She put up a hand as the demon came close. "You need to stop." It didn't. She touched its psyche and felt only a blinding rage. *Shit.* Her heart started pumping even crazier than before and her inner demon began to panic. The entity was almost on her and—

A shower of embers, sparks, and ashes burst to life in front of her . . . almost like a shield. It popped and snapped and made Harper's face go slack.

"How the hell are you doing that?" asked Keenan.

"I'm not," said Harper in a stunned whisper.

The archdemon didn't seem impressed. It punched through the shield, and there was a harsh sizzling sound, like hellfire eating flesh. But the entity didn't pull back, apparently not bothered about a little pain. The embers and sparks winked away, and the ashes disintegrated. Then the demon's hand snapped tight around her throat. The sentinels lunged for her, but a wall of flames abruptly shot out of the ground to surround her, pushing them back and blocking their access to her.

Harper grabbed onto its flaming wrist, hissing at the burning heat, although it didn't hurt her. She tried to free herself, but the demon didn't even loosen its grip. "If you kill me," she managed to wheeze out, "you'll kill the baby. I know the baby matters to you."

Blinding pain rushed out of its hand and filled every part of her. She screamed. She sobbed. She begged it to stop. It didn't. It kept on flooding her with white-hot pain. As she waited for death to come, she silently apologized to the baby for being unable to protect it; for trusting this demon she apparently never should have trusted.

Her skin felt cold, wet. Blood, she thought. The demon was somehow making her blood seep out of her pores. But she didn't smell blood. No, she smelled ... decay. Rot. Sickness.

Harper looked at her arms, realized black liquid was bubbling out of her skin. And she understood. It wasn't attacking her; it was attacking the dark magick that had infected her. She hadn't thought there was any chance that the demon could help; it wasn't built to heal. But this wasn't healing—this was destroying magick. The side effect was that she was healing.

Gradually the pain dimmed, and she let out a shaky breath. The fire started to peel away from the demon, starting from its head. But the eyes were black—the entity was still very much in control.

The hand collaring her throat pulled her close, thumb circling her neck. "Mine." It kissed her hard, inhaling her scent ... and then the hold on her throat gentled, and she knew Knox was back.

His hands cradled her face. "Baby ..." Using his thumbs, Knox brushed the tears from her cheeks. He was about to tell her how sorry he was, that he knew he'd fucked up and he'd make it up to her, but then she sucked in a breath and doubled over. He supported her weight as she breathed through the contraction. Once it finally eased away, she fisted his shirt and yanked.

"You need to get me away from here, Thorne! This baby's coming whether we like it or not."

"I can see that." Knox scooped her up. "Go through the portal," he told the sentinels. "Tell Jolene and the others that she's fine so they don't lose their minds."

"What do we tell them when they ask how you got out of here?" asked Keenan.

"Tell them I made one of the incantors open a second portal that leads straight to my home right before I killed them—I don't care. I'm taking her straight home."

Harper watched as, with nothing more than a single sweep of his gaze, the fire began to calm and thin out. Still, she knew it would look much like a strip of dead, blackened land.

Golden flames built around them, licking over her skin without harming her. Soon, the fire faded and they were in their living room. Everything was set up, ready. Plastic sheeting and old towels and bed sheets were all laid out. Blankets and clean warm towels were set aside, along with Dr. Rodgers' bag. There was even an incubator in the event that the baby might need it, and that made her feel slightly better.

Meg literally dived at her, hugging her and muttering in Spanish. Swiping a tear from under her eye, she stepped back and Rodgers came forward.

"Harper, Knox—this is my mate, Sharon," he said. "She's a midwife, and she's here to help."

Harper forced a smile for the curvy brunette. "Shame we had to meet for the first time under these circumstances."

Knox carefully positioned Harper on the covered floor, and her hand shot out in a panic to grab his own. "I'm right here, baby, I'm not leaving your side," he vowed. As the doctor and midwife examined her, Knox kept his focus solely on Harper. He'd wanted to be with her every step of the way, and he was going to make up for the fact that he so far hadn't been. He'd keep his fears and concerns to himself. This was all about her.

"I wouldn't bother with the heating pad or anything, Meg," said Rodgers. "The baby's crowning already."

Seeing fear glimmer in Harper's eyes, Knox squeezed her hand. "Just think, we'll finally see the baby soon. You'll finally know if it's a girl or a boy—I know that's been driving you crazy." Her mouth quirked, and just the sight lightened the guilt weighing on his shoulders. He might be pissed at himself, but she wasn't pissed at him.

"It's been driving you insane too, admit—" Harper cut off with a moan as a contraction seemed to slam into her womb. She hadn't thought the pain could get any worse. She'd been wrong.

"Once the baby's in your arms, you'll forget all about the pain," Sharon promised. "Now get ready. We're going to need you to start pushing in a few moments." As soon as the next contraction began, Sharon said, "Okay, *push*."

Harper pushed. Nothing happened. As time went on and the pushing achieved jack shit, she clung to Knox's hand, so fucking glad he was there and so fucking surprised she hadn't crushed any of the bones in his hand. Even at home, away from danger, she felt completely out of her element. Utterly out of control.

His touch was strong and reassuring; his words were encouraging and supportive; and his presence was calming and made her feel safe. She needed that right then. Needed the way he squeezed her hand, rubbed her back, whispered in her ear, and didn't complain when she dug her nails into his skin.

Drained, she sagged against him. "I can't do this anymore, I just can't." She'd pushed and pushed, but nothing was happening.

He kissed her temple. "You *are* doing it, baby. I'm watching you do it and I'm proud of you." He smoothed her hair away from her face. "I know you're tired, but you're doing great." Turning to

Sharon, Knox scowled. "Should she really be in this much pain? And should it really be taking so long?"

Sharon gave him a pitying look. "Sweetie, it ain't called 'labor' for nothing."

Rodgers smiled at Harper. "Just visualize your cervix opening like a flower—"

"Stop, just stop," Harper snapped. He'd done nothing but make dumb and often wildly inappropriate comments until he'd lost all credibility to her. It was just her luck that she'd end up with a doctor who used humor to get himself through tricky situations.

Another contraction came, and she dug her fingers into Knox's arm.

"Okay, Harper, time to push again," Sharon declared.

Harper pushed. There was a loud farting sound. Her mouth dropped open in mortification, but then Rodgers gave her a sheepish look and said, "Sorry about that. I had chicken korma before I came."

Unable to deal with him right then, Harper held up her hand. "You are not here. You're just not."

Sharon chuckled. "Ignore him, honey, I do it all the time."

Harper did exactly that, concentrating on pushing and breathing while Knox whispered encouragements in her ear and told her he loved her. And when Rodgers announced that one more push would do it, Harper's heart skipped a beat. Still, she pushed. *Hard.* With what even she could admit was a blood-curdling scream, the baby's head was out. It took just one more push for the rest of the baby to come out. And there it was.

Rodgers grinned. "You have a baby boy, congratulations."

Awe and wonder crept over Harper, and her throat seemed to close over. Still, she somehow managed to ask, "Why isn't he crying?"

"Oh, he will," said Sharon. "Don't doubt it."

After the cord was cut, Rodgers took the baby aside, checked him over and then, yep, the baby started *bawling*.

As Sharon covered Harper up, Rodgers gently rested the baby on her chest with a little blanket and said, "He's fine. Ten fingers, ten toes, and he has a big set of lungs on him. Good luck with that."

Harper's heart stuttered and her chest clenched. To others, he probably looked like a prune. To her, he was the most beautiful, perfect thing she'd ever seen. She spoke in a low, soothing voice. "Hey there. You're here," she marveled. "And you're a boy." He was familiar in the strangest way. She smiled at Knox. "Can you believe we made this little person?"

Knox gently pressed a kiss on the baby's head, and then pressed another on Harper's temple. Looking at them, an overwhelming sense of pride flooded him. There was also a deep sense of relief. Harper was fine. The baby was fine. "You're both amazing," he said a little gruffly.

"You okay?"

Okay? He was . . . overwhelmed. Had no words. It all seemed to have happened so fast that it was surreal for Knox. It was hard to absorb the reality that the baby was finally here. But he didn't need to tell her that; she knew him well enough to understand and gave him a knowing smile.

"I get it," said Harper. The way she was feeling right then . . . it was hard to describe, hard to even process. She had a lot of emotional chaos going on in her mind. Even her demon was a little off-balance, though it was also proud as punch. Gently, she shifted the baby towards him. "Have a hold."

Knox tensed. Very few things had ever made him feel nervous. But holding a baby? Yeah, that did it.

She smiled. "You're a badass. You can manage." She wasn't

the least bit surprised that Knox scooped up and cradled the baby as effortlessly as he did everything else—no awkwardness or fiddling. He was the most competent person she'd ever known. The baby immediately stopping fussing, to her amusement, and looked up at Knox, seeming fascinated by him . . . which meant she and the baby already had something in common. Awesome.

"He's so small," said Knox. Tiny. Vulnerable. His demon settled inside him, content now that the only people that it considered important to it were fine.

"He is small," Harper agreed. "Like a little doll." The baby's tiny fingers clasped one of his, and every line in Knox's face smoothed out . . . and Harper was pretty sure she'd just watched Knox Thorne fall instantly in love.

CHAPTER TWENTY-ONE

———◆———

Harper woke up the next morning to see Knox in the rocking chair that had been placed beside their bed, gently rubbing the back of the swaddled sleeping baby resting on his chest. And her heart just melted. Yep, right into a puddle of goo.

Eyes of dark velvet met hers, and Knox smiled. There was pride, contentment, and ... peace there. "Morning, baby," he said quietly. "How are you feeling?"

She sat up as she took stock of herself. "Good, all things considered." A little sore, but she knew that wouldn't last long, since demons healed fast. "Tell me I didn't sleep through him waking up for a feed."

Knox shook his head. "You've both been asleep for a long while."

Which was no doubt why she no longer felt drained, she thought. Demons didn't need much sleep, after all.

"You literally dropped to sleep like you'd been dealt a blow to the jaw," Knox told her, unable to hide the amusement from his voice. He hadn't initially found it amusing, though. "I was worried at first, but then I figured it wasn't such a surprise, given that you'd not only been through labor but were probably psychically exhausted after using your gifts."

Harper nodded. "Psychic burnout is never fun." She'd fed the baby shortly after he was born—though it had taken a little work since he'd simply refused to cooperate and suckle—and no sooner had Knox taken him to have another hold than Harper lost the battle she'd been fighting against the need for sleep.

Standing, Knox said, "Shuffle over."

Once she did so, he slid onto the bed beside her, careful not to jostle the baby. Unable to get rid of the silly grin on her face, Harper shifted his little hat slightly just to press a quick kiss to his downy head. His hair was as dark and silky as Knox's was, to her utter delight. She inhaled deeply, taking in his baby fresh, sweet scent. Few things smelled better than a newborn baby, she thought. It made her want to gobble him up.

"Where's mine?" Knox asked, mouth curved.

"Right here," whispered Harper before giving him a soft, lingering kiss that he quickly took over—deepening it, yet keeping it gentle and almost . . . reverent.

Pulling back, Knox curled her hair behind her ear and stroked his thumb over her cheekbone. "I needed that." Moving the baby from his shoulder to his chest so that she could see his little face, Knox said, "You do realize that we still haven't settled on a name for him yet, don't you?"

"There was only one name we agreed on, remember. That name still good for you?"

"Yeah." Knox looked down at their son. "He looks like an 'Asher'."

Harper nodded. "Then Asher Knox Thorne it is. Damn, he's just you with a lot less hair."

The resemblance was clear to see, Knox thought. And that only fed the pride he felt each time he looked at Asher. "I still hope he has your eyes."

"Then you're an idiot."

Knox shot her a mock glare. "Your eyes are unique and beautiful."

"They're a pain in my ass—*that's* what they are." She stilled as Asher shifted, but he didn't wake.

Knox sighed. "He keeps pulling his knees up and trying to curl into a ball."

"Like he's still in the womb." Harper stretched, yawning. "I really need coffee. And food."

"I told Meg that you're awake. She'll bring us breakfast soon and formula for Asher, since it's likely he'll wake up soon too. While we wait, you can tell me what happened yesterday."

Her stomach plummeted. "Do we have to talk about it?"

He breezed his thumb along her jaw. "I need to know, baby. I can understand why you wouldn't want to talk about it, but—"

"Not knowing is driving you crazy, I get it."

"I know a little from McCauley." He quickly relayed the child's version of events to her. "I need to hear the rest."

"Okay." So, she told him how Nora had taken her, and how Linda had then stayed inside the circle with her while the incantors chanted, infecting her with magick and inducing labor. "Nora wasn't working with the other Horsemen. She said they wanted to lie low for a while. Unfortunately, that was all she said about them. I got the feeling she didn't want the attention being taken from her." Harper cocked her head. "How did you get to me?"

"Thatcher reopened the portal."

She blinked. "Thatcher?"

"I didn't like accepting his help. For all I knew, he was stalling for Nora. That was why I had Levi contact his incantor-friend. She said that Thatcher was doing exactly what she would have done, only he was doing it faster, so I didn't interfere and just hoped to God he wasn't playing me." It was the fear in her telepathic voice that had made Knox take the chance. He hadn't been able to bear it.

"So, you no longer suspect him of being one of the Horsemen?"

"I didn't say that. I'll never dismiss any of them as potential suspects. Not when that would put you and Asher at risk. Did Linda happen to tell you why she helped Nora?"

Harper took a moment to gaze at her son again before answering, "She promised Linda she could have Asher. As you know, all Linda wanted was a child."

Knox frowned. "I don't think Nora would have handed him over to anyone."

"Neither do I." Harper fiddled with her rings. "I said as much to Linda, but she didn't listen. So I killed her," she added a little too cheerfully.

Knox chuckled. "I'm jealous."

"Hey, you got to kill Nora, remember."

"No, my demon did." He exhaled heavily. "I was really hoping it wouldn't kill her. She could have told us who the last Horseman is."

"She wouldn't have told," said Harper. "And, honestly, I wouldn't have wanted to let her live. She was too powerful. I'd have worried that she might escape, especially since it's highly likely that she was able to help Crow escape your prison."

Knox rubbed her thigh. "Then I'm glad she's gone so you don't have to waste another thought on her."

So was Harper. "Does Wyatt know about Linda yet?"

"He knows that she's dead and that she was working with

Nora to some extent, but he doesn't know the full story yet. He will soon. Keenan and Larkin will pay him a visit later today."

"On the one hand, I feel bad for him. It's going to be hard for him to accept that his partner pretty much betrayed us all, but he betrayed her first. Talia was one of the people he cheated on Linda with."

"And yet, she wanted McCauley?" Knox asked, incredulous.

"She wanted a *kid*." Harper lightly stroked Asher's leg over his fleecy white blanket. "How was McCauley when you last saw him?"

"Same as always, but he seemed glad to get back to Elena. I think he'll settle there."

"Good. He might be weird and creepy, and it's true that his demon sent him to warn me for selfish reasons, but he still helped you work out what was happening."

Knox nodded, slightly distracted by how stiffly she was moving. "How sore are you?"

"Not as sore as I thought I'd be."

"Maybe that's because you weren't in labor for very long. According to Sharon, first pregnancies usually . . . why do you have an odd look on your face?" But she didn't answer him. "Harper," he prodded.

"Okay," she relented. Harper hadn't wanted to tell him this, but she didn't like keeping things from him. "Time was different there."

Knox narrowed his eyes. "Different how?"

"A minute to you was . . . an hour to me."

He quickly calculated the time in his head. "You went through that agony for *over fifteen hours on your own*? You were trapped there all that time?"

She took his hand and squeezed it. "I knew you'd come."

Knox swore under his breath. "I hate that you went through most of the labor alone—Linda might have been there but she doesn't fucking count." He clenched his jaw. "I hate that I wasn't there for you."

Leaning forward, she rubbed her nose against his. "Don't go beating yourself up about it, Knox—it wasn't your fault. I wish you had been there, because I feel like you were robbed of the experience. But most guys will tell you that the labor itself is pretty boring anyway." Hoping to shift his mood, she quickly added, "On another note, we're gonna have our work cut out with this kid. He protected me." A faint smile played around the edges of Knox's mouth, to her relief.

"Yes, I remember the shield that slammed up in front of my demon when it tried to get to you. I wasn't sure if it was really Asher, though."

"Oh, it was definitely him. Your demon knew he'd be powerful, didn't it?"

"It would seem so." His demon still wasn't being very upfront about it. He rubbed her thigh again. "Baby, about my demon, about what it did to you—"

"Don't you apologize for it. The pain it inflicted was necessary to make sure I lived, just like all that labor pain was necessary for Asher to be born."

"Intellectually, I know that." Linking his fingers through hers, Knox kissed her hand. "I wish I could say my demon feels bad about it, but it doesn't."

"Of course it doesn't—our inner demons feel no guilt."

"It does wish you were spared the pain, but it doesn't regret what it did."

"Neither do I," she said truthfully. "Just like I don't regret absorbing the vortex's energy to help me use my gifts—which incidentally also helped Asher to use his. It was a risk, but I had to take it. I was out of options. Things might have ended very, very differently if I hadn't done what I did."

"You think I'd ever blame you for that? You did what you had to do."

"And so did your demon," she pointed out. Knox opened his mouth to say something else, but then his brows snapped together and she sensed him speaking to someone telepathically. "What is it?" she asked.

"Meg told the sentinels that you're awake. They're asking if they can come up here."

Harper blinked. "They're downstairs?"

"They camped out in the living room with Jolene and the girls."

"I shouldn't be surprised. Have they seen Asher yet?"

"No. We both stayed here with you." Knox hadn't wanted her out of his sight; probably wouldn't for a while, he thought. "Honestly, I figured he'd wake after a few hours. Maybe he psychically tired himself out trying to protect you."

Harper bit her lip, nauseous all of a sudden. "I don't like that idea."

"He'll be fine. He *is* fine."

"How's your demon doing?"

"Fascinated by Asher, and it's no longer stressing now that you're awake, which is good. What about yours?"

"It seriously adores the sight of you holding Asher."

His mouth curved, but then he sighed again. "Apparently, your grandmother woke up and is now also pushing to see you."

Harper rolled her eyes. "I need to use the bathroom and stuff; then they can come in." After she'd done her business, Knox curled an arm around her waist and brought her to sit on his lap on the chair, careful not to jar Asher. "Thank you for giving me my son."

The wealth of possession in his voice made her smile. "Thank you for giving him to me."

"You were amazing yesterday. I'm fucking proud of you. You went through a lot for the three of us to be right where we are now. I love you, baby."

She brushed her mouth against his. "And I love you." At the knock on the door, she let out a long breath. "Brace yourself." Getting back into bed, she propped herself up against the headboard. She held her arms out for Asher, wanting to have a little hold before they came in and took him, but knuckles again rapped on the door—this time impatiently.

Knox opened it wide, still holding Asher. Jolene entered first and literally melted as she got a good look at the baby. "Knox, he's just you with a lot less hair."

Harper smiled. "That's what *I* said."

Jolene wasted no time in taking Asher from him and, nuzzling his head, then made a beeline for Harper. She kissed her hair. "You did good, sweetheart. He's beautiful. Does he have a name yet?"

"Asher," Knox told her.

"Asher," Raini echoed as she walked in. "I like that."

"Very appropriate, all things considered," said Levi, no doubt remembering the shield of embers, sparks, and ashes.

Everyone filed in, kissing Asher's head and then giving Harper a brief hug, but none succeeded at getting their hands on the baby. Jolene was determined to have her moment with him.

"He smells so good," said Khloë.

"I hope you know that male sphinxes are a handful," Jolene told Knox. "Worse than girls. Hopefully he won't share Harper's ability to infuse hellfire into things. She ruined at least three sofas and once set fire to her own cradle because she wanted out. That's not counting the times she burned her way through the safety straps of her stroller, car seat, and high chair. Really, I pity you if Asher has that ability."

"He's powerful," said Devon. "I can feel it."

Tanner nodded. "We had a peek at the kid in action." He briefly described what happened.

Jolene grinned, proud. "He's definitely a Wallis."

Knox's jaw clenched. "He's a Thorne."

Jolene waved that away, as if the surname was a mere technicality. "You know what I mean. Oh, he's waking up. Well, hello there." As a unit, everyone crowded around Jolene, whispering and cooing at Asher, all the while ignoring Jolene's glowers.

Harper smiled as Asher's mind slid against hers—it was a questioning touch, like he was wondering where she was. She gave his mind a reassuring stroke. "This kid is gonna be demanding."

Knox raised a brow. "You expected anything else?"

She shook her head. "No, not at all."

"Grams, stop hogging him," Khloë complained. With a huff, Jolene passed him to Khloë. Soon, the baby was passed around from person to person.

"His demon just surfaced and took my measure," said Keenan, grinning. "I think I passed my assessment, because it retreated."

Taking Asher from the incubus, Raini turned to Harper as she stroked her finger over Asher's cheek. "Does he look like the baby in those dreams you told me about?"

"No," Harper replied. "Those weren't premonitions. Those were my subconscious telling me to wake the fuck up and realize I was pregnant."

"He's so tiny," said Devon. "He didn't need an incubator?"

Knox shook his head. "Rodgers thought he might, since he was born early, but he's kept up his own body temperature just fine."

"Of course he has," said Jolene. "He's a Wallis."

Knox glared at her. "He's a Thorne."

Jolene again waved that away. "How much does he weigh?"

"Asher Knox Thorne made his grand entrance weighing five pounds two ounces, which isn't bad at all for a premature baby," said Harper.

"Not bad at all," agreed Jolene. "Well, Harper, how does it feel to be a mom?"

Harper couldn't help but smile. "Like everything's right in the world."

Knox took her hand. *Everything is right.* "I'm hoping he'll have Harper's eyes."

She sighed at him. "Knox, why do you hate our son?"

Jolene scowled at her. "There's nothing wrong with your eyes. They're beautiful."

"That's what *I* said," said Knox.

Harper shook her head. "Forget it. How about we just—oh God, no."

Knox frowned. "What?" He tracked her gaze, and could only sigh.

In the doorway, Lou thrust his arms up in the air. "We have ourselves a baby." Stalking forward, he pushed through the crowd until he reached Raini, who was still holding Asher. "Girl? Boy?"

"Boy," Raini told him.

He turned to Knox and raised his hand. "Hey, up high!"

"Well, hello, Lou," Jolene said from behind him.

Lou's mouth tightened and he dropped his arm. "I'm still not talking to you, evil woman."

Jolene rolled her eyes. "You really need to stop holding grudges. Besides, taking things personally when you're dealing with an imp is utterly pointless and—"

"La, la, la, la, la, la, deaf ears."

Harper just looked at him. "I can't imagine what a joy it must be up there in your head."

Lou stroked Asher's cheek. "Hey, little guy. You remember your Uncle Lou, don't you? Of course you do. Who'd ever forget me?" He peered at Harper. "I don't suppose you did the right thing and named him Lucifer."

"His name is Asher," Knox told him.

Surprisingly, Lou grinned. "I like that. It's a good name for a boy who might one day decimate the universe. His demon is taking my measure." He held his arms out. "I want a little hold." But Raini frowned.

"Just let him have a hold," said Knox with a sigh. "It's the fastest way to make him leave."

Lou's grin widened. "I always feel so welcome here." He carefully cradled the baby. "You look just like your daddy. Yes, you do, but don't be upset; we all have crosses to bear."

"Don't think I won't hurt you," said Harper.

Lou's brows drew together. "I was comforting him."

"You were being an ass."

"And this surprises you why?"

Harper just sighed. "I can't do this with you. I don't have the energy."

"I heard labor is tiring work." His brow creased, as if something only just occurred to him. "Hey, I thought the baby wasn't due for another month."

Harper scratched her head. "Yeah, well, the deadline got pushed ahead by one of the Horsemen."

Lou scowled. "Seriously? What happened? What did the—?" His scowl morphed into a look of utter distaste, and he peered down at Asher. "Ew, he just farted right on my hand."

At that moment, the door again opened and Meg strolled in, carrying a tray. "Visiting time is over," she declared. "Mom and baby need rest." She placed the tray on the nightstand, and the scents of coffee, biscuits, and gravy made Harper inwardly sigh happily.

Meg carefully took Asher from a cooing Lou and handed him over to Harper. "There." She then gave her the bottle of formula from the tray. "He'll be hungry."

"Can't I feed him?" begged Devon.

Looking rather fierce, Meg shook her head and waved her hands at the others, urging them out of the room. "Time to leave."

Smiling at Harper, Khloë jerked her thumb toward Meg. "Does she know she's an employee?"

Harper chuckled. "I wouldn't mess with her if I were you."

"Come on, out, they need rest," Meg insisted. "You can come back tomorrow."

Ignoring her, Lou spoke to Harper, "Wait, you haven't told me what happened with the Horse-person yet."

Jolene took his arm. "I'll tell you all about it. Meg's right, they need rest."

He shrugged her off. "I told you, I'm still not talking to you."

Saying their goodbyes, everyone filed out. Apart from Knox, of course. Meg gave him a pointed look.

"Sorry, Meg, you're not kicking me out," he told her, sinking into the rocking chair. "I'm staying with my family."

The latter comment seemed to melt the woman. Smiling, Meg nodded and left the room, softly closing the door behind her.

"He latched on with no problems this time," Harper told Knox, watching the baby drink the formula.

Knox leaned forward, bracing his elbows on the mattress. "That's good." Ignoring the sound of his cell chiming, he added, "We need him to grow and get stronger."

"Aren't you going to answer your phone?"

"It'll probably just be another of the Primes. We've had dozens of congratulatory calls and emails from them."

Harper tipped her chin toward the phone that had been placed on the bedside cabinet. "Any texts sent to my cell?"

Knox checked. "A lot. There's one from Kellen," he added, barely able to hide his annoyance.

"Saying?"

Knox opened the message. "It says, 'Congratulations. I know you'll be a better mom than ours is'." Relaxing slightly, Knox cupped her face and breezed his thumb along her lower lip. "He's right. You will be."

"You wouldn't let me be anything else."

Knox lightly skimmed his hand over the baby's hat-covered head. "There are no messages from Lucian, so I'm guessing he doesn't yet know that Asher's been born."

"I'll speak to him later."

"Just be aware that if he calls our child the spawn of evil again I *will* hurt him." It would be the perfect excuse to finally get his hands on the son of a bitch.

"I think you'll be surprised by his reaction."

"How so?"

"He wasn't happy that I was pregnant, but now that Asher's actually a person—someone who he can see and touch—Lucian won't be such an ass. He likes babies. He just doesn't like caring for them because he's no good at it."

"I'm very aware of that," Knox rumbled, thinking of her upbringing. "I didn't understand his behavior before, and I especially don't understand it now that I have Asher. I *know* I could never abandon him. I know I could never do anything to harm him."

"Do you really want to talk about Lucian?"

"No." Knox touched Asher's little fist. "I'm more interested in knowing if you're going to give me what I asked for."

"Knox—"

"I want to give you my name, baby. I want us all to share the same one."

Her mouth slowly curved. "So do I; you don't have to try to persuade me."

Satisfaction coursed through him, and he kissed her palm again. "Thank you, Harper Thorne."

"That's going to take some getting used to." She looked at Asher. "So is being a parent. I still can't believe we made this little person."

Knox smiled. "He's perfect. Amazing. Just like his mom."

"Just like his dad," Harper corrected. Seeing that he'd drank half his bottle, Harper gently pulled it from his mouth and handed it to Knox. She then sat Asher upright, gently curving her hand around the front of his neck to hold him up while she rubbed his back.

"I can't get over how tiny he is," said Knox. The baby's eyes opened, and his blue eyes bled to black. The demon stared out at him, and Knox's own demon rose to the surface for just a moment before both entities retreated. They had done it once before, shortly after Asher was born. Both times, Knox's demon chuckled—it was a sound that held a secret. "I still think there's something my demon isn't telling us."

"Probably, because this kid's as powerful as people expected he would be." That unnerved her in ways she didn't want to think about. "Do we hide that he's powerful so no one sees him as a threat?"

"We can only hide that for as long as we keep him here, where he can't be reached or seen. It's easy to sense all that power. I'm good with keeping him here for a little while."

"Me, too. I don't think people will be suspicious of that, considering I was recently kidnapped by Nora, who wanted to take the baby."

Knox rubbed her leg. "I didn't think I'd ever have this. Someone who was mine. A child. A family. Didn't see it coming." His face hardened as he added, "I'll fight to the death to protect and keep what we have."

"So will I, and so will our demons. And if anyone out there decides to test us on that, they'll find out that there are much worse things than death."

Knox had to smile. "Have I mentioned that I love how blood-thirsty you are?"

"Once or twice. Never hurts to hear it again."

He chuckled. "You are bloodthirsty, Harper. And beautiful. And smart. And so fucking strong. There's no one like you, and I love that you belong to me."

"Then kiss me and shut up, because you're making me blush."

Chuckling again, he did.